Praise for the novels of Nicholas van Pelt

The Mongoose Man

"Complex plots, clever twists keep you guessing . . . guessing wrong until the end. A chilling glimpse of what our future, even our present could be, written by a man who knows his subject and the characters he brings to life."

—Fred Bean, author of *Black Gold* and *Eden*

Stomp!

"*Stomp!* romps! A sunstruck stream of humor, brains, and vitality has a brutally threatening undertow. This is the sweet, gritty suspense of Nick van Pelt at his finest."

—Katherine Dunn, author of *Geek Love*

"Fast-paced and fifties, this delightful tale features bountiful surprises, including guest appearances by Brenda Lee and Mamie Van Doren. The raunchy, reckless small-town hero gains love and revenge despite the long shadow of his high school nemesis. *Stomp!* keeps the reader eager for more of van Pelt's witty yet poignant fiction."

—Craig Lesley, author of *The Sky Fisherman*

"*Stomp!* is a delightful, clear-eyed, nineties-style look back on the dreamy existentialism of the 1950s. . . . The tension and pacing are strong. Readers will race through to the final unraveling. . . . Just when the story seems to be over and the resolution obvious, more mysteries arise. The tables turn, and nothing is what it seemed. . . . [The author] is a canny observer of life's challenges and choices, so painful during adolescence."

—Faris Cassell, *The Register-Guard* (Eugene, Oregon)

"*Stomp!* is a . . . tale that takes a nineties look at the fifties' existentialist movement. . . . Nicholas van Pelt shows he can scribe an ingriguing book that readers who enjoy something a bit different will devour."

—Harriet Klausner, *Midwest Book Review*

"Nicholas van Pelt's latest novel is laden with atmosphere, delivering a unique, gripping, and intoxicating blend of *American Graffiti, Rebel Without a Cause*, and *Marathon Man*, along with innocence and dark humor, paybacks and paranoia, and a noirish blend of Hitchcockian suspense."
—*Post & Courier* (Charleston, South Carolina)

"Witty and suspenseful."
—*Post-Intelligencer* (Seattle, Washington)

the mongoose man

nicholas van pelt

TOR®

A TOM DOHERTY ASSOCIATES BOOK
NEW YORK

NOTE: If you purchased this book without a cover your should be aware that this book is stolen property. It was reported as "unsold and destroyed" to the publisher, and neither the author nor the publisher has received any payment for this "stripped book."

This is a work of fiction. All the characters and events portrayed in this book are either products of the author's imagination or are used fictitiously.

THE MONGOOSE MAN

Copyright © 1998 by Nicholas van Pelt

All rights reserved, including the right to reproduce this book, or portions thereof, in any form.

A Tor Book
Published by Tom Doherty Associates, LLC
175 Fifth Avenue
New York, NY 10010

www.tor.com

Tor® is a registered trademark of Tom Doherty Associates, LLC.

ISBN: 0-812-54023-9
Library of Congress Catalog Card Number: 98-11582

First edition: August 1998
First mass market edition: October 2000

Printed in the United States of America

0 9 8 7 6 5 4 3 2 1

For Cading and Celing Artes, of Cebu City, Philippines, proud grandparents of my daughter Teresa

What, Evil Spirit, do you want of me?
Brass, marble, parchment, paper? Name it then!
Am I to write with graver, chisel, pen?
I offer you your choice quite free.

—Dr. Faust to Mephistopheles in Faust's Study (1)
   from *Faust,* by Johann Wolfgang von Goethe

one

in tangier

one

A blond man of Northern or Western European ancestry and wearing a grommeted tropical sun hat of the type worn by yachters and fishermen took a seat at one of eight tables on the beige brick pavement outside William Burroughs. This cafe and bar is located at the hub of five alleys fanning out into a shadowy warren of passages and narrow streets in Tangier, an earthy Mediterranean city of ochres and umbers and whites. Here customers could enjoy the balmy air and watch the passing Moroccan men, trailed at a respectful distance by their veiled women. This was a prime spot, and in an effort to thwart the creep of sidewalk peddlers bent on occupying every square inch of unclaimed territory, the cafe's owner had placed two woven reed partitions, like large protective wings, on either flank of his outdoor tables.

The blond man was lean, fit, and about fifty years old. He had pale white skin and hazel eyes and wore a slender, elegant mustache. He had a confident, self-assured way about him. He was dressed in carefully pressed tan chinos, light-brown jacket, polished penny loafers, and a gray, long-sleeved shirt, open at the throat. When he sat, he folded his floppy white hat and slipped it under one thigh, then stashed his dark-green day pack beside one foot; he then placed an order with a waiter wearing black trousers, white shirt, and bow tie.

The waiter left and quickly returned with a tall glass of clear liquid filled with green sprigs; this was sweet mint tea, a Moroccan favorite. It was 9:50 P.M.

Five minutes later, the tea drinker was joined by a slender, dark-complexioned Arab wearing a blue, pin-striped Western business suit. The Arab had a long, narrow face with prominent cheekbones, making him look like a hawk-nosed version of the English actor Laurence Harvey. William Burroughs was named for the American author of *Naked Lunch,* one of a number of famous expatriate writers, including Paul Bowles, who had hung out in Tangier because of the climate, the easily obtainable hashish, and the charms of the local boys. The interior walls were covered with drawings and photographs of Burroughs and his fellow writers. Unlike in Islamic countries farther east, beer and wine were sold in Morocco, although they were expensive. The proprietor employed English-speaking waiters to accommodate the European trade; William Burroughs was the particular favorite of German and French travelers—especially those with an interest in literary history.

As the Arab sat, the blond man removed a slender cigar from his jacket pocket; burnished with age and black as midnight, the cigar was as long as a corona but not as large as a Churchill. It was a punch, after Punch, a brand of stogie made in Cuba and Honduras. He retrieved what looked like a miniature guillotine from his pocket. He said, "If you want, you can call me Bill. This is a Bill kind of day, don't you think? A straightforward, down-to-earth kind of name."

With his left hand, Bill inserted the tip of the cigar into the hole where a prisoner might have stuck his neck; with his right hand, he snapped the blade shut. This made a neat, satisfying snip, full stop. The tip of the cigar tumbled onto the table. He said, "Would you like a cigar? They're really very good. Nothing like a cigar for conducting a little business."

The Arab shook his head.

"Some mint tea?" Bill retrieved the cigar tip and put it in his pocket. Eyeing the Arab, he lit the cigar with a wooden match. He nursed the flame to life with three quick puffs. "I feel like having a bowl of pumpkin soup. They make a squash soup of some kind in nearly every country. You hungry?"

The Arab cleared his throat. "The tea would be nice, thank you, but I shouldn't linger."

Bill caught a waiter's eye and tapped his glass, holding up two fingers. "A tea for the gentleman, please, and I'll have a bowl of pumpkin soup." He took another puff on his cigar.

"Are we clear?" the Arab asked.

Bill held the smoke in his mouth, savoring it. "If we weren't clear, we'd probably be dead by now. But you're correct to be careful, I respect your caution. I agree: we should do this quickly. And the answer is?" Bill, watching the Arab, assessing him, blew a neat little circle of smoke.

The Arab frowned. "They said no, I'm afraid."

Bill was clearly disappointed, but remained calm. He blew another circle. " 'They?' You mean 'he' said no. 'He' decided."

The Arab waited while the waiter served the mint tea and Bill's bowl of pumpkin soup. "For the moment, he's not in a position to jerk the Americans around. He's been seeking international concessions, and he wants to keep himself clean so he can look good in the media—a sober-minded, responsible leader and all of that. If any of those products are used by a freelance, the entire world will almost certainly go, how would you Americans put it . . . go . . ." He looked at Bill, seeking help.

Bill blew on his soup. " 'Ballistic' is one expression I've heard used. So pissed that one launches ICBMs."

The Arab smiled. "He would naturally be at the top of the list of suspects."

"Or close to the top," Bill said.

"He is amused by your . . . your wicked imagination. That's so. He wishes you all the best, but he doesn't want to be linked to you in any way. Surely, you can see it from his point of view. He did not get to where he is by being foolish or rash."

Bill looked resigned. He sought solace in his cigar, taking another puff. He held the smoke in his mouth, thinking.

The Arab added quickly: "If you can figure out a way of talking him into helping you out, please, be my guest. I will always listen respectfully. He has made it clear that I am to hear you out. It is my job."

Bill observed the growing length of white ash on the tip of the cigar. He took another puff. "How? How do I talk him into it?"

The Arab scratched his head. "You will first have to assure him there'll be no risk. We all learned a lot when Pan Am 103 went down over Lockerbie. The FBI agents were meticulous and tenacious. The evidence they gleaned from the wreckage was nothing short of amazing. Since you're a potential link, you can't be personally involved. You'll have to operate at a safe remove. Assertions won't do. You'll have to demonstrate this ability in advance."

Bill regarded the ash on his cigar again. "I can see the concern. How would I demonstrate my alibi? By having lunch with you or one of your people while the hit was made elsewhere?"

"It would take that or something close. I am under instructions to exercise extreme care."

"Fair enough. Assuming I alter my MO to his satisfaction, what would be the cost?"

The Arab smiled faintly. "We know you're clever with a computer and have the ability to manipulate electronic deposits, but he has oil to sell. He can get all the money he wants. Your best bet would be some form of barter."

"A swap? Swap what? Goods? Services? What?"

"Oh, I don't know." The Arab, looking thoughtful, pursed his lips. "You'll have to offer him something he can't resist, although I have no idea what that might be. You Americans are supposed to be creative. Use your imagination. Look around you. Think about motive and proceed from there. Right now . . ." He stopped. "Right now, I'm afraid he doesn't have any compelling reason to sell you what you want. I'm truly sorry. This is an extremely delicate business."

Bill sighed.

The Arab said, "Dangerous. Very, very dangerous."

"I have no criminal record of any kind, and no motive."

"No motive?" The Arab looked dubious. Watching Bill's eyes, he said, "You don't need us for everything. Surely you know that. Some of the formulas are simple in the extreme. People manufacture ballpoint pens and sell swimming-pool supplies in the United States, don't they? Right there you have the ingredients for something that will make them sit up and take notice."

Bill looked thoughtful. "Yes, there's that. With a vile reputation. Crude, but effective."

"I should think so," the Arab said. "Widely used by the Germans in the First World War. Hardly more sophisticated than ammonium nitrate and diesel fuel."

"But I remain interested in a larger, more sophisticated inventory. Far more exotic and dramatic." Bill gave a lazy half-smile.

"I see. Well . . . I've tried to be as clear and straightforward as possible. You know what you have to do. Demonstrate clearly that you can operate without personal involvement, then offer him something he wants very badly and can't get anywhere else. Hard terms, I suppose, but there you have it. Hard world." The Arab took a sip of tea. He savored it for a moment, then stood.

"Can't win 'em all, I suppose." Bill looked resigned, then brightened. "But then again, what you've given me is only a qualified no, isn't it? That offers some hope. I know what I have to do."

The Arab waited for two Moroccan men to pass by the table. When they were well out of earshot, he said, "Yes, you know what is required, or at least part of what is necessary. You also know how to contact me. Beyond that, there's not much I can say. My authority is limited."

Bill suddenly looked upbeat. He smiled lazily and took a

draw on his cigar, savoring the smoke. "Sooie piggy. This is mighty good smoke!"

Sayani stood and quietly fell in behind the passing Moroccans.

Behind Bill, a man's voice said, quietly, "Bobby Pearl!"

two

Jake Hipp's crossing of paths with Bobby Pearl had begun the day before in Seville, in the Spanish Andalusia, where Hipp had been sent to check out a long shot that had originated in Amsterdam. A prostitute in the Centrum, Amsterdam's red-light district, had told the Dutch police that one of her johns was telling her of his plans to visit Seville, one of his favorite cities. Later, the john, in the mood to talk, claimed he was Pearl; this slip of the tongue occurred moments before he beat her unconscious in a sudden fit of rage, apparently leaving her for dead.

A Charlie named Arthur Hill had fielded the tip from the Dutch police and talked to the girl, but his report was awful, and the context in which Pearl had mentioned Seville was unclear. Had Bobby Pearl somehow been bragging to a prostitute? Why? All Hipp had to go on was that the alleged Pearl was a well-built man in his late forties or early fifties. He had strawberry-blond hair and blue eyes, and he was a real mean son of a bitch. Where was the surprise there? Where was that otherwise useless bit of information that would set this snake apart?

Pearl was in Bangkok, the rumors went. Then in Rio de Janeiro. Then Amsterdam. This time it was Seville, which was fine by Hipp, an aficionado of the laid-back Andalusians in Southwestern Spain. But the Amsterdam report wasn't much of a lead. What with forged documents, hair rinses, colored contact lenses, wigs and beards, an uninspired physical description didn't amount to a whole lot, and there was a glut on the market of abusive sons of bitches. Mongoose suspected strongly that Pearl's real name was lost in the mists of his past. The controlling metaphor of his current surname did not escape the terrorist chasers: a pearl formed slowly over time around an irritant inside an oyster. He was the blackest of black pearls, this one.

Seville was home to the cathedral where Tomás de Torquemada, a world-class son of a bitch, had popped the bones and stretched the spines of heretics in the fifteenth-century Inquisition—giving Gypsies and Jews, of which he was originally one, an extra ration of God's sweet embrace. And here, on the Rio Guadalquivir, was *La Torre del Oro*—the Tower of Gold—where the conquistadors' New World riches were stored. Here too was the Spain of Miguel de Cervantes; and *La Plaza de Toros* in Seville was the ring made famous by Ernest Hemingway's short story, "Death in the Afternoon."

But more than all that, Seville was the home of Sevillana, a flamboyant, flagrantly sexy dance accompanied by the hammering of guitars and the stomping of feet. Sevillana was not a concert-hall kind of music; to be properly enjoyed, there should be green-eyed Spanish dancers, ladies with pale skin and long black hair, proud to the point of arrogance, teasing sweating male onlookers with smoldering looks over bare shoulders. *Ay Dios!* When they sent their skirts sailing, showing a forbidden flash of thigh and pantied buns, it was to rejoice in their beauty, a splendid bounty. The men, displaying elegant machismo—chins high, chests out, wrists crossed at the small of their backs—circled about their ladies with a dramatic *rat-a-tat-tat* stomping of their boots.

At night, when the dancers flashed their stuff, the revelers crowded into bars with stainless-steel counters, drinking red wine and eating *tapas*—olives, cheeses, calamares, *chicharones*, and every Spanish snack imaginable; they spilled out onto the sidewalks drinking and laughing. The smell of *puros,* hashish mixed with tobacco, was everywhere. After a wild Saturday night came hangover Sunday, and the price was paid in throbbing heads, confessions, and vows of never again, for this was a religious city, whose many streets were largely named for holy virgins.

On their charts, the ancient mariners had marked the vast reaches of the unknown with the notation: "Here Lie Dragons." Albert Einstein had taught moderns that space and time were inexorably mixed; space was curved, and there were places where time stood still. In Seville, where the barbarous Torquemada had once reigned, Hipp had begun his journey into the darkness of the next century. There lay snakes.

Jake Hipp was a forty-six-year-old, divorced sociobiologist turned terrorist chaser. He had blue eyes, short brown hair graying at the temples, a strong jaw, a hint of a cleft or dimple on his chin, and remarkably full lips that were not Mick Jagger, but close. Internally, he was a firestorm of ideas. Externally, he was an unmade bed. He had been forever thus. His needs were Spartan. His imagination was Darwinian. Everywhere he looked—traveling the fields and forests, flying in the air, swimming in the water, and wearing suits and ties—he saw beasts.

Hipp was unimpressed by the who of rank, position, or fame. He was indifferent to the what of fashion. The when and the where looped back on themselves. He was a quester of why. He believed that the great conflict of the coming century would not be between warring armies as in the past but in the struggle to bring down terrorists. Hipp knew that terrorists would never stop popping up. Their obsessions were too complicated to understand completely, but in the long run, there was only one possible defense against them: they had to know they couldn't get away with it. A foray into terrorism had to be made a no-win proposition, guaranteed.

Hipp's life had become an odyssey of understanding the motives of terrorists and of running them to ground. As such, he had become as Victor Hugo's Javert in *Les Miserables;* he was implacable, indomitable. Whenever a chickenshit killed at random from ambush, Hipp had vowed on his mother's eyes to bring him down. He, Jake Hipp, would see to it. He would have the creeps. They were his meat. He would not be denied. He was no superman, no high-kicking Bruce Lee or coolly lethal James Bond, but he never quit, never.

Yes, there were well-financed and skilled organizations, including his employers, who were also dedicated terrorist chasers. They too never quit. They had every kind of high-tech investigative tool imaginable, and they were linked internationally by computers. But theirs was an institutional mission. Hipp believed that the pursuit of a phantom quarry was ultimately a creative enterprise. Individuals were creative; institutions rarely were. Hipp's obsession was personal. He hated the motherfuckers.

Hipp decided to watch faces and the sevillana dancers in *La Casa de Pancho.* He found an empty stool at the bar by the *tapas,* a real score, and nursed his favorite Spanish cocktail, the unaccountably civilized combination of *ginebra y Coca Cola.* He assumed that only a country that had produced Salvador Dali could have thought of such a superb drink. Even more civilized were Andalusian bartenders, charming gentlemen who felt they embarrassed themselves if they did not pour long and with gusto. *Ay!* What was gin and Coke for if not to get *"un poco borrachito?"* This phrase, literally meaning to get "a little drunk," was deliberately ironic; it meant to get totally pissed.

Hipp saw nothing that would suggest Bobby Pearl in *La Casa de Pancho,* but two Northern European women, leggy blondes in their early thirties, momentarily caught his attention. One of them seemed somehow distracted. Was she concerned or worried about something? Her companion was engaged in heavy conversation with a Spanish macho man, complete with a rope of gold around his neck and the top three buttons of his white shirt unfastened to show off the fleece of curly black hair on his chest. She had poise and a certain flair about her; she was likely well educated, yet her choice in males was unremarkable.

Hipp enjoyed watching the human animal at play and speculating on the evolutionary song to which the partners danced. Was it intellect and empathy that women sought, or was it power and control? Hipp's conclusions were not uplifting.

He was nursing a gin and Coke and eating slices of dark, reddish-brown *jamon serrano,* mountain ham—a treat not unlike the dry, salty Smithfield hams in the United States— when the distracted woman tapped him on the shoulder. When she spoke, it was with a German accent.

She said, "Excuse me, sir. My name is Greta Mann. I was wondering if you might be able to help me out." She had a look in her eye. She was afraid of something.

Hipp, still chewing on a piece of ham, swallowed quickly. "Sure. But I suppose it all depends."

"I have a problem with a certain man."

Hipp grinned.

"His name is Roger. I had an, uh, embarrassing incident involving him three days ago. He's been following my girl-friend Frieda and me ever since."

"Following you?"

Greta said, "We've been planning this holiday for two years, and he's ruining it. Everyplace we go, there he is, star-ing at me."

"I see," Hipp said.

"He has silver hair, but please don't look for him. He scares me. What if he's crazy or dangerous? You see my girl-friend talking to the Spanish man?"

"Fine-looking lady."

"That's Frieda. She's having fun and doesn't want to go home, but I do. I'm tired of seeing Roger wherever I go. I was wondering if you would escort me back to our hotel. I don't want to catch a taxi alone. There are all those people on the sidewalk, and what if he should follow me?"

"How do you know I'm not crazy?"

Greta smiled. "I don't. But I've been watching you. You seem only interested in the *tapas* and watching the dancers."

"They're beautiful. That black hair and pale skin. Those long legs." Hipp groaned in appreciation.

Greta smiled. "I'll pay for the taxi."

"The cab's on me, no problem. I was ready to go home

anyway. I'll drop you off on my way." He stood and gave her his elbow. "My name is Jake Hipp. Shall we go, then?"

She took his elbow. "Thank you, Herr Hipp."

Hipp steered Greta to her friend to say good-bye. Then— seeing no silver-haired men—he guided her through the crowd to the street outside, where a queue of taxis waited for celebrants wanting a ride home. He opened the door to the backseat of the lead cab and slid in beside Greta. As the taxi drove off, he snuck a quick peek back. In the crowd, he saw a silver-haired man staring after them, but Hipp was too far away to see his features clearly.

Greta said, "Is he back there?"

Hipp gave Roger a quick bye-bye wave of the hand. "He's there." They rode in silence for a moment, then Hipp said, "You spoke of an embarrassing incident with Roger. I was curious."

Greta bit her lower lip. "He really is quite good-looking and charming in his way. He speaks fluent Spanish. You know, the way they speak it in Mexico or South America. I went with him to his hotel after we had been dancing."

She seemed disinclined to say anything more, but Hipp prodded her. "What happened?"

Greta gave him a lazy half-grin. "Unfortunately, nothing happened. Poor man. He . . ." She hesitated, obviously wondering if she should tell Hipp. "I suppose we all have our problems, don't we?" She shook her head sadly, then perked up. She wanted to change the subject. "You are an American, Herr Hipp?"

"Yes, ma'am. From Missoula, Montana, originally. Lately from Washington State."

"I'm from Munich. We get the snow." Greta sank back in the seat, relieved to be rid of her admirer. "Thank you," she said. "I mean that sincerely."

"We Americans aren't all bad," Hipp said. "Are you a football fan?"

"Why, yes I am. My ex-boyfriend was a midfielder for Bayern Munich."

"I like Ajax," Hipp said. Greta seemed surprised that an

American would know anything about the famous Dutch side. If Gina knew he was sitting in the backseat of a cab with a beautiful German woman, she'd come crashing through the window, fangs bared.

Hipp saw the driver eye him in the rearview mirror, wondering if he was going to make a move on Greta. A Spanish man would have a hand on her thigh by now. A casual hand, mind, but there nevertheless. Hipp decided to do his countrymen's reputation a favor and avoid embarrassing himself. He would go back to his hotel and get some sleep. Let Fraulein Greta Mann pass on the myth of having encountered an American with savoir faire.

Five hours later, at 11:32 P.M., Eastern Daylight Time, the FBI's International Terrorist Watch had intercepted fragments of a telephone call. The call, between a man in Paris and a Sudanese Intelligence operative assigned as a political officer in Sudan's Washington Embassy, mentioned "*. . . ob . . . earl*" in *"Seville."* Seville was the only complete word in the conversation. In addition to *. . . ob . . . earl* in *Seville,* the pieces of words included *nel . . . ayani . . . up . . . en . . . sat . . . ay . . . m . . . bur . . . ier.* The snatches of sound were gleaned from transmission by an ultra-high-speed decoding software that was rapidly overcoming the current Sudanese security scrambler. Spy versus spy had evolved into cryptologist versus cryptologist; it was the modern world.

The Watch forwarded the data to Mongoose at the CIA, as per their working agreement. Both The Watch and Company computers suggested that *nel . . . ayani* was likely Sudanese Colonel Hasan Sayani, an Intelligence officer and surrogate for Moamar Qadhafi. The National Security Agency program said *up* was most likely the middle of supper; *en* was part of 10:00 P.M.; *sat . . . ay* were fragments of Saturday; *m . . . bur,* the apparent spot for the meeting, was unknown; and *ier* was the tail end of Tangier.

At 11:52 P.M. in Washington, 4:52 A.M. in Spain and Morocco, Joe Woofter, Hipp's control at Mongoose, phoned the American consul in Tangier, waking her up to ask if she could identify *m . . . bur.* She yawned and said sure. A popular new bar for European travelers was named for William Burroughs.

The computers had concluded that Bobby Pearl would travel from Seville to Tangier and meet Sudanese Colonel Hasan Sayani in William Burroughs at 10:00 P.M. the next night, a Saturday.

The alarm on Jake Hipp's computer woke him up at 5:04 A.M. He opened his secure file from Mongoose—transmitted through facilities at the NSA at Fort George G. Meade, Maryland. The keyboard was more secure than voice transmission. Joe Woofter sent Hipp the fragments of conversation, the conclusion of Mongoose's computer, a photo of Colonel Sayani, and ordered him to Tangier immediately. *"Find the rendezvous of Rattler Four. If at all possible, use your snake kit to bring him back alive. If not, spike him."*

Congress had written laws to prevent assassinations by its Intelligence services, but there were times when laws were overridden by common sense; even congressmen knew that. Use of the kit was preferred; that went without saying. A spike, or kill order, was rare to the point of being almost nonexistent, and was not issued except in the most alarming of circumstances. Hipp typed back: *"Received your message. Please repeat order."*

Hipp watched the letters march across the screen as Woofter keyed them in. *"Use your kit if possible. If not, spike him. We're talking Rattler Four here, and you're operating solo. But remember always: in a minute, there is time for decisions and revisions."*

"Which a minute may reverse"—Hipp finished the famous line from T. S. Eliot's "The Love Song of J. Alfred Prufrock." Woofter was saying that Mongoose could yet change its mind. In the meantime, the responsibility of spiking Bobby Pearl was Hipp's. Woofter had delivered his instructions in such a way that if the spike went sour, both sides could later claim miscommunication. Say nothing directly, even in an alleged secure transmission; that was the rule.

Jake Hipp had taken care of the bill at the hotel desk and begun stowing his belongings in the trunk of his rented Fiat. He had a three-hour drive ahead of him on the winding road from Seville past Cadiz to Algeciras, the Spanish town circling the small bay just west of Gibraltar. Here, ferries regularly crossed the Strait of Gibraltar to Tangier, a four-hour trip.

three

That Jake Hipp should come to be on the spot in Seville could ultimately be traced to a famous meeting of the National Security Council, when, after years of delay and denial, the American antiterrorist response had been formally coordinated in an effort to pacify an increasingly anxious American public. There had been antiterrorist units for years, but these had been rump groups, splintered among several bureaucracies, each of which was reluctant to yield its part of the action. To assure the voters that something creditable was being done in their defense, a proper war on terrorism had to be fought with identifiable armies.

At this meeting, the President had brokered the sharing of the turf among the Pentagon, the FBI, the CIA, and lesser alphabet law-enforcement agencies. A war on terrorism meant increased budgets; increased budgets meant increased power.

To blunt right-wing claims that the Justice Department was establishing an antimilitia gestapo, the director of the FBI argued that the Bureau should be allowed to call its antiterrorist task force "The International Terrorist Watch." The director knew this would be annoying to foreign governments, but foreigners didn't vote in American elections.

Of course the director of the CIA knew about the proposal in advance, and of the President's probable response—the chief executive was notoriously, even laughably, reluctant to offend single-issue voters. The director of Central Intelligence, feigning indignation and suppressed fury, said he would consider resigning if the President approved; the FBI was clearly poaching on the Company's traditional overseas domain!

The DCI was no fool. Having made his point, he didn't press the issue. Better stealth than bravado. He knew that the President and the Bureau director, having gotten their way on the FBI's use of the word "International," couldn't very well object to the Company's right to name its own unit. In victory, they were both gentlemanly and courteous. Certainly, they said. Give us a name.

Well, the DCI said, consider a terrorist as a kind of snake. Snakes are mentioned in the Old Testament as Satan incarnate. They glide silently. They blend into the terrain. They strike by surprise. Some of them carry the most toxic poisons on the planet. Also, they molt; that is, they periodically change their skin, literally sloughing off their old exterior. Terrorists were skilled at crossing borders with forged documents and at altering their appearance with cosmetics. The DCI said the CIA wished to call its antiterrorist unit "Mongoose." Mongooses ate snakes. Mongoose would call its operatives "Charlies," for chasers.

Charlies were what the American soldiers called the Viet Cong in the Vietnam War, and there had been an Operation Mongoose to assassinate suspected Viet Cong operatives; the DCI had been an army captain in Vietnam, an agent of the Defense Intelligence Agency. Both tactically and strategically, this was a kind of Vietnam, he was saying; it takes a Charlie to catch a Charlie. In 1944, the folks back home had been able to chart the competing front lines on maps posted on the wall at the office. One for Europe. A second for the Pacific. Times change. Now the enemy was everywhere.

Both the President and the director of the FBI knew immediately that they'd been trumped. Where was the FBI that had loosed The Untouchables against Al Capone and Pretty Boy Floyd? International Terrorist Watch was old-fashioned and stodgy. From a public-relations standpoint, it was plain dumb. Mongoose would appeal to the public imagination and to the media, which was the modern route to a larger budget and more power.

So the Company formed Mongoose. For internal memoranda and external communications, all terrorists were given snake codes, depending on their habits. Rattlers were terrorists who gave warning before they struck. The IRA was noted for rattler behavior, giving Londoners a half hour to evacuate a particular tube or department store. Muslim fanatics just triggered the chomp and slithered into the darkness. These were vipers.

Since weapons of terrorism were low-tech and widely available, mass killing, as opposed to solo serial killing, was the spooky next step for a psychopath operating alone and for reasons that were specific and individual, thus impossible to predict. Following the madness of the Unabomber, the crazy snake was the unspoken fear at the National Security Agency. This fear was never articulated in public lest it trigger the imagination of the wrong person, and nobody wanted talk-show hosts spooking the public with speculation.

Bobby Pearl was thought to be a crazy snake. He used the telephone or the World Wide Web before he struck, and was suspected to be a molter—a reference to his habit of changing identities. Since Pearl was the fourth major rattler encountered by the Mongoose antiterrorist unit since its inception, he was designated "Rattler Four."

It was a blustery day, with Gibraltar looming large on Jake Hipp's left and whitecaps on the deep-blue Mediterranean, but he did not go below. Never mind the wind whipping his hair and beating against his jacket; Hipp wanted to savor the sight of that famous rock on the port side of the ferry. Gibraltar was splendid in the late afternoon sun. The impregnable Rock. Symbol of an insurance company. Actually, this was the west face, opposite the famous profile most associated with the Rock. On this side, the Juanitos, as the residents of Gibraltar called themselves, lived and ran bars and eateries supported largely by the tourist trade. Hipp popped on a 200-mm lens and snapped a few shots.

On the upper deck there were about fifteen or sixteen travelers, hippie-looking young people traveling in twos and threes, and a few middle-aged men traveling alone, including Hipp. The tourists were down below, out of the wind, listening to their tour guide explain the Moroccan customs.

Hipp was leaning against the port rail, watching Gibraltar's famous profile, when a fellow solo traveler joined him, a slender, amiable Brit with spectacles and curly hair. After introductions, the Brit, whose name was Nigel Beauchamp, said, "I was in a pub in Gibraltar yesterday. They had a book of Gibraltar facts for tourists, so I made some notes. Interesting stuff."

Hipp was in the mood for some company, and Beauchamp had a likable way about him.

Beauchamp dug his hands into the front pocket of his baggy corduroy trousers and pulled out a wadded piece of paper. On this, in small, handwritten letters, was a series of sentences arranged in a list.

Beauchamp began reading from the paper. "Fourteen sieges over the years. That's beginning with the Moors in"— he read from his notes—"seven eleven A.D. Thirteen centuries ago. In seventeen twenty-six, the king of Spain attacked the Rock with an international brigade of mercenaries. They fired fourteen thousand rounds in four days. The barrels of their cannons melted, so they had to withdraw. The British on Gibraltar lost only twenty-six men." He glanced up, grinning, "Really let 'em have it, eh? Take that! Boom! Boom!"

Beauchamp turned to the reverse side of the paper, where the printing was smaller. "Here we are. The Great Siege, from seventeen ninety-nine to eighteen hundred and two. In July, seventeen ninety-nine, the French and Spanish surrounded Gibraltar with a hundred and twenty thousand men and all the cannons they could lug. The next day they fired sixty thousand thirteen-inch shells and a hundred and fifty thousand cannonballs at the place. The British plowed up the streets to keep the cannonballs from skipping."

Hipp said, "You British know how to endure a siege, I'll give you that. Stiff upper lip and the rest of it. Look at what you put up with in the Battle of Britain. German bombs and

V-One rockets day and night." He cocked his head in admiration.

Beauchamp was pleased. "That pounding of Gibraltar was just a warm-up. The French and Spanish kept Gibraltar surrounded and hammered away at it for three more years. Finally, they held a competition for the best way to overrun the defenders. That was won by a" —he checked his notes— "a Frenchman, Chevalier d'Arcon." He looked up at Gibraltar, now receding off the ferry's stern. "D'Arcon proposed to float batteries into position on huge platforms built atop cut-down ships. It was to be a floating menace composed of just about every kind of vessel imaginable." He pointed astern. "Right back there is where it happened. As the French and Spaniards struggled to get their batteries into position, a crowd of journalists and the curious began gathering on the surrounding hills to watch. The British general ordered that his cannonballs should be dumped in charcoal and heated. Am I telegraphing my story?" Beauchamp grinned.

Hipp laughed. "I say he set the mess afire. Clever Brit."

Beauchamp grinned. "You got it. Fifteen hundred Spanish and French sailors were killed. Over the centuries, nobody could drive the Gibraltans out. They tried and tried and tried again, but nobody could make it."

Beside them at the rail, a male voice with an American accent said, "Ridiculous drill. Why didn't the Spanish just slip ashore in the small hours and slit their silly throats?"

Both Hipp and Beauchamp were startled because they hadn't seen the mustached, pale-complexioned, blond man who had edged up to the rail beside Hipp. He wore a grommeted yachting cap and a blue-nylon windbreaker and had a small, dark-green day pack slung over one shoulder. He idly slipped a knife out of his pocket. A spring-loaded blade popped out, quick as a viper's tongue.

He casually reached out and put the tip of the knife at Hipp's throat, pricking him gently.

Hipp blinked, trying not to move his head.

"See there. Easy enough to do," the man said. He eyed Hipp over the tip of the blade. "Surprise is the thing," he said. "See how effective it is? A sweet tactic. You can't plan for it or anticipate it." He pushed the knife gently into Hipp's skin.

Hipp's eyes widened. He rose to the balls of his feet. He found himself barely able to breathe.

"This is a carotid artery here on your neck. A pumper. One little nip and the blood just shoots. Squirt, squirt, squirt."

Jesus Christ, what is this? Hipp was stupefied. What should he do?

The man said, "The Spanish and French were stupid. All that fair-play horseshit. Right?"

"Right," Hipp said. He felt like somebody was sitting on his chest.

"I just bet you'd agree with anything I said, wouldn't you?" The man looked amused.

Hipp licked his lips. His mouth was dry.

The man looked disgusted. "I thought so, Mr. Macho. Why, just look at you now!" He shook his head. He pushed the tip of the knife against the rail, returning the blade into the handle. He said, "Have a good day, Champ." He drifted away and went below.

Hipp thought his knees were going to buckle.

Beauchamp, shaken, glared after the knife-bearing intruder. "Bloody sod."

Hipp's hands began to tremble. His heart was thumping like it was out of control. "Jesus!"

Beauchamp smiled weakly. "Almost peed my pants."

"I almost did more than that," Hipp said.

"Who in the sod is that?"

"I have no idea."

"You don't?" Beauchamp looked puzzled. "He was after you, not me. He sounded like he knew you."

Hipp bit his lower lip, thinking. "As far as I know, I've never met him before in my life."

"Well, if he wasn't sore at you, what on earth brought that on, do you suppose?"

Hipp took a deep breath. "I don't know."

"Was he just crazy? Was that it?"

"Had to be. Nobody carrying a full load would act like that."

It took a half hour for Hipp's stomach to stop churning and for his hands to calm down. He couldn't forget the knife at his throat. The look of pure, raw hatred in the man's eyes was unforgettable. Beauchamp was right; it did seem like the man knew him. Had Hipp seen him somewhere without knowing it? What could he have conceivably done to piss him off like that? He couldn't figure it.

The knife-man was right about one thing; it was more difficult to catch snakes swimming ashore and sliding about unseen than it was to defend against foreign invasion. There was precious little glory fighting terrorists, neither banners to fly nor stirring parades. It occurred to Hipp that the United States had invested its future in a form of siege defense, in the manner of the Juanitos. From Hadrian's Wall and the Great Wall of China to the Maginot Line and Gibraltar, the myth of the impregnable fortress had had a long run.

As he leaned against the rail looking out over the water, Hipp thought back to his childhood, of having to get up in a raging blizzard in Montana to milk cows or to help his father deliver calves, of having to buck bales of hay that weighed more than he did. While other boys his age were good at hitting jumpshots or handling a curve ball, Hipp had one singular ability that had propelled him from Missoula through scholarships at Washington State University, and eventually to a Ph.D. at the University of Virginia. Now he was carrying the people's spike, defending the common ground against an out-of-control predator. He was a man of the cortex. Based on his reaction to having a knife poking him in the throat, he wondered if someone more attuned to the reptilian brain stem might be more qualified for this job. But he knew he was wrong. He had been faced with the prospect of getting his throat cut. Instinct had served him well. To survive, he had done what he had to do, which was nothing.

When Hipp and Beauchamp finally went below, the predator with the knife was nowhere to be seen.

Later, as Hipp waited for the Moroccan customs officials to check his passport, he suddenly smelled full, robust cigar smoke.

Behind him, a man said, "Had a good time with the German girl, did you? Don't turn around."

Hipp recognized the voice. Mr. Big Knife. Then it came to him in a flash of intuition. He understood why knife-man had been so pissed. The blond, mustached man with the knife was the Roger who had stalked Greta Mann in Seville. He had changed the color of his hair from silver to blond. Was he smoking a cigar? Hipp said mildly, "All I did was take her home."

The man said nothing. The line inched forward.

"Figured me out, eh?"

"It just now came to me."

"Have a good laugh at my expense? Greta gave you an earful, did she? Ha, ha, ha! Laughed 'til you thought you'd die."

Hipp said, "I beg your pardon?"

"Just had to give me a little wave, didn't you? Couldn't resist."

Hipp was thankful it was his turn to have his passport inspected. He set it on the table and opened it for the Moroccan official to examine. While the man gave the passport a vigorous chop and signed his initials, Hipp—doing his best to ignore Roger—admired the gorgeous white Mediterranean buildings set on a ridge above the small bay. The very name Tangier was mysterious and exotic, and Hipp's first view of it matched his expectations.

He locked onto Nigel Beauchamp for protection, and the two of them pushed quickly through the crowd of young men offering their services as guides or procurers of whatever scam they were hustling. Hipp felt insecure at being in a crush of bodies, where one thrust of a sicko's blade could screw up his meeting with Rattler Four. He took the lead, forcing Beauchamp to trot. Hipp found open space and stayed there. He glanced back once, checking for Roger the knife-man, but the spooky son of a bitch was not to be seen. He was no Eagle Scout, that was for sure. How many people changed the color of their hair overnight and packed around a blade like that?

four

Dr. Jake Hipp had originally embarked on an academic career as a sociobiologist on the faculty of the University of Maryland in College Park, and later at Lewis and Clark College, in Portland, Oregon. In both places, he had expected that the tepid spaghetti in the faculty dining room would be enlivened by good talk and ideas. He would get to find out what physicists and chemists were doing and what English professors were reading and writing. There had been some of that, but the talk was mostly of faculty politics: who got hired and fired; who had power and who did not; what program got a boost in its budget.

That had been a disappointing turn of events for Hipp. After a failed marriage that had produced a daughter, he was in his late thirties and restless. His being an academic had been his ex-wife's idea, not his. She had liked the idea of being a professor's wife. He had concluded that he was probably better suited doing something else, but he wasn't sure what.

Then one warm spring afternoon, a small man in his late fifties with intelligent blue eyes and short graying hair showed up at Hipp's office at Lewis and Clark College. By nature gentlemanly, self-effacing, and extremely polite, Joe Woofter carried with him a dossier that included both Hipp's counterintelligence training in the army and his education.

After politely introducing himself, Woofter gave Hipp a brief introduction to T-Cell, the Mongoose antiterrorist think tank. T-Cells fought infection in blood. Betas, for brains, were T-Cell scholars and researchers. Populations were getting larger and more diverse, Woofter said, and movement across international borders had become routine. Since the first perimeter of defense was to identify potential perps, T-Cell was the unglamorous front line of the struggle against terrorists. The field agents, Charlies, were the second line of defense, followed by the final perimeter of gates, guards, metal detectors, dogs, and the rest of it.

Hipp immediately wanted to be a Charlie, but assumed that Woofter was likely there to recruit him as a Beta, and he was right. He accepted anyway, thinking that later, when Mongoose got to know him, he would get a shot at becoming a Charlie.

Hipp liked Joe Woofter, who in time would become his good friend and mentor. A graduate of Cornell University at age sixteen, Woofter had spent most of his early and middle years in think tanks speculating on the future. He could speed-read the Romance languages, and spoke fluent German and serviceable Arabic. Still with only a bachelor's degree, he had become a full professor at Harvard by the time Mongoose was formed in the wake of the Trade Center bombing, Oklahoma City, and TWA Flight 800. Mongoose had recruited him as a Beta futurist, although it turned out that he had a genius for directing Charlies in the field. Of all the influential friends to have in the Mongoose brain trust, it was hard to beat Joe Woofter.

In T-Cell, Hipp studied alongside psychologists, sociologists, and anthropologists of every theoretical stripe, plus experts in cults and religions, demographers, statisticians, and more. It was Hipp's assignment—with as much remove as possible—to view terrorists solely as hairless primates with outsized brains that were only sometimes put to good use. Some sociobiologists, passionately enthusiastic Darwinians and lovers of academic quarrels, described humans as genetically programmed robots. Hipp avoided such inflammatory terms; he didn't think the robot metaphor was completely accurate, but it was a close call.

The romantic Charlies came home with stories of sweaty nights in Rangoon and train rides in Siberia, while most of the Betas lived in the Virginia suburbs of Washington, with few thrills greater than throwing a Frisbee around on the weekend. There were rare Betas who did not dream of one day becoming a Charlie, but the Mongoose bureaucracy, wearing the Company silks in the institutional struggle against the FBI, felt compelled to construct a mythical elite. Mongoose issued invitations to potential Charlies, thank you; it did not encourage applications.

Within three months of going to work in T-Cell, Hipp submitted an application to work the field. He was turned down. He submitted a second application. Again he was denied. Then a third and a fourth. He was rejected each time. He became a nag, almost a joke. He wanted to become a Charlie, dammit, not sidelined as a Beta. He refused to quit.

On the afternoon following Hipp's eighth turndown, Woofter had dropped by for a second visit that was to change Hipp's life. "Another application, eh, Jake? Stubborn."

Hipp had looked rueful. "Can't blame a guy for trying."

"Your dossier says you're a slightly introverted, open-minded intellectual. You're analytic. Classic Beta material. Not the usual profile for a Charlie."

" 'Slightly introverted' means I have sense enough to listen before I make a fool of myself. 'Open-minded' means I don't believe in absolutes. 'Analytic' means I test all sides of an idea. So what? Be creative for once. Try something different."

Woofter smiled. "That's exactly what we've been thinking."

Hipp's mouth dropped.

"Got boring turning you down, so we decided to throw you out there in the mud and the blood and the spit to watch some snakes in their natural habitat."

Hipp had been jubilant. "A Charlie? Really?"

"We'll see how it goes," Woofter said.

It didn't take Hipp long to learn that chasing snake rumors was a laborious, time-consuming business. The Mongoose computer sorted out reported descriptions, looking for a match as transnational snakes slithered across borders. But computers couldn't do everything. Garbage in, garbage out;

it applied to Mongoose's programs the same as to everybody else's.

In the end, Mongoose's success depended on two skills that happened to be nearly identical to one of Charlie's natural adversaries: journalists.

A good Charlie could sit down at a laptop and go beyond the photos he had taken; the best Charlies were highly skilled at seeing and appreciating the nonverbal communication of wannabe snakes: their facial gestures, the rhythms of their speech, their choice of costume, and the whole panoply of tics, habits, and preferences that describe human character. The old bell-shaped curve applied to writing skills with a vengeance; Charlies were required to describe their observations in consistently accurate, thorough agent reports, or ARs. Some Charlies, with high verbal skills, wrote incisive, even artful, ARs that were fun for their Mongoose superiors to read; others were tin-eared, blind to nuance, and unable to write a clear sentence.

Joe Woofter enjoined his Charlies to "give me little stories and surprises. I want character revealed." By character, Woofter meant "emotional fingerprints," which he believed were nearly as important in running down a snake as physical ones.

The second requisite skill was photography. Charlies took lots of pictures of snakes. These weren't art shots. They had a purpose. Individual faces were scanned and entered into Mongoose computers programmed to catalog features; the contours of faces were as idiosyncratic as whorls on a fingerprint. The Watch, aided by Mongoose, was inching ever closer to that wonderful day when all snakes crossing an American border would be required to face a camera plugged into that vast bank of data. A fingerprint scanner had already been put in place along the border with Mexico to prevent deported aliens from coming back over. The scanning of faces was next. At all ports of entry.

There was a catch to this, and everybody at The Watch and Mongoose knew it: since a snake's taste for the extreme was internal, unknowable, and unpredictable, the faces of crazy snakes—those operating outside the bent logic of ideologues and rabid religionists—went almost entirely uncharted.

Jake Hipp's transition from Beta to Charlie surprised and pleased the Mongoose bureaucrats who had scorned him for so long. He was second in his class at the Mongoose training school at Camp Edwards, and he turned out to be remarkably skilled in the field. His reports were clear and detailed. He was good with a camera. He found the mud and the blood and the spit far more congenial and fascinating than the sterility of a college classroom or a room filled with Beta computers.

It was for all those reasons that the Mongoose man spent that balmy evening in Tangier.

As Jake Hipp rounded a curve in the narrow street and the William Burroughs sign came into view, he spotted Colonel Hasan Sayani immediately. He was sitting at an outdoor table with . . . Roger, the knife-man! Hipp was momentarily stupefied. Both men had glasses of tea, and Roger, who was smoking a cigar, had a glass bowl before him, perhaps of soup.

Hipp's encounter with Roger in Seville had been by accident, but their encounter on the ferry was not; they had both been on their way to the same rendezvous. The remark about the strategic weakness of the Rock. The business of the knife, and going from gray to blond. The neurotic fury at Hipp's having left *La Casa de Pancho* with Greta. Crazy snake stuff. Now Sayani. This man's name was not Roger. This was Bobby Pearl. Oh, my God! Now he really felt the fear of the knife prick. *Bobby Pearl!*

Hipp, staying in the shadows, moved to his right around the perimeter of the intersection of narrow streets and even narrower alleys; he pretended to be interested in the tooled-leather wallets and ceramic beads being peddled by sidewalk vendors.

He knelt by a pile of Oriental rugs, seeming to be studying them.

He moved on from the rugs. Keeping an eye on Pearl, he stepped into a deserted, narrow alley that branched out from the intersection. The alley was shielded from the tables by two partitions of woven screens.

He squatted behind the partitions, peering through the crack between the panels. He quickly screwed a silencer onto the inch-and-a-half barrel of his .38 Smith & Wesson revolver.

Directly in front of him, Pearl's mood was suddenly upbeat. He took a drag on his cigar, savoring the smoke. He released it with a half-smile, saying, "Sooie piggy. Mighty good smoke!"

As he did, Sayani finished his tea and rose.

Pearl was not going to just sit there like a paranoid stump; he was going to eat while he watched passing faces.

Hipp cocked his Smith & Wesson.

Sayani strolled casually up the street.

From the crack between the panels, Hipp watched Pearl blow on his pumpkin soup to cool it. The alley behind him was deserted—a perfect escape into the labyrinth of passageways. He had a wad of hundred-dollar bills in his pocket to buy his way out of any momentary jam. He was less than ten feet from the craziest of crazy snakes.

He raised the pistol with his right hand while he eased the partitions apart with his left.

This was clearly Hipp's snake. He said softly, "Hey, Bobby Pearl."

Hipp's mark straightened. He turned. Seeing the pistol and recognizing Hipp, he looked surprised, if not outright stunned. The man from *La Casa de Pancho* and the ferry! He raised an eyebrow. Watching Hipp, he took a sip of tea.

The adrenaline surged. Hipp, looking at Pearl over the cocked hammer, struggled to keep his hand steady. His finger froze on the trigger for seconds that were centuries. And froze. Jesus! He did not doubt that this was Pearl, a man who had murdered close to eight hundred people from ambush. He was the closest thing imaginable to pure evil. And yet . . .

Buck fever was the source of much hairy-chested har-har-

har laughter in Montana saloons, where the ability to coolly
drop a mule deer was regarded as a test of manhood. To kill
was to be a man. Hipp was a sociobiologist by training. He
had always assumed he would be genetically prepared for
this moment. But no. Was he plain old chickenshit? What?

He had no idea.

The blond man understood immediately. The hammer
was to remain cocked.

He smiled faintly. He taunted Hipp with his eyes. He blew
a circle of smoke straight at Hipp, a mocking bull's-eye.
Then, cigar in his mouth, he used both hands to dump his
soup and tea and simultaneously scoop the glass bowl, eating utensils, and ashtray into the day pack.

He strolled away, taking his fingerprints with him.

Hipp, his heart pounding, uncocked his pistol and slipped
it back into his shoulder holster. He tried to follow Pearl, but
Rattler Four slithered into one of the dark alleys fanning out
from William Burroughs and was nowhere to be seen.

Hipp was shaking like a dog shitting peach pits. Buck
fever! For all his resolve and determination, he had choked.
He had embarrassed himself. He was furious. This terrible
turn of events was just awful. Now he bore the responsibility
of Bobby Pearl remaining on the loose, free to strike again.
When Pearl killed again, as he inevitably would, the deaths
would be Hipp's. Sweet Jesus, how had he allowed that to
happen? Why, oh why, oh why? What was wrong with him?

Beyond that lay an even bigger question: why was Bobby
Pearl talking to a surrogate for Moamar Qadhafi? What was
he after?

Hipp hurried back to the table, disconsolate. He arrived at
the same time as an annoyed waiter with a sponge and plastic pail; on the tabletop were sprigs of mint draped over
chunks of yellow squash. The waiter started cleaning the
table.

"Aw, fuck!" Hipp muttered.

"Sir?" the waiter said.

Hipp grimaced and slumped onto the chair vacated by
Pearl. He said, "You sell wine here?"

"Yes, sir."

"Red wine?"

"Yes, sir, from Spain."

"I'd like a bottle of red wine, then. Also, can you get me a small pipe and some hashish? I'll make it worth your while." Hipp dug into his pocket and retrieved one of his emergency one-hundred-dollar bills. He wanted the hash and wanted it now. He didn't want to deal with reasons why he shouldn't smoke hash in front of William Burroughs. He laid the bill on the table.

The waiter's eyes widened. "A bottle of wine. A pipe and some hashish. Yes, sir, I can get you that."

A few minutes later, with a bottle of Spanish *tinto* on the table, Hipp, in a gloom of despondency, lit up and proceeded to get stoned. He had begged Woofter to allow him to become a Charlie. Although his profile was wrong, Mongoose had finally relented. Now this.

Jake Hipp vowed that his pursuit of Bobby Pearl was not yet over. He would get him. He would not quit, ever.

five

Carl Czez, pronounced "Chez," had traveled on so many passports that he risked screwing up when somebody asked him his name, but that couldn't be helped. He would just have to stay alert. For the moment, he had settled on Sal Amarando, which fit his dark complexion and curly black hair. He could easily be an Amarando. Or a Silva; a Rodriguez, for that matter. Until there was a reason to change again, he would remain Sal Amarando. What was in a name, after all? Although today he would use his Charles Walesa passport. An exception already. There were never enough names, it seemed. Czez smiled.

Riding in a cab negotiating the traffic on Nathan Road going north, toward the New Territories, Czez stared out at the endless shops on the Kowloon Peninsula. He had always been bewildered by the economics of Hong Kong. How on earth could there be enough tourists buying eyeglasses, binoculars, cameras, jewelry, and pirated CDs, tapes, and computer software to support what appeared to be thousands, if not tens of thousands, of shops? And who, other than neurotic shoppers with the imagination of Pac-Man, would care? It was beyond Czez.

Czez did not pretend to understand the Chinese psyche, having been told repeatedly that the aging comrades in Beijing were the legacy of an ancient civilization that was probably beyond his comprehension. Whatever the mysteries of Chinese culture, he had feared, wrongly, that the heavy-handed bureaucrats in Beijing would completely destroy Hong Kong when they took it over in 1997.

The Chinese had bragged that Hong Kong would become the Wall Street of their empire, and so it had. However conniving their reputation, the apparatchiks from the north were not so stupid as to destroy such a good thing as the commercial jewel they had so long coveted. The tourists kept coming, fooling themselves that because they had spent a couple of nights in an overpriced high-rise hotel in the Admiralty and strolled down the hubbub of Wanchai late at night, they had actually been to China. To some of them, eating a bowl of noodle soup in a sidewalk hole-in-the-wall was high adventure.

Czez was relieved that the comrades hadn't completely overdone the neat and orderly routine as had the barbarous shits who ran Singapore. Hong Kong's British colonialists had been both tidy and civilized. Hong Kong was now distinctly more Chinese, but it had a momentum and culture of its own, and the buying and selling continued unabated. That, ultimately, was its charm. Whatever you wanted— from scrimshaw to tiger-penis wine and pirated computer software—it was for sale in Hong Kong.

Just past the Hong Kong Club, where the ladies and gentlemen of the Empire had once played tennis in splendid whites, the driver turned left down yet another narrow, cluttered lane and pulled to a stop in front of yet another small cafe that sold noodles.

Above this cafe, in a Hong Kong version of a loft, was the studio of James Chan, a special-effects and makeup artist for Sing Sing Boyd, whose famous Boyd Productions had survived the Chinese takeover. Boyd's sets and contract facilities were spread out in numerous locations on the expensive Kowloon real estate; from disparate editing labs, costume-and-equipment warehouses, and special-effects studios like Chan's, Boyd's film crews churned out low-budget, highly profitable horror, adventure, and romance movies.

Czez made his way up a narrow stairwell to the left of the noodle shop. Two flights up, he turned left down a hallway until he came to a door bearing a brass nameplate: JAMES CHAN STUDIOS. He stepped inside.

A pretty receptionist in a tiny office that contained her desk, a potted plant, and a single chair, looked up from her work and glanced at an electric clock on the wall. "Mr. Walesa?"

"Yes, ma'am."

"You can go right on in. Mr. Chan is expecting you. Have you been here before?"

"Yes, I have," Czez said. He proceeded through another door and entered James Chan's remarkable workspace. The walls of the studio, which were about sixty feet long by twenty feet wide, bore an impossible clutter of wigs, beards, mustaches, swatches of hair and fur, horns, antlers, masks, heads, artificial limbs, lips, tongues, tails, ears, and noses. At the base of the walls were boxes of glass eyes, false teeth, fangs, and claws of one sort or another, plus boxes of latex and silicon, and jars of pastes, putties, and paints.

Czez picked his way down a narrow, littered trail to a well-lit workbench at the far end—itself a heap and confusion of hobbyist drills, soldering irons, awls, punches, knives, chisels, needles, brushes, spatulas, spray cans, jars and tubes of paint and glue—where the estimable James Chan, a middle-aged man with a potbelly and thick eyeglasses, sat on a metal stool with a padded, swivel top.

Chan turned on his stool, eyeing Czez. He hesitated, then said, "Mr. Walesa?"

"Pleased to meet you, Mr. Chan." They shook, and Czez looked around at the amazing walls of Chan's studio. He liked them.

Chan picked a thin rubber mask from the table. "Here it is, as promised. You want to try it on and check it out." He gestured at a full-length mirror at the side of his workbench.

Czez tried on the mask.

Behind him, Chan said, "That's him, all right. The mask is made of a new form of silicon compound. Better than latex. More realistic, and more comfortable for our actors. It's accurate down to the pores, and you can wear it for hours at a stretch with no problem. You'll have to change the color of your hair. Black hair won't go with his complexion."

Czez grinned.

"It should pass the muster of movie close-ups, security

cameras, or an eyewitness, but I'm not sure I would try it on an ex-wife. You just roll it back and pull it down over your head. If I got it right, it should be a perfect fit."

Czez did as he was told, adjusting the lips and ears and eyebrows. His mask, betraying not a hint of the artificial, smiled slightly. He looked at the photograph, then checked the image in the mirror. "It's perfect, I have to admit."

Chan said, "You look exactly like him."

Czez turned in front of the mirror. "And we're entirely clear as to the rules of business. There should be no misunderstanding."

"I value my life," Chan said mildly. "Also, you're paying me ten times what I'm making from Sing Sing Boyd. I'd be foolish to forgo profit and possible future business out of some misguided sense of justice. I'm a Chinese, Mr. Walesa, not an American."

"A professional in an age of slop. I admire that." Czez stripped off the mask and weighed it in his hand. "Do you have the gloves?"

"Yes, of course." Chan opened a drawer from under his workbench and removed a pair of thin, nearly transparent gloves with lifelike veins and hair on the back of each hand and fingers. "They're made of the same silicon compound as the mask. You'll find that the fingerprints check out, no problem. You'll have to learn how to put them on. Watch carefully now."

Chan carefully pushed back the thumb of the right-hand glove, or artificial skin, then continued with the forefinger, middle finger, ring finger, and little finger. When he had rolled all fingers of both hands into tight, condom-like circles at the knuckles, he put the gloves on the table. "Work from thumb to little finger or from little finger to thumb, but not from the middle. You'll need to do it slowly to avoid wrinkles."

"I roll the fingers on like little rubbers down to the palm?"

"That's right. Same order, thumb to little or little to thumb. It makes no difference which. Then you pull on the palm, followed by the wrist."

Czez picked up the left-hand glove and did as he was told. When he was finished, both gloves appeared to be made of human skin, just like the mask. His former fingerprints, the ones before the surgery. Wonderful. He flexed his fingers. "Like my mother would say, nobody will notice the difference on a galloping goose."

"All you have to do is wear a jacket or a long-sleeved shirt. If you have to wear a short-sleeved shirt, you can blend the gloves in at the wrist with makeup. Easy to do. If you wish, I can show you how."

six

Elephant Dan Merrill, the driver, was forty years old, a large-chested, husky man with a ruddy, round face. His curly brown hair was cut in the manner of classic Roman gladiator movies, Victor Mature in *Quo Vadis,* or Charlton Heston in *Ben Hur.* Around his neck he wore a gold chain at the bottom of which was a slender, sharp-pointed, yellowish-white object that looked something like ivory. This object, which was about an inch-and-a-half long, was Merrill's lucky toothpick. It was, in fact, a dried raccoon penis, and upon close examination, a tiny hole could be seen in its pointed tip. The penis was Merrill's talisman; he rubbed it for good luck much as one would Ho Ti's belly, and once in a while, when he was loaded, he actually used it to pick his teeth.

Elephant Dan's companion, Slick Smith, was two years older. Smith, who was six-feet-four-inches tall, had a substantial gut and was handsome in a sodden, dissipated sort of way; it was obvious from the slightly bloated tone of his flesh and his red eyes that here was a man who liked his booze almost as much as his next breath. Smith greeted every morning with a gentleman's measure of bourbon before he brushed his teeth. He ordinarily got roaring drunk by noon and continued slamming it back until he passed out at night.

Elephant Dan Merrill and Slick Smith were traveling in a Chevrolet Astro minivan, painted a lackluster blue; this was an older model, clean and in good condition, but containing no fancy hubcaps, add-ons, or decals.

Elephant got his nickname because of his unusual ability to mimic an elephant's trumpeting, or bugling, a talent he had perfected while doing time. He trumpeted by clenching his jaws, tightening his cheeks, and blowing through tightly compressed lips. He put his entire face into it, bearing down as hard as he could. This was not pretense trumpeting. Merrill could get right up there and wail pachyderm jazz straight out of a Tarzan movie. He had a collection of tapes of movies with squealing elephants, including some early beauts with Johnny Weismuller and Maureen O'Sullivan—Mia Farrow's mom—in skimpy little Jane outfits that left her almost naked. He could emit squeals and wails straight out of *Hatari,* wherein the big-eyed former model, Elsa Martinelli, lured John Wayne into her bony arms. Dan was proud both of his trumpeting ability and his coon-dick toothpick.

When other people exclaimed or issued expletives, Merrill trumpeted, bugled, or squealed. When he wasn't driving, he liked to swing his right arm as though it were an elephant's trunk.

If Elephant Dan had a failing, it was that he was cheerfully willing to do almost anything for a buck if he thought he could get away with it. The reason for this anomaly in his otherwise amiable and commendable character was his love of gambling. The cycles of his life revolved around seasons and point spreads: baseball was quickly followed by football and then basketball, with hockey thrown in for good measure. He loved calculating spreads, although—as his girlfriends all told him before they moved on—he wasn't worth squat at it.

Smith was a talker, and when he was in a zone of boozy confusion, which was pretty much most of the time, he was given to put-on braggadocio about his imagined skills, adventures, and exploits, into which he tucked balls-up snippets of truth about himself. His friends loved him despite this weakness, or perhaps partly because of it, and humored him by encouraging his tales of derring-do. Smith never failed to respond. Yes, sir, by God, he was Slick Smith. His friends all allowed as how he truly was an odd piece of work.

Smith's biggest problem, other than his deteriorating liver, was that he slipped easily from reality to fantasy, in which he fancied himself this or that hotshot, and under the grip of these misguided, boozy bursts of optimism, he had gotten himself into some deep manure.

It was in one of those boozy bursts that Smith had talked his companion into throwing in with him to solicit work on the Internet. "We cast our bread upon the Web," he had said. "It's the modern way. You don't go advertising your services in *Soldier of Fortune* magazine. The next morning, you'll have FBI agents reading your mail and listening in to your phone calls. Five hundred bucks for a used laptop, a little imagination, and you're in business. Face it, the government couldn't possibly have enough people to trace all the action in cyberspace. The whole fucking planet is hopping like popcorn with people and proposals. It's wild out there. It's the future. We don't remain stuck in the past."

"Couple of dinosaurs."

"That's right. Big, dumb dinosaurs. Brains the size of walnuts. We join the action."

"I've read where folks with brains the size of grapefruits got themselves into a tub of trouble communicating on the Internet with people they didn't know." Merrill trumpeted loudly, full stop.

Dan Merrill regarded himself as a professional at calculating odds. He always checked the rearview mirror before changing lanes. He never failed to review a pony's recent performances before getting worked up over a colorful name. When football season rolled around, he knew all the turfs in all the stadiums. Candlestick Park—fuck that 3-Com Park bullshit—was natural. The Silverdome was artificial. Never, but never, bet an artificial-turf team on natural grass in the play-offs. He noted that the sportswriters analyzing the action in the newspapers never talked about turf; put an artificial-turf running back on grass and he might as well be running in glue. Merrill was convinced sportswriters withheld that critical little tidbit to maintain the drama, but what it really did was allow bookies to make a fortune off stupes who bet out of emotion.

Now, eye on the rearview mirror, Merrill moved to his

left. "You know, Slick, I'd feel better about this business if we knew who in hell we're working for. I know the money spends and everything, and I've got the World Series and the football season coming up. If I'm gonna lose, better to have something to lose than having loan sharks stomping on my toes and stuff."

"He's paying us a cool one million dollars each. He knows it costs money to have a guy set aside his conscience for something like this."

"He *says* a million each."

"He gave us a wad up front, didn't he? You got a hundred thousand bucks of walking-around money in your pocket. In my book, that's showing good faith."

"Good faith is half the action, Slick, not ten percent."

"Oh, for Christ's sake. If he gave us half, he wouldn't be showing much in the brains department, would he? If we want the rest of our money and a shot at more work, we keep our end of the bargain."

"And if we don't want to end up dead," Merrill said.

"There's that, too."

"I just don't understand, I have to admit. There must be ten thousand guys out there advertising their services just like us."

Smith looked scornful.

"Seriously. You ever stop to think of that?"

Smith slumped. "Oh, for Christ's sake, what difference does it make how he picked us? Maybe he threw darts or flipped a coin. The point is, he gave us the nod. We lucked out. It's like winning the lottery."

"Sure it is," Merrill said.

"You know the difference between you and me, Elephant? You're convinced the glass is half empty. I see it as half full. Half-empty guys never get anywhere. You're a gambler. I'm surprised at you."

Merrill gave a quick squeal. "What if we're really working for Saddam Hussein or the Iranians or somebody like that? Their own guys were so stupid as to try to retrieve their deposit on the van they rented in New York for the Trade

Center Building, so they figure what's to lose. Do you think they give squat about what happens to us? We do their dirty work, then they flush us down the toilet. Fall guys. Dumb, fucking saps. Or what if it's Bobby Pearl? I mean, Jesus, what if it's him? Do you think he gives a rat's ass about Dan Merrill and Slick Smith?"

Smith rolled his eyes. "Bobby Pearl! Oh, hell yes. That's gotta be it." Smith took a swig. "By God, you take the cake, you really do. First off, Bobby Pearl blew up Delta 666 and the IRS Building. He didn't use gas. Second, he always gives a warning first. Have you seen or heard anything about him threatening anybody recently? No, you have not."

"Long as the money's good, I suppose. A million bucks. That'll cover a lot of bad bets. Jesus!"

Smith took another hit of whiskey. "You seen any spy movies, for Christ's sake? The agents never know the whole story so if one of them gets caught and tortured by Odd Job or somebody, their scam is still secret. It's how it's done. Our mysterious employer wanted professionals, didn't he?"

"Or she. Don't be sexist, Slick." Merrill trumpeted vigorously.

"He. She. Whatever. The point is, we're professionals. It's a matter of attitude. What do we care about motive?"

Merrill gave a disdainful snort. "Right."

"If you want to be a professional, you have to think like a professional. Whoever is out there scrubs his hands before he eats. Jesus! He does everything in cyberspace. No footprints on the Web. He can wheel and deal without leaving a trace. How in hell do you think he came up with the two million bucks? Do you think he went into a bank with pistols blazing and security cameras rolling? Get real. He just lifted it out of somebody's account electronically. It's done all the time. There was a story about it on CNN a couple of weeks ago. Nobody wants to admit their losses."

"He's spending other people's money?"

"Correct. He doesn't give a flying fuck who we are other than a couple of slimebags who'll do anything if the price is right. Check that: thoroughly modern slimebags who'll do anything if the price is right."

" 'He'? You're telling me one guy?"

"He. They. Same diff. Somebody out there with some bucks and access to stuff who knows how to work a computer. All we need to know. If we can't figure him, nobody else can either."

"No motive. That's the only good part about it."

Smith said, "Right. Motive is the first thing dicks look for. Our man obviously has got bunches of motive, or he'd do it himself. This way, he keeps his distance."

"We got no mo?"

"No, sir. No mo at all. None. We mix the shit and deliver it just like he says. And we don't roar out of town like that shitbrain in Oklahoma."

"Plenty of mo there."

"Had it plastered on him like frosting on a cake. Give the Feds a hint of mo and they'll track you to the ends of the earth. We're just guys traveling around minding our own business, see."

"The only secret we got is we're all the time farting." Merrill squealed vigorously again. "I guess you're right. As long as we get our money." He began shouting and laughing at the same time, "Gimmie my goddam money! Just gimmie my goddam money!"

"That's the spirit. The money spends. We got all the Benjies for whiskey and bingo we could possibly want. You're talking with Slick Smith here. Stick with me. I know what I'm doing."

Merrill rolled his eyes. "Sure you do. Jesse Fucking James."

Smith looked offended. "You don't believe me? You don't believe me? You really know how to insult a man, don't you?" He treated himself to another hit off the flask.

Merrill slammed on his brakes to avoid rear-ending a Volkswagen Beetle. "Listen, Slick, I can't drive, watch, and listen to you jabber all at the same time, for Christ's sake. As far as I can see, you've only got two moving parts, your mouth and your asshole, and they both work the same."

"Well, if you'd slow down, for Christ's sake." Smith suddenly twisted his neck, his attention riveted on two teenage girls walking down the sidewalk in blue jeans and UCLA T-shirts.

"I'd give either one of 'em a meat injection for a nickel." Merrill trumpeted like he was summoning greyhounds to the line.

"No time for that shit now. We got work to do."

Merrill compressed his lips and gave a bluesy, mournful elephant's squeal. "Then keep your eyes off the goddam women."

Smith unscrewed his flask and took another nip. "We don't need to get into an accident; that's a fact. I'm watching. It'll be coming up on our right. No problem." He studied his AAA road atlas.

Merrill leaned forward. "There it is, Aztec Swimming Pool Supplies. I thought you was paying attention. Cochise and everything."

"The blue sign. By God, you got a set of eyes on you. You really do."

Merrill slowed the van. "Can't go swimming in no dirty water."

Smith smirked. "Oh, hell no. Can't have no fucked water. We're a mighty clean pair of puppies, and we want to stay that way. Got to have that chlorine."

"Kill off all them germs," Merrill said. "Learnt that from our mamas."

"Regular gentlemen," Smith said.

"Wash our hands after we pee and everything. The full nine yards." Merrill pulled the van to a stop in the parking lot; he waved his arm over his head and trumpeted triumphantly.

Standing beneath a promotional poster in the front office of the Omar Khayyàm Pen Company in Azusa, California, Elephant Dan Merrill found it difficult not to giggle as he weighed the sleek pen in his left hand, shining the flashlight beam on it with his right. He compressed his lips and gave a quick squeal. "Ninety bucks a pop. Ninety bucks! Can you imagine? What a racket!"

"Those're executive pens, asshole. An executive's got to have himself a proper pen. Sign all them big deals." Slick Smith's face was flushed. He was three sheets to the wind.

"You're the guy with two years of community college. You want to tell me what kind of executive in his right mind would pop for ninety bucks for an Omar Khayyàm when he could buy himself a perfectly good Bic or Scripto for a couple of bucks? There's gotta be a six-bit explanation there somewhere."

Smith laughed. "Elephant. Elephant. My man. You learn that in Economics 101. It's elementary."

"What's so fucking elementary?"

"Curves of marginal utility."

In block letters, Merrill wrote a big *FUCK YOU, TURD SUCKERS* on the counter.

"Curves of marginal utility explain buyer behavior. It's all perfectly logical."

"Right," Merrill said dryly.

"Most of the time, folks operate in their best interests. But what's really good for them doesn't always make a whole lot of sense, to be honest."

Merrill grinned, pretending to be amazed. "Ahhh, no! You wouldn't bullshit an old buddy, would you?"

"A businessman fancying himself to be a genuine executive 'stead of just another suit ain't gonna buy no cheapie plastic pen at a Seven-Eleven. That's bourgeois."

"Bourgwhich?"

"Bourgeois. Pieces of shit like us."

Merrill trumpeted loudly. He unfolded the small piece of paper that came in the pseudo-leather box containing an Omar Khayyàm pen. On the paper was written, in a fine script, Khayyàm's famous poem, which Merrill read aloud:

> " *'The Moving Finger writes; and, having writ,*
> *Moves on: nor all your Piety nor Wit*

Shall lure it back to cancel half a Line
Nor all your Tears wash out a Word of it.'"

Merrill furrowed his eyebrows. "What kind of crappola is that?" He trumpeted loudly.

Smith said, "That's class, asshole. Something you'd never understand."

"They want wit? We'll show 'em wit." Merrill wrote *UP YOUR NOSE WITH A RUBBER HOSE.*

Smith frowned. "Come on, let's get on with it. The stuff we want ain't gonna be here in the front office. It'll be in the back someplace where they make the stupid things. If we fuck around too long, the bars'll close, and then where will we be?"

seven

Olivia Dunthorpe, a slender, alert black woman, was on duty at the FBI's ultramodern communications center in Washington, D.C., watching the Internet hotline monitor. Dunthorpe was about to take another sip of coffee when the screen turned pale blue. A single iridescent pearl, rolling lazily, tumbled in slow motion from the top left of the screen toward a swirling sea of red at the bottom. This pearl was quickly joined by a second, then by another and another, until a deluge of pearls cascaded in slow motion.

She quickly set her coffee down and tapped the trace sequence, although she knew that in the case of the falling pearl, this would be an exercise in futility. The person on the other end was a phantom of cyberspace.

As in the warnings preceding the downing of Delta 666 and the collapsing of the IRS Building in Ogden, Utah, the falling pearl was accompanied by the Mormon Tabernacle Choir singing Handel's *Messiah*. The same deep, rumbling, electronically altered voice delivered the message:

> *I wish to announce a change in my MO. Boom-boom is boring. Sometime in the next few days, I'm going to enliven the spirit of paranoia.*

The first of the pearls plunged into the sea at the bottom of the screen, sending blood flying.

> *Mongoose calls me a snake.*
> *Hallelujah! Hallelujah!*
> *Snakes slither silently.*
> *Hal-le-lu-u-jah!*

> *Hallelujah! Hallelujah!*
> *So does gassssssss.*
> *Hal-le-lu-u-jah!*
> *Stealth death.*

The endless stream of pearls continued its descent into the blood.

Dunthorpe reversed the action and stopped the first pearl. She enlarged it. Pearl obviously did not want adolescent hackers and pranksters muddying the waters of his dubious achievement. Bobby Pearl gave his signature pearl a distinctive pattern, visible only when it was blown up. For this protection against copycats, at least, the FBI was grateful.

Dunthorpe studied the enlarged pearl, then grimaced. She reduced the pearl and let it continue to drop as she punched up her superior.

In the back of their van, Slick Smith opened his laptop and turned it on.

Watching him, Dan Merrill said, "Jesus, Slick, I still don't know about this business."

"Relax, for Christ's sake. This is like popping your cherry. You're bound to be a little nervous first time." Smith checked his watch and waited. "Exactly eight A.M., not a minute sooner or a minute later. This is a fail-safe."

"Fail-safe! You've been watching too many spy movies. James Fucking Bond. Right?" Merrill rolled his eyes and laughed.

"Laugh if you want, shitbrains, but this is how it's done. If we don't contact him exactly on time, we might be somebody else. How's he supposed to know? The guy's professional. He's very, very careful. You should be glad he's putting us through the drill."

Merrill gave a quick snort. "What the fuck do you know about professionals, besides hookers?"

Smith kept an eye on his watch. "Note that he started with the basics. He told us what to steal."

"Chlorine and thio, whatever the fuck that stuff is."

"Thiodiglycol. Then he told us how to hook up two separate tanks so we could mix the stuff without frying ourselves, after which he sent us the right decals for the delivery tanks. He sent us the remotes that release the valves. He sent us the correct uniforms and receipt pads. Now he's going to tell us precisely when and where to deliver the tanks. What does that all tell you?"

"It tells me I'm in over my head. I'm probably being had."

"Bullshit! It tells you that this guy wants to keep a safe distance. He doesn't want to be fingered. He doesn't want us getting fingered either."

Merrill snorted again. "You can't imagine how much money I've lost on sure things. A pony can be sired by a derby winner and have speed, endurance, a helluva record, the right trainer and jock, everything. A can't-miss. So I get excited and bet the north forty, never mind the short odds. What happens?" He shook his head sadly. "Fucked again. Believe me, pal, I've been there."

Smith looked disgusted. "Oh, stop it already. This guy truly is careful. Now how in hell do you suppose he found out how to buy the correct uniforms, decals, and receipt pads?"

"Beats the fuck out of me."

"He did it with his computer, just like he contacted and hired us. He does everything at a safe remove. He sends the shit we need to a rented mailbox that he's already scouted, so he knows we can retrieve the stuff without being seen."

"Looks good, I know. Still . . ." Merrill gave a plaintive snort.

"Our guy has thought this all through. We're clean, clean, clean."

"Doing backstrokes in Pine Sol."

Smith said, "We do what we're told, exactly as we're told. Nothing more, nothing less. We don't deviate. It's almost time. Don't want to screw this up." He called up the people search. He keyed in "P. L. Ear." With Merrill observing over his shoulder, Smith watched the sweep hand of his watch. Without taking his eyes off the dial, he tapped the enter key exactly as the sweep hand reached the twelve.

The reply was immediate.

Who are you?

"See there," Smith said. "He wouldn't have replied if we'd been early or late. Now we give him exactly the right answer. Anything else and the deal is off." He tapped: "E-Dan and Big Slick."

He tapped the enter key again.

Although he didn't spend a whole lot of time contemplating Thanksgiving or "The Last Supper," Herbie Goldberg intuitively understood the symbolic power of serving and sharing food. Goldberg, a secular Jew originally from Brooklyn, liked to eat so much himself that he'd had to have two operations to clear the fat out of the valves in his heart. He'd had any number of jobs in his time, many of them unmentionable in the presence of officers of the law, but the okay ones included being a fry cook and a bartender.

Despite his condition of being eternally broke, Goldberg genuinely was a jolly man. People could not help but love him, truly, and not in the manner of the fashionable "I love. you, man" crappola that had become a cliché since the charming conniver first appeared in the Budweiser Lite ads several years earlier. Herbie's friends, laughing with shared pleasure, had contests imitating his Brooklyn accent.

"Yeah, man. I am the handsomest. The very handsomest," he liked to say. He was not.

"I am the Most Golden. The very Most Golden." That he was. In five minutes, he could change the mind of the most rabid anti-Semite, living proof that stereotypes of blacks, gays, or whatever minority of choice were the first recourse of demagogues and scoundrels. In flesh and blood lay joy and grief; in numbers and abstraction lay bombast and dreck.

Goldberg's main source of income was from selling falafel at arts festivals, harvest fairs, and flea markets in the San Francisco Bay area. He supplemented this income in the off-season by prowling garage and estate sales for RPM records of classical music dating from the 1960s, which he sold to collectors, and old paperback novels with wild covers; the best, dating from the 1940s and 1950s, featured voluptuous women with torn bodices. Goldberg lived in Point Reyes, in Marin County just north of San Francisco, and it was his assertion that the Golden Gate Bridge was named for him.

Goldberg's falafel mix, made from ground fava beans and chick peas plus garlic, dried parsley and other spices, was the real deal. He had a little made-in-Israel stainless-steel scoop that he used to fashion the tiny balls before dumping them in the hot oil. He had never been to Israel, but proclaimed that no better falafel could be found in Jerusalem or Tel Aviv.

The San Francisco Food Fair was the profitable high point of the circuit. Here, in a city famous for fog, the 49ers, and haute cuisine, San Francisco's cosmopolitan mix gathered to celebrate its many splendid gifts to the world food culture. Everybody had something to offer—from the Changs, Chans, and Wongs of Chinatown to the sons and daughters of Africa, India, Italy, Japan, Korea, Mexico, the Philippines, and Thailand.

The bearded Herbie loved to scope the passing women as he mixed and shaped his falafel. There were women everywhere at the summer fairs, most of them wearing hardly anything at all, and a few looking positively horny. Herbie amused his coworkers with nonstop banter as he watched the passing parade of females. They were like Cinderellas searching for the Most Golden Rod, he maintained. Looking for the perfect fit. He alone possessed this rod. If just one of them tried it on, he would turn into a handsome prince. Dream on, his friends all said.

The two deliverymen arrived with more tanks of propane at 4:00 P.M. on a Saturday afternoon, when the fair was packed with people having a good time. Not only was there interesting food to be had, but there were musicians, artists, and entertainers ranging from tumblers to jugglers, all picking up a few spare bucks.

As the deliverymen arrived with the tanks, Herbie was

dumping more falafel into the huge vat of hot oil used for deep-frying. He wiped his hands on a towel and signed the requisition form. He gave each man a sandwich made of pita bread stuffed with falafel, chopped onions and tomatoes, and shredded lettuce—all of this topped with delicious tahini, a sauce made of sesame seeds.

He grinned. "You're gonna love this, man. Wait and see."

One of the deliverymen tested his falafel, and in appreciation, imitated an elephant's squeal.

"Hip elephant," Goldberg said.

The deliveryman trumpeted again.

His companion glared at him.

The elephant man took a bite of falafel. "Good stuff. You're gonna love this propane, too."

"Wait and see," his companion said.

When the deliverymen left, munching on their sandwiches, Goldberg returned to his chores. A few minutes later, eyeing a girl with outsized boobs and a succulent butt, he smelled garlic. "Hey, where's the garlic coming from? Lotta garlic. Oy!"

He screamed, a single screamer in a chorus of screaming that suddenly erupted among the vendors and fair-goers.

His eyes went wide. A sea of green. What the hell was this? He clutched his throat. His face turned purple. He writhed, wild with pain.

Still clutching his throat, he toppled into the boiling oil with the falafel. The oil was positively cool compared to the blister agent that had seared his eyes, ears, sinuses, throat, and lungs.

He stopped moving.

He began to cook along with the falafel.

Herbie Goldberg turned brown, then browner, his skin slowly bubbling into a rich golden brown, then a mahogany color. Herbie was just one of the scores of victims, none of whom had done a thing at all to deserve this most cowardly of cowardly ambushes. Up and down the aisles of the festival, people twisted and rolled on the ground, screaming, begging for relief from the terrible blinding, burning gas that seared their skin and fried their lungs. They inhaled fire. They could not escape it. They all burned. Old ladies. Little kids, darting in and out of the crowd. Families on a weekend outing. Lovers strolling hand in hand. All the victims had their stories. Nobody was spared the horror that spread outward from the propane tanks at Goldberg's falafel stand.

The burning! The burning! Sweet Jesus, the awful burning!

two

bang!

one

The speech had been announced. The pool cameras were in place. While the President waited for air time—that is, for viewers on the West Coast to get home from work—he sat behind his desk in the Oval Office with his chin held high so his makeup artist could do her usual number on his face. Ever since Richard Nixon had betrayed a five-o'clock shadow and sweat on his upper lip during his debate with the cool and charming John Kennedy, proper cosmetic makeup had been mandatory.

There had been a time, before the money and the power of the tube, when the White House was reserved for elder statesmen of the party and those who had demonstrated their mettle in public service. This was no longer the case, and the President had had his brownish hair colored silver and the age lines accentuated just a tad to show that here was the commander-in-chief, not an ambitious twerp pretending to lead the country. The makeup artist, who had been with him since those first cold days in New Hampshire, had the thoughtful, caring Presidential Look refined to an art form; although some male voters remained skeptical, most women were thrilled.

As the makeup girl did her job, he reviewed his speech. This was one of those unifying duties all presidents faced from time to time—in this case, giving the facts of the San Francisco tragedy and making a Churchillian call for national resolve in the face of a cowardly enemy.

The President was able to scroll the speech up or down, and as he waited for the appointed hour, he did so, looking for a memorable luck-out phrase that would reverberate through the ages as in Abraham Lincoln's "Four score and seven years ago" gem at Gettysburg.

When the rattler Bobby Pearl had first sent his signature E-mail message threatening to release mustard gas, there had been a flurry of activity by the CIA's Mongoose and the FBI's International Terrorist Watch, all part of an automatic response to real and bogus threats that sucked up hundreds of thousands of man hours and millions of tax dollars every year. As in Pearl's previous warnings, the communication was studied and analyzed to exhaustion. Although it was unlikely that anybody would recall a misfit reading war poetry, queries were once again sent out as to the current activities of nutballs and militia groups under surveillance by Mongoose and Watch operatives. Justice Department computers coughed up lists of religious and political ideologues, searching for one with an education, employment, or interest associated with chemistry, to which investigators now added poetry. Rattler Four, like the Unabomber, was obviously an educated individual.

When the investigative drill was completed, there was not a whole lot Mongoose, The Watch, or anybody else could do except hope that investigators got a lucky break, as they had after a mere thirteen years in the case of the Unabomber. Boom-boom was bad enough. The fact that Pearl had altered his MO to include a chemical-warfare agent was an unusually disquieting turn of events.

Both the Marine Corps and the Army had dispatched anti-chemical and biological-warfare units to San Francisco. But these marines and soldiers, equipped with high-tech gas masks and antidotes, were trained to analyze a disease and contain its spread. The marine units were based at Camp Lejeune, North Carolina, and the soldiers at Fort Ord, California. They responded to a crisis; they did not defend. Defense was altogether another matter.

The President faced a political firestorm if the public knew that Pearl could make his own mustard gas. Yes, it had been widely known that diesel fuel and the fertilizer ammonium nitrate could be made into a bomb, but nobody took the threat seriously until terrorists knocked the face off the Federal Building in Oklahoma City. The low-tech nature of mustard gas was the current open secret, and it wasn't the only chemical-warfare agent within the grasp of freelance terrorists. Containing it was like trying to juggle water.

After considering the alternatives and the change in Bobby Pearl's MO, the President decided to keep his warning message secret to buy time for investigators; until the Justice Department learned otherwise, anger directed out there, at Arabs or whomever, was easier to manage than the debilitating fear of a homegrown psychopath.

For the President, this was a calculated risk. He had learned quickly at the beginning of his administration that any fact known by more than one bureaucrat was no longer a secret. Also, the mass media, peddlers of cheap thrills and gossip, were no longer deterred by ethical or moral restraints. It had not always been thus.

The President knew that in World War II, the War Department and the Roosevelt administration had kept secret the dramatic victory at Midway on the grounds that if the public knew that the Japanese Navy had been effectively destroyed, it would get complacent in the face of a long struggle ahead. In fact, a reporter for the *Chicago Tribune*, who was not an accredited war correspondent and so not bound by the agreed-upon rules of the time, accurately recreated the battle from accounts by sailors he met on his way back from Australia. After the *Tribune* published his account of the battle, the Justice Department charged him with treason but, in the end, quietly dropped the case.

Editors and publishers had never been Eagle Scouts, but the erosion of institutional discipline in the media had accelerated with a rush during the previous forty years, beginning with the assassination of President Kennedy and continuing through Watergate and the emergence of internal terrorists. By the closing days of the century, concepts of responsibility and notions of taste had almost entirely disintegrated. Editors and producers now believed that their readers and viewers were entitled to know everything at all times. No secret, for any reason, was beyond their ken, a right granted them by the First Amendment.

The President, who had studied political philosophy at Cambridge University, understood the origins of his dilemma. The Constitution had been written in the late eighteenth century, the end of the period historians had dubbed "The Age of Reason." John Locke, whose ideas had been particularly influential on the Founding Fathers, had asserted that government is a trust; its purpose is the security of the citizen's person and property, and the subject has the right to withdraw his confidence in the ruler when the latter fails in this task. The President was Constitutionally charged with the duty of defending and protecting. But how, pray tell, was he supposed to meet his end of the bargain when the Fourth Estate of the realm, the mass media, operated independently of Locke's formula? Surely, the Founding Fathers had not anticipated this turn of events.

The facts of Bobby Pearl's lastest strike were simple enough. One hundred and eighty-seven people were dead and 344 were in the hospital following the release of mustard gas from propane containers at a San Francisco food fair. The remote releasing valves were fashioned from components purchased at Radio Shack.

In the Pearl drama, the assumptions of the past were being put to test by the circumstances of the new millennium; it was that and little else.

The President's speechwriters had done a creditable job with the brave rhetoric: "As the gap between haves and have-nots widens, cant and ideology, fueled by anger and resentment, have joined forces with technology. Our country is in a state of siege from invisible, uncivilized cowards, who can move about undetected. Their communications can't be traced . . ." Et cetera.

The President's chief-of-staff, Charlie Boso, a pale-skinned man with dark brown hair and a neat mustache, slipped into the Oval Office. He glanced at the clock on the wall, then squatted by the corner of the President's desk. "I've got some wonderful news to cheer you up while you wait. They're telling me that a chemical-and-biological-warfare expert on NBC told the viewers how to make mustard gas out of chlorine and ink produced for ballpoint pens. It was like giving them a recipe for baking a cake. Isn't that sweet?"

The President looked astonished. "He what?"

"Proving his point that anybody can make this shit."

The President puffed his cheeks in fury. "Jesus Christ Almighty! That kind of crap can have little kids and old ladies wetting the bed."

The producer said, "Thirty seconds, Mr. President." This was a message for Boso to clear out.

Boso stood, shaking his head in disgust. "Thought it would cheer you up. Give 'em hell, Mr. President."

The President watched Boso retreat from the office. He understood why his chief-of-staff had given him that little piece of news. Boso knew that the President performed better when he had fire in his belly. The President had never once addressed the republic following an airline crash, a riot, a terrorist attack, or any other situation requiring that he calm the populace, without loathing the mass media within minutes. This time, thanks to Boso, he was furious before he even delivered his speech.

As he waited to begin his address, he drifted into reverie.

His job truly would be a lot easier if reporters would cooperate just a smidgen. The celebrity reporters wouldn't have to be running-dog lackeys of his administration, or any kind of Goody Two-shoes, but if for once they used a little common sense, it would go a long way. There were some reporters whom he suspected would swap their mother for a twenty-Nielsen scoop. But if their butts were on the line, not someone else's, he bet they'd shape up mighty fast.

He wondered as he waited: what if someone knocked off one of the motherfuckers? Just shot the son of a bitch? Pow! The posturing, sanctimonious Joaquin Hurtado would make a wonderful target, and most of the public, sick and tired of narcissistic reporters and the televised Circus Maximus, would probably applaud the killer. Certainly nobody would think the President of the United States would simply take matters into his own hands and give tit for tat.

The President knew that the public and the mass media would leap to the conclusion that the assassin was an out-of-control militiaman. The militiamen, obsessive patriots, were famous for hating what they regarded as the knee-jerk liberal media. A couple of them had blown up the Federal Building in Oklahoma City to strike a blow against the government that had laid siege to the religious compound in Waco. Easy to imagine that one of them, locked in the grip of paranoia, might start dropping reporters in a national emergency.

The hit would be simple enough to arrange. The Watch and Mongoose had informants and agents watching all manner of creeps, and in some cases, had them under electronic surveillance. They had hundreds, if not thousands, of criminals, assassins, and political zealots in their computers who would just love to waste a few hotshot journalists. Some of them would do it for free, but if they insisted on being paid, there was plenty of drug money that could be laundered for the tab.

Finding an experienced assassin was well within the realm of possibility for the President. On the off chance that confidential access to the FBI's internal data might one day be useful, the President and Charlie Boso had taken the precaution of placing Boso's younger brother Tom, a computer management specialist, in a strategic position in the Bureau. Owing to Tom's skills on the Web and his knowledge of government taps currently in place, there were some heinous, downright demented perps with whom it was possible to communicate anonymously but not catch.

The President smiled at the thought of reporters running to him with their knees banging like shutters in a high wind. *How can we help, Mr. President? What can we do to cooperate?*

"Mr. President! Thirty seconds, Mr. President!"

The President, thus jostled from his pleasant fantasy, looked momentarily foolish. "Sorry, drifted off there."

He scrolled the speech back to the beginning.

Just shoot the sons of bitches. That'd do it. Put them on the receiving end and see how they liked them apples. Nobody would suspect him of being behind it. That would be too outré, even for a politician with the chutzpah and hustle required to claim the White House. After all, look at the century just past; think of the sacrifice of blood made by soldiers defending the national interest—the boys in the Ardennes and at Bastogne, on Pork Chop Hill and at Khe Sahn.

Maybe he'd broach the idea to Boso. Pose it as a humorous what-if and see how Charlie responded. Charlie was a broad-minded, imaginative kind of guy just like his brother. Why don't we just kill one of the sons of bitches? Ha, ha, ha.

The President licked his lips. He waited.

The red light came on.

"Good evening, my fellow Americans . . ."

His message to the country completed, the President kicked back with Charlie Boso in his private office on the second floor of the White House to mellow out with a little Meyers dark rum laced with a squeeze of lemon, the President's drink of choice. It would take at least an hour for the administration's polling firm, Grigorich and Wells, to complete its flash check of the public reaction to his speech and digest the data in its computers.

What were the numbers? Were the favorables up or down, and by how much? The questions were always thus. This was the long wait.

"Well, whaddaya think, Charlie? Will they buy it?"

Boso smoothed his mustache with his forefinger. "I don't think Franklin Roosevelt could have done any better. At a time like this, people want to believe."

"Propane tanks at a food fair. Jesus!"

Boso clenched his jaw. "I know. I know."

"The Bronx would've been okay. Trim the welfare rolls. Save us all a few bucks."

Boso grinned. "And they elected you president! You sick son of a bitch."

"The State Department hates terrorists. At least in the Cold War, we had a predictable competition. All that spy-versus-spy stuff. There was a need for Henry Kissingers and James Bakers and the rest of them. Brent Scrowcroft. But these chickenshits are pinheads. No geopolitik here. No balancing of power and interest. Geography is irrelevant. Nothing for the diplomats to do but play with their pee-pees, and nothing for the Pentagon to do except assign more marines to guard duty and train more response units." The President looked grim. "And that business about telling people how to make mustard gas is too fucking much. It's just unreal."

"I know. I know. Several years before the bombing in Oklahoma City, the Department of Agriculture sent brochures out to farmers telling them how to blow up tree stumps by mixing ammonium nitrate and diesel fuel. The federal government taught people how to make bombs! Now we've got the media getting in on the action." Boso freshened the President's drink.

The President sighed. "You know, Charlie, when I tell people everything will be all right, they know damn well I'm lying through my teeth. What we're talking about here is an agreed-upon national fiction. When it comes to terrorists, everybody knows that the United States, a world superpower, has no choice but to talk big and brandish a little weenie."

"Welcome to the new century."

The phone on the President's desk beeped. Boso snatched the receiver from its cradle.

"Well?" the President asked. He chewed on his lower lip.

"Brooks Grigorich with the numbers," Boso said. He grabbed a pad and pen. He listened, nodding. He made a quick note. "Got it. Got it." He made another note. "Good job, Brooks." He hung up, grinning broadly, teasing the President by making him wait.

"Are you going to tell me, or are you going to sit there looking like a dog eating a turd?"

"They loved it. Fabulous numbers all the way across. Ninety-percent positives. The Republicans will have to stick with you on this one or suffer the consequences."

The President poured himself and Boso another hit of rum. "All right! The sons of bitches might choke on their own vomit, but they don't have any choice except to back me all the way. Fuck 'em all but six, I say. We'll need them for pallbearers."

Boso paused, his hand at his chin. "But you gotta find Bobby Pearl before the inevitable leak that he warned us in advance. If the leak comes first, those numbers will go south so fast it'll make your head swim. There's gotta be something we can do to calm down the media. There's just gotta be."

The President put his forefinger on his lips, looking pensive. "You know, I've been thinking of an idea that's perhaps a trifle unpresidential, if not outright dangerous. Not your ordinary course of action."

Boso looked interested. "Oh?"

The President pursed his lips. "We might check out the possibility just for the fun of it. A discreet inquiry. Nothing more. We have to keep in mind, Charlie, desperate times sometimes call for desperate action. We've got a spooked country on our hands."

Boso waited.

The President said, quickly, "We don't have to get carried away or make any commitment. Just test the water to see what would happen."

"Well? Go ahead. Tell me."

"A what-if kind of thing, Charlie. That's all. We might want to think about it somewhere down the line. Of course we'd have to be very, very careful with the first step, maybe take it without telling me, so I'd have plausible deniability. And remember, just because we make an exploratory contact, it doesn't mean we're obliged to follow through with anything." He licked his lips nervously.

Boso frowned. "Oh, come on, for Christ's sake. There's nobody here except for me and thee. There haven't been any hidden microphones in the Oval Office since Richard Nixon. Out with it."

two

The nightmare again. The same old ghastly thing.

First came the cocked hammer of his pistol at William Burroughs. Gunmetal gray. Directly in front of him. But the hammer was poised at him, not at the round in the cylinder. The pointed tip, eerie, drifty, ghostlike, floated in psychic space, ready to strike Jake Hipp right between his eyes. It seemed like he was forced to contemplate the cocked hammer for hours, although when he finally woke up, his mouth dry, he knew it was probably for only minutes. Night after night, the image of the cocked hammer repeated itself like an errant tape in his synaptic underworld. It tormented him.

That was just Part One of the nightmare. His guilt was merciless and unrelenting. Part Two, Lynn Vaughn, ordinarily came after he finally got back to sleep. Hipp's favorite newscaster had always been the breathy-voiced Vaughn on CNN. After the hammer, it was Vaughn's turn to insinuate herself into his subconscious, and then the whole awful thing began again.

In these haunting shards of memory, Vaughn always wore the same off-yellow sweater with a jagged brown stripe running across her chest. Her opener was always the same. A photograph of the San Francisco Food Fair popped onto the screen as she said, *"This just in from San Francisco."*

Behind her, paramedics loaded the bodies of the stricken victims of mustard gas into ambulances. Mustard gas!

"For the third time, the elusive terrorist Bobby Pearl has kept his promise. He said he'd do it, and he apparently has. This despite a concentrated fourteen-month manhunt since Pearl collapsed the IRS's regional headquarters in Ogden, Utah . . ."

Hipp woke up sweating. He looked down at Gina Jumero, sleeping peacefully beside him. Gina, an uncomplicated, undemanding lover, was the best thing that had ever happened to him, and she looked extraordinary in the moonlight. He was her man, and she loved it when he was in Cebu. He did too. He swung his legs over the bed and sat up, shaking Lynn Vaughn from his mind.

He got up and walked into Gina's kitchen and sat on a stool, looking down into the darkness of her walled courtyard. He flipped on the light and squinted momentarily to let his eyes adjust. The barred window was open, and outside the air in Gina's small courtyard was hot and wet and filled with the moist and earthy smells of life, death, and regeneration.

He went into the bathroom to relieve himself, then studied his face in the mirror above the sink. He returned to the kitchen and poured two fingers of Tanduay rum into the bottom of a water glass. He took the barest sip, savoring the taste. He packed the bowl of his bamboo bong with some Filipino weed and took a leisurely hit. He snapped the light off and sat in darkness.

He took another sip of Tanduay. Good rum was delicious.

The bereaved, enraged families of Bobby Pearl's latest 187 victims—a modest strike by Pearl's standards—had bought a two-page spread in *The New York Times* to display tiny photographs of their loved ones. Hipp padded back to the bedroom in his bare feet and retrieved those two pages, which were folded up beside his passport in his day pack. He returned to the kitchen and spread the pages out on the table. The faces were always the same. A bald suit. A young woman with dangling earrings. A little boy in a cowboy hat. Rows and rows of faces.

Here we are, the pictures said, *look at us. We aren't numbers. We're flesh-and-blood people, with friends and families. We did nothing to deserve the ugly horror of mustard gas. We had no quarrel with any political or religious cause. We were merely having a good time at a festival, eating lamb korma and chicken adobo and sushi. Why us?*

Staring at the faces that he alone could have spared, Hipp's stomach twisted. He took another hit of pot and slipped back into bed beside Gina.

He felt himself closing in on sleep. If he could suppress Lynn Vaughn, he had it made.

In the year that had passed since Tangier, Hipp had replayed a mental tape of his encounter with Rattler Four hundreds of times. Of all the details in his humiliating failure, he never forgot what the snake had been eating; he sometimes thought about the cigar, but after Bobby Pearl mentioned the pumpkin soup and mint tea in his *My Side* interview, they had become the stuff of nightmares.

He remembered calling out, softly, "Bobby Pearl!"

Pumpkin soup and mint tea.

The Beta who had begged to become a Charlie had quietly been sacked. From Mongoose's point of view, the attempt to turn a Beta into a Charlie had been a ghastly error. The aptitude tests had said the appointment likely wouldn't work, and it hadn't.

Outside, a lizard, staking out prime bug-catching territory underneath a night-light, made its distinctive *fuck-you, fuck-you* warning to competitors. These were geckos, which the Cebuanos called *tokus*.

Lying there, Hipp traced the chain of events following Tangier. He had gone back to Seville in a long-shot attempt to find Greta Mann. He checked every hotel and pensione in the city. Nothing. He had known that his search for Roger's hotel was also a long shot; a man like Pearl changed his name as casually as he did his shorts. Hipp had found a Roger booked into a downtown hotel, but this gentleman was in his late sixties and carried a British passport. Yet Hipp's chance encounter with Greta had yielded two things about Bobby Pearl that Hipp hadn't known before: Pearl spoke Spanish with a New World accent, and he carried some sort of secret that the discreet Greta had nevertheless hinted at very strongly.

In going from Amsterdam to Tangier, Pearl had likely dawdled in Spain because he spoke fluent Spanish. He was good-looking. He was charming enough to have lured an English-speaking German girl to his hotel, and not just any German girl. Greta was an educated beauty, attractive enough to have her pick of numerous admirers.

After Bobby Pearl had first struck three years earlier, Mongoose and The Watch had checked birth certificates, IRS data, and INS records, looking for an American with the surname of Pearl—not only in English, but in all the languages in Europe and several in Asia. There were more than nine hundred Pearls in six languages in the United States, but none fit the profile of the terrorist.

Although the FBI kept several dozen Pearls under loose surveillance, none of them were exciting prospects. Both Mongoose and the International Terrorist Watch concluded that Bobby Pearl was a nom de guerre. The question was, why had he chosen the surname Pearl?

After Tangier, Hipp had begun to consider a theory. The terrorist's signature warning featured pearls tumbling into scarlet at the bottom of the screen. Was that image intended as a macabre prophesy for the next century—a coming deluge of terrorists tumbling into a sea of blood? Was Pearl sending the message that these victims were sacrificial martyrs, surrendering their lives so that their countrymen could learn a necessary lesson?

A pearl evolved from a grain of sand or other irritant caught between the mantle and the exterior of an oyster's shell. As this irritant was rolled about by minute contractions of the mantle, the annoyed oyster covered it with layer upon layer of soothing calcium carbonate. But the irritant would not go away; remaining free of the shell, it became symmetrical over time and grew larger and larger. It was the calcium carbonate that gave a pearl its iridescent quality.

Was the grit part of the puzzle?

How was the oyster to protect itself from grit without forming deadly pearls from within?

What was the grit?

Hipp believed there were two possibilities. One was the grit that Pearl *thought* was behind his actions, some ennobling political or ideological justification for killing innocent people. The second was the real grit, some personal or psychological irritant that had evolved into a murderous compulsion. Hipp remained struck by Pearl's initial fury on the ferry from Algeciras and his later obsession with Hipp. Had Hipp inadvertently tumbled onto some embarrassing psychic pain or tic? Had Pearl beaten up the prostitute in the Centrum because she knew about it? Was that why he had pursued Greta after dating her once—waiting to silence her also?

Embarrassed by what? What nagging pain would not go away?

Pearl had no obvious regional American accent, nothing Southern, Boston, Baltimore, Chicago, New York, or New England; this meant he was likely from the Midwest or Far West, where the speech more closely mirrored the standard English of television newscasters.

Pearl was lean and fit for his age. Was he a former athlete or soldier?

Joe Woofter had done his best to convince the Mongoose bureaucrats not to overreact to Hipp's failure in Tangier. The fact remained that Mongoose needed Hipp, he said. Despite Hipp's terrible choke, he remained the only Charlie who had seen the way Pearl moved and heard the pitch and cadence of his speech. By sacking him, Mongoose forced its remaining Charlies to work from secondary sources. But the bureaucrats had refused. Hipp had to be held accountable for the screwup. This was a lesson all Charlies had to understand. The best they could do was to offer Hipp his old job as a Beta, which offer Hipp declined.

However much Hipp was sore and disappointed, he also understood the decision. In the shoes of the Mongoose Grand Pooh-Bahs, he might have done the same thing. On one point, he thought they were completely wrong. They believed that his analytical mind and his understanding of Charles Darwin were pointless qualities for a field agent. Hipp passionately believed the opposite; this was his strength, not his weakness. He felt—and he knew Joe

Woofter agreed with him—that it was precisely *because* of his understanding of the human animal that he had the best shot at running Bobby Pearl to ground.

He was convinced there would come a day when good sense prevailed and he would be asked to return. In the meantime, there was nothing to do but get on with his life. He had used his severance money to buy a cabin in Long Beach, Washington, and a bar with his girlfriend in the Philippines, and he kept himself busy writing magazine articles and shooting travel pictures. One thing he would not do was to return to academic life, which he now regarded as no life at all.

He never stopped thinking about Bobby Pearl.

If the image of pearls tumbling into blood were intended as a form of prophesy, then Pearl and Hipp, curiously, were thinking along the same lines. Hipp had lately been reading about the Mayans, whose religious and social life had revolved around recurring prophesies made by their priests. Hipp had even been thinking about producing a modern version of the Mayans' twenty-month-long calendar. He was convinced that the wives of prosperous suits would spring for an overpriced Mayan calendar if the photographs caught their eye.

Now, thinking of tumbling pearls and blood; he decided that he would go to Belize and the Yucatan to shoot the pictures for the calendar. The Mayans had used the past to predict the future, a sensible insight by a culture that had gone out of business.

James Chan was sitting on his swivel stool as always. He grinned when he turned, recognizing his visitor. "Well, well. Back again. Busy man."

Carl Czez grinned. "Always been a hard worker." He boosted the ice chest onto the table beside Chan. He opened the top and stepped back so Chan could look inside. He said, "Can you do a mask and pair of gloves from the head and hands of this gentleman?"

Chan leaned over the chest, looking amused.

Czez said, "I took the precaution of taking some good color photos so you can get the complexion right." He retrieved a batch of photos from an envelope.

Chan studied the pictures. These were live photos of the man whose head was in the ice chest.

Czez bent over the opened container, looking inside. "This gentleman was extra careful when he was sober, a man of professional habits, but when he got to drinking?" He shook his head sadly. "Talk, talk, talk. Brag, brag, brag. At first I thought he was one of those congenital liars you meet in a bar once in a while, but that turned out not to be the case. He really did have a history."

"Perhaps he was insecure," Chan said.

"Bullshit artists is what we call them where I'm from, but every once in a while you run into somebody who mixes the truth in with the hoo-hoo."

Chan picked up the frozen head and turned it in his hands, examining it closely.

"Lucky he lived as long as he did," Czez said.

Chan turned the head farther, studying it. "I can work from this."

Czez said, "I want to be able to make a life mask myself from an unconscious form, say from somebody who has been drugged. No sense killing someone if I don't have to. Can you teach me to do that?"

Chan placed the frozen head on his workbench and cocked his head, grinning. "You're one of my best customers. Of course I can do that."

three

Jake Hipp stood ankle-deep in water at the bottom of a sluggish drift in a shallow tropical river, the Macapal, in Belize, a few miles from the Guatemalan border. He had no companions; there was just himself and the smell of his armpits and the clicking and snapping of bugs and the heat of the late afternoon sun. He readied an ultralight fishing rod and flipped a purple-plastic worm upstream; he retrieved the worm slowly, giving it a slight action with his wrist.

He wore dark glasses and a floppy white-cotton hat pulled low over his ears; this hat, which provided shade for his face and neck, looked like a sailor's hat but was actually made for Australian cricket players—perfect for a long day in the tropical sun. He wore light tan–cotton walking shorts, a pale-blue shirt with patches of sweat under the arms, and a multipocketed khaki vest of a type worn by fishermen and photographers.

Hipp heard the sound of a motor in the distance. He glanced up.

He heard the door of a vehicle, a muffled thump. He had a visitor. Or visitors.

He flipped the plastic worm upstream again.

He retrieved the worm and mopped the sweat from his forehead before he tried again.

A strike! The ultralight carbon rod, which was about a yard long and hardly thicker than a matchstick, was nearly bent double by the hit. Hipp tilted the tip of the rod up so that the rod—not the silky thin line—took the action.

The rod tip bounced wildly as the fish made a good run.

The fish broke water.

On the shore, a voice said, "Give him some line, Jake. Play him."

Jake Hipp glanced up at a figure squatting at the base of a mamey tree. The man had a computer hardly larger than a skinny book. Eyeing the computer, Hipp said, "You! Joe Woofter."

"Me."

"God, you guys are everywhere, aren't you? Can't leave a guy alone." Hipp concentrated on his fish.

"What have you got? A real fighter?"

Hipp played the fish. The tip of his rod bent in a sharp arc as the fish made a determined run for freedom. "Here, it's called a tuba. I've heard them called peacock bass. Fun catching them on light gear." He unclipped a small net from his belt.

Hipp scooped up the fish, which had bands of yellow, green, red, and white on its underside. He waded across the bottom of the pool and unhooked a string of tuba—all of which were eight to ten inches long. As he did, he looked up at Joe Woofter, who was wearing rumpled chinos, a wrinkled, short-sleeved shirt, serviceable, unfashionable shoes, possibly never shined, and a panama that looked like it had been sat on numerous times. Woofter mopped the sweat from his forehead with a red handkerchief, looking vaguely uncomfortable at being out of doors on a hot and humid tropical day with bugs everywhere.

Hipp added the new fish to the string and studied his visitor. "Well, well, fancy meeting you here. How do you like the tropics, Joe?" He knew there was only one reason why Woofter had come all this way to see him.

Woofter rolled his eyes. "Too hot for my taste, I'm afraid. I don't know how you do it."

Hipp wanted to get straight to the business of Bobby Pearl, but he decided to let Woofter tell him in his own way. He said, "How's your family?"

"Harriet is now the principal of her school, and I have another grandson. And your daughter and significant other?" Woofter lit a cigarette.

"Laura is in the fifth grade—still lives with her mother. Gina still runs Most Hipp. How many men own a bar in the Philippines? It actually makes money. Not a lot, but it keeps me afloat."

"Charlies coming in from Asia are telling me it's the best expat bar on the circuit. It's the books that does it. The Wiener schnitzel is good, too."

In Most Hipp, customers could either buy the paperbacks that lined the walls or swap two for one. "Gotta lot of German customers. We even taught a Filipino butcher how to make German sausages. Gina's uncle, Felix."

Looking at the ground, Woofter took a drag on his cigarette and nudged a stone with the toe of one shoe. He was always polite and well-mannered, and ever curious. "Still got your place in Long Beach?"

Hipp nodded. "Spent last summer there. Mostly, I've been yo-yoing back and forth to Most Hipp with more books. Isolation gnaws at our expat customers. They crave something to read."

Woofter sighed. "My daughter-in-law has your 'neat bugs' number in her office at Stanford."

"Homage to Charlie Darwin, a beetles man from childhood."

"I liked the huge-horned number from Africa. The one that eats elephant dung. Looked like a rhino." Woofter shook his head; he gave the rock a flip with his toe. "You always were good with a camera. Beautiful stuff. Densely meticulous, Jake, I mean that. Lush and harsh at the same time."

Hipp said, "Between Most Hipp, travel articles, and the calendars, I stay afloat. I just scored an article in *Vanity Fair* called 'On the Road with a Paranoid Cheapskate.' " He looked rueful. He wished Woofter would get on with it.

Woofter laughed. "That's gotta be autobiographical."

"My agent is trying to peddle that idea in one of those coffee-table books with photographs of travel in the Third World. Something suits and their wives can enjoy while drinking white wine."

"Oh?"

"An overcrowded ferry about to founder. Men squatting to defecate beside a temple. A pee-and-semen-stained mattress on the floor of a Spartan room. A visual adventure. You get the idea. Adventure at a tidy remove. No suffering the bad-food quicksteps or getting ripped off at airports and borders."

Woofter looked amused. "You should do the Kama Sutra ruins in India. That'd sell." He glanced at Hipp with troubled eyes.

Hipp could take it no longer. "Bobby Pearl?"

Woofter looked back at the ground. "Someday you should also do a Cosmic Motherfuckers calendar." He cleared his throat and kicked another rock.

Hipp reeled in his line and fastened the hook. "What do you say we go to a bar I know in San Ignacio and have us a cold beer? Too damned hot out here."

"Good idea," Woofter said.

Hipp said, "Come down here by the water. There's something I want to show you."

Looking puzzled, Woofter joined him at the water's edge.

"Watch," Hipp said. He submerged his forearm in the water. "See 'em?"

"I do indeed," Woofter said.

Hipp's arm had been set upon by diminutive fish, each no more than half an inch long. They appeared to be chewing furiously. "First time I did this, I was spooked. Figured the little bastards were going to eat me up, but they can't do any harm. Their mouths are too small. Go ahead, stick your hand into the water."

Woofter hesitated, then did. In seconds, his hand was covered with the tiny fish, nibbling furiously but too small to actually bite anything.

"Eager eaters," Hipp said. He stepped into a pair of aged made-in-India sandals.

Woofter yanked his hand out of the water. He cleared his throat. He lit another cigarette. "Unnerving little bastards."

"You know, Joe, there are probably hundreds of thousands of these little eaters in this river. They're all hungry. They wiggle and they chew. They all look alike. Suppose there was a poisonous mutant among them. Tough job sorting him out." Hipp squatted by Woofter and stuck his hand into the water again, watching the diminutive fish attack his fingers. "Did you know that the exact same gene in both Homo sapiens and ants correctly puts the head in place? By tinkering with an ant's genes in the lab, they've been able to put a leg where an antenna ordinarily belongs. What's he threatening with this time?"

"Isopropyl methylphosphonofluoridate." Woofter paused to grind out his cigarette with his heel.

Hipp raised an eyebrow. "I beg your pardon."

Woofter looked surprised. "Sarin."

Hipp's shoulders slumped. "Oh, shit." He looked at the diminutive computer. "You want to show me what you've got?"

Holding the computer in his left hand, Woofter opened the slender screen. "Sent it over the Web, just like before. Same rush of pearls. The Mormon Tabernacle Choir singing Handel's *Messiah*." He tapped a button. The screen turned pale blue. The now-familiar iridescent pearl tumbled from the top left of the screen, followed by an avalanche of pearls, all rolling in slow motion as they fell. The deep, rumbling, electronically altered voice said:

> It's me again, your old pal, Bobby Pearl. Surprised? I bet not. I've now got all kinds of goodies on my shelf. Sometime in the next six months, I'm going to give you a modest hit of sarin to show you what I can do.
>
> Hallelujah! Hallelujah!
>
> I can also deliver tabun, soman, hydrogen cyanide, and VX. Biologicals, too. Anthrax. Botulism. Pick your poison.
>
> Hal-le-lu-u-jah!

* * *

The pearls plunged into the blood.

> *Go ahead now, put on your thinking caps. Try to
> find me. Go through your pathetic drill.*
> *Hallelujah! Hallelujah!*
> *You kept my last warning secret. Are you going
> to keep this warning secret, too? I bet that secrecy
> business won't last forever.*
> *Hal-le-lu-u-jah!*

Hipp said, "You want me back, then."

Woofter nodded. "The Pooh-Bahs don't like sacking
somebody for a gross fuckup and being forced to take him
back in. It rubs their bureaucratic fur the wrong way. But in
this case, they don't have any choice. If they don't take you
back, they risk waking up some morning to read an editorial
in *The Post* or *The New York Times* asking why don't they
use every possible resource. You're the only Charlie who has
seen him and heard his unaltered voice."

"They want me back as a Charlie, not a Beta?"

"As a Charlie, yes. But this is only a temporary thing,
Jake. A one-time job."

"I go for Bobby Pearl?"

"Yes."

"If I nail him, they take me back permanently or no deal."
That wasn't true; Hipp would have returned to the hunt on
any basis, but he knew he had them by the short hairs.

Woofter sighed. "That too. I told them you'd want that."

Jake Hipp grinned broadly. "Well, they'll eventually get
used to the idea, especially after I nail Pearl. Screw 'em, I
say. Give me five." He gave Joe Woofter's hand a slap. "I'm
going to run that son of a bitch down, Joe. You watch my
smoke. Yes!"

"A real Charlie in action," Woofter said.

"A bloodhound and then some," Hipp said.

"I know how much you hate him," Woofter said. Then he

added quietly, "I've got something at stake here too, you know. It was me who convinced them to take you on in the first place."

They trudged up the trail through the sticky heat, but Jake Hipp remained pumped. He had his shot at redemption. "I knew it. It was too much to expect that Bobby Pearl would quietly retire after frying those people with mustard. This is an ego thing with him. He thinks he's teaching us all a lesson."

Joe Woofter said, "It took some effort to lay his hands on sarin. Can't just buy it at your local Kmart. That had to be the reason for the delay. The question is, who gave it to him, and why?"

"Sarin. Jesus!" Hipp clenched his teeth.

Woofter shook his head grimly. "What happened in Tangier could have happened to anybody, Jake. You can't blame yourself forever."

Hipp looked annoyed. "But it didn't happen to anybody, did it, Joe? It happened to me." He stopped for a breather in the cooling shade of a mamey tree.

Woofter said, "We can't undo the past, Jake. We have to live with it."

They both sat. A cooling breeze momentarily rustled the leaves above them.

Hipp said, "When I saw him in Tangier, Bobby Pearl was talking to a Sudanese we thought was fronting for Moamar Qadhafi. Joaquin Hurtado interviewed Qadhafi in Libya a few weeks after the San Francisco mustard gas—a two-hour special, as I recall. No other guests, just Qadhafi. I take it you talked to Hurtado about that."

Joaquin Hurtado's *My Side* was the ratings flagship of a twenty-four-hour news channel, New Era Television, called The NET, owned by Elia Khardonne, a Canadian who had emerged from Sundre, near Calgary in Alberta Province, to challenge the supremacy of Rupert Murdoch's Fox Television News and Time-Warner's CNN. On *My Side,* controversial, obnoxious, demented, and downright criminal figures got to tell their stories without the clutter of bothersome objections or pointed questions. Joaquin Hurtado, the charming and inoffensive host, went where the action was, no matter where it took him.

Woofter used the edge of his hand to squeegee sweat from his forehead. "We tried, but no soap."

Hipp was surprised. "No?"

Woofter looked at him mildly. "That's partly why I'm here, Jake. The show's producer, a woman named Dani Bernardi, says Hurtado will talk to us if we send you to do the debriefing. She wants a follow-up to Hurtado's interview of Bobby Pearl."

"To find out about the pumpkin soup and mint tea?"

"Plus she obviously read the piece in *Esquire*," Woofter said. *Esquire* magazine had published an article about Mongoose a few weeks after Hurtado's interview of Bobby Pearl in the Philippines. The article had detailed Mongoose gossip about a Beta turned Charlie who had choked big time in Tangier, after which he was canned. This Charlie's lack of *cojones* in Morocco had allowed Bobby Pearl to release mustard gas in San Francisco.

Hipp said, "The intellectual who should have stayed in the library. They know how to cut a guy down."

"We told Ms. Bernardi we had no idea where you were. Last we heard, somewhere in Australia shooting pictures of aboriginals for a magazine article. She said we could find you if we tried hard enough. She was right, of course. Qadhafi was trying to come off as an international Goody Two-shoes, and he somehow conned The NET into spending a fortune promoting it. A real coup for Qadhafi. He got to show the world his mushroom-growing room at Tarhunah."

Hipp rolled his eyes. "Mushrooms. Right. Did Hurtado talk to you about his Bobby Pearl interview?" The interview with Pearl in the Philippines had followed the Qadhafi special by some months.

"No soap there either."

"Ms. Bernardi again?"

"*My Side* was her idea originally, and she's guided it to

success. She calls the shots. Hurtado is a self-important pretty boy."

Hipp said, "Tough to swallow the Pearl interview, I have to say. The motherfucker hiding behind an electronic screen and giving me a transparent bird with half the world watching."

Woofter, watching Hipp, said, "Has to be hard on you, Jake. We all understand that, believe me we do."

"Shit happens. It's something I have to live with. A little humiliation is good for the soul, I suppose."

"You have a tape of the interview?"

"Oh, hell yes. I've got one of the fucking things. Hurtado talked to Pearl at a local beach resort on Negros, one island over from Cebu. Gina knows the man who owns the place. Pearl's choosing the Philippines was no accident, Joe. He was sending a message. He knows my routines."

"Stalking you?"

"You should have seen the look he gave me when he poked my throat with the knife." Hipp stood. "Well, I suppose we shouldn't sit here all day. I've got work to do."

They walked slowly onward, smoking and taking their time in the heat. They said no more until they reached their vehicles, a rusting derelict Chevrolet pickup for Hipp, and what looked like a brand-new Toyota Land Cruiser for Woofter.

Hipp, eyeing the Toyota, said mildly, "Ahh, it's the good life."

Woofter dug for his keys. "Air-conditioned. Rented it in Belize City. A big gouge, but the taxpayers are good for it."

"Poor fucking taxpayers. I'll drop my clunker off in San Ignacio." Hipp climbed into his pickup and fired up the engine. He led the way down the gravel road, glancing in his rearview mirror as Woofter followed in the Toyota.

Jake Hipp was back, and as far as he was concerned, Bobby Pearl was one doomed scumbag.

four

Jake Hipp drove the Toyota Land Cruiser over the aged Hawksworth Bridge spanning the Macapal River. They would drive northwest through the Belizean capital of Belmopan on their way to Belize City, where they would catch a plane to Miami and switch to a flight to National Airport in Alexandria, Virginia, just across the Potomac from Washington. Hipp would have more detailed briefings at Company headquarters in Langley, Virginia, and at the Justice Department headquarters on Pennsylvania Avenue in Washington, D.C.

Hipp said, "After I talk to Joaquin Hurtado and his producer, I'll retreat to my cabin in Long Beach. Washington D.C. or Washington State. What's the difference in a case like this? I've got my laptop and a scrambler for my phone."

"Long Beach it is." Looking out at the modest houses of the impoverished Belizeans, Woofter lit a Camel. He thought for a moment. "Pearl has to get this shit somewhere. You already know about Qadhafi, so let's go over the other players. Where do you want to start?"

"I don't know. The North Koreans?"

"The North Koreans have everything on Pearl's list, and they desperately need the money. They're not picky about who they sell it to, as long as they're convinced it'll be used on somebody else."

"China?" Hipp geared down for a curve.

"Beijing signed the Biological Weapons Convention in nineteen eighty-four, but continues to produce all the standard gases and poisons in quantity. The Chinese've been selling both chemicals and equipment to Iran, but we think they value our market too much to risk an American hit being traced to them."

The two-lane highway curved through gently rolling hills. In the distance, a limestone cliff rose above the tropical undergrowth. Hipp said, "Iran and Iraq? Soldiers of Allah leading us boldly into the next century?"

Woofter eyed him mildly. "Either Iran or Iraq could be Pearl's supplier as long as there's no way of linking it to them."

"Maximum chickenshits. Praise Allah!"

"In his war against the Ayatollah in the eighties, Saddam used aerial bombs of tabun as well as mustard gas. Tabun is a good battlefield gas because it disperses quickly. You deliver the hit and send your troops in after the air clears. The Iranians answered the tabun with sarin and mustard gas. Saddam didn't use g-agents in the Gulf War, but we found ordnance stores of sarin and mustard in Kuwait. If we had pursued Saddam's army up the Tigris River in an attempt to topple his regime, there's no telling what would have happened. Saddam had nothing to lose. What then?"

"Nuke Baghdad?" They passed through the shadow of a limestone outcropping jutting up from swampy grassland.

Woofter looked grim. "It was a difficult chore for George Bush to put together the coalition in the first place, Jake."

"Ultimately, the g-agents worked for Saddam, didn't they? They saved his skin."

"We've calculated that Saddam had accumulated about five hundred metric tons each of tabun and mustard by the time he sent his troops into Kuwait. God knows how much sarin he had. The UN later destroyed twenty-seven thousand chemical-filled bombs, rockets, and warheads, and another five hundred tons of precursor chemicals. Then we found out that Iraq had produced ninety thousand liters of botulinum toxin and more than eight thousand liters of anthrax. They claim to have destroyed it after the war, but we don't know that for a fact."

Hipp slowed for a herd of goats being urged across the

highway by two small boys. "Destroying it voluntarily doesn't sound very much like Saddam."

"No, it doesn't," Woofter said. "The Arabs may be crazy, but they're not dumb. They know the Japanese cultists delivered sarin in plastic bags. And if you've got eight thousand liters of anthrax stashed away, where's the harm in selling a few liters of it to somebody like Bobby Pearl?"

"As long as it can't be traced."

"That goes without saying. We're talking about definitive chickenshits here." Woofter lit another cigarette, watching the passing countryside.

Hipp geared down for a curve again. "I take it that India and Pakistan would have to be on our list."

"Yes, they would. Although fairly low down, I would think. Their motive is hard to figure."

"And the Russians."

"Not the government. The Kremlin is stroking our pee-pee because it wants foreign aid and is afraid of NATO expansion into Eastern Europe. The problem is, they don't have the rubles necessary to keep their stocks secure. We know that Russian gangsters have been stealing and selling both sarin and soman. Turning a profit is enough motive for them."

Hipp started to pass an aging pickup truck, but quickly pulled back in as a car whipped by in the other direction. Then he pressed his foot hard on the accelerator and passed the pickup. "You never know where the shits are coming from."

"Or when you're going to be flattened," Woofter said.

"I take it Qadhafi is at the top of our list of possible suppliers."

"Not necessarily. Qadhafi's trying to get back in the good graces of the world community. If we link him with Bobby Pearl, it would be a disaster for Libya, and he knows it. He's on our list only because we caught Pearl talking to Colonel Sayani in Tangier."

Hipp said, "Pearl presumably made contact with all the major players."

"We have to assume that," Woofter said. "North Korea. Iran. Iraq. They've all got the stocks. They all hate us. Any one of them could have struck a deal."

Hipp drove in silence, thinking. The appearance of Bobby Pearl was an old story that was repeating itself endlessly. The familiar beast decked itself out in this or that righteous costume to justify its actions—the glistening shoes of rhetoric, the underwear of greed. As tribute to the greater good of ego-gone-wrong, snakes killed without regard to proportion. Political fanatics, extortion artists, and movie directors loved the big boom of explosives as pyromaniacs loved fire; but gas and disease were far more terrifying to the public imagination.

Hipp said, "Before I hung it up, I looked at photographs of possible Bobby Pearls until I nearly went blind. We know he's good with a laptop, and we suspect him of supporting himself through theft on the Internet. We turned to college yearbooks looking for a sociopath who'd studied computer science."

"Couldn't find him," Woofter said.

"I know it's intuitive and unscientific, Joe, but he just didn't look like your usual hacker or computer nerd. Those people spend their lives in an interior world. He was neat and in shape, with a recent haircut. He cared about his appearance."

"A former military man."

"That's what I've been thinking," Hipp said. "Someone who knows the ropes of the international arms market. You have I.D. photos of soldiers assigned to the National Security Agency at Fort Meade, don't you? And the Defense Intelligence Agency in the Pentagon? Why don't we start there this time?"

Up ahead, a group of four turtles was plodding across the highway.

"Their counterintelligence people are professional paranoids, so it'll take me a few days."

"Goes without saying."

"This country is like a Rube Goldberg engine with pistons

poking out at every angle imaginable. You want the pictures on proofs again?"

"Easiest way. You can beam them to me on the Internet." Checking his rearview mirror again to make sure he wasn't going to get run over himself, Jake Hipp geared to a stop. He watched the determined turtles, wondering why they were bent on crossing the road—same swamp on either side.

five

The silicon mask covered everything, including Carl Czez's ears and lips, and his hair was now a rich, lustrous brown. Dressed in a camel blazer, light-gray shirt, dark-blue slacks, and polished black wingtips, and carrying two valises, he looked stylish and prosperous as he pushed his way through the heavy brass-and-glass revolving door into the lobby of the Southern Comfort Hotel in Atlanta, Georgia. He caught a glimpse of his reflection in a mirror. He paused momentarily, smiling. James Chan had done a beautiful job of reproducing the face of a frozen head. Czez laughed. The mask laughed perfectly. Well . . . hello, Ralph Snow!

The lobby was quiet and sedate. The beige carpet was soft under Czez's feet. This was the habitat of suits, not a fifty-buck-a-night kind of place, which was more to his taste. He proceeded to the reception desk and set his valises on the carpet, all polish and confidence.

The clerk, a young black woman with a round, pleasant face, wore a brown skirt and blouse with PAMELA embroidered above the pocket on her right breast. If she noticed anything unusual about Czez's face, she didn't show it. "Yes, sir?" she said with a soft Georgia drawl.

"Do you have any openings higher up? Something overlooking Sumpter Avenue?"

"Higher up?"

"I like to look out over the city. And I like to smoke."

Pamela pretended to check a directory, although it was obvious from the full panel of key boxes behind her that the Southern Comfort had plenty of empty rooms. There were no conventions in town, and the Braves were on the road. "Let's see, a smoker overlooking Sumpter."

"I like to have a cup of coffee in the morning and watch the sunrise."

"I see. Yes, we can give you a room on the tenth floor above Sumpter. Just you?"

"A single, that's right."

"That would be one hundred seventy-five a night, including tax. We have twenty-four-hour room service. You'll find a menu with our hospitality package in your room. We have a sauna, Jacuzzi, and a fully equipped gym."

Czez dug his wallet out of his pocket. "I'd like to pay in advance."

"Of course, sir."

He brandished a wad of greenbacks.

Pamela looked momentarily confused. Almost all the guests used a credit card at the Sumpter. This was part of the profitable expense-account racket ultimately borne by the taxpayers.

Czez, watching her face, smiled. "Hate plastic," he said. "These'll do, won't they? They'll spend. That'll be what, something over twelve hundred bucks? Is that right?" He started peeling out the hundred-dollar bills, the newest version with the larger picture of Benjamin Franklin. Benjies, Czez called them.

Pamela pushed a registration form toward him, and Czez, using his left hand, signed in as Gene Beaver, 1421 Chicory Lane, New Orleans, Louisiana. When he finished, he said, "I have to book a flight to Los Angeles. Could you recommend a travel agent?"

"Certainly. Old South is just down the street. They'll give you the cheapest rates possible." She slipped him a pamphlet from behind the counter and wrote her name on the corner. "Just give 'em this brochure and they'll see that you're taken care of."

A bellhop, also black, was immediately at his side, eager to assist any new guest with a wad of greenbacks like that. Talk about long green! The nameplate on the lapel of his brown uniform identified him as Louis.

Czez followed Louis to the elevator; as they were whisked

silently to the tenth floor, he said, "Can you recommend a good bar around here? Nothing fancy. Just a place where a guy can have a beer and chew on buffalo wings or whatever."

"Sure. There's Peaches just across the street on Sumpter. They've got pool tables and dartboards, and the waitresses have these big uh-huhs. You know, the very best Georgia peaches." Louis grinned broadly. "You like peaches?"

"Love 'em. Yuppie place?"

The elevator stopped and the door slid open. "Here we are. Not really. It's a hangout for the people who work at CNN just around the corner. Not the stars. Technicians and writers mostly. Cameramen, sound people, that kind of thing."

"The enlisted types."

Louis laughed. "That's right. The officers have their own place." He grabbed Czez's valises and headed for the room. As he walked, he cleared his throat. "Say, you're not any kind of cop, are you?"

"Me? A cop? No, no, no."

"If you're ever in the mood for company or a little something, you should let me know. Maybe I can help you out. You know, with whatever."

"Little weed?" Carl Czez didn't smoke pot, but he knew Ralph Snow had. If he bought it, he didn't have to actually smoke it.

Louis smiled. "I've heard it's the number-one cash crop in Georgia. Better than peanuts."

"Who knows, maybe I'll give you a call."

Once inside, Czez laid a couple of Abes on Louis; when Louis was gone, he stripped off his Ralph Snow face, but kept on the silicon gloves with Snow's fingerprints. He put his belongings away, then poked his head into the bathroom and checked out his face in the mirror. The scars had sunk back into his skin, just as the good doctor had said they would. Unless you knew they were there, or had a magnifying glass, you would never notice them.

Czez returned to his bedroom, mounted a Nikon with a 200-mm lens atop a tripod by the window. He snipped the end from his cigar with his little guillotine cigar trimmer. Puffing thoughtfully, he studied the street below. Then he took a few shots of the customers entering and leaving Peaches.

After that, he put his Toshiba laptop on the coffee table, plugged it in and opened his Microsoft 2000 software. He was soon hard at work, nursing his cigar and looking thoughtful as he tapped the keys; a list of names and job titles popped up on the screen. He scrolled leisurely through the names, studying them.

Peaches, despite a room containing six pool tables and another half-dozen dartboards, was not a neighborhood bar where middle-aged males talked about baseball and bitched about ex-wives and child support. In a neighborhood bar in Atlanta, you could escape your empty apartment and score a Bud Lite for a buck seventy-five; in Peaches, a midscale hangout for thirtyish men and women with a few bucks in their pockets and an optimistic future, one had to pony up three bucks.

The extra buck twenty-five was presumably to keep the riffraff out and to pay for the wonderful fruit on the chests of the waitresses. Whether your taste in peaches was for strictly European ancestry or the darker, African-American variety, the waitresses all sported remarkable, if not downright inspiring, fruit. This was Georgia, and if the feminists had descended in righteous fury on the sexist motif, they had not yet triumphed. The buck nearly always beat civility.

Peaches was not so boorish as to allow its customers to inflict adolescent music on other people with a loud juke-box. A house tape played Rod Stewart, Elton John, Steely Dan, The Eagles, Jimmy Buffett, and other rock-and-roll with soul and rhythm. At one end of the bar, a television monitor showed CNN with the sound turned off.

Carl Czez had to smile when he stepped into Peaches, which was packed with a hubbub of talking and laughing men and women. Czez made his way to the bar and ordered a Michelob from the bartender, a young man in a white shirt and black bow tie. He said, "Lucky this isn't the chestnut or acorn state."

The bartender said, "Isn't that the truth."

Czez glanced up at the silent set. "You always show the news with the sound turned off?"

The bartender smiled. "We get a lot of folks in here from CNN just down the street. Some of them edited these stories before they got off work. They like to see how they turned out."

Czez nursed his Michelob and watched the pool players. One table was reserved for challengers. Here one put a quarter in a line on a small sill by the coin slot. A winner could play all night for free if he was good enough. He watched the players for an hour. Finally, he got up and added his own quarter; when it came up, he got himself a fresh bottle of Michelob and stepped over to the table and introduced himself to the current champion, a tall, slender redhead in a Georgia Tech T-shirt.

"I believe I'm up. Ray Peckinpah," he said, shaking the redhead's hand.

The redhead said, "Bill Paige. Pleased to meet you, Ray."

Paige set about racking 'em up as Carl Czez sang an old tune:

> Rack up the balls, boys, put away the cues.
> Old Father Time is on your tail, and he ain't a
>   gonna lose.

six

After a day of debriefings on Bobby Pearl and updated reports from Interpol at CIA headquarters in Langley, Virginia, Jake Hipp had a Greek salad in a neighborhood cafe, then settled back in his room at Virginia's Best, a sleazy motel just outside the beltway near McLean. Hipp could have stayed anywhere he wanted to on the Company's tab, but he felt bored and uncomfortable in the hangouts of traveling suits. He had grown up working-class and had come to realize, with the passing of years, that he would be forever ill at ease in the trappings of middle-class success. He was an unembarrassed intellectual, which, in a fundamental way, transcended class and national boundaries. He preferred to be alone, thinking, rather than in the company of people talking about profit and loss. He did not scorn profit and loss of the conventional ledger; he was just not interested in it. And yet Hipp knew he was a treasure hunter in his way. He sought the elusive *why*.

Back in his room, he uncapped a Guinness stout, got out his tape of Joaquin Hurtado's interview with Bobby Pearl in the Philippines and popped it into the VCR.

Clenching his teeth at the memory of his humiliation, he punched the play button.

A solemn Joaquin Hurtado, wearing a Los Angeles Dodgers baseball cap and dressed in Birkenstock sandals, Banana Republic walking shorts, and a multipocketed safari jacket—all new and neat and crisply pressed—walked slowly down a muddy beach. He was there, wearing his adventurer's getup, on behalf of his viewers. He was Joaquin Hurtado, a serious, caring man, and his demeanor was serious and caring in the extreme. In the background, a scattering of Asians, knee-deep in grayish-black goo, were gathering something.

As he walked, Hurtado said, "We are less than a mile north of Bacolod, on the western side of the island of Negros in the Philippines."

He gestured at the figures behind him. "The tide is out, and the Filipinos you see are gathering clams. If you had been in this spot on the morning of March 12, 1945, you could have seen American warships preparing to send soldiers ashore against the waiting Japanese Army." Hurtado turned and pointed behind him. "In May of that year, some thirty miles north of here, that bitter struggle ended as American soldiers drove the remaining Japanese from Mount Tamalon in a bloody battle. The locals will tell you that Mount Tamalon, now occupied by the insurgent New People's Army, is where General Yamashita buried part of his storied gold, although none of it has ever been found."

Hurtado faced the camera again. He had a grave and necessary duty to perform.

"We are here to interview the terrorist Bobby Pearl, who, authorities say, threatened to blow up an airliner, then did; threatened to blow up the IRS headquarters in Ogden, Utah, then did; and who threatened to release mustard gas on an American city, then did—three devastating acts of treachery that cost a total of five hundred and twenty-three lives. He's still free despite a coordinated international effort to run him down. But *My Side,* in an effort to tell the full, unedited story, sought him out. We found him, and he has agreed to an interview."

Hurtado wheeled and pointed with his finger. "Bobby Pearl is waiting for us there, to tell us his side."

A man with an electronic mask sat in a bamboo cabana on a tropical beach. Wearing a short-sleeved blue shirt, he had a red bandanna tied around his forehead as a sweatband. Grinning at the camera, he waved a fly away with his hand.

Hurtado, looking intense and grave, said, "Why did you do what you did, Bobby Pearl? And will you do it again?"

He looked the camera straight-on with his sincere brown eyes. "We'll have his answers to those two questions when we come back. Don't go away."

Hurtado was replaced by a burly actor, naked to the waist, pounding metal at a forge, the heat glowing against his sweaty body. He put down his hammer and picked up a bottle of Douse. "Too much burning after a meal? Worried about getting ulcers? Can't eat food that really tastes good? Douse the flames! Douse is now available with no prescription needed."

After advertisements for a new miracle paint and gold-plated bathroom fixtures, Bobby Pearl was back. Pearl finished off a San Miguel. He swatted at another fly. When he spoke, it was through an electronic scrambler that gave his voice an odd, warbling pitch, or echoing burble, as though he were speaking through a long pipe or tube.

He said, "You want to know why I blow people up, and you want to know if I'll do it again. Those are both reasonable questions, Mr. Hurtado." He waved for another beer. "Di! Di! Nothing beats an ice-cold San Miguel." He scooped some peanuts from a shallow dish and popped them in his mouth; the peanuts had been cooked with their skins on. Chewing on the peanuts, he said, "These are good, too. Cooked with garlic. They grow them between rows of sugarcane."

Pearl leaned back to accommodate a slender Filipina delivering another sweating bottle of San Miguel. "Thank you, Di. First of all, who *says* I did those things anyway?" He laughed a weird, burbling laugh and took a swig of beer. "You might as well forget all your fancy psychological theories. I am a professor of hard knocks. I do it to teach the meaning of purpose, discipline, and loyalty to the Great American Fool."

Hurtado was apparently incapable of embarrassment; a cutaway showed him listening intently to Bobby Pearl's every important word.

The electronic mask did not affect Pearl's enthusiastic

body language. This was his moment, and he was incapable of masking his pride. He burbled on: "When the history books are written, you'll find my name in the index: 'Pearl, Bobby, instructor of necessary lessons.' The lives lost are a form of national tuition, a modest payment for truths learned. I will remain in encyclopedias and dictionaries long after people have forgotten about Jack the Ripper and Adolph Eichmann. Hundreds of years from now, I will stalk people in their dreams. Perhaps, one day, they will understand and thank me for my modest contribution. Does that answer your first question?"

Hurtado looked grave.

"As to your second question, will I do it again? Does a bear shit in the woods?"

"I—"

Pearl cut him off with his spooky burble. "I'd like to say hello to the good folks at The Watch, and to all the Charlies from Mongoose who are watching this thinking they're going to figure out where this old bear is going to squat next. Say, Jake Hipp, did you save that pumpkin soup and mint tea so it could be analyzed? How are you doing out there? Getting a good night's sleep? Learned how to pull a trigger yet? The old choke artist."

Pearl held up his hand like he was aiming a pistol. "Boom! Boom!" he burbled. "See there. Nothing to it. Remember those old ads for Nike shoes? Just do it. Getting a good night's sleep, are you? All those dead people on your conscience."

Hurtado said, "Mr. Pearl, we were wondering—"

"I'm afraid that'll have to be it, Joaquin. I know you came halfway around the world and everything, but I also know that half the cops on the planet will be studying this tape, and I do cherish my neck. So now that I've told you what I'm doing, go ahead, try to stop me. Adds to the mystique. Be my guest!"

"Pumpkin soup and mint tea? Jake Hipp?"

"Listen up now, everybody. Get a pencil. I'll say it again.

You want to stop the tumble of pearls? There is only one way, through purpose, discipline, and loyalty. Blow me off, and you are doomed."

Pearl wiggled his bottle of San Miguel. Another empty. In his warbling, echoing voice, he said, "Damn, this stuff is good." He had successfully used *My Side* to do a little showboating. His burble said, "It's been a pleasure meeting you, Joaquin." The burble masked timbre, but his meaning was nevertheless clear: "It's been fun screwing you, dumb pecker."

Bobby Pearl signaled to the waitress that he wanted another beer; his interview with Hurtado was finished, and he was thirsty. He said, "Di! Di!"

Jake Hipp shut down the VCR and turned his attention to the menu of skin flicks offered by the motel. *L.A. Ladies. Asian Sensations. Brown Meat. Big Bunned Women. Oral Action. Lotta Boobs. Anal Delights. Hunks. Boys Having Fun.* He tapped a number on his remote. On the screen came *L. A. Ladies,* displaying two lithe young ladies as the credits rolled. One ran her hand over the other's rump.

Hipp lit a cigar. Watching the girls, he immediately got an erection. He grinned. He wasn't in the mood for pulling his noodle, but he soon would be if he continued watching. He punched off the set. He sat thinking.

What motivated Bobby Pearl?

In the Darwinian world, everything was secondary to the survival of the species. To promote this survival, individual males sought to reproduce themselves as many times as possible. In the interest of passing along the strongest possible genes, females of the species felt compelled to accept the advances only of males they had been programmed to regard as superior. Out of this tension came the familiar dances of display and demonstrations of prowess. This was the endless tournament of sex and power.

The tournament was clearly expressed in myth and lore, from Homer through John Wayne and Aristotle Onassis.

Succeeding champions claimed not only the laurel of the moment, but the pretty girls as well.

In the human species, the tournament was now masked by the gilt of civilization, but the outsized human cortex had inadvertently sidestepped—or overrun—the evolutionary process. Any human male so inclined had the wherewithal to capture the champion's laurel; it was as though both bulk and winning snout were available to the most cowardly male on the beach. By combining easily obtainable chemicals, Bobby Pearl could command the attention of an entire planet.

Hipp felt there was no doubt that Pearl was fueled by the same genetic urge that had produced a history of wretched excess, from Vlad the Impaler to Ted Bundy. This led to another disconcerting conclusion: *Jake Hipp and the other Charlies were not chasing phantom anomalies; they were chasing the dark side of themselves.*

When would all this stop?

The answer was unsatisfying to most people, Hipp knew—especially since technology multiplied the danger geometrically.

He tapped on the set and found the young women again. They were young and lithe. Beauties. Horny to watch. His gentleman leaped quickly to attention. Perhaps on second thought . . .

With Elephant Dan Merrill driving, the minivan rolled east on Ohio State Highway 32, a four-laner, past Gibbons, Roads, and Hebbardsville. This was gentle Midwest farm country, with field after boring field of corn. Slick Smith uncapped a bottle of Johnnie Walker Scotch and used a funnel to pour it into his flask. He capped the flask, stored the bottle under the seat, and took a satisfying hit. "Tastes better when it's in a flask. I don't know why, but it does. Feels neat in your hand." He checked the map. "We should be about ten or twelve miles out. Closing in."

"Maybe if you hadn't had so many DWIs, you could take

your turn at the wheel. Let me sit there and get bombed."
Merrill squealed.

Smith bunched his face. "No thank you. I like it just the
way it is. Not every man has a personal driver, face it. You're
talking to Slick Smith here. Professional." Smith offered a
hit to Merrill, but Merrill shook his head. Smith said, "Got
Old Crow this time. Figured biblical symbolism and all that.
Try some."

"Last thing we need is to get pulled over by a state bull."
Merrill trumpeted. "What do you know about biblical symbolism anyway?" He slowed for a pickup horsing its way
onto the highway.

"What do I know?" Smith burst out laughing. "Why, my
daddy was a hell-fire-and-damnation Baptist preacher.
Didn't I tell you that? If I didn't do right, he whupped me
proper, reciting scripture all the while. Wouldn't let me get
away with anything. No, sir! He hit me with old boards,
pieces of rope, whatever he could lay his hands on. Once he
broke three of my ribs with the blade of a shovel."

"Jesus!"

"Said it was the Devil in me. Compared to me, Linda
Blair had it easy in *The Exorcist*. Remember that movie, all
that vomiting and stuff? Better to have a priest shouting
scripture at you than your old man beating on you. Catholics
have this forgiveness thing. Baptists aren't into that. He
made me read the Bible a half hour every night before I went
to bed. Wanted me to be a good boy."

Merrill grinned a toothy grin. "You liked your daddy,
Slick?"

"Mostly I just stayed out of his way. I was pretty good at
it too, until I got busted for putting the eye out of a woman's
registered poodle. Stupid little thing. The ugly old bitch
claimed it was worth a hundred bucks, which was a lot of
money in those days. One thing I learned, though."

"What was that?"

Smith looked surprised. "A BB gun won't do a whole lot
to a poodle. Just enough to make it feel uncomfortable." He
giggled. "I once used a BB gun to prang a whole litter of

rabbits in their cage. They couldn't run or anything. I just kept pumping shots in there while they squealed and kicked and jerked. Another time I knocked off a pair of lovebirds hanging in a cage by the postmaster's porch. Worthless birds."

"God, you're bad, Slick." Merrill gave a high-pitched peal of trumpeting.

"I used to catch turtles and prop their mouths open with little sticks, then throw them back in the water." He pretended to chuck a turtle. "Seagulls were fun, too."

"What did you do to seagulls?"

"Seagulls are flying rats, Elephant. They'll eat anything. What you do, see, is you catch yourself a fish three or four inches long. You ram a hook down its gullet with a stick and throw it out on the river, so it just floats. The seagull dives down and scarfs up the fish, and there you go!"

"There you go what?"

"You've got a seagull on the line. You play it like a fish, only it flies around in a circle. You gotta have a twelve to fifteen-pound test line, or risk having it snap. The real sport is if you have a buddy. One plays the fish, see, while the other tries to knock it out of the air with a twenty-two automatic." Smith pretended to be shooting at the sky. *"Pam! Pam! Pam!* I've folded a lot of seagulls in my time. Yessir! Make a satisfying *plop!* when they hit the ground." He grinned at the memory. "It was them lovebirds that was my downfall, I have to admit."

"Oh, how was that?"

Smith turned and pulled up his shirt to reveal ugly scars across his back. "My old man nearly beat the living shit out of me. Said it was for my own good. The way he saw it, family values are what made this country great. I got one hell of a dose of family values, that's a fact."

Merrill burst out laughing. "Is your old man still alive?"

Smith shrugged. "Naw. Somebody beat the son of a bitch to death a couple of years ago. Did a proper job of it, too."

"Jesus!" Merrill emitted a piercing squeal. He glanced at Smith. "I take it you had an alibi."

"They couldn't break it," Smith said. "Tried like hell. But all they had was circumstantial evidence. Couldn't get past shadow of a doubt. A good lawyer knows how to stretch those shadows of a doubt. It was like I was sittin' under a big old cottonwood tree."

"Lotsa doubt there."

"You bet."

Merrill said, "I ought to load up on gas before we get there. I don't want no foolin' around with gas on our way out of Athens."

"Our man told us what to do at Ohio University, so we do it. We just ease into Athens and find the apartment. We have the address and a duplicate key. We do our thing, then glide right on out of town. We know what we're supposed to do in West Virginia. We've been through that before. No problem."

"That's what I thought when I got busted for sticking up that jackass liquor store."

Smith glared at him. "Listen, our man was straight-up with us in the San Francisco job, wasn't he? He told us what to steal and how to safely mix the shit. We delivered the propane tanks and cruised on out of town with nobody the wiser. Nothing went wrong, because we're working with a professional. All communications are done in cyberspace. We look into the future and it is us. Think of it!"

"The edge of the fucking envelope." Merrill let rip a high-pitched squeal.

"And by God, there'll be none of that elephant shit when we get to Charleston. You do that and people will remember. We'll wind up behind bars, sure as hell. All it takes is one fuckup. If you're going to be a professional, you goddamn it have to act like one."

Merrill grinned and emitted a wild trumpet.

"Sure, sure, keep it up."

seven

Jake Hipp was on the trail of Bobby Pearl again, a predator following spoor; he felt alive and confident. He had failed to pull the trigger in Tangier, yes, but he knew that would not happen again. Something inside him had changed in a profound way. Where once he had been an intellectual who had watched too many thrillers on his VCR, he was now a Charlie in Beta clothing. This time he would not fail.

The night before his interview with Joaquin Hurtado and the *My Side* producer, Hipp checked into a wonderful, spread-out, three-floor motel, The Planet X on Santa Monica Boulevard, that was abuzz with the comings and goings of hookers and their johns. The rooms contained VCRs as well as television sets, the better for the gentleman and his lady to watch skin movies for warm-ups. In a fancy drive-in across the street, pimps hung out in big mo-fo Caddies while they kept an eye on their string of bitches.

After he had stashed his gear, Hipp took a stroll down the heart of West Hollywood crazy country, and on his return, had a drink at a piano bar called Amazonia. He found himself in the company of regulars speaking a slurred version of Portuguese.

A Brazilian bar in Los Angeles! Hipp said, "All right! Rio. Carnival. Pele. Rain forests." He raised his glass to toast things Brazilian.

At close to midnight, Hipp, carrying a six-pack of Brazilian beer, Brahma Chop, headed back to the Planet X Motel. On the sidewalk outside the motel, a dozen sloe-eyed ladies lounged in check-these-tits blouses and come-fuck-me boots. Three white teenage girls were mingled in among the black girls, who had squeezed sensational bodies into outfits two sizes too small. One of these, a young woman with an amazing rump, gave Hipp a look intended to make his balls stir. "Date tonight?" She turned, the better for him to appreciate her outstanding buns; they weren't floppers; they were solid as hardtack and poked right out.

"Believe I'll pass. Belly's full of black beans and rice," he said. He patted his stomach and kept trucking. The other girls, seeing the failure of the first, ignored him with noses high. They didn't understand men who checked into the Planet X merely to sleep. What was wrong with him? Weren't they good enough for him?

In his room, Hipp opened a Brahma Chop, flipped on the tube, punched mute, and there was the movie *Butch Cassidy and the Sundance Kid.* Paul Newman and Robert Redford, Butch and Sundance, the last of the Hole in the Wall Gang, were high up in the rocks, looking down at the never-quit railroad detectives coming after them bearing rifles with telescopic sights. Hipp didn't have to turn the sound up to remember Newman's famous line, "Who *are* these guys?"

The American frontier was underpopulated and a criminal could get lost in its vast space, with communication taking weeks, or months. In 1868, each new face in a frontier town was immediately noted and remembered. Even in the cities, neighborhoods had meaning and strangers were known to all. In the short space of twenty years, the telegraph had changed everything. In the end, Butch and Sundance had gone to Bolivia in a futile attempt to find space.

Hipp flipped off the tube. *Butch Cassidy and the Sundance Kid* was a movie about change. Bobby Pearl hung out in cyberspace. The operative word was *space.* Space, as Hipp saw it, was a form of frontier. The railroad dicks pursuing Butch and Sundance had used technology to eliminate space.

Overpopulation was now a fugitive's best friend; individual faces had become increasingly hard to remember. The Carloses, Libyans, Abu Nidals, Trade Tower bombers, Unabombers, and OK bombers simply blended into a great, buzzing, milling landscape of strangers, the loneliest of lonely crowds. This form of tall grass was the natural habitat of snakes and serial killers; simultaneously enjoying the refuge of space and the cover of numbers, the snakes, unseen, lethal, slid silently among the innocent.

What of sarin, which, if released in a crowded place in sufficient quantity, could kill thousands in a terrifying cycle of agony: dizziness, blood shooting from the nose and mouth, cramps and spasms, followed by death?

Did not rattlesnakes kill by poison?

Joaquin Hurtado had interviewed Bobby Pearl for *My Side* in the Philippines three months after the incident in Tangier. Since Hipp and his girlfriend owned a bar on Cebu, one island over from Negros, Hipp was convinced that this was no coincidence. Pearl did not want to be seen and remembered; he had privacy on Negros, which he knew was close enough to Cebu to be bothersome to Hipp.

Jake Hipp slipped the tape of the Bobby Pearl interview into the VCR and watched it one more time. He nearly had it memorized, and yet he watched it again and again, looking for something he might have missed. Each time he listened to Pearl's mocking burble, singling him out for ridicule, he became more determined to one day cut the man's fucking heart out.

When the interview was finished, Jake Hipp punched off the VCR and the tube. Unsettled at the idea of Bobby Pearl hanging out in the Philippines, possibly casing Most Hipp, and even eyeing Gina Jumero, he sat alone in the darkness, thinking.

Hipp understood the ratings game of television, and with it, the fame and money that motivated Hurtado, and yet he found it nearly impossible to reconcile unlimited freedom of expression with the dangerous facts of the twenty-first century. The cultural seeds for *My Side,* which solicited story ideas and interviews at the end of the program, had been sown years earlier with the popularity of Oprah, Sally Jessy, Jenny Jones, Ricki Lake, and the rest of the daytime talk-show hosts. It had been only a matter of time before the profitable notion of the viewer as voyeur was expanded from quarreling lovers, bikers, fat people, humpers of animals, fetishists of every imaginable description—or whatever pathetic, bizarre, mind-numbing story was out there in the national menagerie—and extended to at-large rapists, murderers, arsonists, thieves, and outright dangerous creeps and deviants. And sure enough, *My Side* had joined the freak show with enthusiastic abandon, going so far as to promise electronic masks and voice alteration, if requested.

Hipp thought he understood the logic that propelled this parade of the bizarre and outlandish. To forever command a footnote was to achieve a form of immortality, so celebrity had become currency. A poor man is he who dies unknown; a rich man is famous. *See me. I exist. Never mind what I am or what I have done. Remember me, and I will live.*

If Mr. Darwin's genetic robots occasionally had crooked wiring, the human model was capable of entertaining odd and oftentimes dangerous notions of prowess. While other men might flash brains, cars, or length of dick, Bobby Pearl displayed a surfeit of infamy; in this, he was not so much an anomaly as the logical extreme, an unequaled demonstration of prowess. *I am on the front page of every checkout rag on the planet.*

Victory!

Hipp regarded Rattler Four as the archetypal enemy of the future, a kind of lethal jack-in-the-box. While celebrity journalists played their profitable game of Nielsens, psychopaths like Bobby Pearl popped up every few years and did something monumentally shitty to innocent people—other people, not celebrity journals, the chosen ones.

eight

With apologies that Joaquin Hurtado and Dani Bernardi would be a couple of minutes late, the receptionist at the *My Side* studio ushered Jake Hipp into Dani Bernardi's office, the walls of which were covered with scores of framed, glass-covered photographs of a small woman with enormous brown eyes, full lips that were close to Sophia Loren's, and short black hair, posing with the famous and infamous who had appeared on *My Side*. These included Moamar Qadhafi, standing rather stiffly beside her. Qadhafi had the serene, possibly demented look of a man who never doubted himself. There was Bernardi with Saddam Hussein, sporting his little potbelly, and Bernardi with Ali Muhammad, the current Iranian strongman. If she could have posed with Adolph Eichmann, or the evil Gletkin from Arthur Koestler's *Darkness at Noon,* she presumably would have.

In one picture, she was standing arm in arm with a younger woman who looked exactly like her except that she had darker, copper-colored skin and her nose was slightly broader at the bridge. There was almost certainly African blood somewhere in her ancestry.

Bernardi's office was light and airy, with clean, lean Scandinavian teak furniture. Aside from the scores of photographs of Bernardi and the celebrity rogues, the only decoration on the walls were two paintings: a watercolor of a Mexican coastal village, and an acrylic mural of Asian peasants standing in a sugarcane field with their cane knives; both paintings featured solid and heavy figures as might have been imagined by Diego Rivera. And one calendar— Jake Hipp's offbeat take on Lagos, a seaside town on the Algarve on the southern coast of Portugal.

As Hipp was looking at his own calendar, Joaquin Hurtado and Dani Bernardi came into the office.

Hurtado, dressed in a stylish Italian suit, looked like a skinny, vain rooster trying to fluff up its feathers in an attempt to look larger than it was. He seemed constantly aware of his appearance, as though the walls were one-way mirrors through which he was being watched by the amassed millions of his adoring fans, and he arched his back in a transparent attempt to look as erect as possible; this posture was so exaggerated, even absurd, that Hurtado seemed about to topple over backward. Hipp wondered if he had calluses on the heels of his feet.

"Mr. Hipp." He shook Hipp's hand vigorously with his chin held high, as though he were looking for a fly on the wall.

As Hipp had figured, Ms. Bernardi was the woman in the photographs on the walls. She wore a form-fitting black tube dress and dangling red-ceramic earrings that set off her black hair and fair complexion. She had all the female equipment. A well-designed model, she was one of those small women who got better with age; she was likely in her early forties. Teenage voluptuaries were almost always doomed to matronly thickness. Bernardi was not matronly. She was sexy as hell.

Bernardi extended a small hand, watching him with her intelligent, almond-shaped brown eyes. "So you're the estimable Beta turned Charlie, Jake Hipp."

Hipp said, "I don't know about estimable, but yes, ma'am. Former academic. One-time Beta. Sacked Charlie. The man Bobby Pearl mentioned in your interview and the sorry schmuck in the magazine article. Coming in from the heat of Belize to do this one job for the Company."

"One job?"

"They said you wouldn't talk about your interview with Qadhafi unless I asked the questions, so here I am." He wondered how the *My Side* crew felt about Bernardi. Did they think the black tube dress could have used a red hourglass on the stomach to match her earrings?

"Well, then," she said, "won't you take a seat, and we'll see how we can help you."

Hipp smiled and sat in a comfortable, flowered easy chair and accepted a glass of sherry, which he thought a civilized, vaguely British gesture. He knew she had put the calendar on the wall for his benefit. Still, he was pleased. It was one of his best efforts, and he was proud of it. "I like your taste in calendars."

Bernardi took a seat behind her desk, and Hurtado, looking like the Pope receiving a pilgrim, sat in a chair that matched Hipp's.

Bernardi turned toward the calendar. "Ahh. Discovered it in the course of our research."

Hipp remembered the fun he'd had shooting and selecting the twelve shots for the calendar—from a woman eating snails with a wooden pick to overweight German men playing volleyball on a nude beach. "A wonderful little town," he said. "I wanted to show people simply enjoying life—totally unconcerned with the Big Picture." Hipp said that knowing that Bernardi and Hurtado likely didn't agree or they wouldn't be running a program like *My Side*. They had ambition and basked in the warming glow of achievement and fame. He gestured at the picture of Bernardi and the dark-complexioned woman. "And that's your sister, I take it."

"My sister, Frances. She lives in Nicaragua."

Hurtado said, "I hope you understand that we're breaking a rule in this case. We can't have people thinking we're CIA spies. If people knew we were even talking to you, it could ruin us." He sniffed, a form of sanctimonious punctuation. His chin remained high, as though he were still searching for that elusive fly.

Hipp said, "Say, this is good sherry. It's been a while."

Hurtado was having nothing to do with changing the subject. "We showed everything worth seeing on television," he said. "We held nothing back. Nothing. We ask questions that people can't ask for themselves."

"I'm sure you showed everything you could."

Hurtado straightened. He tilted his head indignantly. Was

his integrity being questioned? "Do you think we'd hold back on our viewers?"

Hipp wished Hurtado would lighten up. Did the man actually think Hipp was so stupid as to buy all of his horseshit? Hipp watched Ms. Bernardi light up a Virginia Slim, her eyes never leaving him as she lit the cigarette with a brass lighter in the shape of a seal. He said, "I'm sure you reported everything Qadhafi wanted you to report. I was wondering why you gave him a full two hours. You ordinarily interview three guests in one sixty-minute slot. It seemed like you promoted your Qadhafi special for weeks. Here was Moamar bouncing a baby on his knee. There was Moamar handing out food at an orphanage. Good old Moamar. Just a regular kind of guy. Why the special treatment?" He wanted to say why the sucking up to a raging megalomaniac who had shielded the snakes who blew up Pan Am 103?

Bernardi's laugh was warm and throaty. "Special treatment? No, no, no. Hot score. You have to remember, Moamar Qadhafi is one of the Arab devil incarnates who helps prime the money pump for the Pentagon. If it weren't for people like Qadhafi and Saddam Hussein, how on earth would the Defense Department justify its budget? There has to be sufficient reason to waste all that money."

Hipp smiled. "Yes, I guess so."

"The renegade president of Libya took us into his bosom, even gave us a tour of his alleged nerve-gas factory. You don't think viewers were curious about that?"

"The evil one in his lair. I see what you mean. Did it pay off?"

"All those promos are expensive, Mr. Hipp. We don't go to that much effort to lose money."

"I suppose not." Hipp thought for a moment, noting that she hadn't answered his question directly. If the Qadhafi special had been that good, wouldn't she have given him the program's Nielsen ratings? "Will you tell me how you got from Tripoli to Tarhunah?" He did his best to sound cheerful.

Hurtado looked at Bernardi. The Filipinos had an expression for Hurtado's relationship with Bernardi. He was "under the *saya*," that is, under the skirt. Back in Montana, where folks were no doubt retarded in catching up with civilizing changes in the larger culture, the expression was "PW," for pussy-whipped.

"They took us there in a helicopter," Bernardi said mildly.

Hipp regarded Bernardi in a new light. Somebody with a brain. Okay! He said, "Who arranged the interview?"

"The Libyan Embassy contacted us through the E-mail address we give at the end of the program," Bernardi said. "I followed through."

"Thank you. How long did it take to work out the details?"

Bernardi hesitated, thinking. "Several months. They were worried that we were a front for the CIA, but there were mushrooms in there, just like Qadhafi says."

"How long was the ride from Tripoli to Tarhunah?"

She shrugged. "I don't know. More than an hour."

"Day or night?"

"Night."

"Thank you again," he said, and meant it. He gave Hurtado and Bernardi copies of the same photograph. "Would you take a look at this, please?"

Hurtado and Bernardi each studied the photograph.

Bernardi said, "Taken from a satellite?"

Hipp nodded yes and studied his own copy of the photo. A wide dirt road entered the lower center of the photograph at a forty-five-degree angle from right to left and led to a broad, flat area at the base of what looked like an open-pit mine or quarry. There were nine small buildings, perhaps administrative offices and storage sheds, at the lower left center of the photograph. A large pit or quarry at the right center revealed four terraces carved into solid rock. At the bottom of this pit, two tunnels with thick, rounded concrete tops led into the rock. The road at the bottom of the picture continued past the surface buildings to a spur leading to the right, straight to a third tunnel at the bottom of a smaller pit with a single terrace. "Is this where they took you?" he asked.

Bernardi, taking a drag on her cigarette, said, "That's the place. The helicopter landed in the open space in front of the lower tunnels."

"Which tunnel were the mushrooms in?"

"The upper tunnel," she said. "We walked up the road there. That was the only tunnel we saw."

"Did Qadhafi say where he got the water? It takes lots of water to grow mushrooms."

"He said he has a deep well," Hurtado said.

"Is that rock basalt?" Hipp asked.

Hurtado glanced at the picture, then at Bernardi. "Basalt?"

"Some kind of lava maybe," Bernardi said. "It was dark. There were only a few lights out front."

"How many levels did you see?"

"One," Hurtado said.

"How far back into the mesa?"

"Maybe a hundred yards."

"I saw your report on television. But the tunnel went farther back, did it not?"

"I think so."

Hipp sighed.

Hurtado looked indignant. "Do you think we're making all this up? We saw the mushrooms."

Hipp regarded the famous face, a professional Mr. Sincere, a Latino Eagle Scout. "Mr. Hurtado, have you ever heard the expression 'popped up like mushrooms?' You get a late summer rain, and the next morning there are mushrooms all over the place. The mushrooms you saw, *agaricus bisborus,* popped up overnight all right. The Libyans bought them in Italy and moved them to Tarhunah in six refrigerated trucks the night before you showed up for your interview. We have a copy of the bill of sale if you would like to see it."

The Company tap had led straight to the Italian mushroom dealer; the resident agent in Milan later took pictures of the mushrooms being loaded on trucks leased by a Libyan front.

Bernardi shrugged. "If Joaquin comes on like Perry

Mason or Mike Wallace, nobody will talk to him. If we could lay our hands on the Green River murderer, we'd hear him out, too." She picked up the decanter of sherry and topped off their glasses.

No matter? The Green River murderer? "Promise him anonymity, too?"

"Of course promise him anonymity. How else would we get him on the show? My goodness, we're journalists, not cops!"

"Why didn't Qadhafi dig his fancy underground grow-room in Tripoli, close to docks with shipping containers? Did he explain that?"

Bernardi frowned. She wasn't about to let Hipp change the subject. "I remember the numbers. We scored a thirteen. That's with the Miss America Pageant on ABC. We're in the business of delivering viewers to advertisers, Mr. Hipp. You're in another game entirely. We should work together, complement one another. Nothing wrong with that. Once you understand the function of television, our program is perfectly logical. I bet you terrorist chasers watch it all the time."

Hurtado said, "Tell us, exactly what do you think Qadhafi has in those tunnels? If you don't mind my asking."

Hipp said, "In the late nineteen eighties, Moamar Qadhafi swapped naval mines to Iran for sarin, which he proceeded to use against Chad. The operation was so successful that Qadhafi built his own chemical-manufacturing plant at Rabta in northwest Libya, where he produced at least a hundred metric tons of nerve and mustard gas. Unfortunately, Chad was supported by the French, who led an international protest. Qadhafi simply burned the Rabta site and moved his production facilities underground at Tarhunah. He was afraid of the Israeli Air Force and our Smart bombs."

Hurtado furrowed his brow. "Say, what's all this interest in nerve and mustard gas? Do you know something we don't?" He glanced at Bernardi.

Hipp said pleasantly, "Mr. Hurtado, the sole reason for these questions is that you and Ms. Bernardi are the only persons we know who have actually been in one of those tunnels. Since you travel on an American passport, we thought you might want to help the cause."

"The cause?"

"Saving human lives."

Hurtado hesitated. Being indifferent to the loss of human life was not the image he so assiduously cultivated for his trusting viewers. This was the empathetic Joaquin. He wasn't just another pretty boy. He *cared.* He gave a damn. He said, "Those tunnels are dug into solid rock. It'd probably take a nuke to destroy the place, if that's what you're thinking."

Hipp smiled. "No, no, we don't have mayhem or other villainy on our mind. We just like to keep an eye on our raghead friends. They sometimes appear to have spent too much time humping camels under the hot sun. Begging your pardon, ma'am."

"Nice talk," Hurtado said.

"I'm a spook, not a diplomat. Tell me, have you ever heard of sarin, and do you know what it does to its victims?"

Hurtado shook his head. Bernardi didn't know either.

"Sarin acts on the central nervous system," Hipp said. "You get dizzy and your eyesight starts going at the same time. Your mouth waters a heartbeat before blood shoots out of your nose. You get disoriented. You're twisted by muscle spasms. You twitch and jerk, out of control. You're dead in about five minutes. It's not pretty at all, I assure you."

Bernardi perked up. "Is somebody out there threatening to use sarin? Who? Tell us."

Hipp raised an eyebrow. "Do you propose to interview him on *My Side*?"

"Maybe we could help," she said.

On the surface, the velvet-voiced Bernardi seemed civilized and intelligent. She wore no wedding band, so Hipp assumed she wasn't married. Did she have a boyfriend? Hipp thought she was a very sexy woman, but complicated in the extreme. He wondered what lay beneath that gilt of warmth and charm. He said, "I sincerely thank you both for answering my questions. I mean that. I assure you, it is not my intention to challenge your professional integrity." He thought about saying that he understood their position, that he knew they had a job to do, et cetera, but he thought that would be going too far. Better to quietly retreat and retain his dignity.

Bernardi tilted her head, studying him with her large eyes. "Tell us, Mr. Hipp, what did you think of the *Esquire* article?"

Watching her, Hipp ran his fingers down his jaw. "Interesting stuff about Mongoose, I suppose, but a lot of it was inaccurate."

Bernardi studied him. "Could you do it if you had another chance?"

"Could I do what? Shoot Bobby Pearl?"

"Yes. If you had another chance."

Hipp smiled. "I don't suppose you'd talk to me about your chat with him. The electronic mask and altered voice kind of ruined it for me. If it hadn't been for the business about the pumpkin soup, I wouldn't have known it was him."

Bernardi raised an eyebrow. "Are you really retired, or is that just Mongoose hoo-hoo?"

What a voice she had! She made Suzanne Pleshette sound like Minnie Mouse. "I hung it up," Hipp said.

She smiled. "Compared to you, Gary Cooper was downright talky. We've been hearing rumors from The Watch and Mongoose about a new warning from Bobby Pearl. What do you know about that?"

Hipp shrugged. "If there is one, they're not telling me about it."

Bernardi waited, but it was obvious that Hipp wasn't going to volunteer anything. "Are you going to tell us about the pumpkin soup incident? Joaquin and I are both dying to know about the soup. We want you to give us an interview, tell us your side of the story."

Hipp smiled. "I'm not sure what I have to tell. I'm not sure I understand fully what happened myself. In any case, it's between me and my conscience."

She said, "There are two sides to every story. Always. I'd think this would be a real opportunity for you."

Hipp laughed. "The failed Charlie, sandwiched between a serial rapist and a banana-republic thug. I'll pass, thanks."

Bernardi opened a fresh package of Virginia Slims. "How about supper with me, then? A consolation."

Hipp paused, thinking of the uncomplicated Gina. But he had a job to do. He said, "Sure. Why not?"

Bernardi smiled. "You pick the spot. Anyplace you want. It's on me."

Carl Czez, driving a year-old Buick sedan registered in California under the name of Harry Murray, checked into the Pony Express Motel in Victorville, California; Victorville, eighty miles east of Los Angeles, was on the edge of the Mojave Desert along Interstate 15, leading to Las Vegas and points east.

The Pony Express was an American classic—a U-shaped motel dating from the late 1950s. This was cheap living, but not for somebody who required that paper tape be wrapped over the toilet lid each morning to show that it had been cleaned. Czez was a private, even secretive, person; he didn't like strangers pawing through his place, whether they bore brushes and toilet-bowl disinfectant or search warrants.

Hindus ran the Pony Express. They had been polite to Czez when he'd checked in and hadn't bothered him with questions or demands. Their frugality enabled the Pony Express to remain cheap. Skinny little Hindu kids with large brown eyes watched his comings and goings with curiosity, but they kept their distance; Czez assumed they too would one day settle along a bypassed highway and run an old motel with kitchenettes and coin-operated porn.

Czez considered Hindus to be a clannish lot. Most of the women ran around with a stupid red dot on their forehead and looked overweight, although it was hard to tell what they were like under those loose-fitting saris. Czez had heard that Sikhs, as a religious practice, kept small knives in their turbans. He wondered if that was true. He had seen them standing guard outside banks in Hong Kong; he'd concluded they were trustworthy or the Chinese bankers wouldn't have hired them.

Czez didn't approve of most dark-skinned people, whose increasing numbers, he felt, were screwing up the country. The worst were the shiftless coons, so fucking dumb as to free a double murderer, O. J. Simpson, just to score a political point. That was the final straw as far as Czez was concerned. Whenever the big lips started their whining and bitching, all Czez could think about was O.J.

Although he liked their food, he thought the Mexicans who had overrun the Southwest were Popers, good for picking apples and artichokes and not a whole lot else.

Czez walked across the street to the Chijuajua Cafe for lunch, where a jolly, middle-aged couple, Epifania and Jose, hustled to serve a counterful of customers. He studied the plastic-covered menu and when he was ready, Epifania arrived, pad in hand, to take his order.

Czez ordered chicken mole and a Dos Equis beer and glanced at the service window between the counter and the kitchen where the cook was at work, a young Latino woman in her early thirties. The cook wore an apron over a simple cotton dress, but it couldn't hide the soft, fluid curves of her figure. As she put a plate of food on the shelf at the bottom of the window, her eyes caught Czez's. She looked quickly down at the food she was cooking.

Epifania, who had seen the moment, said, "That's Rosalina. She's my niece. Beautiful, isn't she? Hard for her to hide her figure."

Czez looked momentarily flushed. He couldn't help himself.

Epifania said, "She's a widow. Her husband was killed two years ago when a truckload of cantaloupes he was driving ran off an embankment into a dry streambed. *Dios mio!*"

Czez hesitated. "You're right. She is beautiful."

"She has a little boy, Pepe," Epifania said, watching him. "He's four years old."

Czez forced himself to look away from Rosalina.

He turned and pretended to be interested in the darkening clouds outside. "Looks like more rain tonight." But he wasn't thinking of rain. His imagination had been seared by the sight of Rosalina moving under her cotton dress.

He ate his lunch, aware that Rosalina was watching him from the kitchen. He couldn't stop himself from checking her out again. He called softly, *"Su comida es muy deliciosa, Señora."* She smiled broadly, pleased at the compliment.

There was another woman in the kitchen with Rosalina. This woman, a little older than Rosalina but looking very much like her, held a little boy in her arms. She too grinned broadly at Czez.

Epifania, watching his face, said, "That's Rosalina's sister, Teresita. She takes care of Pepe while Rosalina works."

Teresita murmured in Pepe's ear, and little Pepe, looking embarrassed, waved timidly at Czez. Czez waved back. *"Hola, Pepe! Como esta?"*

Rosalina stepped to the service window. *"Mi nombre is Rosalina."*

Czez, barely able to take his eyes off her breasts pressed against the edge of the service window, inadvertently licked his lips. "Harry Murray. *Habla Ingles usted?"*

"Pleased to meet you, Harry," she said. "I speak *un pocito Ingles,* but I still think *en Español.* I want Pepe to think in English so he will have a future."

"Well, you speak good English, Rosalina, almost without an accent. *Usted esta bella."*

Rosalina flushed. *"Gracias.* Your Spanish is good, too."

"Es usted Mexicana?"

"Si. I have *cinco meses* until I can become a U.S. citizen. I am studying for the test. I am from Merida. Do you know where that is?"

Czez said, *"Es en la Yucatan por la Golfo de Mexico.* I've been there." *Her* breasts. *Her.* The softness of the pronoun quickened his breath.

Back in the Pony Express, Czez lay propped on the bed.

He lit a large black Cuban Punch and smoked it slowly, savoring the smoke. He sat for a moment thinking of Rosalina. He punched up CNN and took calming puffs on the cigar as he watched the news.

nine

Dani Bernardi leaned back in her chair as a slender Asian waiter in a white apron delivered their food, a bean-sprout salad for her and a huge bowl of noodle soup for Jake Hipp. "Plastic flowers. I like the decor. No pretense here."

Hipp grinned. "Just honest food. There are entire streets in Ho Chi Minh City that sell nothing but noodle soup. To them, it's what the hamburger is to us. No pumpkin soup, thank you, but I'll take the noodles any day." Hipp emptied the contents of his bottle of Stella Artois into a mug and lifted it in a toast, tapping it against Bernardi's glass of white wine. "Well, here's to it."

"Indeed, here's to it," Bernardi said, looking around with her large brown eyes. "I said I'd spring for anyplace, Jake. But I never expected this!"

"My kind of place," Hipp said. "Those fancy foo-foo places in Beverly Hills make the palms of my hands sweat. Born on a farm, always a farm boy, I suppose." He sprinkled slices of hot pepper on top of his noodles. "The noodles are made from rice, but sometimes they make them from mung beans. The Vietnamese have added a lot to this country. The French were in Indochina there long enough to teach them to appreciate good food. You think French colonial officers were going to put up with lousy food? You get the Malay mixed in there with the Chinese, and with just a soupçon of French, why, hey!"

"And Stella Artois is made where?"

"Belgium."

"You don't think I'm too Rodeo Drive, do you?" Bernardi looked down at herself. For the occasion, she had chosen black slacks, white blouse, and a stylish camel blazer.

Hipp smiled. "I bet there's not a male in here who wouldn't like to back you into a broom closet. Who knows, maybe a couple of females, too. I take it Elia Khardonne chose Los Angeles for New Era because of the entertainment industry."

"Better than Atlanta. Down there, it's all the fried chicken and grits you can eat, and then it's time for a nap. Ted Turner and Jane Fonda can have all the football and rednecks they want, and New York is barbarous, face it. A Third World country with Wall Street. Southern California is the future. Hunks, beauties, and money beyond imagination."

"If that's your idea of a good time."

"Elia understands the attraction. Good thinking, too. Our numbers are right up there with CNN, and Fox never had any zip, face it. In another year or two, with the right breaks, we'll cruise right past both of them. They're just too stodgy."

Hipp said, "I'm curious. Tell me something. You're good-looking. You're obviously smart as hell. You've got a good, rich voice. You've got presence. Why aren't you behind the camera instead of Mr. Twit? Respectfully, ma'am. Begging your pardon."

Bernardi hesitated. "I . . ." The question had somehow jolted her.

Hipp said, "I bet you'd be really good. I'd think that would be apparent to everybody."

She sighed. "I guess I took the wrong career path. I spent almost five years of my life pushing that program to the top over every conceivable objection. I suppose Elia's people came to think of me as an executive, not a performer."

"I see," Hipp said, although it was obvious that he didn't. "Hard to believe you spent all that effort to make a star out of Joaquin Hurtado. Runs against human nature, I'd think."

She frowned. "I wanted to be the host, that's so. The money people thought they had to have a proven star behind the camera. A bankable personality and all that. Cut the risk."

He said, "Being on stage or in front of the camera is a logical female ambition."

"Oh? How is that?"

"It's display cubed. Instead of being admired and judged by a handful of males, you get several million scoping you out. I don't mean that as any kind of put-down. It's not wrong or unbecoming in any way. It's just the way the world works. Good for those who can pull it off."

Bernardi smiled, thinking about that. "Yes, I see what you mean. Maybe so. The magazine article said you were divorced, like me."

Hipp said, "If you haven't been divorced at least once, you're still a virgin."

"Do you have a family?"

"I've got an older brother Carl in Missoula. My dad's dead. My mother is in a nursing home in Missoula. She's got Alzheimer's. Can't recognize either Carl or me. And you?"

"My parents died in a car accident two years ago. You saw a picture of my sister, Frances, in my office. She's six years younger than me. Our maternal grandmother was of African ancestry—she was a dancer—and Frances got her skin."

"Gives her an exotic look. Sexy. You said she lives in Nicaragua?"

"She was a botanist originally, Dr. Frances Bernardi, but she wound up running a company that makes designer furniture out of tropical hardwood. Frances and I have never gotten along, which I suppose is putting it mildly. We have a case of . . . intense sibling rivalry." Her face tightened momentarily. "The picture in my office was taken during one of our occasional truces."

Hipp thought it was better to change the subject. "In Portland, you can buy a bowl of Vietnamese noodles for three-fifty. A complete meal. Delicious broth. The noodles are good for you. A little beef for protein. What more can you ask for?"

"What more?" Bernardi laughed, obviously relieved to get off the subject of her sister. She had a rich, husky laugh.

"And they know how to make coffee. A legacy from the French."

Bernardi took a sample of her bean sprouts. "Not bad."

"It's the peanut dressing. They grow a lot of peanuts on the Indochina peninsula."

"Most people would jump at the chance to be interviewed on *My Side*. You know that? What do you do up there in the place where you live? Where is it?"

"Officially, in Long Beach, Washington. It really does have a long beach, twenty-eight miles long."

"Up by Canada, or closer to Oregon?"

"It's on a narrow peninsula just above the mouth of the Columbia River. But I only spend the summers there, if that. I fish and dig clams and hang out in a local tavern with some friends. It rains a lot, but I don't mind. No, I amend that. It rains a whole bunch. But when it rains too much, I go to Cebu City in the Philippines, where I own an expat bar, Most Hipp."

She smiled. "With paperbacks lining the walls, even in the toilets. I know. We went there on our trip."

Hipp inadvertently licked his lips. "Recommended by Bobby Pearl?"

She shook her head. "A friend recommended it. What a place! British Penguins. And foreign-language editions, too."

"German, Swedish, and Dutch. In addition to the Aussies, Canucks, and Brits, that's who most of our customers are. And the Americans, of course. Travelers and expats. Very few tourists."

"No French or Spanish?"

"They don't get out to that part of the world for some reason. Are you going to come popping in on me in Long Beach someday with your video cameras humming, or do you propose to catch me in Cebu?"

"I was just wondering. I was also wondering why you agreed to have this meal. To learn more about our trip to Libya? I don't think so."

Hipp raised his hand to signal for another beer. "What kind of question is that? Look in the mirror. I'm male, after all. But you're right. I'm also interested in your interview with Bobby Pearl."

"Ahh, your nemesis."

"A raging asshole, begging your pardon."

Bernardi smiled. "People don't watch our program to hear Joaquin interview choirboys. Pearl contacted us through our e-mail address. We met him at a place on the beach just outside of Bacolod on the island of Negros."

"One island over from Cebu and my bar. A coincidence, do you think? Why would he choose the Philippines, of all places? Did he say why?"

"If you saw the tape, you saw just about everything that happened."

"And maybe something that didn't happen. Did he smoke a cigar?"

Bernardi thought for moment. "Why, yes he did, as a matter of fact, but not during the interview. You just gotta let us do you, Jake. Mongoose fired you. Defend yourself. Tell your side of the story. Like I said before, there are always two sides to everything."

If he let them, Hurtado and Bernardi would turn him into a walking joke. "I had a chance to spike Bobby Pearl, and I didn't get the job done. Mongoose doesn't have a whole lot in the way of patience for someone who lets a serial terrorist walk away whistling Stephen Foster songs. I bet your viewers will be able to endure the disappointment of not knowing every little detail of my embarrassment. To know absolutely everything is not necessarily a social good, is it? I thought that's why we all wear clothes."

She smiled. "And here I thought it was to keep warm. The CIA has received another warning from Bobby Pearl, hasn't it?"

Hipp looked about mildly. He had been trained always, but always, to refer to the Central Intelligence Agency by euphemism. It jarred him to hear the name used in a public place. He cleared his throat and looked confused. "The which?"

Bernardi knew why he was momentarily discombobulated. "Okay, okay, I won't mention your employer again.

But it's Bobby Pearl, isn't it? That's why you've returned to Mongoose. They've taken you on again, haven't they?"

Hipp sat back in his chair. "Yes. But the question is not so much of who I'm after, but what."

"What, then?"

Hipp blinked. He leaned forward, his body tense, his face tight. "I want Bobby Pearl's nuts."

Bernardi sat up, looking startled.

"I want to pickle 'em and put 'em in a jar like those eggs they sell in taverns."

Bernardi arched an eyebrow. "Maybe Joaquin and I can help you flush him out. Have you ever thought of that? We could work together."

Hipp perked up. "Bobby Pearl? You'll help me nail Pearl? How? How can you do that?"

Bernardi shrugged.

"You could offer him another interview. He loves to show off."

Bernardi shook her head. "He'd never do it again, but there may be other ways we can help. Tell me, Jake Hipp, would you like to spend the night at my place? I have some wonderful sticky green. Hydroponic stuff. Plus silk sheets. Have you ever slept on silk sheets?"

Hipp accepted another Stella Artois from the Vietnamese waitress. "Nope."

Dani Bernardi cocked her head, watching Hipp with her brown eyes. "Well?" The question was put to him in the manner of Lauren Bacall at her sultry-voiced best.

Carl Czez, looking around at the shelves of ceramic cows, accepted a cup of coffee from Epifania, who had little Pepe clinging to her leg. There were easily more than a hundred cows, cute little holsteins, cow salt-and-pepper shakers, and cow creamers. The Artis house was small, but cozy; except for the cows, it was furnished entirely with furniture *hecho en Mexico* and paintings of Mexican peasant scenes. On the outsized Sony television, a young blond man, looking more

Southern California than Mexico, held a dark-eyed beauty in his arms. He said, *"Te amo, Lucia."*

Lucia struggled to free herself from his grasp. *"No entiendo. Por favor. Por favor."* She burst into tears.

Epifania grinned. "Soap opera from Mexico. We get fifty-one channels by satellite, and it's just about the only one that isn't talking about Bobby Pearl. That's an awful business, but I get tired of listening to them talk about it. The same stuff over and over and over again. If they had anything new to report, it'd be different. All the relatives of the victims saying how awful it is. Of course it's awful."

Czez shook his head, looking grim.

Epifania picked up the remote and punched the mute. "Rosalina said she'll be ready in just a minute. You know women."

Czez smiled an I-know-women smile. "No problem. Rosalina is worth the wait."

Epifania said, "She's a real nice girl. *Muy simpatica y bella tambien.* Jose went down to the Kmart to buy some tomato settings. He'll be back in a few minutes."

"I saw your garden on the way in."

"It's a beauty. We get a lot of sun here and a year-round growing season. If you can get water on that sand, you can grow some beautiful vegetables."

Czez looked around at the shelves of ceramic figurines. "I see you like cows."

"We had a cow when I was a girl in Mexico. I helped my father feed her and take care of her. After I married Jose, I began collecting ceramic cows. Pretty soon I was getting cows for every birthday. You see the result." Epifania sighed. "But I've been in the United States forty-five years now. You are in what line of work, Mr. Murray, if you don't mind my asking?"

Czez smiled. "No, no, I don't mind. I've spent the last fifteen years working as a roustabout on Indonesian oil rigs. Nothing to do but save my money. I eventually got tired of it. I want to settle down somewhere, maybe buy a business of some kind. Maybe a cafe like yours."

Epifania brightened. "A cafe? Really?"

"Years ago, I had a buddy in the Marines who was from Victorville. He brought me home one Thanksgiving, and I thought what a good place to settle down one day. I've always liked the desert. Got the Mojave on one side and Los Angeles on the other for a taste of city life now and then. A straight shot to Las Vegas if you want to have fun in the casinos."

Epifania looked surprised. "You want to buy a cafe here in Victorville?"

Czez shrugged. "It's always possible. I like the sun, and I don't mind a little heat if it isn't humid. Of course I'd have to get somebody to show me the ropes."

Epifania liked the sound of that. "I don't think you'd have to worry about that. Here, let me get you some more coffee." With Pepe trailing behind her, she headed for the kitchen. From the kitchen, she said, "Where is your friend now?"

"He stayed in the Marines and was killed when an Iraqi Scud missile struck the barracks in Riyadh. He was a gunnery sergeant. A lifer. A short-timer when he got killed. Had just six months to go."

Epifania arrived with the coffeepot and poured him some more coffee. "If you're thinking of starting a cafe, I expect you'll be wanting to settle down and start a family, too."

"A family? Well, that's not out of the question. You never know. Have to find the right woman first."

Epifania suppressed a smile. "I don't expect you'll have much trouble with that if you put your mind to it."

Rosalina stepped in from the bedroom dressed in a yellow Mexican fiesta dress, cut low over her breasts and showing bare shoulders. She had a yellow ribbon in her black hair and was wearing a turquoise bracelet with matching turquoise earrings. With a hint of blush to her cheeks, lipstick, and a judicious touch of mascara, the shy cook at the Chijuajua Cafe had been transformed into a striking beauty. Stand aside, Rita Moreno. "Sorry, I made you wait, Harry," she said, looking shy. Sexy shy.

Czez laughed and put his cup on the coffee table. "It was

worth it, believe me. You're beautiful, Rosalina." He couldn't wait to yank that dress the rest of the way off her shoulders.

Rosalina blushed, and she took his arm.

Epifania beamed. She approved of Harry Murray. Rosalina and the man who wanted to start his own cafe, and maybe start a family. Such a couple they were. Good endings were scarce as hens' teeth, but not impossible.

As Czez and Rosalina stepped out of the door, the grinning Epifania said, "Have a good time and don't be too late." She punched on the sound to her soap opera. The young blond man and Lucia had made up; they were kissing passionately as the strains of violins soared in the background.

ten

She was a twister. She was a leaper. She was a squealer and a screamer. She was a get down and dirty fuck-me, fuck-me, fuck-me kind of big-eyed, pale-skinned, television-producer lover. She had exquisite, smallish breasts with brown nipples that poked out larger than the end of a man's thumb. And her rump?

Would you do a guy a favor and show me that ass again?

She had a scar in the shape of a fishhook on her tailbone. Even had a barb on the end.

A little wider. That's a girl.

Liked to get down there and forage with her mouth.

Hey, watch those teeth!

Knew enough stunts to please a presidential assistant.

Easy on the balls, lady!

She was an unembarrassed lover, undeterred by moronic social prohibitions. She loved the passion. Surely no inhibited twenty-two-year-old could compete with a grown-up woman expressing herself sexually.

Jake Hipp, high from sticky green, went for the kink, as he believed most males, except for the timid and the dishonest, were wont to do.

When they had popped their cookies, they lay back, sweaty and feeling good. Hipp turned on his side, admiring her amazing nipples. "You've got a scar in the shape of a fishhook on your tailbone. Did you know that?"

She grinned. "My sister knocked me off my feet at the beach and I landed on a broken Pepsi bottle. Talk about blood and hysteria. My sister bawling and saying it was an accident and she didn't mean it. My father was pissed. My mother rushed me off to the car."

"Ahh, the scars of sibling rivalry. Glad I didn't have to go through that. Tell me, Ms. Bernardi, you people gave Bobby Pearl an electronic mask and altered his voice. How are we to know it was really him? Maybe it was an impostor playing a hoax, or a shill designed to jack up your ratings, begging your pardon."

"You think it was a scam?" Bernardi shook her head. "What about the pumpkin soup? How would he know about that?"

Hipp said nothing.

"He was the real deal." Seeing that Hipp's eyes were on her chest, she casually trailed a hand across one breast. "Like these, do you?" Delivered with her rich, deep voice, it was an evocative question, grandly delivered. Ava Gardner, Hipp thought. She had Ava Gardner's big, dark eyes and similar high, broad cheekbones. She had Ava's presence. She even had a dimple on her chin like Ava's.

"They're wonderful."

Bernardi reloaded the bowl of her glass bong. She took a hit, holding the smoke in her mouth.

She said, "Give me an interesting question for sociobiologists. Make it about sex."

Hipp thought for a moment. He said, "When did women lose estrus, and why?"

She cocked her head and exhaled. "Estrus?"

"All other female mammals, including primates, have estrus, or what we indelicately say of a bitch, she's 'in heat.' Human females don't have estrus. Over the years, evolution has given them a formidable advantage over males. They can choose to have sex or not to have sex, which option has turned sex into a form of commodity."

She laughed. "Hey, that's good. How do you Darwinists explain it?"

Hipp scratched his jaw. "The 'liver theory' is a commonly used phrase. For most of our past, we were hunter-gatherers. Men hunted and scavenged for meat, while women gathered seeds and roots and took care of the kids. Each hunter got a share to take back to his family. Somewhere along the line, we believe, smarter females began finding ways to delay returning hunters."

"For an extra ration of liver?"

Hipp grinned. "Sure. They got more protein and so more of them survived than females who had to have estrus to be in the mood. As the years passed, all human females eventually lost estrus. Sex is a form of power. If a man is getting it on the side, his wife is in a weaker position, so in most cultures, she takes care of the household budget. No surprise there."

"Gotta weigh the liver."

"You have to understand that the value of the commodity depends on the desirability of the female. The impressive breasts and rumps on you females didn't happen by accident."

"No? How then?"

"As the tens of thousands of years rolled by, males impregnated more curvy females than straight ones, so more big-boob and impressive-butt genes got passed on. We males designed you. Took a couple million years, but in the end, we came up with one hell of a model." Hipp gave his companion a lopsided grin.

He rolled his eyes. He was stoned. Sex and power. Yin and yang. His mind drifted. Then a flash of memory, a connection, welled up from the synapses. He said, "I remember a drill sergeant at basic training at Fort Ord eyeing a formation of us recruits one morning and telling us what it meant to be soldiers. 'This is your piece,' he told us, tapping his M-16, 'and this is your gun.' He unzipped his fly and looked down at himself. He said, 'I want every swinging horn to remember that. Your piece and your gun are different. They are not to be confused. I say again, this is your piece. It destructs.' He held up his rifle. 'And this is your gun. It constructs.' He grinned at us and tapped his unzipped fly." Eyeing Bernardi, Hipp said, "Did Bobby Pearl make a pass at you in the Philippines?"

She looked surprised. "Why, no. Should he have?"

Hipp said, "Sure. You're a good-looking woman. You

came halfway around the world to see him. He fancies himself a big man: Bobby Pearl, immortal serial terrorist. I'd have thought he'd come on to you. Why didn't he?"

Bernardi shrugged. "I have no idea. There's no accounting for taste, I suppose." She smiled. She exhaled. "You like these sheets? I promised you silk sheets." She ran the back of her hand across the sheets.

"Slippery," he said. "I like queen-sized beds. Give a person room to maneuver."

She laughed. "Have you ever thought of doing a calendar of nudes?" She reloaded the bong and gave it to him.

Hipp put his mouth to the bong and lit up. With his lungs full of smoke, he said, "I wouldn't rule it out, but it'd have to be more than boobs and buns. I like to frame a calendar around an offbeat theme or motif. 'Naked Female Television Producers Eating Ice Cream Cones.' That might do it. Ms. January, Ms. February, and so on. You have a picture of you and Bobby Pearl on your office wall?"

Bernardi shook her head. "He wouldn't let me take his picture."

"I bet he wouldn't. I'm surprised that he let you take the videotape. By the way, who was there besides you and Hurtado? I take it you took a production crew."

Bernardi shook her head again. "Just Joaquin and me. I taped the interview. Pearl said that if we showed the tape without the screen, he'd kill us both. We believed him."

"Good thinking."

"You've told me something about how males select females. What about the other way around?" She regarded him with amusement, wondering what kind of answer he had for that one.

Hipp ran his hand up Bernardi's thigh and over her hip. "Females of all species are genetically programmed to pass on the best possible genes to their offspring—mammals usually go for the biggest, baddest available male. Among humans, wealth seems to be an aphrodisiac, although there are women who are drawn to muscles or musicians or whatever. Hunks, brains, or money. You get the idea. Jesus, lady, you are a fine specimen of the species, I have to say."

Bernardi, enjoying his touch, closed her eyes. "We're, what's the term, a tournament species?" She turned so he could enjoy looking her over.

Hipp ran his fingers lightly down her groin. "Females compete, too."

"They do?" She turned again and opened her thighs so Hipp could enjoy that view.

Hipp said, "They display sex, right down to flashing their stuff in ritual tournaments like the Miss America Pageant."

"This is fun."

"Theory and practice." He placed his palm gently on her vulva. "A successful male like Mickey Mantle could have it with thousands of women."

"Or like Einstein."

"Or like Einstein, yes." He bent over and kissed her gently on the thigh, running his tongue up her leg. He paused, looking up at her between her breasts. "There you've got it. We males compete on baseball fields and in boardrooms. It's all in our genes, and it's nearly all about sex. You can watch tournament species do their thing in animal documentaries almost any night on the Discovery Channel. If you want pair bonders, check out the ducks and geese. Partners for life."

"Always the Beta at heart, eh, Jake?"

Hipp laughed. "I still know my Charles Darwin. But that was the old Jake Hipp. Tangier changed that. I still know that stuff, even though now I'm all predator."

"I like the practice better than the theory."

"Me too," Hipp said. He reached for Bernardi's breast and leisurely twisted one brown nipple.

Bernardi sucked in her breath and smiled. "Ready for another round?"

His old pal was standing right up there, rigid and ready for action. But Hipp was stoned. His attention drifted again. The rumor placing Bobby Pearl in Spain had come from the

Centrum, Amsterdam's red-light district. He said, "You ever been in Amsterdam's red-light district?"

Her eyes were lazy from being high. She shook her head. "Tell me."

"In the Centrum, the women sit in sexy costumes in diminutive bedrooms at street level. Each little bedroom has a tiny stage by a large window facing the sidewalk. Here milady sits demurely in her chair, the better to display her costume, or lack of it, in addition to her several womanly charms. Does the gentleman prefer boobs or buns? Does the idea of leather turn his mouth dry? Perhaps his taste runs to string bikinis or pierced this or that? It's like strolling through a sexual supermarket. String beans or potatoes? There's a woman for every taste."

Bernardi laughed. "You men must love it."

"When a customer comes calling, the lady simply pulls the curtains over the window that separates her bedroom from the street. Some even have truck mirrors mounted outside so they can relax between gentlemen strollers. Why sit there posing when she doesn't have to? She can watch television or something. A voyeur's paradise. I've strolled those narrow streets and back alleys many times, enjoying the sights. This is display in its pure form, by the way. Far more civilized than Bangkok, where the girls are in a room behind a window with numbers hanging around their necks like some kind of human buffet."

Hipp wondered: was Bobby Pearl an habitué of the Centrum? What did he like to do in addition to beating up the girls? Pearl had stalked the German girl for three days, following her everywhere.

The mongoose and the snake. The mongoose and the snake. In the pit of survival. In the dark, dark pit.

Hipp suddenly had an idea. "You know, Dani, I just thought of something. I might be talked into an interview after all."

Bernardi perked up. "Oh, how is that?"

"I'll let you interview me if you agree to send a private message from me to Bobby Pearl at the end of your program. A simple line, followed by my e-mail address. *'Bobby Pearl, Jake Hipp would like to communicate with you. Establish your bona fides if you wish to reply.' "*

"Establish his bona fides?"

"Things we both know as a result of our encounter."

"But not known by copycats watching *My Side*."

"There you've got it. He'll understand," Hipp said. "Bobby Pearl has two ways of hiding out in cyberspace. He can use one of those anonymous codes that people use to advertise unusual sex, or he can hack his way into somebody's account and use that. We think the latter, which means it's just about impossible to run him down. I propose to goad him into communicating directly with me. *My Side* is shown around the world. I bet he's a fan. He was a *My Side* star, after all."

"How long do you want me to run your message?"

"Give me a month, after which I'll let you interview me one way or another. A deal's a deal."

Bernardi arched an eyebrow. "Done. We'll run your message on Friday night, our next show. What are you going to say to him?"

Hipp shrugged. "I'll think of something. I say that's enough talking about Bobby Pearl for one night. Ms. Bernardi, I have to tell you in all honesty, you're an absolutely fabulous model of the human female species. An extraordinary commodity. Put you in one of those little rooms in the Centrum and you could command top guilder." He could say that without lying. She *was* hot, right down to the fishhook scar on her tailbone, which was oddly sexy in its way.

"Really! Thank you."

"You look like Ava Gardner in her prime, and that's a fact."

"You think so?" She was pleased. Her voice was a rich, welcoming contralto.

The stark, white moon was large and full, a lonely cyclops eye. Carl Czez, doing his best to keep under the speed limit, clenched his jaw as the desert zipped by on either side. What Czez needed now was a good stiff drink somewhere quiet, no women present. Someplace where he could shoot pool with guys who drank Budweisers from the bottle and talked about the Angels and Dodgers and told racial jokes. Good wholesome fun.

Why? Goddam it, why?

Czez still couldn't figure why Rosalina had been a shouldn't. She'd had a real body on her; that was a fact. It had been breathtaking. My God, those tits! Shit, oh dear! If Rosalina wasn't a should, who the hell would be? Were the shoulds gone forever? Maybe it was because she had a kid. That was the only thing Czez could think of. Another psychological no-no to add to the growing list. No pushy loudmouths. No feminists. Tight butts only, thank you. Good set of jugs. Now, no kids. What in hell had gone wrong? Would it never end?

He punched on the radio. Texas Ed was singing his current country-and-western hit, "Blubber on My Rubber," that Czez ordinarily found amusing.

> *I've felt the ruts*
> *Down six long roads*
> *Left six women*
> *Like six squashed toads.*
> *Kip, ka-dop, kip, ka-dop*
> *Hop, hop, hop*
> *Kip, ka-dop, kip, ka-dop*
> *Listen to 'em pop*
> *Blubber on my rubbbbbber!*
> *Blubber on my rubbbbbber!*

Carl Czez slammed his hand against the radio, silencing Texas Ed to lament the blubber on his rubber. Ordinarily he would have been amused by Ed's lament, but tonight just wasn't a good time to listen to country-and-western music. Oh, woe is me. Woe is me. Czez wasn't in the mood for it. He wanted to have a good time and forget.

Czez checked his rearview mirror. Clear. He knew he'd have to lay low for a couple of days until that business in Victorville settled down. He knew it wasn't safe to stay on the highway. He saw some lights up ahead. A truck stop?

As he drew closer, he saw it was that and more, a desert wayside. A red neon sign blinked "The Lariat Room." Another sign advertised "The Mojave Motel—Satellite Television, Swimming Pool, Jacuzzi. Traveler's Oasis."

He slowed his car. This looked just right. He'd have a few beers in the Lariat and get a room in the Mojave. He would get himself an early morning treat of steak and eggs in the truck stop. There would be a zillion channels on the satellite link. Maybe he could find a ball game to watch before he went to sleep. Maybe that would help him forget what he'd done to Rosalina. It's not like he'd had any choice in the matter.

If they hadn't managed to screw things up, Elephant Dan and Slick Smith should be closing in on Charleston. He smiled at the thought of anybody being so shockingly dumb and uncivilized as that pair. What a world!

eleven

In the distance, above the tops of field corn, Elephant Dan Merrill and Slick Smith could see the upper girders of a bridge painted a pale green. Smith opened his road atlas and checked the map of Ohio. "Let's see. Meigs County. Here we are. That'll be the Ohio River coming up. West Virginia on the far side."

Merrill emitted a short, plaintive squeal. "I'm hungry. What do you say we find ourselves a tavern and have ourselves a couple of big cheeseburgers with lots of onions?"

Smith emptied the last of his flask. "Cheeseburgers. Yes, dammit. And some more whiskey, too. Man's gotta have a little whiskey." They started across the bridge. Below them, a coal barge pushed upriver. Smith said, "Ravenswood. Isn't that a neat name for a town? A wood filled with ravens. A copse filled with black birds. Copse. That's a good word too, just one letter away from corpse. The raven was the first animal off the ark, did you know that?"

"It was?"

"Oh, yes. Lots of folks are under the impression that the dove went first, but that's not so."

Merrill cocked his head. "You going to tell me what happened?"

Smith laughed. "Sure. After forty days on the ark, Noah released the raven to see whether the great flood had yet subsided, but it hadn't. A week later, he released the dove, but the water still had not receded, and the dove returned. After another week, he set the dove free again, and the dove returned with an olive leaf. In another seven days, he sent forth the dove a third time, and the dove never came back. It took a full six months before the world was dry enough to release the rest of the animals."

"What happened to the raven during all that time?"

"It was out there flying back and forth, presumably with no place to rest. It's sometimes translated as flying 'to and fro.' Same diff. Just like us, Elephant."

"Nothing to do but fly around and get in trouble."

"Exactly right! You'll find the raven story in Chapter Eight of Genesis. I remember listening to my daddy preach. When you're so damned dumb as to believe that kind of high-sounding nonsense, then thinking requires physical effort. Have to move your lips when you read. The poorer and more fucked-up people are, the more credulous they become. 'What does it mean?' they ask themselves." Smith dropped his mouth open in the presumed manner of a gullible fool. "My old man worked 'em to the max. He was good at parting stupes from their money, I'll give him that. The best raven line is in the thirty-eighth chapter of Job, if I remember it right:

> *"Who provideth for the raven his food?*
> *when his young ones cry unto God,*
> *they wander for lack of meat."*

Merrill drove around the looping curve of the West Virginia off-ramp of the bridge. He slowed for the stop sign on the road flanking the Ohio River; a right turn north led to the small town of Ravenswood.

Smith said, "The women like to ponder that one. 'Young ones' crying for lack of food! Whatever will happen to my young ones? Oh, my goodness! Whenever there was Christmas or a birthday coming up, my old man scoured the verses relating to birth, newborns, and children."

Merrill looked at him. "Say again?"

"Women are forever worrying about their offspring. Born into 'em. That's how a preacher bulks the collection plate. My daddy knew all the tricks. They should cut out huge ravens from plywood and put them on the tops of the buildings along Main Street. Biblical stuff. Brooding emblems of evil, watching."

They passed a narrow park on the banks of the Ohio River on their left and a sewage-treatment plant on their right with Canada geese strolling about. They crossed a small bridge over a creek thirty feet below. Up ahead was the town's single traffic light. This was a nineteenth-century town onto which had been grafted the accoutrements of the twentieth century, including a Gino's Pizza on one corner.

Merrill pulled to a stop at a red light. Looking around at the three- and four-story redbrick buildings, he said, "You don't suppose this is a dry town, do you?"

"Looks like a sensible little town. They can't be that damn crazy," Smith said.

"There are dry towns in this neck of the woods." Merrill suddenly waved his trunk over his head and trumped so long and loud his face turned nearly purple from the effort. "There it is. Mulberry's." He hung a left onto Mulberry Street. "Look at this, people parking against the traffic." He pulled the minivan to the curb and turned off the key. "Come on, Preach," he said. "Let's have ourselves a drink. It's almost time for Sunday-night baseball on ESPN; maybe I can scare up a little action. The Dodgers and the Cubbies. It's Steve Sanger's turn in the rotation, and he's always had the Dodgers' number. These rubes won't know that until Joe Morgan tells them. All they know is that the Cubs are forever losers in August." He gave a little squeal and unbuckled.

Merrill and Smith got outside and strolled down the hot sidewalk to Mulberry's, which was in a stone building painted white with a green door, windowsills, and awnings.

They stepped inside Mulberry's. On their left were coin-operated game machines; on their right, a coin-operated pool table. The bar, straight ahead, burned and browned by cigarettes and smoke, looked like it had survived a hundred years of the drinking wars. On a television monitor above the right side of the bar, the CNN anchor was giving the news. The story of the hour was out of Victorville, California, in which someone had torched the Chijuajua Cafe, killing its Mexican-American owners, the cook, and six customers, plus decimating the Pony Express Motel across the street, killing its owners, their five children, and seven lodgers. Separately, the residence of the Chijuajua's owners had been burned, and the sister of the Chijuajua's cook had been murdered. Nothing like this had ever happened in Victorville, and the local police had called in the FBI for help.

The bartender was a young blonde in tight, white shorts with "Can't Beat 'Em" printed across the boob line of her T-shirt. "What's your poison, gents?"

"We'll have straight shots of Old Crow with a Budweiser back."

Merrill watched the bartender pour the whiskey. "If them shorts was any tighter, they'd lift her feet right off the floor." He trumpeted in appreciation.

As the bartender served their whiskey, she leaned over, examining Merrill's toothpick. She looked puzzled. She reached for the little penis. "What's this?" she asked.

twelve

David Karr liked to slip out of his office on a dog-day afternoon and enjoy a little skin at Bo Peep's in Charleston, West Virginia. At night, when the bearded, ponytailed good ol' boys came down out of the hollers to whoop it up and have a good time, the Peep's was impossible. Karr was put off by all their obnoxious shouting, Boone County jokes, and blathering on about how drunk they had gotten the previous weekend. Karr could not comprehend how getting drunk could be the subject of intense, prolonged interest to any rational human being. Drunk himself into a stupor, har, har, har!

As an afternoon regular, Karr had lately become an open admirer of a dancer who called herself Baad Betty. Her butt was largish, but didn't have a hint of cellulite. She was tight, tight, tight, and there was something about her that positively made Karr's mouth water.

Karr found that the ambiance at Bo Peep's shifted radically at night and was not to his liking. At night, the girls did their thing staring through the bluish haze of cigarette smoke with professional smiles, their eyes fixed just above the sea of upturned baseball caps perched on the noggins of the good ol' boys. After flashing their puss and a little undulating, they hustled quickly offstage and hid out in their dressing room to count their take.

In the afternoon though, if you gave them a decent tip, the girls got to know your name and what you were all about. When they danced on the bar, the fun spot less than a foot in front of your upturned face, they'd give you an extra ration of pink to think about when you went back to your office to decipher legalese. Karr, an afternoon regular and big tipper, called the waitresses by their first names and sat at the dancer's bar, where things were most up close and personal.

Elephant Dan Merrill, sitting with Slick Smith in the darkness behind Karr, gave a toothy grin in appreciation of the slightly overweight dancer. "Ain't this one got a hot butt on her? Give a man something to grab onto. Give them things a proper swat and watch 'em wiggle. Hoo, boy!" He started to tighten his lips, but Slick quickly clapped a hand over his mouth.

"Goddam it, I told you. None of that elephant shit. Are you crazy? You might be wearing a mask, but every con in San Quentin knows about the asshole who whiled away the hours squealing like an elephant. There'll be none of it. None! I mean that." Smith unwrapped a Snickers and started eating it.

Merrill, chastened, said, "Baad Betty, her name is. Nice set of jugs, too. Look at them nips."

"Baad Betty. Right." Smith chewed with contentment. "Boy, these are good. Nothing like a Snickers for a little pick-me-up. I'll strike terror into their hearts, Elephant. Yes, sir, I will. They'll wish they never crossed paths with Slick Smith. No, sir. I'm by God, Slick Smith, and I'm good at drinking and jacking!"

"I bet you're a real champ at jacking. Old Lady Five Fingers. Probably got calluses on the palm of your hand."

Smith opened and closed his right hand, pretending to admire it. "Lovely lady she is. Never gives me shit. Man practices something long enough, he's bound to get good at it. You know, Nolan Ryan throwing those fastballs year after year. Larry Bird practicing his jump shots. I especially know how to jack, I will tell you. I'm a fucking professional. Nobody, but nobody, jacks like Slick Smith." He threw the Snickers wrapper on the floor and puffed out his chest. "Nobody. Want me to show you a couple of strokes?"

Merrill looked disgusted. "Just keep your goat in his pen, and I don't want you puking in the middle of all this. That'll draw attention to us just as easily as my elephant calls."

"Not to worry. Not to worry," Smith said. "Got a Snickers on my stomach, so I'm okay. I'm just beginning to see things clearly. I'll strike terror into their hearts. Yes, sir, I will."

Merrill surveyed the room. "Do you think it's safe?"

Smith looked scornful. "Of course it's safe. We're just a couple of middle-aged men out of fifteen or twenty having a beer and enjoying the skin. Nobody will remember us. On our way out, we stash the jar in the wastebasket there beside the NASCAR video game. We drop one load here as punishment for the sin of lust; that'll justify the second two hits."

"Your daddy would approve."

"Punish them sinners. Yes, he would. Yes, he would for a fact. We've got a fortune sitting on the table in front of us, Elephant. All we have to do is take it. We don't look around. We just drop our package and drift on out of here."

The music stopped, and Baad Betty, down to pasties and G-string, knelt on the bar beside a coin-operated jukebox. She said, wearily, "You gotta spring for the music if you want me to take the rest of it off." She sighed. "Gentlemen. Please. I know it's a grind, but it's the drill." She held out a languid hand to the man sitting closest to the bar, but perked up when she saw the suit sitting next to him.

Smith said, "You see that suit down there by Baad Betty? That guy looks like he has a few bucks. Look at him bullshit with the waitress. A fast talker. Asshole. He's a regular here. Gotta be."

"You suppose he'll go under?"

"That's like betting which bird will be the first to fly off a telephone line. It's a form of chance. Existential."

"Exiwhat?"

"He either stays or goes. If he stays, he was in the wrong place at the wrong time. Not much more to be said. His decision whether he goes or stays. Not our fault." Smith looked around coolly, his face flushed with booze. "Let's do it. We don't want to get hung up in traffic on our way to Wal-Mart." He stood and strolled toward the NASCAR game machine.

As he passed by it on his way to the exit, he slipped a paper bag into a domed garbage can with a swinging lid.

Baad Betty danced on the bar right above David Karr. She knew he'd lay a ten spot on her if she would do the split a foot in front of his face. Small price to pay for a gift for her niece. She played with the hook of her G-string.

The wonderful pink was coming up. Hoo, boy! Karr knew he wouldn't go back to the office until he saw Baad Betty one more time. Or a couple of times. To hell with it. Loved that pink. Like to get his mouth in there and really chow down. Brrrrrrrr. He flubbered his lips at the thought of it.

Mary Beth Staats and Annabelle Hopkins, second cousins, and best friends since they were little girls, were, as the saying went in West Virginia, good people. With four kids each palmed off on grannies for the day and a few baby-sitting bucks in their handbags, it was time for some fun—lunch, a little shopping, and a whole lot of gossip.

The round-faced Mary Beth, a real mountain mama, had a huge rump that bounced *ka-lump, ka-lump* when she walked, and breasts like overstuffed pillows. Her husband Tom, a carpenter, claimed that her remarkable behind was as wide as six ax handles and a plug of tobacco. But then again, he acknowledged with a grin, he liked lots of meat with his potatoes. Annabelle was just about the opposite, scarecrow-thin, with shoulder blades that poked out of her cotton blouse like old boards. She was nearly breastless and had buns that were hardly more than a pinch, but her husband Tommy, who worked in a grocery-store warehouse, held to the clichéd dictum that the closer to the bone, the sweeter the meat.

Mary Beth and Annabelle started out with a lunch at the Mountaineer Cafe—fried chicken, mashed potatoes, gravy, cole slaw and biscuits—before proceeding on to Wal-Mart, where, feeling good, they crossed over the bright-red, six-foot-wide smile circle in front of the entrance. Three large signs hanging from the ceiling directed shoppers to the various sections of Ladies' Wear: Career Wear, Trends, and Body Wear.

Mary Beth and Annabelle skipped Career Wear, hardly considering themselves career women, and browsed through Trends on their way to Body Wear. In Trends, they checked out an *hecho-en-Honduras* flowered shirt by White Stag, $11.95; a made-in-Bangladesh denim vest by Cilano, $13.95; and a made-in-Mexico flowered blouse by Niki Lee, $13.95.

Then it was on to Body Wear to look at bras and panties.

Annabelle, holding up a lacy mint-green Bill Blass offering, looked momentarily wistful. "A waste of money buying something like this, even if I really needed it. Tommy used to like to take stuff off; now he just wants to get in and get off so he can get some sleep. 'The old in-out,' he calls it." She shook her head.

Mary Beth smiled. "Ain't that the truth? Mine's the same way. Couldn't get enough of it for the first couple of months. Acted like that old cocker we used to own, Sandy. Remember him? Chased every bitch in the county like there was no tomorrow. Once he even tried to hump the mailman's foot. You shoulda seen that poor man's face, standing there with a fistful of throwaways from the Baptist Church." She giggled at the memory. "And now . . ." She shrugged her plump shoulders.

Smith walked down the Wal-Mart aisle with a spring in his step and Merrill at his side. "Let's go to Sporting Goods first. You know what I like best about a store like this? Fishing lures. When I was a kid, we had spinners and snelled Eagle Claw hooks and maybe a couple of bass plugs, and that was it. And we had to go dig those crappy worms ourselves. Now they've got all these great plastic worms in different colors and scents. Orange. Yellow. Blue. Purple."

Merrill shook his head. "I seen on TV where they got plugs that smell like horny female fish. They got batteries in them that glow and make fish noises underwater."

Smith, with Merrill close at his heels, hung a left around a large wire basket of Gerard giraffes, the wildly popular Gerard being the subject of a recently released Walt Disney movie. They quickly arrived in the fishing-lures section. Smith grabbed a small packet of purple plastic worms. "See. What did I tell you? Here, feel." He gave Merrill the packet.

Merrill kneaded the package of worms between his fingers. "Isn't this neat how this feels? You know, a person would think that brown would be a lot better color. You know, something natural-looking, not purple. But they tell me purple is the favorite color of professional fishermen. Bass just love 'em."

Merrill looked thoughtful. "If you're willing to spring for it, you can buy lures with little guards that keep 'em from snagging on the weeds. That ought to make a man think. First off, why didn't they market snagless lures years ago? The answer is, they wanted you to lose lures. The more lures you lose, the more money they make. It's the same reason the drug manufacturers aren't into developing vaccines. They make money off sick people, for Christ's sake, not healthy ones. You think we learned how to fly close to a hundred years ago and still couldn't come up with a snagless lure? Bullshit! I don't believe it."

Smith grabbed a small box that contained a lure that was visible through a cellophane window. The box was covered with fine print explaining this lure's many features. "Here it is. See here. It has a miniature computer inside." He grinned, shaking his head in disbelief. "Computer? Come on, don't give us that crap." He read the explanation: " 'It glows, emits fish odor and fish talk all at the same time. You use it at night and take home your limit of bass, trout, or other predator fish.' I tell you what, Elephant, there is a lesson to be learned here, as there is almost everywhere."

"And this one is?"

"Take your money out of snelled hooks and put it into high-tech. Without weed guards." Smith glanced past the fish lures and down a wide aisle that led to the women's section. He said, "See that fattie and her friend there?" He put the lure in his hand back on the shelf.

Smith led Merrill down the aisle toward lingerie. They glided by the large woman and her friend. As they passed,

Smith whistled a little tune and sang, *"Two more birds sitting on the line. Will they stay put or will they be mine?"*

"The exi-thing."

"Existential," Smith said.

Mary Beth looked annoyed as the two men cruised by. One of them was playing with something on a gold chain around his neck. The other, looking drunk, muttered some kind of nonsense poetry. She glanced back at the retreating figures. "Creeps," she muttered. She held up a Playtex bra that advertised an eighteen-hour comfort strap. "Eighteen hours of comfort?" She weighed her breasts with the palms of her hands. "With boobs like these, it'd take a mattress and a forklift! You know something, 'Belle, I'm hungry again. What do you say we go back to my place? I've got Rice Krispies and marshmallows. We can make some candy."

Annabelle said, "Fine by me. Don't have much money anyhow, and we've got two more hours free of the kids."

They followed the two men out of the store but kept their distance, not wanting anything to do with the drunk and his stupid poetry.

The diminutive Playland was built around a huge, curving slide that was a large tube made of bright plastic—red at the top, then yellow, pink, green, dark blue, aqua, red, fuchsia, and light blue. Sitting at a round plastic table with attached stools, Bill and Ellen Corbin ate Big Macs and dipped french fries into little paper cups of ketchup while their three-year-old daughter explored the territory.

Tamara was one of those rare genetic jackpots, a toddler with a fabulous face and hair that hung in natural Shirley Temple ringlets; plus she had outsized, perfectly shaped lips, baby Sophia Lorens. Wherever the Corbins went, people stared at little Tamara and fussed over her, calling her "a living doll." For Bill and Ellen, it was like dragging a diminutive movie star around.

Now as they ate their Big Macs, they watched Tamara staring up at the tube slide.

Bill Corbin said, "Go on. Climb up there and try it out."

Tamara stepped back from the entrance of the colorful slide. She was uncertain.

Ellen said, "I'd just as soon she stays right where she is. If it's possible for her to find a way to bang her face, she'll figure it out." She glanced inside, where two men were watching them.

Tamara looked back at her parents. She smiled shyly.

"Go ahead, Tamara," Bill called.

"I don't think she should." Ellen bit her lip. "Do you see those two creeps watching us?"

Bill said, "Aw, they're not hurting anything."

"I don't like them staring at us like that. Don't they have anything better to do?"

Tamara gave her parents a huge smile, then came running back to their table.

Ellen, bursting with pride and relieved that her beautiful daughter was not going to try the slide, wiped some ketchup off the corner of Tamara's sensational mouth.

Munching on Big Macs, Smith and Merrill watched the little girl through a plate-glass window.

Smith said, "We agreed on the Playland, Elephant. We're professionals. Professionals don't let sentiment get in their way. Lotsa little girls in this world. Too damn many, in fact. Do you know what little girls do when they fart?"

Merrill couldn't keep his eyes off the tot. "What?"

"They release methane gas, that's what. Methane gas rises up in the air and fucks up the ozone. Yes, that's right. That little girl out there is worse than a refrigerator with Freon in it. I bet she's got a cheeseburger working through her system right now producing more methane."

"Jesus, Slick."

"I got that from reading a book about why we shouldn't eat meat. The author said that bovine flatulence was screwing up the ozone. Too much methane. Pretty little girls. Plain little girls. They all let farts. By wasting one of 'em, we're helping save a tree. Responsible citizens." Smith looked amused. "Regular Greenies. Ralph Nader'd love us."

"Listen, Slick, no need to stash our last jar here. There are plenty of McDonald's around. If you just gotta have a McDonald's, we can find another one."

Smith looked shocked. "And destroy our professional objectivity? What are you talking about?" He shook his head vigorously. "No, no, no. I am Slick Smith, professional. Drowning cats for candy bars or wasting little farters for a fortune. All the same to me. Our employer wants a McDonald's, by God, a McDonald's he's gonna get. Keep them Benjies coming in."

"What's the difference if we decide to make the drop or if a coin decides for us? You said yourself there was no accounting for fucked luck."

Smith straightened. His eyes were red. He glared at Merrill. "You want to be an amateur for the rest of your life? Huh? Is that it?" He looked disgusted. "Where are your balls, for Christ's sake?" He glanced outside at the playground, looking at the little girl. "By God, I could use another drink."

Merrill retrieved a quarter. "Heads, we stash it here. Tails, we drop it at another McDonald's." He flipped the coin with his right thumb, caught it, and slapped it on the rear of his left hand. Seeing what it was, he tightened his lips to trumpet, but the alert Smith elbowed him sharply.

"Hey, dammit!"

"Sorry, Slick."

"Sorry, my ass. You want to go back to the joint?"

David Karr looked up at Baad Betty, peering down at him from between her breasts as she undulated her bare pussy less than a foot in front of his upturned face. Karr struggled between flirtations, knowing eye contact and openly coarse, honest staring at her crotch. Betty, the daughter of a Logan County coal miner, was both pleased and amused that she was able to dangle a hotshot Charleston lawyer on a hormonal string. Baad Betty had learned early on that men were men; whether or not they had fancy university degrees and drove Japanese cars, it made not a whit of difference.

In those moments when Karr was able to wrest his attention from the pink, she gave him a little wink and squeezed her breasts. This was the flirtatious daily game between lawyer and dancer. It was a deal for both of them. Karr got a memorable sight that he could recall for a satisfying jack later on, a break from the by-the-numbers drill of married sex. Betty—nursing the fantasy that a man like Karr would lose his mind and spirit her away to a fancy house one day—was able to pay the rent on her HUD apartment and buy herself a stash of pot now and then.

On the jukebox, Sally O'Malley, a throaty hank of hair, sang her long-running hit, "Body Honey."

> *Mama's very best. Just waitin' for you.*
> *Don't it smell so sweet? Don't it smell so good?*

Karr began to feel dizzy.

> *Dip it with your finger. Lick it. Lap it.*
> *Special stuff. Special stuff.*

Above him, Baad Betty faltered.

> *Body honey. Bawdy honey. Don't cost money.*
> *Got plenty of boaaaaawdy honey. Just for you.*

"Are you okay?" Karr said. His vision blurred. Betty shook her head. "I feel dizzy."

> *All over your face. A sticking to your nose.*
> *Body honey. Bawdy honey. Nature's own.*

Betty toppled off the ramp, taking Karr with her as they crashed to the floor.

> *You like it. You like it. Smell it. Smell it.*
> *Got plenty of boaaaaawdy honey, just for you. A*
>   *treat for you.*

Karr felt his own blood as he saw it rushing from Betty's nose and mouth. He began to twitch and jerk, as did Betty, lying next to him. He reached out and took her hand, and they squeezed hands tightly as their bodies twisted with cramps and spasms.

> *Body honey. Bawdy honey. Don't cost money.*
> *Got plenty of boaaaaawdy honey, just for you. A*
> *treat for you.*

In minutes, David Karr, Baad Betty, and seventeen other customers and employees of Bo Peep's lay dying in a macabre dance, jerking and flailing on the floor with blood shooting from their mouths and ears and noses.

thirteen

The wind slapped a light rain against Jake Hipp's rain gear; he had it all—boots, rubber trousers, hooded slicker. Inside the waterproof exterior, he was layered in stocking cap, long johns, jeans, cotton shirt, and wool coat. He even had clear plastic goggles to keep the saltwater out of his eyes. The sky was slate-gray, and the wind off the Pacific pushed huge swells toward the mouth of the Columbia River. The Oregon shore, five miles distant from Cape Disappointment, was shrouded in gray. This treacherous span was one of the most violent estuaries in the world, a challenge both to freighters bound for Portland and fishermen putting out from Astoria, on the Oregon side, and Ilwaco, on the Washington shore.

Hipp braced himself against one of the wet boulders and once again flipped the spinner out into the water, turning his face against the buffeting wind as he retrieved the lure.

A hit! Hipp slipped against the rock and landed on his butt. He had a real fish on. His heart raced. He held the tip of his rod up so that the rod, not his line, took the pull, but it was too late. The line suddenly snapped and he reeled it in, disappointed. What could have been that big? A salmon? A steelhead?

The wind and the rain suddenly picked up in intensity. He glanced to the west, where the blackening clouds were roiling and boiling. He unfastened his string of perch and sea bass and climbed up the huge rocks to the top of the jetty; with the wind lashing rain against his back, he trudged slowly back toward shore.

As Hipp walked along the jetty, he thought of the thrill of having a big fish on, of the adrenaline rush as he literally pulled the life from a fish. When he was a kid, he had gotten a thrill out of shooting animals. He had been able to knock a squirrel off a limb with his .22 automatic, or send a jackrabbit rolling. No more. He liked to watch fishing programs on ESPN, but flipped the channel when hunters aimed shotguns at geese, or high-powered rifles at deer or elk. He assumed this was a post-forty phenomenon; now, on the down side of his ration of years, he appreciated and valued life as he had not when he was an adolescent, but the genetic rush of having a fish on a line remained.

By the time he got back to his Ford pickup, Hipp was trotting in a raging gale. He stowed his gear in the plastic box in the bed of the pickup and hopped up onto the driver's seat. He sat for a moment listening to the rain pound against the cab. He turned on the radio, hoping to pick up the public station in Astoria; he quickly tuned in on a breaking news story that turned out to be on every station on the band. Unknown terrorists had released the nerve gas sarin at three locations in Charleston, West Virginia—at Bo Peep's, a tavern featuring exotic dancers; in a Wal-Mart store; and at a McDonald's fast-food outlet.

Hipp sat stunned, listening to the reports. A Justice Department spokesman said the government had no idea of who was behind the attacks, but Hipp knew better. Bobby Pearl. The motherfucker had struck again. He checked several stations, but nobody had anything new to offer. The exact body count was uncertain. There were no known witnesses to the identity of the terrorists, who had left canisters of sarin with timed release devices in trash cans.

Bobby Pearl. Jesus!

Hipp punched off the radio. He started the engine and turned on the heater. In a few minutes, he'd be getting a call from Joe Woofter, who would fill in the details not released to the media. He retrieved his cellular phone from under his seat and punched up the number of Most Hipp in Cebu City. Got right through. Hot! "Gina, is that you?"

"Jake! Where are you? Belize still?"

"Naw, I'm back in Washington State. I'm sitting in a rain squall at Cape Disappointment." He unscrewed the lid from a blue thermos bottle on the seat and poured himself a cup of coffee.

"You're at the jetty where you took me? How did you do?"

"Got enough perch for supper. Porgies, they call them here. Not as good as Lapu-Lapu, I admit, but they're not bad. How are Cading and Celing and everybody in Labangon?"

"Oh, they're fine. Papa's gout is better. He's on Bohol, buying carabao. Mama loved the watch you sent her. Are you finished with Guatemala and Belize? When will you be coming out?"

Hipp cleared his throat. "I'm going back to work, Gina. Joe Woofter ran me down in Belize." He fished an Oreo out of a paper bag.

"What?"

"For one job." He bit into the Oreo.

"To run down Bobby Pearl." It was a statement, not a question.

Hipp said nothing, which meant yes. He fished another Oreo from the bag.

Gina remained silent for a moment, then said, "You promised."

"I know I promised, but sometimes there are things in life you just can't dodge, and this is one of them. I was the only Charlie to see and hear him. I have to do it."

"Oh, Jake."

"There's no turning back on this one. I'm doing it for me, not just for them."

"Be careful, Jake."

"I always am."

"Sure you are. Bobby Pearl is dangerous, Jake. The magazine was right. You should have stayed in the T-Cell library."

"We all have reptilian brain stems, Gina. I'm theoretically capable of being as much of a bad ass as the next guy."

"I thought you said Bobby Pearl always gives a warning. I don't remember hearing any warning about these. Maybe it's somebody else."

"It's him, Gina."

"They've told you that?"

"No. But I expect to hear from Joe shortly."

Gina sighed. "You're eating something. What are you eating?"

"An Oreo. They're good. I'll bring you some."

"I want chocolates with lots of nuts and those little cherries, same as always."

"Little cherries. I know what you mean. Mmmmmm."

Gina laughed. "Aren't you getting horny?"

"Well, you know, Gina. I can always yank my noodle."

"Sure you can. Just don't drag anything back to me, or I'll tear you limb from limb. You know that."

Hipp laughed. "Yes, I know that, Gina."

"I don't need to study monkeys or go to graduate school to know about men. I'm a Filipina, remember. We Filipinas know how men think. Just because we know what you men are doing when we're not around doesn't mean we won't make you pay if we catch you at it. Are you walking around in yesterday's underwear? You get yourself a clean pair of shorts, Jake."

"They're clean. They're clean, really."

"I know you. And watch the cholesterol and saturated fat. No eggs. No cheese. I read this article. I know how you like pizza."

"It's nice that you care."

"You're getting older, you know. You have to take care of yourself. You might think you're quick as a mongoose, but you're more like a carabao in a rice field."

Hipp took a sip of coffee. "I'm hardly in the grave yet. I love you, Gina. Keep the San Miguel cold."

"Did I tell you a shipment of mustard finally arrived from Germany? Lots of mustard. Also, Felix has learned to make Australian sausages. The Aussies say they taste just like home."

"Is the john camera still working?" Hipp had installed a knothole camera in the toilet at Most Hipp. Whenever a cigar smoker went in to take a leak, the cashier punched a button, activating a camera that snapped a picture of the next customer through the door. If Bobby Pearl made an appearance in Most Hipp and smoked a cigar, they'd take his picture.

"I've got another roll of cigar smokers for you to develop."

"Put 'em in the mail. I'll eventually get him, Gina. It might take time, but I'll get him. In the end, it just might be that camera that turns the trick. Love you, Gina." Hipp meant it. He did love Gina. She was a sweetheart.

"I love you, Jake."

Hipp hung up and sat alone with his coffee. Bobby Pearl. Who in hell was Bobby Pearl, and where was he? And why was he doing this? Why?

fourteen

"No more slop. Next game, no slop." Elia Khardonne looked dapper in his tan slacks and double-breasted blue blazer with yellow ascot. He snagged another drink from the tray of a tuxedoed waiter. "Have to call the numbers. Whaddya say?" Khardonne looked around, grinning. He was a small man with a large forehead and darting brown eyes. "Anybody can luck out. No slopsies. Make it a real contest."

His proposal was met with laughter. Of course there would be no slopsies for the next game. Khardonne owned the board, the sensational lodge, the waiters, the handsome spread on the deck overlooking the Ghost River, and the souls of most of the players.

Khardonne, who had sprinkled communications satellites in the heavens like so many profitable sequins, loved few things as much as buying more media property. One of his other pleasures was playing darts with his friends and anybody who presumed to do business with him. Another was "Out of Here," his fabulous retreat on the Ghost, a branch of the Red Deer River, about fifty miles west of his hometown of Sundre, Alberta Province, Canada. Of course Khardonne loved money and the power that it brought, but that went without saying. He also liked to dip his wick into the sweet young things who gathered to him as flies to honey. That too went without saying; it was one of the perks of being rich and powerful.

Now, on the day following the release of sarin in Charleston, Khardonne had gone to Out of Here to celebrate his sixty-first birthday. There were close to a hundred invited friends, employees, and hangers-on at the party, most of them outside on the huge deck with the food and booze to enjoy the sunset over the Canadian Rockies.

Khardonne said, "Same partners? Bill, you game again?"

Bill Johnson, a childhood friend from Sundre, was the caretaker of Out of Here. The slender, rugged Johnson, who had been a rodeo cowboy in his youth, said, "Sure, if I don't have to hit all the numbers this time."

Everybody laughed at that, too. Johnson, the best player in the room, had been Khardonne's cricket partner all afternoon. Khardonne didn't like to lose at anything. If Johnson was around when he played darts, Johnson was his partner. Khardonne didn't mind being carried at darts as long as he won. Making money was his game. One of those old barons of print—William Randolph Hearst, was it?—had observed that owning a newspaper was a license to print money. Hearst was born too soon. He simply had no idea of what the future would deliver.

Johnson toed the hockey to middle for the diddle.

Khardonne smiled as Johnson nailed the double bull.

One of their opponents, who was in Canada to negotiate the sale of his broadcast television station in Phoenix, stepped up to the line and sailed a dart high and to the right, a three. The American had never played darts in his life, but had demonstrated by his success that he knew how to suck when he had to.

Never mind that the man from Phoenix was a beginner; Khardonne was pleased that he and Johnson would go first.

Johnson stepped up to the hockey. "Twenties," he said, concentrating on the top of the board.

A tuxedoed waiter came striding toward them bearing a cellular telephone. "A call for you, Mr. Khardonne."

Khardonne looked sour. "I'm playing darts. I thought I said no calls."

The waiter said, "It's the American President, sir. He says it's extremely urgent."

Khardonne was cool. "The President. I see. Well, okay, I guess it won't hurt me to make an exception now and then."

This was met with laughter from Khardonne's impressed guests. He put the phone to his ear—the Big Man graciously interrupting his dart game to listen to another suck up. "Yes, Mr. President. This is Elia Khardonne. What can I do for you?"

"This is a private call, Mr. Khardonne. Between you and me."

Khardonne looked around at his guests, who were all curious as to why the President of the United States would be calling Khardonne at his Canadian retreat. "Private? Oh, sure." He gave his guests a knowing look. Private? Right.

"Mr. Khardonne, Joaquin Hurtado has been promoting some kind of major scoop in the sarin story to be aired on *My Side* tonight. If Hurtado has what I suspect he does, I would sincerely ask you to please help us out."

Khardonne blinked. "Help you out? How would that be?"

"I want Hurtado to sit on his story. For the good of the country. No, I amend that. For the good of everybody. Canadians. Americans. We're all in this together."

"I would like to help you in any way I can, Mr. President. Joaquin Hurtado doesn't call me with every scoop he comes up with. I'm not an editor. Perhaps you should call Ms. Bernardi, the show's producer. By the way, what story are you talking about, Mr. President?"

"It's a tape, Mr. Khardonne."

"A tape. Are you going to tell me more than that?"

"I . . . no, I don't believe I should. But if it is the tape, it's dangerous, if not treasonous, for Hurtado to make it public."

Khardonne pursed his lips. "Treasonous, Mr. President? I don't believe Congress has declared any kind of war. We both know you have no legal authority to tell Joaquin Hurtado what he should or shouldn't put on his program. If he slanders someone, I suppose you could take him to court later, if you want."

"No prior censorship. I know. I know."

"The Supreme Court made that abundantly clear thirty-odd years ago with *The New York Times* publication of the Pentagon papers."

"We're involved in an ongoing, continuous state of war with terrorists, Mr. Khardonne. We both know that. I'm asking you to do this to help us catch one particular terrorist."

Khardonne frowned. "Tell me, Mr. President, can you guarantee to me that none of the other broadcast or cable networks will break the story if Joaquin goes along with your request? Or are you asking Joaquin to sit on it while everybody else totals their Nielsens?"

The President fell silent. Then he said, "You know I can't do that. I would if I could, but it's impossible. Who knows who might have gotten their hands on that tape? I say again, you have to help. If you don't know anything about the story, you can find out. There's a half hour left before Hurtado's show begins. Barely enough time to call him."

"Ah, well . . ."

"When you know what he's got, you can guess the consequences. If you want more information from me, just call me back. I'm willing to work with you on this. Listen, Mr. Khardonne, there's a time for the bald truth and a time, in everybody's interest, to sit on it for the moment. We all have to pull together with something like this. Call him and ask him. Please."

Khardonne shrugged. "Okay, Mr. President, I can go that far for you. Won't hurt me."

"Thank you, Mr. Khardonne. I mean that sincerely." The President sounded relieved. "Will you call me back? I'd appreciate it."

"Well, sure, if I can get to Joaquin and Ms. Bernardi before they go on the air."

"Then let's waste no more time flapping our jaws. We've got limited time. Let's do the sensible thing. Make your call, then get back to me and tell me what you think. I'll be eternally grateful." The President hung up.

Khardonne handed the phone to the waiter and said, "Please get this thing out of here. I said no calls and I mean it. I'm playing darts." He turned back to the game. "You want to get us our twenties, Bill?"

Bill Johnson hesitated. He was curious about the call, as

was everybody else in the room. The guests were momentarily silent.

The Ghost River could be heard gurgling past the deck outside.

Khardonne said, "Joaquin has apparently been hyping a hot Charleston story all day. He's got the President so worked up he's about to dump a load in his shorts." He grinned. "Not a whole lot of fun being president at a time like this. Worry, worry, worry." He glanced at his wristwatch. "*My Side* is due up in a half hour. We'll watch Joaquin and see what the fuss is about."

Khardonne, pretending to be ignorant of what he had just done, picked up his darts. "Are you going to throw those things, Bill, or what?"

For Khardonne, this was a win-win situation. What was the sense of accumulating all that money and power without showing it off now and then? Twenty to thirty people in the room had witnessed the conversation. They'd all tell their friends what happened, and the story would be passed on, exaggerated in each retelling until it was elevated to the level of myth. This was what triumph was all about.

Elia Khardonne, having casually blown off the President of the United States, went back to his dart game.

Lugging a plastic bag of take-out enchiladas and a six-pack of Carta Blanca beer, Carl Czez returned to the Pacifica Motel in Glendale, just east of Hollywood, to watch the media circus that had followed the release of nerve gas in Charleston.

Czez first punched up Joaquin Hurtado, but found that the self-conscious twit was enough to gag a maggot. He tapped the remote again, this time to NBC, where the balding, mellow-voiced Charles Horton—a kind of sincere national uncle—was interviewing two experts on chemical and biological warfare. Nuclear-Biological-Chemical. NBC on NBC. What a wonderful world it was! Czez grinned broadly.

Dr. Stephen Adkins, a thin, intense man with thick spectacles, was on-screen, from his book-lined office at Johns Hopkins University in Baltimore. Adkins' spectacles did not fit, and kept sliding down the narrow bridge of his substantial beak. He had passion and oily skin. The glasses slid. He pushed. The glasses slid.

Dr. John Wheeler, a tweedy, silver-haired chemistry professor at Vanderbilt University, sat across from Horton in NBC's high-tech news studio. In the background, writers toiled at computers and people strolled around, presumably going about their business.

On the screen, Adkins said, "Sarin is an acronym for Schrader, Ambrose, Rudriger, and van der Linde, the German chemists who accidentally discovered it in nineteen thirty-eight while researching agricultural pesticides. The Third Reich turned it into a chemical-warfare weapon. Less than a minute drop on human skin can kill a victim within five to fifteen minutes, and there are unconfirmed reports that the Nazis tested it on inmates in their death camps."

Horton raised his eyebrows. "Five to fifteen minutes?"

"Just one third of an ounce of sarin can kill up to five thousand people," Adkins said.

Czez scooped up some refried beans with a tortilla, then made a remonstrative clicking sound with his tongue at the roof of his mouth. Five thousand people. Tsk, tsk, tsk!

"The problem is that anybody can make this stuff," Wheeler said. "In Pentagon jargon, it is 'accessible technology.' "

Czez, chewing, leaned forward.

"John is right," Adkins said. "The ingredients for sarin are easily come by. All you have to do is buy yourself some insecticides at your local hardware store. The formula is available in the British Patent Office or in the reference library of any large American university."

"And on the Internet, don't forget," Wheeler said. "All you have to do is call it up on a laptop."

"On the Internet? Really?" Horton exclaimed. "I see it's time for a break. When we return, we'll learn more about nerve gases and biological-warfare agents, including, perhaps, how they're made. And we'll take some calls to see what questions you, our viewers, might have."

"Questions you might have. Right." Czez rolled his eyes; unzipping his fly, he headed for the toilet.

The sponsors, coveting the attention of retreating viewers, hounded them with increased decibels. Standing at the toilet, lacing the water with recycled beer, Czez was forced to listen to a woman tout a new chocolate-flavored diet drink. Those who drank it, she said, would lose one pound a week and feel better or they would get their money back.

Czez shook his one-eyed snake, repacked it, and returned to his meal as NBC was hawking the thrills and chills to be had by watching its Saturday-night movie.

He took a bite of chicken, watching Dr. Adkins push his spectacles up on his nose with his forefinger. Adkins said, "Sarin is related to tabun, also developed by Gerhard Schrader, and to soman, which was developed by Soviet scientists and stockpiled during the Cold War. Tabun disperses easily, making it the gas of choice in combat. Soman is heavier, more poisonous, and more persistent than sarin. In the literature, these gases are called g-agents."

Wheeler looked grim. "You have to know what you're doing, and you have to be careful and have the proper equipment, but they're easily made."

Czez raised an eyebrow. "No shit, Sherlock," he murmured.

Horton said, "You say the terrorists at Aum Shinri Kyo made this sarin themselves?"

"Yes, they did," Wheeler said. "They also made hydrogen cyanide, which would require twenty-five ounces to kill five thousand people. Easy enough to make, but it results in a terrible death—it inhibits breathing so the victim slowly suffocates. And they made an oily, nonvolatile liquid called VX, that can linger for weeks, producing a slow, painful death. Steve has recently published a paper on its recorded uses by the military. Steve?"

Adkins said, "The Japanese used g-agents, which they

apparently got from the Germans, to eliminate tens of thousands of Chinese in the Second World War. More recently, both the Iraqis and the Iranians used a form of mustard gas in their eight-year-long war in the nineteen eighties, and Saddam Hussein used both sarin and mustard gas against dissident Kurds."

Horton said, "Say again? Anybody can make this stuff? Are you serious?"

Adkins said, "The Pentagon generals have known this for fifty years, but they've not talked about it. It doesn't take an ICBM to deliver an ounce of sarin. The government's attitude has been that if there isn't anything you can do about it, why frighten people?"

"Perhaps this is a good point to take a call," Horton said. "Hello, Gene, in Walla Walla, Washington. What's your question, Gene?"

Gene cleared his throat. "I don't really have a question, just an observation. The Second Amendment militants and the National Rifle Association argue that guns don't kill people, criminals do. Isn't it true that what we're facing here is that precise logic cubed? Fertilizer chemicals don't blow up federal buildings, terrorists do. We can't ban the sale of ammonium nitrate, because it's essential to an agricultural industry that earns our largest export income. What can we possibly do to protect ourselves when anybody can make sarin or brew anthrax and botulism? That's the only question that really matters, and you're telling us it can't be answered. Isn't that right?"

Horton looked at the screen. "Dr. Adkins?"

Adkins said nothing.

"Dr. Wheeler?"

Wheeler started at the table in front of him.

"Our next call is from George, in Albany, New York. You have a question, George?"

"Sure. You people tell us it's madness not to face the truth. Let me ask this: suppose I've got a chip on my shoulder or extortion on my mind, and I want to covertly manufacture and deliver a deadly gas. What, specifically, would be within the realm of dangerous possibility? I'll need some kind of logical cover for this and a method of delivery. You tell us anybody can do it. Prove it. Are you telling us the truth or just blowing smoke?"

Horton glanced at Adkins and Wheeler, uncertain of how to continue. "Following the logic of the caller from Walla Walla, this would be like telling our viewers how to manufacture an assault rifle."

George said, "Cubed, which is how the gentleman from Walla Walla expressed it. Let's see how brave you really are."

Horton said, "Well, I'm not sure."

Adkins, looking determined, pushed his glasses up. He'd been challenged. He shrugged. "Okay, here's one that's already been described on television, so I'm not breaking any new ground. You buy thiodiglycol, a chemical used to make ink. Thiodiglycol is legal to buy and no records are kept, but you can steal it if you want to be safe. You chlorinate it, a single, simple chemical process. *Voilà!* You have mus-tard gas."

"Like the terrorists released at the food fair?"

"Precisely."

"Wait, wait. Stop. That's a cop-out. 'Chlorinate' it. A 'single, simple chemical process.' What does that mean? How simple?"

"You add chlorine in an enclosed container."

"And how do I deliver it?"

"The terrorists in San Francisco used propane tanks. You release it with a remote; they did. Does that about cover your question?"

Horton blinked.

Adkins said, "Ink is manufactured around the planet. China. Iraq. Iran. Name the country. Companies that make ink go in and out of business every day."

In the Pacifica, Czez said aloud, "Well, for Jesus Christ's sake, tell the whole fucking world, why don't you?"

Wheeler said dryly, "We should all remember that the terrorist said he can do biologicals, too." He licked his lips. He continued, eyes unblinking. "What, you ask, would he need to brew up some botulism or anthrax? For the botulism, he would require fermenters, which are routinely used by wineries and breweries. Think of the wineries in the Napa and Sonoma valleys in California, or in western Oregon or Yakima Valley, Washington, or the Finger Lakes region in upstate New York, and of the proliferation of microbreweries producing designer beers. They're everywhere. Numerous research laboratories and makers of antibodies, insulin, and enzymes of one sort or another require centrifuges and purification equipment. Right, Steve?"

Adkins repositioned his sliding spectacles. "In nineteen eighty-nine, the German government found a cell of the Baader-Meinhoff gang with a culture of clostridium botulinum, and by nineteen ninety-one, the Iraqis had four plants brewing botulism, anthrax, and clostridium perfingens."

Wheeler licked his lips. "As a means of delivering death, botulinum or anthrax are far more efficient than sarin or mustard. Production of disease, which can kill more people over a larger area—the city of Chicago, say—is measured in kilograms. Nerve gas or blister agents, which can eliminate all life in a specific area of combat, are measured in tons."

Adkins flopped a slick, dark blue magazine on the desk. The camera cut to the magazine, *Proliferation: Threat and Response,* then returned to Adkins, who looked at the red light straight-on. "This is an unclassified Pentagon report published for the benefit of members of Congress serving on the National Security Committee, which used to be called the Armed Services Committee. Let me read you what the happy generals have to tell the men and women of the Congress about delivery systems. Quote, 'A number of delivery-system options are available for terrorist or paramilitary delivery of NBC weapons,' end quote. You suppose it took Sherlock Holmes or Columbo to figure that out?"

Adkins looked up. "By the way, NBC is short for Nuclear-Biological-Chemical." He looked down and continued reading. "Quote, 'States that want to employ NBC weapons to support military operations are likely to make

use of combat aircraft, ballistic missiles, or cruise missiles,'
end quote. What's missing from the second sentence? You
want to tell them, John?"

Wheeler said, "What's missing is any mention of how
NBC weapons are delivered by individual terrorists. And
consider the phrase, 'are likely to make use.' Likely? Why on
earth should a nation state resort to combat aircraft, ballistic
missiles, or cruise missiles if it doesn't have to? If Saddam
Hussein wanted to give us a hit of sarin, why not simply have
his people smuggle it across our borders, or better yet, hire
someone? In fact, there are so many ways of delivering lethal
gases and diseases that they're impossible to list in a neat little paragraph. The Aum Shinri Kyo cultists used plastic bags
that they punctured with the sharpened tips of umbrellas. In
Charleston, the terrorists used quart fruit jars with a remote-
controlled mechanical releasing device on top.

"And check out the phrase, 'to support military operations.' The cultists from Aum Shinri Kyo weren't conducting
military operations. Was the bombing of the Federal Building in Oklahoma City a 'military operation?' Maybe in the
sick imagination of the terrorist, but not in any sensible definition of the phrase. And it's what Mark Twain would call a
'stretcher' to deduce any military operation from the release
of sarin in Charleston. This stuff is being used as a form of
blood sport."

Horton said, "Both of our callers made good points, then."

Adkins took off his glasses. "Yes, they did. Very good
points. Unless John and I had answered the second caller's
question candidly, nobody would have taken the first caller
seriously, and they should. It's foolish to make public policy
according to agreed-upon lies. What can we really do?"
Shaking his head sadly, he tapped the Pentagon's publication with his forefinger. "The anonymous Pentagon authors
write about the 'accessibility' and 'military efficacy' of g-
agents and anthrax. It is ghastly, low-tech death, is what it is,
and it is here, now, released by zealots, psychopaths, or outright idiots."

Czez looked amused. He was finished with his meal. He got up to retrieve another Carta Blanca from the refrigerator.

The beeper on his computer went off. He twisted the cap from the bottle and strolled casually to his computer. He flipped it on and tapped a key to find out who was on the other end. When the code of his correspondent popped onto the screen, Czez slapped his thigh in amazement and burst out laughing.

He watched as a question appeared on the screen.

Scarcely concealing his glee, he glanced at his watch and typed a reply: *"Hell, yes. I can do it tonight. Got plenty of time."* He tapped the enter button, sending his message on its way; then he laughed even harder.

fifteen

Jake Hipp poured himself another cup of coffee and sat by
the cabin window. Beyond the window he could see the
angry white of huge breakers crashing onto the wide beach.
Open the door and it was a forever roar. A stiff wind buffeted
the salt grass on the sand dunes and pushed more low, dark
clouds in from the Pacific. In the clouds were shapes: he saw
stampeding caribou; huge, antlered bulls thundered over
dark tundra. Then the caribou dissolved, replaced by Roman
legions clashing with barbarians. Hipp saw helmets and
heads and horses. Men lay dying.

Ultimately, the grit that formed Bobby Pearl was likely
sexual. If it wasn't, so what?

Hipp turned on his laptop and tapped out a message:
*Bobby Pearl, I've been wondering about your sex life. Been
getting the old end in?*

He reread the message. Thousands of curious viewers of
My Side—not to mention reporters from the weekly newspapers to the television networks—would be checking Hipp's
e-mail address, wondering what message he had left for
Bobby Pearl. The media were desperate for any tidbit of
information about the elusive Pearl. Any message Hipp left
for Pearl would be multiplied on the tube—instant grist for
barroom and beauty-parlor bullshit throughout the land.

It occurred to Hipp that here was a real opportunity. Pearl
already had given Hipp an amusing in-your-face on *My Side.*
*How are you doing out there? Getting a good night's sleep?
Learned how to pull a trigger yet? The old choke artist.*

Turnabout was fair play, wasn't it? Why just prick the
bastard's carotid with the tip of the rhetorical knife? Better
to show him what maximum chickenshit was all about. Hipp

did not know for a fact what Pearl's problem was, but he could make an educated guess. He grinned devilishly. He tried again:

Bobby Pearl, I've been wondering about your sex life—or lack of it. Have you been getting your end in, or you still out there following women around with that pathetic, hang-dog look of yours? The German girl was disgusted at your behavior. Poor, poor man, she called you. Listen, pal, killing from ambush sure as hell doesn't make you a stud. You must be getting bored with pulling your pee-pee. Same Old Lady Five Fingers. Calluses on the palms of your hands? They tell me these conditions aren't impossible to manage. Fix the problem, don't take your frustration out on innocent people. If you want, I can put you in touch with a shrink who can give you some help. The taxpayers will spring. No problem. Just drop me a line.

P.S. Greta was hot, I agree. Hard to forget those long legs of hers. Mmmmmmm! And horny! Damn near wore me out.

Whether or not Pearl had a sexual problem, that cute little in-your-face would piss him off royally—especially after it became public knowledge around the planet.

When the phone rang, he knew it was likely Joe Woofter. He sighed and picked up the receiver. "Joe?"

"Me, Jake. You've been watching the news?"

"Got the gist of it on the radio after I came back from fishing. When they started repeating the details, I punched it off."

"Good thinking."

"I keep expecting Bobby Pearl to step out of the rain and waste me with a gatling. Charleston, West Virginia. Why in West Virginia, for Christ's sake? Can you figure that?"

"He probably opened an atlas at random. This way, everybody thinks they could be next, not just New Yorkers or Washingtonians. Eu Claire or Carson City. All the same to Bobby Pearl. He gets more people rattled that way."

Hipp took a sip of coffee. "That's one explanation, I suppose. Have you come up with any leads?"

"Well, yes, we did, as a matter of fact. Watch investigators found themselves two women who were in the Wal-Mart a few minutes before the gas was released. They said two guys cruised by them while they were looking at lingerie. One of them was playing with something on a gold chain around his neck, possibly a crucifix or a small figure of Jesus. The other was a drunk who gave them a little couplet on his way by. These are two country women, Jake, but one of them, a regular Ten-ton Tessie, has a real memory on her."

"Well, there you go, Christian screwballs. Killing for the love of Jesus. A common enough phenomenon."

Woofter said, "That's what we thought at first, until one of our people interviewed a bartender in Ravenswood, West Virginia, which is about an hour north of Charleston on the Interstate."

"And?"

"She described the same two men, only she got a close look at the crucifix. Something about it was different, and she was curious. Wasn't a cross, turns out. Christ was crucified on a cross made out of dogwood. This was a dried coon's dick. Or at least that's what the guy told her."

Hipp paused. "Say again?"

"A dried coon's dick. He said he uses it for a toothpick. Demonstrated for her right there at the bar. Picked some Polish sausage out of his teeth. This same guy is good at imitating elephants. He can squeal and trumpet with the best of them. Turns out this matches the description of two men at a McDonald's in Charleston. An elephant man and a drunk."

"A McDonald's, not the one that was hit?"

"A different one, but we definitely think these may be our guys."

"A drunk and a guy with a dried coon's dick around his neck who likes to imitate elephants. A dynamic duo if there ever was one."

"All three women had a session with a portrait artist. The fat woman and the bartender described a man who looks remarkably like the Bobby Pearl you remembered, but it's hard to tell with those things. Unless the mark has distinctly irregular features, they have a tendency to look pretty much the same."

"Which one looked like a fit?"

"The drunk."

Hipp thought about that for a moment. "The Bobby Pearl I saw looked like a loner to me. Hard to imagine him doing a job loaded or having a partner going around snorting like an elephant. They remember anything else?"

"The plump lady remembered the couplet. *'Two little birds sitting on a line. Will they stay put or will they be mine?'* We put the description on the local radio and television stations and got a call from a man and his wife who had been sitting at a McDonald's Playland—not the McDonald's that got hit—who say two men were watching them from the dining room inside. Their description matches that of the men in the Wal-Mart. 'Creeps' was the way the woman described them."

"Guy with a dried penis around his neck. Jesus!"

"Speaking of penises, I read your report on your trip to L.A., Jake. Good work getting Bernardi to let you challenge Pearl with an E-mail address. What are you going to say?"

"I'm going for his balls, big time. If that's not his problem, it'll still piss him off, which is the point of the exercise. By the way, Joe, I think you should have someone go back to Amsterdam and talk to that prostitute again. I've read Art Hill's report several times, but I think there are some more questions that need asking. Art's a fun guy and I like him and everything . . ." Hipp left the sentence unfinished.

"But his ARs leave something to be desired. I agree."

"For one thing, the exact context in which Pearl mentioned Seville is not clear. What were they talking about? Were the Spanish girls allegedly sexier or better lays than Dutch girls? Did he want the girl to go with him? Does he get his kicks beating up on people? What? We know something is seriously wrong with this asshole. We need every possible clue."

"I'll get somebody on it."

"I hate to sound like Columbo or somebody, but we have

to pay attention to details. We just have to. You can contact me at my E-mail address to see what I've left for our friend Pearl. If it doesn't draw a response out of him, I'll kiss your bootie."

"Jesus, Jake, what did you do?"

"Go ahead, check it out. See for yourself."

"Any luck fishing?"

"I caught some perch, locally called porgies." Hipp hung up and poured himself more coffee. A snake like Bobby Pearl could slip through the slightest crack in an AR. A Charlie could be smart as hell, an ace linguist, good at tapping phones, a terrific shot, and the rest of it, but if he couldn't communicate what he saw to Mongoose, none of that mattered. To remove ambiguity from ARs, Mongoose went so far as to require that all personal pronouns referring to a snake, or a suspected snake, be put in caps, and schools of journalism were favorite sources of Mongoose recruiters. Art Hill was a veteran Charlie, but some of his reports were close to incomprehensible. And he left things out. For example, he said the girl "had been burned before she had been pulped." Not good. How badly had she been burned, and with what?

Jake Hipp thought about the smell of cigars. Thus encouraged, he retrieved a Filipino cigar, a Tony Valenzona panatella, out of the glove compartment. He dug his Swiss army knife out of his pocket. When Gina had learned of his new interest in cigars, she'd sent him a box of Valenzonas as a joke; the box looked fancy, but Filipino businessmen were notoriously mischievous if there was a peso to be made. When Gina asked him how he liked the cigars, he replied that San Miguel was the best cheap beer in the world. Since then, he had come to like Valenzonas. No, he wouldn't want to tear one open and examine its insides with a microscope. Better simply to sit back and enjoy.

Jake Hipp opened the knife and nipped the end off the cigar. He now smoked cigars because Bobby Pearl smoked them.

sixteen

Joaquin Hurtado, wearing his trademark Sincere Face, solemnly addressed his viewers straight-on. "Well, that's Bobby Pearl as he was when I interviewed him nine months ago. I asked him if he would do it again. He said, 'Does a bear bleep in the woods?' At the beginning of the program tonight, I promised that *My Side* would make public the administration's secret of secrets in the Charleston tragedy. It's our lives at stake, and it's our government sworn to protect us from all enemies, foreign and domestic. We have the right to know all the facts, no matter how unsettling."

Hurtado strolled to his left, addressing a tracking camera. "An informant in the Justice Department has given *My Side* a CD containing two messages from Bobby Pearl to the FBI. One just before the mustard gas was released in San Francisco, and the second this summer. Here, watch these."

On *My Side's* monitor, the avalanche of pearls began their descent into red. When the mustard-gas warning was finished, the pearls began a second plunge. This time Pearl boasted of his new stock of chemical- and biological-warfare agents and threatened a demonstration release of sarin.

When the second message was completed, the camera returned to Hurtado, who closed his eyes.

He opened them again.

Hurtado clenched his teeth and strode to his left, chopping the air with his hand as he addressed the tracking camera. "Bobby Pearl! The FBI's International Terrorist Watch and the CIA's Mongoose terrorist chasers have had the sarin warning for six months. Pearl says he can deliver any of the chemical- and biological-warfare agents that are being discussed in the news. Here, listen to Pearl's warnings again and judge for yourselves whether or not we should have been fully informed."

Hurtado sat, looking intense, as Pearl's messages were played a second time. When they were finished, he said, "I ask again: is this what the twenty-first century will be like? Is this our future? Assaulted by phantom terrorists. Kept in ignorance by cowards."

Hurtado bunched his face in disappointment. The bravest of brave Eagle Scouts had done it again. Time to promo. He faced another camera. "For years, the American government has been insisting that Moamar Qadhafi is making nerve gas underground. Well, that alleged underground chemical research-and-production facility is at Tarhunah. Last year I was taken on a tour of at least part of the Tarhunah facility." He looked around, cocking his head. "And what did I find?" He turned up the palms of his hands. "Why, just what Colonel Qadhafi said I'd find."

He started walking again. "Mushrooms! For the Italian market, Qadhafi says."

Hurtado stopped, looking grave, a cue to his viewers that grim stuff was coming up. He pursed his lips. This was the concerned, responsible Hurtado, his mind ever on his countrymen and how he might best serve them. "Was Moamar Qadhafi trying to use *My Side* for his own nefarious reasons? Hard to say. I don't vouch for the truthfulness of people we interview. You're big boys and girls. That you have to decide for yourselves. Next week, I'll replay key portions of Moamar Qadhafi's side of the story as he told it to us in Libya last year, and you'll get to ask yourself: is this man capable of telling the truth, or is he living his life in a fantasy world of eternal treachery? Don't miss it.

"Also, I will interview General Otot Imbubwe, the renegade Tutsi commander who is bent on eliminating the Hutu people from central Africa. Imbubwe, a graduate of Oxford University and trained by the British military academy at Sandhurst, is said to have been responsible for the slaughter of nearly a quarter of a million Hutus last month—this amid stories that the controversial Imbubwe and his commanders are keeping a harem of young Hutu girls for their amusement. I flew to a military camp in the mountains of Rwanda, where General Imbubwe is on the run from United Nations troops.

"Imbubwe says that what he does or doesn't do is an African affair, none of the business of the United Nations, the United States, the European powers, or anybody else. The Hutu, once the majority tribe, attempted to kill all Tutsis in nineteen ninety-four, he says, and this is simple justice. Watch *My Side* and see how General Otot Imbubwe responds to charges of genocide and the keeping of sex slaves."

My Side ended with a list of ways that potential guests could contact Joaquin Hurtado: a toll-free telephone number, a fax number, and an E-mail address.

A legend scrolled across the bottom of the screen:

> *No matter who you are, what you have done, or what you know, Joaquin Hurtado will go any-where, anytime, to hear your story. If you work in a company or in a government bureaucracy and you know something you feel should correctly be shared with the public, we can alter your voice and provide you with an electronic mask. Your confidentiality is guaranteed.*
>
> *Will the serial rapist in Houston please contact us? We'd like to share your side of the story.*
>
> *We're still waiting to hear from whoever has been burning churches in Virginia and North Carolina. You have to be doing this for a reason. We would like to know your story. Don't be shy. Speak up!*
>
> *Bobby Pearl, your story has now changed dra-matically. If the government won't tell us what they've learned, My Side will have to ask the obvi-ous questions. We'd like to talk to you about chem-ical- and biological-warfare agents. Did you make*

the mustard gas and the sarin, or did you buy them on the market? Also, the Charlie, Jake Hipp, has a personal message waiting for you at Hipp@Goose.Com. He says that if you wish to reply, please establish your bona fides.

Joaquin Hurtado, glowing with triumph and expectation, turned and admired his profile in the makeup mirrors in his dressing room. There was a mirror in front of him, and mirrors were set at an oblique angle on either side—all of them lined with diminutive lightbulbs. He straightened, his spine erect. He liked what he saw. He smiled at himself.

He sat and flipped on the switch to the bulbs around the mirrors. Close up, under the unsparing barrage of light, a pimple looked like Vesuvius and a wrinkle was turned into an ugly crevice. The pancake, which eliminated the flaws, gave Hurtado an unreal, corpselike appearance under the makeup lights, but he had to wear it on-camera or close shots aged him twenty years.

Hurtado loved winning. It made him feel alive and vigorous. He had risen from the barrios of East Los Angeles to this! So many adoring fans. And the women! *Ay, chijuajua!* He was amazed at his own success.

Hurtado had come to enjoy the ritual of removing his makeup. It was during this ten-minute chore of cleaning his face that A. C. Nielsen's first flash report was totaled— points on the scoreboard of life. It was Dani Bernardi's nightly chore to deliver the preliminary numbers, which in recent years had been retrieved more quickly and with more sophisticated demographics. The bottom line was still simple enough: the more viewers, the more profit; the more profit, the bigger the nick for both Hurtado and Bernardi.

Hurtado wondered how his scoop had been received in the White House. He was fascinated by the fact that as his own numbers soared, the White House favorables, recorded by Grigorich and Wells, would likely plunge. Rarely did Nielsens and political favorables rise and fall in harmony; it was as though the quantification of journalistic and political success existed in inverse proportion to one another, making them competitors on every public issue. The good news and bad news of poll numbers rose and fell like the surf. Joaquin Hurtado regarded himself as a bad-news surfer. The bigger the disaster, the bigger the thrill; covering a nerve-gas terrorist was like riding the banzai pipeline on Oahu's north shore.

Hurtado glanced at the clock on the wall and reached for the cleansing cream. He unscrewed the lid on the dark-blue jar. Empty.

He frowned and called, "Nadia!"

A slender young blonde appeared in the open door behind him. "Yes, Mr. Hurtado."

He held up the empty jar. "Every night it's the same, Nadia. I have to have this stuff or I can't get this goo off my face. You know that. I hate to be a nag, really. I don't ask for too much, do I?"

Nadia Heimbigner looked dismayed. "Sorry, Mr. Hurtado. Be right back with another jar."

Hurtado found it hard to be sore at his assistant. If his promos had delivered the viewers for his Charleston scoop and he had kept them watching to the end of the program, he stood to move well to the front of his competition. He was aware that the traditional broadcast network biggies regarded him as a lightweight. Well, let them suck these Nielsens.

Heimbigner was behind him again, bearing a full jar of cream. "Here you go, Mr. Hurtado. From now on, I'll check the jar every night. I promise. I don't know what I was thinking about."

"No problem, Nadia. Nothing bothers me in the mood I'm in. What did you think of the show?"

"It was hot, Mr. Hurtado. It truly was. Slick how you replayed the Bobby Pearl interview, then hit them with the tape the government has been keeping secret. I bet the President would like to get his hands on you."

Hurtado grinned broadly. "I just bet he would, wouldn't he?"

He unscrewed the lid and scooped out a wad of cream

with the fingers of his right hand. He closed his eyes and plastered the cream on his face. As he smeared it over the pancake, he said, "The government has known about this threat for six months. They kept it secret from the American people. They didn't tell a soul. Can you imagine? The arrogant bastards."

Hurtado did not understand the concept of irony, or if he did, he never thought it applied to him. He leaned over the sink and turned on the water. "Gotta save the best stuff for the last if you want people to stay in front of the set. Can't have 'em taking a leak or fucking on the sofa when the ratings people call."

As he washed the brownish cream from his face with hot water, Dani Bernardi arrived beside Heimbigner with a computer printout fastened to a clipboard. "Got 'em, Joaquin," she said.

Hurtado snagged a towel and began drying his face.

Bernardi teased Hurtado by deliberately making him wait.

Hurtado, his voice muffled by the towel, said, "Come on. Come on, Dani. Let's have 'em."

Bernardi grinned. "We got an eighteen, more than seventeen million households—thirty-one percent of all households."

Hurtado wadded the towel and threw it against the wall. "Yes! By God, yes! All the networks were hot on Charleston and I still kicked butt. Is Elia going to love this or what?"

"The best numbers in the history of *My Side*. I checked. The advertisers will be happy. Elia will be pleased. Good work!"

"Genuine eighteen Nielsen, seventeen-million-household butt! Hot! Can you imagine the poor damn President about now? Nadia and I were just talking about it. All those show-off favorables down the toilet. Probably puking his guts out."

"Nobody else was close to us, Joaquin. We were way, way out front."

"Ten of the largest media markets in the country on both coasts wondering if they're next on Bobby Pearl's list. And they'll all be watching us, because they know we've got hair, and they'll learn it here first. Talk about a story! Next week we'll replay the Qadhafi interview and throw in Otot Imbubwe for good measure."

In his enthusiasm, Hurtado slipped his hand between Nadia Heimbigner's legs and gave her crotch a playful grab. "The real question is not when will the government catch Bobby Pearl, but when will the goose replace the hand-shake? Right, Nadia?"

Heimbigner's face froze. She clenched her jaw.

He grinned at Dani. "Dani?"

Dani Bernardi pretended to be studying the figures on the clipboard. "Right," she said, without looking up.

Joaquin Hurtado, looking pleased with himself and with an extra spring to his step, strode from the side door of New Era's studio to a waiting limousine. Sure, maybe he wore elevator shoes, but now he was the Stud of the Western World. Killed 'em. Creamed 'em.

A tinted rear window slid down. A gorgeous blonde inside smiled up at Hurtado. "You were wonderful tonight, Joaquin. Socked it to 'em."

Hurtado grinned his famous grin, showing beautiful teeth. "A knockout. Best numbers in the history of the show."

"We should celebrate."

"Oh, yes indeed, we have to celebrate. That goes without saying," Hurtado said. "You know, hon, Nielsens like that make me really horny."

The blonde grinned. "That's the kind of talk I like to hear. I don't see any problem there."

Hurtado laughed. "I mean really horny. You know what I mean. A night like this calls for something special."

The blonde cocked her head. "I see. You naughty boy. You want I should call Veronica to join us."

Hurtado grinned. "Now you're talking. A celebration like this calls for Veronica, too. Bring along those tits of hers. No doubt about it. Double our fun."

"I'll give her a call." The blonde reached for the cell phone.

What then happened, happened in silence.

Police investigators later determined that the unknown marksman, using a silenced rifle, fired two rounds from the twentieth floor of an office building more than a quarter of a mile away. The rounds were of a type designed to shatter into multiple fragments on impact, causing maximum damage to the target.

Hurtado's head snapped back. His brains and most of his skull hit the sidewalk. *Splat!*

The blonde did not see this; she was punching Veronica's number on the phone.

Hurtado's corpse dropped to its knees.

"Veronica?" the blonde said cheerfully. Smiling, she turned toward Hurtado.

What was left of Hurtado's head disappeared. *Splat!*

The blonde blinked. What was this?

The headless corpse toppled backward onto the bloody sidewalk.

The sidewalk, splashed with happy crimson, looked like a Jackson Pollock original. It took a moment for the blonde to comprehend what had happened. Only then did she break the silence with a long, wailing scream.

The E-mail message addressed to the editors and reporters of *The New York Times, The Washington Post,* and the broadcast and cable networks, arrived twenty minutes after Joaquin Hurtado hit the pavement with a 9-mm slug in his brain:

> *To the ladies and gentlemen of the mass media,*
> *Well, now, aren't we in a pretty fix? We've got Bobby Pearl out there blowing people up and killing them with mustard gas and sarin, and you all just love it. Such a story. You've got the entire world clinging to your every word. Your Nielsens*

are soaring. Your circulations are up. You're making a fortune.

Joaquin Hurtado died with his Guccis on and his Nielsens up, that's a fact, but ask yourselves this: was Hurtado a martyr to the freedom of the press, or a greedy, uncivilized little ignoramus? This is a question we all have to confront if we are to survive as a democracy.

You obviously respond only to legal arguments. Civility, respect, and common sense don't count. Tell your readers and viewers that I am Bang, the no-more-bullshit man. Keep on jabbering and see what happens.

seventeen

As a trained observer of animal behavior, Jake Hipp had never been surprised by the permutations of the never-ending tournament. Television reporters, no less than dung beetles, sought the nourishing shit, and Joaquin Hurtado, a triumphant Nielsen warrior, had wallowed in the excrement of scandal and exposé. Sweet, sweet, sweet was the smell of fame. Hipp felt that the popularity of sports owed to their simplicity. The competition was limited, and there were rules to assure fair play. After nine innings of baseball, whichever team had scored the most runs won the game. If the teams were tied after nine innings, they kept playing until one or the other won.

The Nielsen tournament—protected by the First Amendment to the Constitution—had evolved into a free-for-all, but there were still unspoken rules. As the people's eyes and ears, reporters were exempted from the direct wrath of the players. In murdering Joaquin Hurtado, Bang had stepped way outside the bounds of fair play, threatening to destroy the tournament entirely. This was all wrong! This wasn't the way things were supposed to go. The remaining Nielsen competitors were understandably furious. They all wanted the outrageous Bang stopped pronto so they could return to the profitable story of the International Terrorist Watch and Mongoose versus Bobby Pearl.

Hipp, thinking of Bobby Pearl and Bang and the new century, was watching The NET with the sound turned off when Joe Woofter summoned him to his laptop. Hipp's military photographs were ready.

Hipp opened a bottle of Henry Weinhard's beer and began downloading the pages of photographs of soldiers from the

National Security Agency and the Defense Intelligence Agency. Each face, less than an inch square, was shown straight-on and in profile. For security reasons, each photo was identified by code; this included a number identifying the page, a letter identifying the row, and another number identifying the face. Thus NSA-16-C-2, was the second face of the third row of the sixteenth page of NSA faces. All told, Hipp was given fifty pages each of NSA and DIA faces—a total of 4,500 faces. If Hipp found a match with Bobby Pearl, it would be up to Joe Woofter to pry the identity out of the NSA or the DIA.

Hipp got out his reading glasses and began with page one, row one, of the NSA faces. He chose the National Security Agency first because the folks at Fort Meade specialized in encoding and decoding computer security systems, and they monitored communications around the world. He proceeded carefully, keeping in mind the possibility of colored contact lenses or a change in hair color and minor cosmetic surgery—a rearranged nose or the sudden appearance of a dimpled chin. With only memory to go by, this was a long shot at best. Hipp used an ink pen to mark an X over each face that he examined and excluded as being that of Bobby Pearl.

The President, with the secure cellular telephone at his ear, took a deep breath. Looking at Charlie Boso, he shook his head in disgust. He mouthed "Guess who?" and took a bite of toast.

"Let's see." Boso shrugged.

The President, chewing on the toast, began mouthing the Canadian national anthem, "Oh, Canada, Oh, Canada!"

"Elia Khardonne? Wishing us a good morning, I take it."

The President rolled his eyes. He gestured to the conference phone, inviting Boso to listen in.

"Now it starts," Boso said. He punched the on button.

Khardonne shouted, "The country can't tolerate some imbecile running around shooting television reporters. Killing the bearer of bad news won't catch Bobby Pearl. All we do is report the news. We don't make it, for Christ's sake.

I want you to get the son of a bitch who killed Joaquin Hurtado, and to get him pronto."

The President said, "Imbecile? You're calling Bang an imbecile? Just who in hell is the fucking imbecile, I want to know. You didn't call me back, Mr. Khardonne. I phoned you with a reasonable request under the circumstances. You said you would check with Hurtado and call me back. No call. I took you at your word."

"That's irrelevant now."

"Irrelevant. Is it? Secrecy is a part of war, and Bobby Pearl is roaming around on our soil with a laptop, access to nerve gas, and a warped imagination. What the hell is that if not war?"

"We're dealing with a single terrorist, or maybe a handful of terrorists at most. This is not the Red Army."

The President said, "We don't know who this is for sure, do we? If you'd listened to me, maybe Joaquin Hurtado would still be alive. But no, no, no. You just can't pass on scoring an extra buck for your wallet."

"How was I supposed to know there was some maniac out there with a high-powered rifle? You get him. We just cannot have this."

The President remained calm. "Bang is killing journalists one at a time. Pearl is taking people by the goddamn fistful. This is a kind of security triage. We use our resources to save the most lives possible."

"I want the prick who killed Joaquin Hurtado."

"You think I don't? And I want Bobby Pearl, too. I will do whatever is necessary to run that son of a bitch to ground. What do you think should be my priority? Catching the murderer of a single reporter, or someone who is killing people at random and in numbers? Listening to you, I'd have to concede that Bang at least has a motive, however twisted. Probably fancies himself a patriot, and he's not entirely wrong."

"What did you say?"

"You heard me."

Khardonne said, "You like this, don't you? This son of a bitch is doing what you'd like to do."

"I say again: whatever I have to do to get Bang and Bobby Pearl, I'll do. Never doubt that."

"Will you shoot journalists who leak government secrets? Is this what we've come to?"

"What are you saying?" The President's voice rose in anger.

Elia Khardonne was not a little sore himself. "You want to see someone with motive? Look in the mirror."

The President paused. "I tell you what, Mr. Khardonne. I have a thought here that's entirely appropriate to the situation." His voice was calm.

"Yes?"

The President murmured, "Fuck you and the horse you rode in on."

"What?"

The President shouted, "I said, 'Fuck you and the horse you rode in on,' asshole!"

"That's what I thought you said. You like that kind of talk, do you? Check out *My Side* tonight. Joaquin Hurtado might be down, but we've still got Dani Bernardi. Never, but never, underestimate a pissed-off woman. Oh, and Mr. President, don't forget to bend over while you watch."

The President hung up.

eighteen

Dani Bernardi, wearing a simple black dress, looked the camera straight-on. "Owing to the despicable murder of Joaquin Hurtado, we are departing from our weekly format tonight to give you a special edition of *My Side*. We do this so that we may honor Joaquin and to serve notice to his murderer that we will not be intimidated. As a longtime producer of *My Side*, I stand before you as a temporary and grossly inadequate substitute for a genuine American hero.

"Today, through television, we are able to communicate directly and immediately to millions of people around the globe. One thing does not change, and that is the courage and resolution of journalists who believe, as John Milton did in his famous essay *Aeropagitica*, written in sixteen forty-four, that when truth is put to the test against falsehood, truth will always prevail." Bernardi smiled grimly. "Sometimes we may wonder about that. Our faith, it seems, is put to the test almost daily.

"Joaquin rose from the barrios of East Los Angeles to the pinnacle of his profession. He fought the good fight so that the rest of us might be informed about the public events that shape and alter our lives, and for that, he was taken under by a coward." Bernardi's lower lip began to bob. Then the tears came. She wept openly and without embarrassment. Struggling to regain her composure, she swabbed the tears with her forearm.

"Sorry," she said. She straightened, eyes reddened. She clenched her jaw, looking resolved. "To quote that patriotic American, Tom Paine, this is not the time for summer soldiers and sunshine patriots. 'These are the times that try men's souls.' If we here at *My Side* did anything other than push forward in the name of truth, we would stain our good name. The truth was not just Joaquin's battle. It is yours and ours. Together, we will take the beach. Together, we will push forward. Together, we will plant our colors on the mount. First, a moment of silence for Joaquin."

She bowed her head and waited. When a minute was up, she looked directly at the camera.

"Tonight I will report on another government secret in the hunt for the terrorist Bobby Pearl—a discovery made by FBI agents at a student's apartment in Athens, Ohio, home of Ohio University. The government won't like this report made public, and neither will the misguided patriot who murdered Joaquin Hurtado. But if I sit on the truth, I would dishonor the memory of Joaquin, and that I will not do. Truth *will* prevail over falsehood. Truth *will* triumph over secrecy. Now is when we stand tall and defend our right in a free, open, and democratic government—the right to the truth. The latest secret, revealed by confidential sources in the Justice Department, after this message."

Bernardi was replaced by three commercials and one NET promo. The first commercial was of a middle-aged man tormented by hemorrhoids. His answered prayer was an ointment called "Cease." The second ad, surely a new miracle, was for fatless potato chips, better than previous brands that caused diarrhea in some people; a skinny rube wearing coveralls stuffed fistfuls of potato chips into his mouth, saying, "Hog them babies down." The third was for GM's new electric car being offered to urban commuters at what was touted as an affordable price; a prosperous-looking suit with a briefcase slipped behind the wheel of the car while his envious neighbor started up a gas-guzzling barge. The promo was for NET's Sunday-night news special on Internet theft.

Then Dani Bernardi was back. Facing the camera, her chin high with pride, she said, "Listen to this, whoever killed Joaquin Hurtado. You will not stop us. From unimpeachable sources, *My Side* has learned that the FBI, acting on an anonymous tip, today searched the apartment of an Israeli student, Avi Feuer, at Ohio University in Athens, about a sixty-minute drive from Charleston, West Virginia. Feuer, it turns out, is the younger brother of the fast-rising Likud politician, Kimi Feuer, who remains incensed at the forced Israeli withdrawal from Hebron and the Jewish settlements on the West Bank.

"What did investigators find? Well, for one thing, they found an empty canister of the type used to hold chemical and biological warfare agents; this canister was fitted with a remote releasing device. For another, they found a piece of paper sewn in the waistband of underwear found in Feuer's closet, giving detailed instructions, in Hebrew, on how to get to a Mossad safe house in the Virginia suburbs of Washington, D.C. Mossad is the Israeli counterpart of the CIA. This raises the question: Is Bobby Pearl an agent of Mossad?

"Why would the Israelis sponsor terrorist attacks on American soil? One obvious possibility is that Zionist hardliners are bent on destroying Arab attempts to rehabilitate themselves in the court of public opinion. But *My Side* sources say the administration isn't buying that logic. The search of Feuer's apartment was the result of an anonymous tip that investigators from the International Terrorist Watch believe was planted in a sick attempt to sow confusion. But was it? Who on earth would go to the effort of planting something like that? Bobby Pearl? Not likely, say our sources.

"Those questions and more are tormenting investigators from the International Terrorist Watch today as they fan out from Charleston, West Virginia, looking for clues to the elusive Bobby Pearl. *My Side* would like to add one more question: Is the International Terrorist Watch avoiding the unspeakable truth for fear of offending the powerful Israeli lobby in Washington?"

When the *My Side* newscast was over and Dani Bernardi had given the administration another salvo of truth in the name of Joaquin Hurtado, she strode from the set, making her way amid the cheers and unabashed weeping of the studio crew. As those present would later say, they all felt proud and part of a team. They were soldiers of truth. Together with Dani Bernardi, they had given the murderous Bang an in-your-face demonstration that they would not be intimidated.

Nadia Heimbigner, herself fighting back tears of pride, followed Bernardi into the dressing room for the post-show removal of makeup, as had been her ritual chore when Hurtado was alive.

NET's security cameras tracked Heimbigner's exit a few minutes later. One camera recorded the opening of Bernardi's dressing-room door. Heimbigner stepped out, her face giving no indication that anything was wrong. A second camera taped her walking down the hall. A third caught her leaving the building.

As she left, the camera outside Bernardi's dressing room recorded the door as it erupted outward. That tape, later a staple on television newscasts, suddenly ended as the camera was knocked out of action.

The reverberating blast plunged the production stage into darkness. NET directors and production assistants, stunned, stood in momentary silence. At the time, nobody knew for certain where the explosion had taken place. Seconds later, the studio's emergency electrical generators kicked in, lighting those areas not destroyed by the eruption.

NET security guards quickly found the center of the explosion, Dani Bernardi's dressing room, although there was virtually nothing left of it. Ms. Bernardi herself had been all but evaporated. The only evidence that she had existed were traces of blood, hair, and bone on the debris that the FBI later studied for evidence of the nature of the explosive device.

It was immediately clear that Joaquin Hurtado's murder had not been a one-time shot by a psychopath. Bang obviously meant what he said. He was a no-more-bullshit man. The demolition of Dani Bernardi's dressing room had transformed the public theater of American journalism into a terrifying theater-in-the-round. The narrators, no longer offstage, had become one with the players.

nineteen

The Federal Government and the airline industry, not wanting to annoy passengers with lengthy searches and delays, had stonewalled the touchy and expensive question of security for years until TWA Flight 800 went down off Long Island in 1996. Until then, the public had preferred to believe that airliners were bombed only in places inhabited by Jews or people who spoke English with a British or an Irish accent. As the new century began, the times they were a-changing—airport security along with everything else.

Food and drink were traditionally outrageously expensive at airports, part of a coarse and calculated screwing of travelers, who were captive consumers. In such circumstances, the much-touted benefits of competition did not apply. The delays in airport terminals following increased security—holding hungry and thirsty travelers like restless penned cattle—had meant boom time for the unembarrassed concessionaires.

In the Los Angeles International Airport, Elephant Dan Merrill and Slick Smith paid no attention to the jolly racket. For the first time in their lives, they had the long green to buy whatever they wanted, never mind the price. They were in a cheery mood as they drank overpriced Gibsons in one of the airport's many passengers' lounges, watching the news on television. The public was locked onto the stories of Bobby Pearl and Bang that had momentarily brought the republic to its figurative knees.

When religious nutballs had released sarin in Tokyo's subways in the early nineties the Americans hadn't especially cared. Their attitude had been that the Japanese, then paying five times the world price for rice rather than buying it from the Thais or from farmers in Arkansas or California, richly deserved a hit of nerve gas. Greedy little scumbags. Now that Pearl had released sarin in Charleston, West Virginia, U.S. of A., Americans were going ballistic, their emotion matched only by that of television reporters, themselves under siege by Bang. The reporters were torn between focusing on Pearl, who was wasting their viewers, or on Bang, who was wasting them. Judging by their reaction, Bang, for the moment at least, was the more outrageous of the two.

Watching all this, Slick Smith was much amused. "Wait'll New York. They think a little sarin is bad. Just wait and see."

Merrill gave a quick squeal. "This is funner than splashin' seagulls, eh, Slick?"

Smith laughed. "Do onto others whatever brings in the green. Now you're talking. Remember, I'm Slick Smith. You can't lose by sticking with Slick Smith. No way. Just ain't gonna happen."

Merrill, eyeing the tube, pursed his lips. "Guy out there wasting television assholes. Don't you just love watchin' them fuckers squirm? They're all for watching the shit hit the fan as long as they're at a safe distance. But now their butts're on the line." He looked amused. "You know, these little pickled onions are sweet to suck on and everything, but we ought to be drinking manhattans. What're they made out of, Slick?"

"Manhattans? Whiskey and vermouth."

"Maybe we ought to drink us a toast to Bang, a gentleman with a sense of justice."

Smith grinned. "Oh, hell yes. He richly deserves a proper toast." Smith caught the bartender's eye. "We'll have a couple of manhattans, please."

"Gonna drink us a toast to Bang," Merrill said.

Smith laughed. "A hero of the people. Gotta give the man his due. Show our esteem and high regard."

"For his stellar accomplishments," Merrill added quickly.

The bartender, a tall, bald man wearing a white shirt and red bow tie, gave them a half-smile. Glancing up at the television, he said, "A toast to Bang? Can you gentlemen handle doubles? You're flying, aren't you? Not driving."

Merrill trumpeted loudly. "Oh, hell yes. We're flying. And you're right. Got to have doubles for a proper toast."

"One for the elephant. One for his friend. On the house," the bartender said. He glanced up at the television set, shaking his head in disgust, then set to work preparing two extra-large manhattans.

Jake Hipp studied the face on the screen of his laptop. David Wong, a middle-aged, round-faced man with tidy pouches under his eyes and a neat little mouth with Cupid lips, was communicating from Darwin, at the top end of Australia. Hipp didn't have to be told that M-I6 had provided Wong with some form of commercial cover that gave him good reason to go in and out of Australia, and that Darwin had a large population of Chinese.

On the screen, the amiable Wong wrote: *You're thinking of Dr. Wu Feng, a plastic surgeon of admirable skill and negligible ethics. We watched him for about ten years, but had to drop our surveillance when Beijing took over.*

Hipp took a sip of coffee, and typed back: *Do you have photographs of his former clients?*

He waited for the answer.

Those before June 1997. For what it's worth, the women all say he's a tit man non pareil. *Lots of actresses running around with Wu boobs.*

Hipp smiled. Pearl would likely have been a post-Beijing client. He typed: *June 1997 is too early for my snake. I have a series of photographs of cigar smokers taken in a bar in Cebu City. Could you download these pictures and see if any of them strike you as familiar?*

Sure. Send them along. Always glad to help our American cousins.

Hipp called up the first photographs from the memory of his laptop, a frontal and a profile of a man standing at a urinal, and sent it on its way. He was about to call the second picture up when a message popped onto the screen.

I recognize the books. Lots of Penguins. Both Alice in Wonderland *and* Leaves of Grass *within arm's reach of the porcelain throne. Most Hipp. You own that bar, if I'm not mistaken.*

Hipp smiled and tapped a quick reply. *It's mine.* Actually, Most Hipp was in Gina's name. It was against the law for foreigners to own property in the Philippines.

Gina's a little beauty. Lucky you.

Hipp clenched his jaw. Yes, lucky Jake Hipp. If a passing M-I6 agent knew that Gina Jumero was his girlfriend, Bobby Pearl almost certainly knew too. Had to. Thinking of his latest challenge to Pearl, Hipp felt a rush of anxiety. Had he gone too far?

There had been enough threats by psychopaths in the past that the main entrance to the CNN studios in Atlanta, a heavy glass door, was closed to unescorted visitors. Owing to time zones, the weekday prime-television time—when a live program could be watched by the maximum viewers on both coasts—occurred on swing shift, from 9:00 P.M. to 10:00 P.M. On weekends, this was shifted to 4:00 P.M. to 9:00 P.M. During the weekday swing, the main entrance was locked and unlocked by Selena Williams, an attractive young black woman who performed her duty from the safety of a bulletproof glass booth. A camera above the glass door taped the entrance of all persons going inside.

CNN employees and those ascertained by Williams to have a valid reason to proceed into the building were required to step through a metal detector operated by a security guard. The metal detector screened for hidden weapons. The security guard on the weekday swing was Matthew Greene, formerly a police officer in Marietta, Georgia.

Only after receiving a go-ahead nod from Greene did Williams punch the button that unlocked the door. If for any reason Greene was challenged or she was suspicious, she punched a button that silently summoned the Atlanta police.

In the aftermath of The NET killings in Los Angeles, Williams and Greene were joined by two helmeted security officers wearing bulletproof vests, bearing shotguns, and presumably pumped with testosterone. The alarm button in Williams' booth was changed to both call the cops and trigger an ear-piercing siren that did everything short of shatter glass.

But Selena Williams did not question the familiar-looking redheaded man who strode cheerily in from the sidewalk, digging his picture I.D. from his wallet. "Evening, Bill," she said.

Carl Czez smiled and put away his I.D. "Another day. Another dollar."

Czez stepped past the helmeted guards and through the metal detector; as he did, the lock on the glass door clicked open.

twenty

As he turned to yet another page of faces, Jake Hipp began thinking about psychologist Carl Jung's pioneering attempt to describe what were obvious differences in the way individuals relate to the world around them. Jung's observations were later transformed into tests purportedly measuring aptitude, by which the military services determined career paths for both officers and enlisted men. The idea was to match individuals with work that they were naturally suited to by temperament and that would give them the most satisfaction. Hipp knew that IBM and other corporations used variations of the same measure.

There were Jungian psychologists in T-Cell who had incorporated some of Jung's ideas in profiling terrorists, but Hipp felt that their attempts at profiling were largely misguided in that they attempted to answer the "why" of aberrant behavior. Following the assertions of Freud, and conceding to politically fashionable cultural concerns, child abuse was high on their list of the root causes of aberrant behavior. But Carl Jung—more popularly known for his theories of the collective subconscious—was in this case not after "why." "What" was good enough for him. He regarded Freud's fancy lingo as a pretentious attempt to appear scientific, and so went the opposite way, using straightforward terms whenever possible. And although there were extreme personality types, most individuals—following the statistical laws of the bell-shaped curve—were somewhere in the middle.

Hipp, a sometime-watercolorist, had always regarded the spectrum as the colors of personality. Each person had different colors on his or her palette. There were earthy people—all ochres and umbers. There were hot people—oranges and yellows and reds. There were cool people—Payne's gray. Hipp regarded himself as Hooker's green.

Jung first developed a series of questions seeking to determine whether an individual was more extroverted or introverted—those who flourished in the company of people, and those who were most comfortable by themselves. In the extreme, these were party animals and couch potatoes. He assigned E to extroversion and I to introversion.

His second group of questions sought to determine whether an individual was more comfortable with the exterior world of sensation—color, smell, sound—or preferred the internal world of ideas. These he labeled sensates and intuitives. In the extreme, these were clotheshorses and bookworms. He designated the former by an S and the latter by an N so as not to repeat the I of the extrovert-introvert axis.

He later added a third line of questions, seeking to discover whether or not a personality was dominated by emotion or intellect. This was the F-T axis, for feeling and thinking. This axis was controversial, inasmuch as there appeared to be clear differences in test scores between genders. Women tended to be Fs and men Ts. Women tended to have higher verbal abilities than men, for which there were evolutionary explanations.

Jung's final measure was whether a person was more comfortable in familiar territory or was adaptable to new experience and ideas. Cs knew what they liked and stuck with it, whereas Ps were open to the possible. The ranks of cops and judges were filled with Cs, who valued order and tradition. Extreme Cs became ideologues and flag-waving patriots. Ps, avoiding intellectual or personal closure, were uncomfortable with cant and dogma; the rolls of artists and writers were heavy with Ps.

Hipp had taken a sophisticated version of Jung's test when he was recruited by Mongoose, and Joe Woofter, knowing he would be interested, had shared the results with him. It turned out that Hipp was an INTP, meaning he was an introverted, intuitive, open-minded intellectual. Introverted didn't mean he couldn't deal with people. He wasn't a recluse; he simply preferred privacy over crowds. The solitary INTP, commonplace in the academic world, loved to build intellectual systems, which is why Hipp was initially assigned to the T-Cell think tank. Comfortable with new experience and ways of thinking, Hipp found expatriate living congenial, and was undeterred by the cross-cultural adjustments necessary in having a Filipina girlfriend. He did not require meat and potatoes at every meal. Fish and rice were fine by him.

Hipp's profile wasn't surprising; once, reading Jung while under the influence of cannabis, Hipp had had the eerie feeling that he was reading himself—Jung's style and choice of vocabulary was nearly identical to his own. He later learned that Carl Jung too was an INTP.

While the language of these personality types remained clear, they were basically descriptive and nothing more. For most of the twentieth century, the tantalizing *why* of their formation proved elusive. What was the biological kiln that had forged both defenders of orthodoxy and revolutionaries, plodders and risk takers?

The answer, in Hipp's opinion, almost certainly lay in the fires of sibling rivalry, that is, in birth order. Over the years, research had shown that firstborns and lastborns showed remarkably different personality traits. Oldests were almost always Carl Jung's Cs, defenders of the status quo and leading candidates for cops, military officers, judges, bureaucrats, and in extreme cases, reactionaries of one sort or another. Youngest were Jung's Ps, open and flexible, given to new ideas— scientists, artists, writers, and in the extreme, revolutionaries. Hipp knew without checking it out that Clint Eastwood was almost certainly an oldest and David Letterman a youngest.

Hipp had always suspected that birth order was given short shrift by academics because it was too obvious. There were few obscure journal articles to be had by rehashing an observation that was so straightforward and logical, namely, that people appeared to spend their entire lives using the tactics that had enabled them to survive the trials of childhood. Finally, at the close of the century, scholars, in an *oh-my-God-really?* burst of enthusiasm, began describing and detailing a truth that was obvious to all grandmothers throughout the millennia. There were even nursery rhymes and folktales based on the observation.

The pecking order of siblings evolved around birth order. The firstborns, logically defending the system and their position at the top, were given to solemnity and seriousness, the stuff of a conservative imagination. The later-born cutups and wild ones logically challenged the order. It thus turned out that second-, third-, or lastborns, successively more open and flexible, had more in common with other second-, third-, or lastborns than they did with their own brothers and sisters. Extreme types, predictably, were the oldest sons and daughters of oldest parents, and youngest sons and daughters of youngest parents.

Writers were soon able to predict the birth order of historically famous figures with stunning accuracy, and one scholar even charted the succeeding waves of rebellion in the French Revolution, led, it turned out, by later-borns and youngests. Researchers ultimately found two wild cards in their studies. One was shyness, which apparently was an inherited characteristic. The other was the only child, or one separated from an older or younger sibling by ten years; the experience of being an only child resulted in an unpredictable mix of personality traits.

Right-wing reactionaries tended to be oldest; left-wing radicals tended to be youngests. The purpose, discipline, and loyalty trilogy of Bobby Pearl's warnings was the telltale bleat of an oldest, uncomfortable in the presence of change and new ideas.

Jake Hipp, ten years younger than his brother, was effectively an only child. As such, he was an anomaly among Charlies, who were almost all oldests or high up in the birth order. T-Cell, on the other hand, was heavy with creative later-born and youngest intellectuals, given to challenging the status quo. He had originally been placed in T-Cell as a result of testing, a standard CIA and Mongoose practice. He had been made a Charlie only by the personal intervention of Joe Woofter, a personal friend who thought there were advantages in career mix and match. Woofter liked to say that making Hipp a Charlie was like Stanley Kubrick casting Slim Pickens as the red-hot B-52 pilot in *Dr. Strangelove*.

T-Cell scholars felt that Bobby Pearl was most likely an ISTC or an ESTC. He was almost certainly an oldest, and maybe even the oldest son of an oldest father. Hipp agreed.

The quiet men of action in the movies, archetypal warriors, were almost all ISTCs—from early movie defenders of faith and hearth such as Gary Cooper, Randolph Scott, and John Wayne to later heroes such as Sylvester Stallone, Arnold Schwarzenegger, and Chuck Norris. The anomalous Indiana Jones character, the adventurous archaeologist played by Harrison Ford—a man who knew how to laugh at himself—was closer to Hipp's own INTP profile.

As Hipp went from photograph to photograph, thinking of the man he had seen on the ferry and sitting at the table in Tangier, he wondered: what was the profile of the man who had become his nemesis? Did Bobby Pearl exhibit the extreme in any of Jung's measures, or like most people, did he reflect the sensible middle of the bell-shaped curve?

Pearl apparently operated solo, which would indicate introversion, but an extreme I was an unlikely candidate for undertaking such a complicated task as buying sarin on the international market. Mongoose knew nothing about Pearl's past. The man could very well have had an occupation requiring him to administer or supervise, which would require E skills. Hipp mentally put him in the middle, comfortable alone or in a group.

Pearl's personal tidiness meant that he was likely a soft S, as reflected by his preference for the exterior. He shined his shoes and got regular haircuts, and although he was a master of cyberspace, he didn't look like the archetypal nerd.

Pearl's rage at whatever real or imagined slight he felt he had suffered from Hipp suggested that he was dominated by emotion. For whatever reason, he was furious enough at Hipp to go out of his way to embarrass him on *My Side*. He was enough of a T to negotiate the complicated world of buying and selling NBC, so give him a soft F.

Passionate Cs tended to have Manichean imaginations—preferring clear-cut whites and blacks, rights and wrongs. A terrorist ordinarily struck for the same reasons cops and FBI agents defended; both saw themselves as defenders of God or country. Until he knew more about Pearl, Hipp felt compelled to assign him a hard C. The word *diversity,* which had been corrupted by political code, might well stand for the Ps, who were comfortable with social, cultural, and sexual differences.

Humans were cooperative predators, and over the millennia, the survival of the species had depended in large part on the willingness of individuals to sacrifice themselves for the greater good. In modern times, this urge to belong translated into an oftentimes rabid identification with groups—everything from place to race, religion to political parties. In one famous extreme case, when a homogeneous culture believed itself to be contained and threatened, this natural identification with group had expressed itself as the National Socialist German Workers Party in Germany during the 1930s.

Who would find it easier to pull the trigger at Tangier, an ISFC or an INTP?

Hipp thought almost certainly an ISFC, although this did not mean ISFCs were bad people. Given the human condition, armies and soldiers were necessary, but passionate ISFCs were simultaneously capable of being heroes or saints.

Hipp felt that his imagination had been so abuzz with moral and ethical questions at the critical moment in Tangier—reflecting his preference for the intellect over physical action—that he had been unable to act.

Then he saw him.

There on the page.

The fair-complexioned blond man, Bobby Pearl.

NSA photograph 3-E-3 stared straight at him.

* * *

Carl Czez restrained himself from wadding up *USA Today*. The editors of McPaper had clearly lost their goddamn minds. They had put Jake Hipp's horseshit E-mail message, boxed, on the front page. Front page! The entire country was now in a frenzy of gossip, speculating about Czez's sex life, or possible lack of it. Eager shrinks and excited callers on every chickenshit radio and television talk show were offering two-bit theories. A nation of bored morons!

There was no doubting that this was Hipp's idea of payback for the Philippine interview. And the business about Greta's long legs at the end was too damn much. Hipp had deliberately gone tit for tat, challenging Czez. Just killing the son of a bitch wouldn't be an adequate reply. Czez would have to come up with something better than that. He was thinking about Hipp's girlfriend, the sweet, sexy Gina in Cebu City, when he saw another sexy lady—an earth mama, she was—sitting across from him in The Lavender Goose.

Had she been watching him out of the corner of her eye, or was Carl Czez only imagining it? Imagining it probably, but until he found out for sure, he wasn't going back to his hotel.

She was in her late twenties, maybe twenty-seven or twenty-eight, sitting directly under the lavender goose on the wall for which the tavern was named. She had a slightly rounded body. In another ten years, she would be fat, but now she was a voluptuary. Properly finished off with a sheen of sweat, she'd be a sweet little seal, all hot and slippery and smelling grand. She wore a simple cotton dress with a low bodice that displayed a sensational pair of knockers. No need for a push-'em-up to display these tits. They were the real deal.

She had pale white skin, huge, flirtatious brown eyes that were alive with curiosity. Her mane of black hair tumbled over her bare shoulders. She was a grinner and an obvious lover of life, given to wonderful haw-haw-haw peals of laughter as she jabbered and gossiped with her two women friends. When she laughed, her entire face mirrored joy. Her eyes sparkled. She had a good set of white teeth, and full, sensuous lips. Loni Anderson lips, they were.

Carl Czez knew her jugs would really hop and bounce if a man slammed his sausage into her good and proper. It had been years since Czez had encountered a pair of genuine rock-and-roll tits. He groaned audibly and took another sip of Heineken's.

She looked at him straight-on. Had she heard him groan? Yes, she had, and she liked it. She cocked her head. She grinned broadly, teasing him with her eyes. She draped a languid hand over her left breast and took her lower lip between her teeth, a naughty little nip.

Czez couldn't help but smile. A hormonal little wench she was, and she was obviously in a playful mood.

Should he, or shouldn't he?

There had been a time when the answer was always should. Then, for some inexplicable reason, the maddening shouldn't-haves had made their ugly appearance. It had started out with one devastating shouldn't for each three or four triumphant shoulds. This was a worrisome turn of events, but not a show-stopper. Slowly, however, the ratio had pulled even. As the months dragged into years, the ratio was reversed; there were two or three shouldn'ts to one should, and Czez became haunted by the sick dread that the day would come when the shoulds failed to return. The anxiety twisted his stomach. Where there had once been confidence, there was now doubt, lingering fear.

But this one was a definite should. Had to be. Those tits of hers! He winked at her.

This elicited a haw-haw-haw peal of laughter.

The groan. The biting of the lip. The wink. The laughter. Their communication was complete. She stood and walked right toward Czez's booth, her hips rolling, her body all round and pneumatic under the cotton dress. No embarrassment for this lover of life. She had a me-girl, you-boy kind of imagination. Her girlfriends watched her with a grin and not a little admiration. She knew what she wanted and went for it.

She was definitely a should. No doubt about it.

Stopping at his booth, she said, "I saw you watching me."

"Hard not to," Czez said.

"I heard you groan."

Czez smiled. "I like girls with rock-and-roll bodies."

"And I like good-looking older men."

"I see."

"No bellies though. No couch potatoes. No pasty-pale skin. And they gotta have eyes that've seen before. More fun than wannabes with fuzz on their cheeks. When boys think rock-and-roll, they've got guitars on their minds. I like men."

Czez grinned.

"Ain't seen you in here before." Her eyes danced. She liked having fun.

"First time," he said.

"You from here in Atlanta?"

"Just got in from the coast."

"California! Cool." She smiled broadly.

"You like a Heineken?" He caught the waiter's attention and tapped his bottle and held up two fingers. It had been years since he had encountered one this straightforward. She was a should. There was absolutely no goddam doubt about it.

"Better than draft beer with the girls." She took a seat opposite him. "Tell me, what kind of girls have you had in your band?"

He shrugged. "All kinds. Chinese girls with skin like silk. Black girls with spankable butts."

"Spankable butts?" She cocked her head.

"Gotta be done right. Warm 'em up a little. Make 'em bounce."

She laughed, watching him with her lively brown eyes. "I bet you're going to tell me experience is the thing."

"That's exactly right. You like to try that out?"

"Maybe. If it's done right."

"It'll juice you right up, guaranteed. My name is Frank."

She leaned back and let it rip. *Haw-haw-haw!* "Oh, yes. The name thing. Donna."

twenty-one

Jake Hipp, listening to the rain beat *ka-slap, ka-slap, ka-slap* against the window of his cabin, used his toes to push his unlaced, wet boots onto the floor. If Gina had been there, she would have howled at his sloppiness. The Filipinos, one of the planet's poorest peoples, were also one of the cleanest.

Outside, the wind whipped the salt grass on top of the dunes just in from the broad beach. The darkening clouds above the Pacific roiled and boiled and rolled, pushing more rain onto the water-soaked coastline. Hipp had heard people say they couldn't stand rain, yet they put up with cold in the winter that made their lips stick together if they weren't careful. There was no better place on the planet to hunt wild mushrooms on the Pacific Northwest coast in October and November.

The phone rang. He knew intuitively that it was Joe Woofter.

He took a sip of coffee and used his shoulder to hold the receiver against his ear. "Joe?"

"Me."

"Quick work. What did you find?"

Woofter said, "You picked a real humdinger of an adversary, I'll give you that. He leave an answer on your E-mail yet?"

"Not yet. Come on. Come on. You did get an I.D., I take it. Who is he?"

"Fun making you wait. We got a name, but it was like pulling teeth. Nobody wants to admit somebody like this was one of theirs. Oh, no, no, no! Not one of us. Couldn't be."

"Can't say as I blame them," Hipp said. "Let's hear it."

"Bobby Pearl's real name is Carl Allen Czez. He is

divorced. No children. His parents are both dead, and he has a younger brother, Jerry, who's a comic-book artist. His father was a professor of military history at Louisiana State University, and his mother, who was in her early forties when he was born, was once an executive secretary to the governor of Louisiana. He is a graduate of a Catholic high school in Baton Rouge, and of The Citadel in Charleston, South Carolina, where he was captain of the shooting team and graduated second in his class. He tests two standard deviations above the mean in cognitive ability."

"Jesus Christ!"

Woofter said, "A duty, honor, and country kind of guy. He may be demented, but there's no denying he's smart as hell. He is now fifty years old. He retired from the army four years ago as a bird colonel after an exemplary career that was cut short by personal tragedy, which is putting it mildly. He studied Spanish at the Defense Language Institute in Monterey, California, and computer science at California Polytechnic Institute, at San Luis Obispo. When he retired, he was commander of a classified unit at the National Security Agency at Fort George G. Meade, Maryland. This unit, comprised of the best civilian hackers money can buy, was in charge of electronic eavesdropping on the communications of both individuals and governments abroad."

"Oh? Which individuals and what governments would that be?"

"Czez's unit was following the money trail of arms merchants and people dealing NBC. His hackers became experts on electronic money transfers. The arms dealers included French, Belgians, Brazilians, and Italians, mostly, selling everything from FAL assault rifles to land mines. The government officials included Iraqis, Iranians, North Koreans—"

"And Libyans and Sudanese."

"Yes, those too. Also Chinese bureaucrats and Russian mobsters of various stripes. The commander at first didn't want to tell me any of this, but when I asked him if he'd like us to hold a press conference and explain to the public why he didn't want to help us identify Bobby Pearl, he relented."

"A spirited public servant. You say Colonel Czez retired. Where does the government send his retirement pay?"

"To an account in Laurel, Maryland. He pays his taxes by computer and invests his money by computer, but doesn't spend any of it."

"No?"

"Not a dime."

Hipp took a hit of beer. "Doesn't want the money traced. How does he support himself?"

"The security systems in Switzerland or the Cayman Islands would be a piece of cake for him. Go figure."

"He likely steals it. And likely steals what he needs to buy g-agents and biologicals from whoever is his supplier."

"That's the way we see it. The banks have improved the security of their data systems over the years, but Czez's NSA unit was on top of every change. The people at Meade tell me it's entirely possible that he knows enough about his unit's system to have continued monitoring its data after he retired. It would cost the army a fortune to reprogram its software after each body moves on."

"And the personal tragedy?" Through the window of his cabin, Hipp watched the wind whip the salt grass on the sand dunes into a fury.

Woofter said, "This is likely the psychic irritant of your pearl theory, Jake. Czez's wife Angelina, a.k.a. Angie, nee Dunn, was having an affair with his executive officer, a Major George R. Hollins, who was his longtime best friend. Czez and Hollins went on hunting trips together: razorbacks in Arkansas, antelope in Wyoming, elk in Montana, mule deer in Oregon, and grizzlies in Alaska. When Czez found out about the affair, he confronted Hollins in the Officers' Club. An ugly brawl ensued. Two days later, Angie and Hollins disappeared. Hollins's car was found parked on a side street in Norfolk, Virginia, but neither he nor Czez's wife were seen or heard from again."

"Oops!"

"Oops big time, Jake. The military held an inquiry. It was ascertained that the affair between Angie and Hollins was an open secret at Fort Meade, but there was no evidence of foul play, and no bodies. Six months later, Czez, still under a cloud of suspicion, resigned his commission and left the service. We're in the process of running down people who knew him, but so far, we haven't found anybody who has had contact with him since then."

"He just vanished."

"Just like Angie and Hollins. That's right. A genius. A marksman. Fluent in Spanish and Arabic. A computer whiz who may have gotten away with a double murder. Although we've just started our investigation, we're getting a clear idea of what he was all about—at least on the surface. The people in his unit all say the same thing. He was smart as hell. He was disciplined—spit and shine all the way. He worked hard. He was ambitious in the extreme. He was on General Schwartzkopf's staff in the Gulf War. He had served a tour of duty as a security advisor to the joint chiefs of staff in the Pentagon before he was moved to Fort Meade. His NSA unit was a special project for the Pentagon, which had long been worried about NBC on the market. Money was the secret, it was felt."

"No secret there," Hipp said. "Well, there we have it: the irritant that formed the pearl. He's a hard C. Nothing worse than a hard C oldest gone wrong."

"What's that?"

"Nothing," Hipp said. "Tell me about his father. Oldest or youngest?"

"Oldest. Carl is the oldest of an oldest. In fact, we're talking three generations of oldests, which has your old T-Cell pals grinning."

"An archetypal defender of orthodoxy. His brother hear from him?"

"Not a word. They were never close in the best of times, and it's been more than ten years since they last talked. Jerry draws a popular series of comic books called *Loopies,* which is a kind of modern Beetle Bailey poking fun at military types. Carl took offense, to put it mildly. Jerry even has a character named Colonel Cornbrain."

Hipp smiled. "A little sibling rivalry there. *Loopies*. Good for Jerry."

"Jerry lives in your part of the world, as it turns out. In Astoria, Oregon. His wife is an artist."

"Astoria's only a half-hour drive from here. I get first dibs."

"I thought you'd say that. Go for it. When you're finished, we'll talk to him again and see if there's anything you missed."

"I take it Carl Czez was on his way to the top when the proverbial shit hit the fan."

"He was on a clear track to become a brigadier general when his wife disappeared, yes."

Hipp thought for a moment. "So he would know who was dealing in chemical and biological warfare agents, and how to contact them. All the details."

"Correct. The names of the operatives and runners, the salesmen. And remember, Jake, the original intercept that took you to Tangier was between a Sudanese in Spain and the Sudanese Embassy in Washington. Colonel Czez would have known better than to risk that. Somebody else's mistake put us on to him, not his. He's probably still swearing at the stupid Sudanese."

Hipp, looking at the surf crashing onto the beach in the distance, said nothing.

"Well, what do you think, Sherlock?"

"I think we still don't know who sold the BCs to him, or why. I also think he's Bang."

"You think what? Bang?"

Hipp said, "I always wondered why Pearl would take a chance on the interview in the Philippines. I know he wanted to brag a little and strut his stuff. But there are risks in letting people see what you look like. Dani Bernardi said he wouldn't allow a production crew to be present, only Joaquin Hurtado and one other person."

"Herself."

"She taped the interview. Besides me, only Hurtado and Bernardi ever set eyes on Bobby Pearl. Now they're both dead. Go figure."

Woofter thought about that for a moment. "Good enough logic as far as it goes, I suppose. There's only one flaw. He almost certainly knows that you own Most Hipp, and he likely knows about Gina. All the regulars there know you, or about you. By letting you live, he has given you an opportunity to identify his photograph, which you have done. Why are you still alive?"

"We call these assholes snakes partly because snakes shed their skins. A Charlie sees him. You want to tell me his logical next step?"

"He molts."

"Same snake. New skin. What Joaquin and Dani knew was not just his physical exterior. He could change that. But what if they had picked up on some telltale nonverbal clue? Aren't you always nagging your Charlies to detail personal tics in their ARs? 'Character,' you're always saying. 'Give me character.' Judging from what we've found out about him, Bobby Pearl sure as hell isn't a dummy. I say he'll murder at least one more journalist to maintain the fiction of Bang, the pissed-off patriot. He was a career military officer. He likes a tidy barracks. Everything in its place."

Woofter fell momentarily silent. Then he said, "He probably considers journalists loose cannons. I see what you mean."

"Didn't Mongoose have reports of a plastic surgeon in Hong King who was altering faces for anyone with enough money to make his fee? What if Pearl availed himself of the services of the good doctor? Lots of places in Asia to hole up in while your face heals. The Philippines is one of them."

"I still don't understand why he would want to torment you."

"We been through this before, Joe."

"Because of the German girl?"

Hipp said, "Colonel Czez is a sophisticated baboon with fancy medals on his chest. He thinks Greta Mann and I were laughing at him. He thinks I somehow deprived him of his honor, so he lets me have it in his Joaquin Hurtado interview—the intellectual Charlie who couldn't pull the trigger. But I didn't take it lying down, I struck back. Now he hates me with a vengeance. His demented next step is what, Joe?"

"Beats hell out of me, but if I were you, I believe I'd sleep with my eyes open and eat with my back to a corner."

She wasn't a professional. She did it because she liked it, and she hadn't asked questions when he had taken her to a hotel that wasn't found in any tourist's guidebook. Watching him with a half-smile in the dim light, she took the hem of her dress in her hands. The neon sign outside washed her body with alternating green, yellow, and red.

Lying back on the bed, Carl Czez knew without a doubt that she was a should. And yet . . .

She turned, and in a single fluid motion, pulled the dress up and over her body. She was wearing black bikini underpants and a black bra. She arched her back and poked her butt out at him as she reached behind to unsnap the bra. "Spankable stuff, you think, Frank?" She tossed the bra away and gave herself a slap on the butt.

"Nice ass," Czez said. He gripped his cock, which rose swift and sure. All right!

She slipped off her underpants.

He gave her a pop on the butt. She squealed in delight. "Oh, you!" She turned, cupping her breasts in the palms of her hands.

A should. Still . . . He said, "Nice. I'm wondering about the tips of those things. Brown or pink?"

She grinned, still cupping her breasts. "Brown. You like brown?"

He smiled. "Dimes or dollars?" There would be no problem here. No, no, no. Sexy Donna was a guaranteed should.

She removed her hands. Enormous brown nipples. Bigger than Eisenhower silvers.

"Those things boogie, do they? Up and down. Up and down."

She smiled. "You bet."

He gave her right tit a gentle forehand and backhand. Bounce. Bounce. She made a little sound in her throat.

He reached out and rolled her nipples between his thumbs and forefingers.

She made another noise in her throat. "I'll give you six weeks to stop that."

He licked his lips. "Fun?"

She bit her lower lip. "Uh-huh."

He slipped his left hand between her legs and deftly, lightly, traced her cleft with his middle finger.

"Ooooooo. You wicked, wicked man," she said. She gently undulated her pelvis.

He worked her gently. She closed her eyes. She shuddered.

"Well, that didn't take much," he said. Talk about a should!

"Never does."

"Can you do that again, or are you a one-time girl?"

Her body tightened again. She sucked in her breath. "All night long," she said.

He rolled her onto the bed and parted her legs.

"Make 'em really rock and roll," she whispered.

He got set to slip it in. It was as though he were outside of himself, watching himself. This was a mistake. He knew not to do that. He knew precisely what to do, and this wasn't it. Concentrate on the girl. Go with the flow. Let it happen. But no. His mind was abuzz. Instead of fucking, he thought about fucking.

Then it happened.

Again.

It wilted. The damn thing wilted. Jesus!

Czez flopped back on the bed. A shouldn't. She was a shouldn't. Who would have thought? Was he at the end of the line? No more shoulds forevermore?

It took Donna a moment to realize what had happened.

She rolled against him, soft, moist, and warm. "Hey, hey. No rush. Not good to go too fast."

He took a deep breath.

"No big deal." She snuggled against him.

Performance anxiety, this was called. The shrinks all said the same thing. It was curable. Relax, they said. Right. Concentrate on the woman, not on yourself. Sure, sure. Don't think too much. Uh-huh. Let the lady go on top. Czez hadn't done that. He should have put her up there and sat back to enjoy, but he hadn't. Find yourself one woman and stick with her. All the little rules and advice. Such bullshit.

Czez sighed. By now, he had some idea of which women were shoulds and which were shouldn'ts. Older women, he had found, were definite shouldn'ts. Mouthy, opinionated women were off-putting, too. Shouldn'ts.

Carl Czez remained baffled. He had no idea of what had started his problem—well, yes, he did have, but it remained a mystery nevertheless. That it was emotional in nature, not physical, there was no doubt. He was vigorous and in shape. His blood pressure was okay, and his plumbing remained perfectly serviceable. All he had to do was open the pages of *Playboy* or pop a skin flick into the VCR and the little general jerked to immediate attention, all hot and bothered and ready for action, thank you. The choke had to do with the unaccountable human imagination and was impossible to treat by pharmaceuticals.

The mental block had started shortly after the business with Angie and George. Career destroyed and recently resigned from the army, he had picked up a young lawyer named Kerri in a jazz club in the French Quarter of New Orleans. Czez had fucked more than four hundred women in his time with no problem whatsoever, and there was no reason to believe that Kerri would be any different. They'd had a good time, had a late-night supper of blackened Cajun shrimp, then retired to his hotel room.

Even now, Czez remembered Kerri walking in from the bathroom while he watched from the bed. She'd been a real package, that was a fact. Had these hard little pointed tits. Mmmmm. But then, come action time, the unthinkable happened. He had been shocked. What the hell was wrong with him? He had assumed that the malfunction was an anomaly, a one-time thing, but the subsequent shouldn'ts were almost all the same. Just as he was about to slide it in, or just as he got it inside, his damn cock suddenly deflated like a flat tire.

Czez assumed yes, that his affliction could be traced to his having murdered his wife and George Hollins. The rage at having been made the laughing stock of Fort Meade—with private soldiers secretly ridiculing him—had slowly, over the succeeding weeks, yielded to the understanding of the real reason for his block.

Donna gripped his balls and began massaging them. His unit responded.

"See there," she said. "Look at that gentleman straighten up. Eager for action. No problem."

Yes! Czez suddenly felt emboldened. To hell with that female-on-top stuff. He was going to put it into her and really make those tits jump. One good, old-fashioned slam-it-to-her fuck would fix everything. He threw her onto her back and was upon her.

He quickly rammed it to her. The warmth! Yes!

She groaned.

His cock wilted. It was like trying to push a piece of wet spaghetti. He pulled out limp.

"It's okay. It's okay," she said. "We rushed it. We shouldn't have rushed it. We'll give it a rest, and I'll show you how to keep that thing hard. I know a couple of tricks, believe me."

It had been unimaginable that the Mexican girl, Rosalina, had been a shouldn't. Czez was equally mystified that Donna was one, too. She was young and sexy, if not downright succulent. No functional male on the planet wouldn't want to jump her.

Czez lay back, sunk into a gloom of despondency. Everybody fucked. Pimple-faced adolescents. Shoe salesmen. Fatsos. Rednecks. Henpecked morons. Swaggering blue gums.

Wimps and losers of every possible description reproduced themselves casually and with impunity. The country was awash with their pathetic offspring.

He remembered the smug Jake Hipp sitting beside the girl in the taxi—looking back at him with a knowing, triumphant look on his face. However his problem had begun, there was no doubt in Czez's mind as to who was responsible now. Hipp was to blame for Rosalina. Donna was Hipp's fault.

Carl Czez felt Donna's lips and tongue begin moving down his body. She was going to try again. After two failures, going for a third would only make it worse, although she had no way of knowing that. He knew she felt pity for him. Pity! God, how he hated that!

twenty-two

Yet another storm. It was raining. The wind was blowing. The clouds were low and dark and swiftly moving. Jake Hipp was in a contemplative frame of mind as he drove his Chrysler minivan past Black Lake on his left. He slowed for the fishing village of Ilwaco, tucked in behind Cape Disappointment. Here brave or foolhardy fishermen in search of salmon and halibut and bottomfish put out through the infamous triangle formed by Clatsop Spit, Leadbetter Point, and Astoria. This was the Columbia River bar, where the Pacific surf was channeled into the entrance of the river that was larger by volume of water than the Mississippi. In the previous three hundred years, this triangle had claimed more than two thousand vessels and seven hundred lives.

Hipp pulled to a stop at the intersection that was effectively Ilwaco's downtown and hung a left for the twenty-minute drive upstream to the bridge across the Columbia to Astoria, Oregon. There were towns that would have added a stoplight at that intersection as a form of status, and he thought that the Ilwacans, or Ilwacoids, or whatever they were, showed some real class in staying with a plain old stop sign.

He drove through the rain, thinking about Ted Kaczynski, whose family had spotted a remarkable similarity between the Unabomber's antitechnology tracts published in *The Washington Post* and *The New York Times* and Kaczynski's familiar obsessions. In the puzzle before him, a career military officer and a comic-book artist who had not spoken to one another in ten years suggested a classic older-younger breach. Was there any chance at all that brother Jerry had spotted one of Carl's tics among the reports of Bobby Pearl?

As he followed the winding road along the river, the wipers silently sweeping the rain from the windshield, he thought about how he should broach the subject to brother Jerry.

Hipp thought it better to simply show up at Jerry Czez's house rather than phone him in advance. Under the best of circumstances, it was no fun having someone accuse your brother of being one of the major assholes of the departing century. He didn't want to give Jerry time to tailor his answers. The old opening line about asking routine questions was obvious nonsense to anybody of intelligence, and it was unlikely that Jerry Czez, clever enough to draw a satiric comic book, was any kind of fool.

In a few minutes, Hipp hung a right at the northern end of the bridge and started across the Columbia, which was three and a half miles wide at this point. On the far side, barely visible through the rain, the old fishing town of Astoria was strung out along the water at the base of a steep ridge covered with Douglas firs.

When he reached the southern end of the bridge, Hipp pulled into a Shell station for gas. Oregon prohibited self-serve gas stations, which, along with its bottle-return laws, Hipp considered to be a hallmark of a civilized state. Exempting food, Washington had a sales tax rather than an income tax and so scored major points there.

While the attendant filled his minivan, Hipp studied his map of Astoria. A few minutes later, he drove up a steep street, checking the map as he drove. He quickly arrived at the residence of Jerry and Lenore Czez, a restored Victorian house perched on the side of the steep ridge above the town. The house, painted a light purple with chartreuse shutters and trim, was a thing of beauty and had a great view of the watery graveyard at the mouth of the Columbia.

Hipp parked his van on the street in front of the house, walked up a path paved with red brick and flanked by evergreen bonsai, and thumped the old-fashioned brass knocker on the door.

A large-bellied, middle-aged man wearing the bottoms of cotton sweats and a Portland Beavers T-shirt with crossed bats opened the door. As he did, he let go an audible fart, a little oopsie. He giggled cheerfully. "Sorry." He had a baggy face, spectacles, a stubble of beard, and an untamed mane of graying hair.

Hipp couldn't help but laugh. "We all do it," he said.

"It's the navy-bean soup. My wife and I love it. We sound like dueling cannons come bedtime."

"My name is Jake Hipp." He started to say he was with Mongoose, but the man held up the palm of his hand to stop him. His face suddenly turned serious.

"The Mongoose man. Won't you come in. I'm Jerry Czez."

They shook, and Hipp, wondering how Czez had figured him so quickly, stepped into a foyer covered with a dark-purple Oriental rug. He followed Czez into a larger room with a high ceiling; this room too was covered with an Oriental rug. But the walls were the eye-catchers. Here was where the fun was. The walls were covered with paintings of men and women fucking and sucking with joyful abandon. These weren't intended to titillate, but rather were celebratory in nature, playful studies of straightforward, honest gropers enjoying one another.

Dead ahead, an aged, tattered, overstuffed sofa and matching chair faced a large bay window overlooking Astoria and the Columbia River. Here were a sofa and a chair that had entertained a lot of tired butts in their day. A coffee table between the sofa and the window was made from what Hipp recognized as a deck hatch from a World War II Liberty ship.

Hipp, with a half-grin, looked around at the paintings with open admiration. "Okay!"

Following his eyes, Czez said, "My wife's work. Horny woman. Horny paintings. She's the one who makes the real money in the family, not me. Who the hell wants to hang a sterile abstraction on the wall?"

"You got that right. I'll take one of these any time."

"Humping and grunting is what life's all about. Or at least

thinking about humping and grunting. Which one do you like the best?"

Hipp considered the many paintings. Then he pointed to one of a couple, each covered with a sheen of sweat, screwing dog style. The woman looked back over her handsome rump at her partner. She had a Mona Lisa smile. The smile said she enjoyed the action perhaps more than she was willing to admit. The man's face spoke volumes as well. However fleeting, he was enjoying a form of earthly heaven. "That one."

Czez looked pleased. "Good choice."

"Looks like the gentleman's got a rhythm going. Does it have a title?"

"Lenore likes imaginative titles. That one's 'Enjoying Milady's Rump, Ka-bump, Ka-bump.' "

Hipp laughed.

From the next room, a female called out. "Who is it, hon?"

Czez looked resigned. "A man from Mongoose."

A redheaded, hazel-eyed woman of about forty appeared in a doorway, holding a paintbrush and trailed by an obese black-and-white cat. She wore eyeglasses, threadbare, paint-stained blue jeans that showed patches of white skin through multiple holes, and a T-shirt that couldn't disguise unembarrassed nipples. She had a lazy, sensual look about her that went with the artist who would have imagined the paintings on the wall. Looking at Hipp, she cocked her head. "Mongoose? The terrorist chasers?"

"Yes, ma'am," Hipp said. It was obvious they knew he was likely there about brother Carl, but he decided not to push it. Better to let them tell him what they had to say in their own way.

"I'm Lenore." She nudged the cat with the side of her foot. "This is Fat Edna."

"Pleased to meet you. I'm Jake Hipp. Hello, Edna." He shook Lenore's hand. "Seems like Edna likes her supper."

She said, "She's spayed. Makes 'em fat. Would you like a cup of coffee? We can watch the rain while we talk."

"Great sport," Czez said.

"Sure, I'd like that," Hipp said. He followed Czez to the sofa and easy chair by the window while Lenore, with Fat Edna waddling at her heels, went to get their coffee.

"Take the chair," Czez said.

Hipp sat in the chair and sank into an enveloping softness. "A sensual chair," he said.

"That describes it," Czez said.

Hipp looked out the window. The town and the bridge were directly below them. In the distance to the left were the pale silhouettes of North Head and Cape Disappointment. "Nice view."

"We enjoy it. Where are you from, Mr. Hipp?"

"Near here, as it happens. I have a cabin in Long Beach, where I live several months out of the year."

"And the rest of the time?"

"The rest of the time I live in the Philippines, where my girlfriend and I have a bar."

Lenore arrived with a platter containing a coffeepot, what looked like hand-thrown ceramic mugs, a bowl of sugar, and a creamer in the shape of a cow. She poured Hipp a mug of coffee and sat beside her husband. Edna settled quickly into her lap.

Hipp, finding it difficult to keep his eyes off Lenore Czez's T-shirt, laced his coffee with a hit of half-and-half and a spoonful of sugar.

Czez said, "If you're wondering, I recognized your name from Joaquin Hurtado's interview of Bobby Pearl in the Philippines."

Hipp took a sip of coffee, watching Czez over the rim of his cup. "Was there something about that interview you want to share with me?"

Czez hesitated, glancing at his wife.

Lenore said, "You have to tell him, Jerry. We can't dodge it forever."

"You think Carl is Bobby Pearl?" Czez licked his lips.

Hipp shrugged. Best to be quiet and listen.

Czez said, "A shrug means the answer is yes, then. You do suspect Carl."

Hipp nodded.

Czez clenched his teeth.

Hipp felt sorry for Jerry Czez. Hard to take news like that about your brother, no matter how obnoxious he might be. Hipp looked about the room. "Carl liked your paintings, did he?"

Lenore burst out laughing. "He thought they were pornographic. All those people shamelessly having a good time."

Czez said, "The guy in the Philippines interview talked about Jake Hipp not being able to pull the trigger." He watched Hipp; he was obviously curious.

"I was supposed to kill him. Had my orders. Had him right in front of me in Tangier, but I choked. For whatever reason, I couldn't pull the trigger. Couldn't do it."

"Couldn't off another human being? Don't apologize. Who could?" Lenore said.

"Carl could," Czez said.

Hipp regarded him mildly. "Do you think he killed his wife and Hollins?"

Czez sighed. "I don't think there's any doubt about it. But nobody will ever be able to prove it. Carl is too smart and careful for that. Everything was by the book for him. By the rules. George and Angie broke the rules. Even worse, they embarrassed him."

"The prosecuting attorney thought he was guilty, but lacked the evidence to take him to court."

Czez said, "Murder is one thing, but releasing mustard gas and sarin on people is something else. What makes you think Carl is Bobby Pearl?"

Hipp thought for a moment. "You're his brother. You're entitled to know why. We learned from a phone tap that Bobby Pearl was supposed to meet a Sudanese surrogate of Moamar Qadhafi in Tangier. I was in Seville at the time—the Charlie on the spot—so I got the assignment. I first met him on the ferry between Algeciras and Tangier."

"A Charlie?" Lenore looked puzzled.

"A field operative. Charlie, for chaser. Mongoose sacked me after the incident in Tangier, but took me back to hunt for Carl because I'm the only Charlie known to have set eyes on him. Later, after San Francisco and Charleston, I spotted his photograph in a military catalog of men who had served tours of duty in the NSA. His unit at Fort Meade was in the business of tracing money laundered by arms dealers, so he knew all the sources and sellers. Everything fits. We think he uses the Internet to hire surrogates to do the hands-on dirty work."

"Where does he get the money?" Czez asked.

"He knows all about codes and the movement of electronic deposits. He steals it."

Czez looked despondent. He frowned. "We were always opposites. He was like my dad and grandfather, everything by the book. God and country. All that. It was like he loved shining shoes. He carried a toothbrush around with him so he could brush his teeth three times a day."

Hipp smiled.

"No, really. I'm serious. He did. Jesus, when he finished second instead of first at The Citadel, you'd have thought the world was coming to an end. The wonderful Carl Czez? Second, not first? How had he allowed that to happen?"

"Your father was a military historian. What about your grandfather?"

"John Czez. He was an artillery officer. He . . . he got seared by mustard in the Ardennes. He still had scars on his face. Carl just loved him. All those stories about battle. The cold. The mud. The trenches. The barbed wire. The stupid asshole Marshal Foch. Boy, oh boy, was he ever hard core. All duty and honor and sacrifice. My father, Leonard, was just like him, and then Carl, another clone."

"Mustard in the Ardennes. When I saw that, I really started wondering." Czez took a sip of coffee and stared out into the rain for a moment, thinking. "I'm not saying that people like Carl and my father and grandfather are all bad, mind you. Most people might see a little of Carl in themselves, and also a little of somebody like me. You know, a mix of imaginations. It's not all cut-and-dried. And a good thing, too."

"A complicated subject, I agree," Hipp said.

"The difference between Carl and me is that he was the president of the student body and captain of the football team, an Eagle Scout who earned every merit badge in the book, and I was his annoying, undisciplined little brother who couldn't handle any of it. I've got nothing against Eagle Scouts, but you get the picture. As for him being Bobby Pearl though, I just don't know. He's my brother, for God's sake. Nobody wants to think his brother is responsible for blowing up and gassing innocent people."

Lenore gripped her husband's knee.

"It's hard to believe." Czez shook his head. "No, I amend that. It's hard to accept." He had a faraway look in his eye.

Lenore looked at Hipp mildly. "Do you smoke pot, Mr. Hipp?"

"Now and then, sure," Hipp said.

Czez took a deep breath and let it out through puffed cheeks. "Good thinking, hon."

"We could all stand to mellow out a bit." Lenore opened the top of a square wicker basket that served as an end table. She retrieved a dark-brown glass bong and a cedar box filled with aromatic cannabis buds, large numbers laced with purple threads. She took a pinch of bud and filled the bowl. She gave the bong to Hipp together with a box of stick matches.

Hipp took a hit and waited for Lenore and Czez to take a turn. Then Czez, his lungs filled with smoke, stood. "Can't put it off forever. Gotta be done. I'll be right back."

When he was gone, Lenore said, "This is hard on Jerry. He had convinced himself that the Philippines interview was a coincidence."

"Could be it's not Carl."

Lenore said nothing. She petted Edna, who purred contentedly; then she refilled the bowl of the bong.

Czez returned with a comic book that he handed to his guest. It was a copy of *Loopies*. "Open it to the first page."

Hipp did. A scowling military officer in a dress uniform and a giant cigar in his mouth, fist raised in fury, was addressing a formation of cowering nerds, boobs, and nincompoops. The officer was so festooned with decorations that the colorful medals and ribbons covered not only his chest, but his stomach and shoulders as well, even continuing down his thighs to his knees. His hair was short. His eyes were blazing. The balloon above him said, "Purpose! Discipline! Loyalty!"

Hipp glanced up at Jerry Czez. "Colonel Cornbrain?"

Czez sighed.

"Carl?"

He nodded. "Brother Jerry letting him have it one more time. I've been at it for years. Earned my living ridiculing him. No damn wonder we haven't talked for ages."

Lenore said, " 'Purpose, discipline, loyalty' is Carl's mantra, Mr. Hipp. It's like a stuck record in his brain." She closed her eyes.

"Colonel Cornbrain repeats it in almost every issue," Czez said. "Colonel Asshole strutting around lecturing everybody. A real giggle for my readers, who're rebellious adolescents for the most part. They identify with the troops. Cornbrain is every sanctimonious, overbearing adult they've ever met. I dump buckets of paint over his head and give him loose bowels in the middle of a military parade. That kind of thing. The kids just love it, and not a few adults as well."

"Oh, wow," Hipp said.

"Once I had the company clerk use a hypodermic to insert Krazy Glue into his tube of toothpaste. At the morning formation, he yelled, "Purpose! Discipline!' Then his teeth stuck together. He couldn't finish it and was beside himself."

Hipp smiled; he couldn't help it.

"I know. I know," Czez said. Then he grinned. "He struggled so hard to get that last word out that his eyeballs popped. I had him taken to the dentist in an ambulance with his face all contorted. In the last panel, when the dentist finally separates his teeth, he shouts, "Loyalty!' "

"Had to finish it," Hipp said.

"Compulsive. That's the Colonel. It was a real kick at the time. Now it doesn't seem so funny."

They fell silent for a minute. The wind whistled through the trees. Rain rattled against the house. The Washington shore of the river disappeared in the mists. The cat on Lenore's lap purred loudly.

Finally, Lenore said, "I believe you regard it as a personal failure, Mr. Hipp, but I think it speaks well of you that you couldn't pull the trigger in Tangier."

Hipp said, "If it hadn't been for me, those people in San Francisco and Charleston would still be alive."

Lenore said, "Yes, I suppose they would." She petted Fat Edna, who purred even louder, rumbling like a B-24 on a run over Ploesti.

"I didn't do my job," Hipp said. "If they had sent another Charlie to Tangier, maybe someone more like Carl, the problem would have been solved. I have to live with that."

"Which painting did he like best, Jerry?"

" 'Ka-bump, Ka-bump,' " Czez said. "Liked that butt up." He took a hit of pot.

Lenore smiled. "Good taste, Mr. Hipp. I want you to have it."

Hipp held up his hands. "Oh, no, hey. Really."

She said, "No, no. I insist. But if Carl is Bobby Pearl and you get another chance, I want you to stop him. This can't continue."

Jerry Czez, his eyes drifty and filled with pain, looked out over the river.

twenty-three

Slick Smith strode down the wide sidewalk on Broadway with an extra spring in his step. Beside him, Elephant Dan Merrill was in good form also, squealing and trumpeting in awe at the sights and sounds of Manhattan. "By God, this is it, Elephant. The Big Apple! The center of it all! Ain't this something? Got plenty of scratch in our pockets and a fancy room at the Waldorf-Astoria. The Waldorf-Astoria! They named a salad after the Waldorf, did you know that?"

"A fuckin' salad. Hot damn!" Merrill gave Smith a scornful look. "Like anybody in New York with bucks in their pocket gives a shit about salad. Grow up."

"I'm serious. A salad. Got apples and nuts and stuff in it. Raisins. Good shit. My first old lady used to make it."

"Fuck the apples and nuts. Let's find us a bar with some take-out twat," Merrill said. "My kind of salad. Lots of dressing. Hold the dingleberries!" He giggled and dug at an itch on his forearm.

Smith glared at him. "Show some class, for Christ's sake. Grow up. Twat, twat, twat. This is Manhattan. Take a look around you. This is where the action is. If you can make it here, you can make it anywhere. Isn't that what they're all the time telling us? We're supposed to be inspired."

"A tight pussy'd inspire the hell out of me," Merrill said. "Speaking of pussy. Jesus, would you look at this?" Making an appreciative gurgling sound in his throat, he sidestepped a young woman wearing a sequined miniskirt.

Smith, relieving an itch of his own, gave him a look. "Don't drag me down to your level. You know, I've been thinking."

Merrill looked amused. "Thinking? You?"

"Laugh if you want, but there's more to life than pussy."

Merrill trumpeted. "Sure there is." He scratched his arm. "Tight pussy."

Smith sighed. "Listen, will you? It's beginning to look like we got a permanent deal with this guy."

"Whoever the hell he is."

"This is our third job, so he obviously trusts us. If we're smart, we'd start thinking of ways to invest our money. I'm Slick Smith, trust me."

"Pierce, Fenner, and Blah Blah. Merrill Lynch and Do Dah."

"No, no, no, asshole. Those people just rip you off with their commissions. Doesn't take a rocket scientist to make money if you've got a few bucks to start out with. The poor bastards who don't have anything are the ones that never get off the ground. I read this article in *USA Today* saying you should only invest in companies where the guy who runs it owns part of it. That way, he isn't playing with other people's money. Stands to reason that the best of all worlds is to bet on yourself. Don't put your money on somebody else's pony."

"I know what I'm going to invest in." Merrill spread his arms and started singing. "I want lots and lots of pussy. Give me lots and lots of pussy."

"Religion's where the real action is. We're talking top bucks here. Just look at your Mormons and Catholics. Multinational corporations."

"Religion?"

"Religion plus technology. Televangelism. A hell of a racket. My old man did pretty good traveling around with a tent. Gave the folks a dose of hell-and-damnation, passed the hat, and moved on to the next piss-ant town. I figure I ought to honor his memory by picking up where he left off. The dutiful son and everything."

Merrill grinned. "The least you could do after having caved his head in."

"You know, I'm building a powerful thirst. What do you say we find ourselves a bar and have a couple?" Smith opened his arms as though to believing masses and said, *"I say it's there! Right there in the Book! Read it for yourself! God says to Abel and Cain, 'You have to hang together if you want to keep your tax-exempt status!' "* He laughed at his delivery. "What do you think?"

Merrill eyed him mildly and sucked air between his two front teeth.

"Good as Jimmy Swaggart?"

"Jesus Christ, I've been itching all damn night." Merrill began pawing at his ribs. "You gotta be good at pounding your pud if you want to keep up with Jimmy Swaggart. Guy had calluses on the palms of his hands. Maximum Jack with a hotline to God."

Smith looked offended. "Hey! I'm talking about an investment here. A future. You have to understand people's needs if you want to make any money. Basic stuff. That's all those guys on Wall Street think about. Keeps 'em awake at night."

"People's needs? They're thinking about people's needs?"

"Correct. You ought to try watching public television once in a while. The guy Louis Whatshisface who interviews the investment brokers. Do you good. What people want, Elephant, is certainty. Better'n cheap chickens, or a cheap drunk even. That's where preachers come in." He attacked an itch on his forearm.

"Delivering certainty."

"Correct again. You can't make real money passing a fucking hat. The problem is, the really big preachers, the ones who rake it in on television, are kind of an informal club, see. It's just like all the really worthwhile scams. You have to pay to play."

"You have to buy all those RVs for the tour and stuff?"

"Exactly right! You can't go driving no used Buick to a televised revival. That's bush. The believers think rich preachers are tight with God, or they wouldn't be so successful. You see how that works? The more bucks up, the more bucks back. Thanks to our anonymous employer, I can afford to deal myself into the action. Slick Smith, entrepreneur."

Merrill said, "I was in the joint with a defrocked preacher. Did I ever tell you that? He was in there on a manslaughter charge. The story was, he got drunker than a skunk and hit a little girl in a school zone. Sent her sailing over the teeter-totters." Merrill laughed at the memory. "Said his prayers regularly, but still had to do his time."

"You can't get away with killing no people, but you can do almost anything else and all the churches'll back you up. Catholics. Zionists. Crazy Ted's Most Holy Rollers. They have to hang together if they want to keep their tax-exempt status."

Merrill brightened. "Look here, one of them Irish bars is coming up. Paddy's."

Smith said, "Let's go for it. Yessir, Slick Smith, rich preacher. I can handle that."

Merrill headed for Paddy's.

Smith led the way inside. "People want somebody to lead them through the darkness. Well, I'm by God your man. I know the way into the darkness and out again, believe me. I even got locked up once because I saw a few bugs one night. Hallucinations, they said. Hallucinations, my ass. Those were fucking bugs, some of 'em as big as potatoes, with spooky, fucking eyes. You should've seen 'em!"

Merrill led the way to the bar, scratching the back of his hand. "What the hell is wrong with us? We've both been digging and pawing at ourselves. What is this, New York lice or something?"

Smith scratched his belly. "I know what you mean. Scratch, scratch, scratch. Dry air, maybe."

Merrill gave a quick squeal. "Need to get ourselves some Oil of Olay. Smooth out the wrinkles and calm them itches."

Smith held up two fingers to the aproned bartender. "We'll have two shots of Canadian whiskey, please. Crown Royal."

"Doubles," Merrill said.

Smith reached down and dug at his ankle. "A successful guru has to understand the primary need of his flock. That's starters."

Merrill accepted the whiskey and gave the bartender a fifty-dollar bill. "You want basics, sell 'em twat. Any pimp can tell you that."

Smith looked disgusted. "Twat, twat, twat. Jesus. I'm serious."

Merrill took a hit of whiskey. "I'm serious, too. Lotta bucks been made peddling twat over the years. I tell you what, Slick. You can go for the guru if you want. Believe I'll spend my share on tight screws and loose shoes. Maybe get myself a big ol' hog-ass Cadillac with a wet bar. Buy American! Hell with giving jobs to a bunch of Mexes." He dug at his forearm. Another itch. He pulled back the sleeve of his jacket. "Would you look at this? I'm getting goddam boils on my arm."

Smith unbuttoned his shirt and looked down at himself. "I've got 'em on my stomach. What the hell's going on?"

Merrill looked concerned. "Shit, oh dear! Don't make any difference how many Benjies we got in our pockets. Ain't no skinch in her right mind gonna sharpen the pencil of a man covered with goddam boils."

Rattler Four's Internet warning to the FBI had the usual beginning: the tumble of pearls into a sea of blood; the chorus singing Handel's *Messiah* in the background.

This was a short rattling, as Bobby Pearl's warnings went:

> *In the first paragraph of Exodus, Chapter Nine, the Lord, god of the Hebrews, tells the Pharaoh to let His people go or He will bring a terrible plague on Egyptian cattle and sheep and goats. In the eighth paragraph, He tells Moses and Aaron to take handfuls of soot from a furnace and toss them into the air in the presence of Pharaoh, saying it would become a fine dust over the whole of Egypt, and festering boils would break out on men and animals throughout the land.*
>
> *Hallelujah, hallelujah!*

Festering boils! Sound like fun? This disease is also called splenic fever, black brain, and malignant pustule. Pustule. Quick, quick, run for the dictionary.

Hal-le-lu-u-jah!

In its acute form, a victim is dead in twelve hours. Don't shake hands with strangers.

Hallelujah, hallelujah!

Time to tell you what this is all about. I am Bobby Pearl, professor of the next century; the lesson to be learned is simple enough:

Purpose. Discipline. Loyalty.

Hallelujah!

Ray Bulloch and Rosemarie Ginther had their dreams just like everyone else. They drove an aged, rusting beater, a 1978 Chrysler New Yorker, but their heart was on owning a pair of brand-new Harley Hogs so they could cruise the country with all that fabulous power throbbing between their legs and the wind batting against their leathers. They had watched Peter Fonda and Dennis Hopper riding the highways and byways in a rerun of *Easy Rider* and had been inspired. They wanted to be freed from the drill of survival. Fuck that shit of pinching every penny. They wanted to get out there on the road and roam. They wanted to see the country. Call it Purpose.

They had spent twelve years saving their money in pursuit of their Hogs. Their diet consisted mainly of spaghetti, meat loaf, beans in their many variations, and whatever beer was cheapest. They were passionate coupon clippers, and cruised yard sales for their clothes. They did what they had to do, and still they were short. Call it Discipline.

Ray and Rosemarie were both twice-divorced, but that was in the past. They were true to each other, except on those occasions when they were so broke they couldn't buy beer, gas, or Wonder Bread and Rosemarie was forced to peddle her butt. Ray didn't like this, but it had to be done, and later, after Rosemarie told Ray what a stupid dork her john was and what a teenie, tiny dick he had, they had a satisfying makeup screw themselves. Call this Loyalty.

Ray was a short, muscular man with kinky red hair and a lined, weathered, vaguely simian face that was highlighted by a pug nose, a small, thick-lipped mouth, and green eyes. An occasional farm laborer and hod carrier, he was known in and around Fresno, California, as being one brick short of a full load. He was thirty-two years old going on fifty.

Rosemarie, a sloe-eyed, strawberry blonde, was nine years older than Ray and taller by six inches. She had a lop-sided, knowing grin, wide, bony hips, buns like flattened pillows, and an outsized pair of hangers on her chest that Ray affectionately called papaya boobs. He was an unabashed admirer of these soft, droopy numbers, velvety smooth they were, and he weighed them appreciatively in the palms of his hands before he massaged her nipples, which was the never-fail key to her engines.

Rosemarie, a sometimes waitress and fry cook—by all accounts, a wild fuck—openly bragged of having once taken on the defensive line of the Southwestern Louisiana Ragin' Cajuns; that's four down linemen plus linebackers—seven gigantic dudes with dicks the size of Louisville sluggers. Whether this was true or it was wishful thinking, Ray was proud of his lady, saying the only difference between Rosemarie and a mosquito was that a mosquito stopped sucking when you gave it a swat.

Some kind of out-of-sight pair were Ray and Rosemarie. They were also a thoroughly modern couple. Although Ray had only made it through the eighth grade, Rosemarie had graduated from high school in Winnemucca, Nevada, and they were curious about the Internet, which they had read about and which everybody was talking about on television. They didn't want to be left behind. They too wanted to see what the hubbub was all about.

And so, holed up in Texarkana, Texas, where Ray was mixing and running mud for bricklayers building a new junior high school, they had bought themselves a used laptop for a hundred and fifty bucks. The access service was cheap enough, and they got themselves some software that was not just user-friendly, but user-slut. Soon they were having as much fun as fancy rich-kid nerds. They liked the sex stuff the best, but then, still dreaming of owning new Hogs, they began to think of establishing an Internet business themselves. Everybody else was doing it. Why not them? The sex ads had gotten them to think about the wonderful world of anonymity afforded by Internet communication. Plain old Ray Bulloch and Rosemarie Ginther could, with a little imagination, transform themselves. No biggie.

When they had run their ad on the Internet, Ray and Rosemarie, then thoroughly sloshed on a jug of cheapie Carlo Rossi burgundy and high on butt-rush Mexican weed, had added a touch of the romantic to their enterprise:

Bonnie and Clyde wannabes will entertain all offers if the price is right. We've got genuine hair and imagination, and not a whole lot of what you would call inhibitions. You can count on us. Check us out.

And hey, within minutes, they had gotten their first response.

Not only that, but after an exchange of messages with a series of oddballs and crackpots, they had a big fish on—or what they thought was a big fish. It was hard to tell. Their mysterious correspondent, who called himself "Nameless," claimed he was interested in hiring them for some simple, highly profitable delivery work. After having asked them numerous questions about themselves, Nameless had dropped communication, but there was something about him that gave Ray and Rosemarie hope. They had a feeling, based on his series of specific questions, that they would be hearing from Nameless again.

And sure enough, now, while they were drinking Lone Star beer and eating Fritos while watching the anthrax story on television, they got another message.

three

snake kit

one

William Tarnauer was a smart, thoughtful black man with a mellow white voice and a sincere manner that had propelled him to the top as a CNN anchor in the space of two short years. He had a way about him that people liked—especially middle-class white viewers, who were important to advertisers. Most white viewers presumably wished that all black men were like Tarnauer, that is, precisely like themselves except for his skin. He was not a pretend black who was obviously half white. He was a genuine African-American. He was not a professional, put-upon victim who eternally whined about racism, but neither was he an ass-kissing Tom. He was simply an educated, respected journalist whose skin happened to be black. He was good at his job and so commanded respect, along with a seven-figure salary.

Tarnauer's partner, Belinda Lovewell, was a slender, elegant beauty; long-faced, pale-skinned, and black-haired, with large, cornflower-blue eyes, she had an aristocratic BBC accent that had been popular at CNN ever since the phenomenal success of Christiane Amanpour some years earlier. She said *beeen* instead of *ben, tomahto* instead of *tomayto, vahse* instead of *vayse,* and went so far as to talk of automobile bonnets and boots instead of hoods and trunks. Lovewell, with her good, rich voice, was British upper class all the way; matching her with the respected William Tarnauer was a stroke of mix-and-match inspiration by CNN's producers. Never mind that the patrician Lovewell had been educated in tah-tah British public schools—read "exclusive private schools"—the proletarian Tarnauer, a graduate of the University of Minnesota, more than held his own.

Now, sitting behind their sleek, blond desk in CNN's new

space-age set—surrounded by high-tech gadgets and television monitors fielding images from all over the planet—Tarnauer and Lovewell solemnly reported the latest strike by Bobby Pearl. Anthrax!

This was, officially, a terrible story, awful stuff—never mind that gross jokes about boils and pus would spread throughout the nation's bars the next day. *Did you hear the one about . . . ?* Years later, the story of the anthrax outbreak would become fodder for speakers' fees as the aged, storied journalists who had reported it in their salad days would recount the details for wide-eyed students. Every detail would one day reap a profit. *I remember I was driving to work on Peachtree Lane in Atlanta on a balmy night, listening to some Golden Oldies on the radio; Elvis Presley was singing "Heartbreak Hotel," when . . .* But now the story was a career thrill—*hot damn, I-was-there* stuff—and it was a mark of professionalism that the television journalists who reported it were able to mask their joy and elation with solemn, melancholy faces. Be there at the center of a story like this and it was a meal ticket for life.

Tarnauer and Lovewell, their faces grim, professional masks, took turns reporting the spate of revelations, firing sound bites like gatlings. First Tarnauer, then Lovewell, and back to Tarnauer.

Tarnauer said, "We are getting new details of the outbreak at the Kennedy Airport on Long Island, and in midtown Manhattan. Added to earlier reports out of Los Angeles, a horrifying picture is beginning to emerge. Belinda?"

Lovewell, her pretty, porcelain-complexioned face solemn, said, "Authorities in both Los Angeles and New York are urging any person who has developed unexplained rashes or pustules on their skin to immediately go to a hospital. There is an antidote for anthrax, but if the disease is left untreated, it could be fatal. Jim, is that you? We now have Jim Bunyan in Los Angeles. Come in, Jim."

Jim Bunyan, a slender, sharp-faced man in his early thirties, was now on the monitor to the right of Tarnauer and Lovewell. He was in the right place at the right time; call him Lucky Jim. "Belinda, viewers should be advised that doctors here are stressing that anyone displaying symptoms of anthrax should avoid all physical contact with other people. I repeat, all physical contact. No touching. We're told that when this disease breaks out among animals, veterinarians avoid autopsies for fear of becoming infected themselves. The usual practice is to cut off an animal's ear to examine its blood. Bill? Back to you."

Tarnauer said, "We'll now have a word from Dr. Gerald Oblinski, deputy director of the National Communicable Disease Center here in Atlanta. Dr. Oblinski, could you please tell our viewers more about this disease and how it works?"

Oblinski, a round-faced man in his early sixties with curly gray hair, spoke from the monitor to the left of Tarnauer and Lovewell. "Anthrax is caused by the bacterium *bacillus anthracis,* which has been known since ancient times. Hippocrates, Virgil, and Pliny all described lesions that we believe were caused by anthrax. We know that some sixty thousand people in southern Europe died of anthrax in sixteen thirteen. There were near-epidemics of anthrax in the United States and Great Britain following World War One. The source of the anthrax spores in that case turned out to be horsehair shaving brushes made in China and Siberia."

Tarnauer said, "Dr. Oblinski, can you tell us exactly how this disease is transmitted and what it does to its victims? Is it always fatal?"

Oblinski scowled to demonstrate his extreme concern. "There are two forms of anthrax, internal and external. A victim is infected internally by eating contaminated meat, say. The external form, which is the case here, is contracted by physical contact with anthrax spores; a rash comes first, then carbuncles, or pustules, form on the skin. If the disease is not treated, the bacillus moves from these sores into the blood and the lymphatic system. This is fatal bacteremia, or bacteria in the blood."

"You say fatal? How long does it take, Doctor?"

"In its acute form, untreated anthrax can kill its victim

within twelve hours. One must keep in mind that while anthrax is treatable by sulfonamides and antibiotics such as penicillin and tetracycline, it is wildly infectious. When the outbreak occurs in crowded metropolitan areas such as Los Angeles and New York, the problem is finding all the victims, having enough supplies of serum and antibiotics, and treating the victims on time. This disease spreads very, very rapidly. Containing it is a formidable task."

Beautiful, serious Belinda was on the screen. "Bill, we're getting word from Dr. Janice Cross, an investigator from the Communicable Disease Center who is in Los Angeles. Dr. Cross, can you give us a preliminary picture of the situation? What do you think has happened here?"

Cross, a bespectacled blonde woman in her mid-thirties, popped onto the monitor to the right of Tarnauer and Lovewell. "Of course, we don't know all the facts now. We can only make an educated guess. It appears that one or more infected individuals boarded a plane in Los Angeles bound for Kennedy Airport in New York. They apparently checked in baggage that was also covered with anthrax spores. This led to multiple trails of infection: clerks who sold them magazines in the terminal; bartenders who sold them drinks; people who handled their baggage. Infected ticket agents passed the disease on to their customers, who took it with them aboard flights headed for other parts of the country. Infected flight attendants spread the disease to other passengers bound for New York. When these passengers spread out to the surrounding areas—you get the picture."

"The trail of infection widened."

"Trails of infection. It appears that way, yes."

"If you'll excuse me, Dr. Cross, we now have your colleague, Dr. Harold Hull, in New York. Dr. Hull, did you hear what Dr. Cross had to say?" Pretty Belinda, her chin held at a patrician angle as though she were ordering wine at a classy restaurant, addressed the opposite monitor with her broad As and nearly nonexistent Rs.

Dr. Harold Hull, a small, plump man standing at the corner of 42nd Street and Broadway, nodded. "Yes, I did. From the preliminary information we have here, the infection in New York spread from the infected mules, as we call disease carriers, plus the flight attendants and other passengers, to multiple locations in the New York–New Jersey metropolitan sprawl. We don't know which of these trails leads to the mules. We have one very strong trail of infection through bars and girlie shows in midtown Manhattan, which suggests males in that case."

"We have yet to receive any threat from Bobby Pearl. Dr. Hull, can you tell us what the feeling is among investigators: was this infection deliberately set, or was it accidental?"

"We have no way of knowing, Bill. If it was deliberately set, it was also suicidal, or close to it."

The camera returned to Tarnauer. In his mellow, sincere voice, he said, "We're receiving an urgent call from our correspondent, Midge Sullivan, at the Justice Department. Midge, let's see what you've got."

Sullivan, a pretty, serious young woman with sensual lips and large, dark eyes, popped onto the monitor to Tarnauer's right. "What we've got, Bill, is the answer to your question to Dr. Hull." Sullivan was quickly replaced by Bobby Pearl's message.

The first pearl tumbled from the corner of the screen, and Pearl began talking about pharaohs and boils in the Ninth Chapter of Exodus.

When Pearl's communication was finished, Tarnauer said, "Midge, can you tell us why on earth, after all the fuss about secrecy, the government would want to keep this tape from the American people? At first glance, this seems bewildering. You've been talking to people in the Justice Department. What's the logic here?"

The camera switched to Sullivan, who looked grave. This was the story of a lifetime, and she was obviously determined to remain cool and professional. "That's a good question, Bill. The story coming out of Justice is that a decision was made to withhold the tape for only a few hours, until the threat was confirmed. To release it earlier, it was felt, would encourage unnecessary panic. Also, the government wanted to make sure of exactly what disease was involved so it could get the necessary serums and antidotes into place. The reference in Exodus to boils and animals could be anthrax; then again, it could be something else. Biblical scholars have always believed it was anthrax, but they have no proof of it. Many other diseases give boils and lesions."

Tarnauer shook his head in dismay. "Hard to believe."

"Excuse me, Bill." Belinda Lovewell, looking concerned, held up her hand. "Bill, we've just had a message from Bang at our CNN Website." Her jaw dropped.

Tarnauer leaned over to read the message. His eyes went wide.

The sleek blond desk exploded, eliminating both William Tarnauer and Belinda Lovewell. The video camera closest to the anchors was knocked out by the blast, momentarily plunging the set into darkness, but the alert floor director instantly switched to another camera, which, unaffected by the explosion, continued to roll.

Viewers watching the unfolding anthrax story now saw a smoking crater where the anchor desk had been, and a set stained by the blood and bodily fluids of Tarnauer and Lovewell.

Elephant Dan Merrill sat on the edge of the bed with his shirt off, his shoulders slumped in disbelief. He swallowed as he looked down on the pus-filled boils that had developed on his arms and seemed to be spreading by the minute over his shoulders and down his torso. "I knew it was too good to be true. Here we are in a fancy suite in the Waldorf-fucking-Astoria in New-fucking-York with all the money we want to spend, and look at us, just look at us. It was just too damned good to be true. I knew it. I knew it. I just knew it all along. Couldn't be true. Couldn't."

The shirtless Slick Smith, displaying ugly pustules of his own, trembled as he turned on their laptop. "He obviously fucked up and got that stuff on the outside of the package, and now we have it. We keep our heads. We don't panic. Thing we have to do now is get rid of it."

"We've probably been spreading it all the way from Los Angeles. Maybe that was his plan, you ever think of that? We're like those bees you see on TV, flying around spreading pollen from one plant to the next. He hired us off the Internet. He doesn't know us. What does he care whether we've infected ourselves or not? We're a couple of disposable stupes, face it. Plenty more where we came from."

Smith looked impatient. "Oh, for Christ's sake. Knock off the paranoia, will you? Show a little patience."

"Patience with my skin rotting right before my eyes? Right. Right. And here I was listening to all your Slick Smith horseshit. Look at me. Just look at me."

"It was an accident. Accidents happen. He gave us an address to contact him in case of an emergency. He wouldn't have done that unless he was worried something would happen. Bitching don't help. The deal is to remain cool and do what has to be done."

Merrill, squinting his eyes, examined his forearm. "Be cool. Right. Fever. Boils on our skin." He slammed the palm of his hand on the bed and gave a plaintive elephant squeal. "And here I had my heart set on two twats at once. Big-titted bitches with tiny little holes. Play motorboat with one while the other sucks my popsicle." He imitated an outboard engine by blowing air between his lips while he moved his face left-right, left-right, on pretend breasts.

"We weren't supposed to release the stuff until tomorrow, so it's an obvious accident. He's the kind of guy who doesn't leave anything to chance. He'll know what we should do, and he'll tell us."

Merrill tested a boil with his finger and winced. "By God, he better. This stuff works fast, that's a fact. I look like a giant dick with the clap." He shook his head sadly. "I almost had it made, Slick. Almost pulled it off. Almost . . . Jesus!" He closed his eyes and puckered his face. "Another fucking-sure thing gone wrong. Ain't no such thing as a favorite in this world. That's bullshit! Bullshit!" He trumpeted loudly.

Smith brightened. "Here it is. See, I was right. He's left us emergency instructions in case something went wrong. Didn't I tell you?"

A reversal of fortunes. Merrill squealed in triumph. "Okay! Lady Luck makes her move in the stretch. She's closing fast, hooves thundering. Hot pony. Hot, hot, pony!" He hurried over to Smith and read the message over Smith's shoulder:

> *If you should develop a sudden fever and boils on your skin, you should take two aspirin, drink plenty of fruit juice, and get some sleep. My mother always put Vicks in a steamer.*

two

Jake Hipp, the telephone receiver tucked between his shoulder and the side of his head, doodled on a yellow legal pad upon which he had written: *Czez. Pearl. Hurtado. Bernardi. My Side. Qadhafi. Tarhunah. Philippines. Most Hipp. Plastics. Mustard. Sarin. Anthrax. CNN. Bang.*

Who?

Why?

Woofter said, "It's ghastly, Jake. Anthrax. The hospitals can't handle all the victims. Jesus. We've been after this guy for three years, and this is the fifth time he's hit us—plastic explosives on the Delta flight and at Salt Lake, mustard gas at San Francisco, sarin at Charleston, and now this. The President is threatening to sack us all, and I can hardly blame him."

"I bet he is. Bang is right about one thing, I'll give him that. The President would have been smart to be up front and open with the public from the beginning. Getting hit with this crap is bad enough, but when people know the government has been holding out on them, they get pissed big time. Hard to blame them."

"Easy to say from hindsight."

"Easy to say from any sight, Joe. We have to keep our perspective. In the end, that's what the democratic experiment is all about, isn't it? Dealing the people in on decisions that have to be made." He drew an arrow from *Pearl* to *Hurtado*, and from *Hurtado* to *Bernardi*.

"I don't know, Jake. I really don't. At times like this, I wish I had stayed in academia."

Hipp said, "You weren't in on the decision to keep things secret, were you?"

"No, no, no. That was made by the President and the National Security Council."

"Judging from what they're saying on the tube, Pearl apparently deliberately infected a couple of mules and spread the disease that way. Is that what you're thinking?" Hipp circled *Philippines* and *Most Hipp*.

"We think that's most likely," Woofter said.

"Okay, tell me again about your Bang find in Atlanta." He wrote *Pearl=Bang?*

Woofter said, "The CNN security cameras tracked everybody entering and leaving their studios. They caught one man leaving the building who didn't enter. This was thirty minutes before the set blew up. The Southern Comfort Hotel just down the street has a security camera above its check-in desk. This camera photographed the same man as he checked in two weeks ago. He returned again the night before the murder."

Hipp drew a large X through *Pearl=Bang?* He chewed on his lower lip, thinking. He said, "Do you know who he is?"

"He called himself Gene Beaver on the check-in register, but the only Gene Beaver we found on a Web check was a maintenance worker for a Kroger warehouse in Dallas, Texas."

Hipp said, "Not very damned professional, I wouldn't think. Letting himself get his picture taken like that."

"And going back to the same hotel. After Hurtado and Bernardi were murdered, the CNN people went to extreme lengths to make sure no screwballs got inside the building. How did Gene Beaver, or whatever his name is, get past the security cameras? And when?"

"Good questions, Joe." He wrote *Greta. Sex. Rogue male.*

"That's not all, Jake. A studio technician with access to the newsroom set is missing. We've got his picture going in, but not coming out. What happened to him?"

Hipp furrowed his brow. "What do you think? Latex or silicon?"

"It's possible he used masks, yes, which means that both the exit and hotel images could be bogus. But think for a moment, Jake. Suppose he did use masks. It takes time to make a mask good enough to fool a security guard, and there are only a handful of artists with the skill to pull it off."

"Movie people?"

"Maybe. Which brings us to another problem. If he used a mask, he'd have to have known about Pearl's hit in advance, wouldn't he? It takes planning. A pissed-off militiaman wouldn't plan anything. If he killed out of passion, it would be on the spur of the moment. 'These reporters are screwing the republic, so I'm going to show them a thing or two.' Et cetera. You see our problem."

"The question is, what do you tell the public?" Hipp said.

"Exactly."

Hipp wrote *Silicon masks?* on his pad. *Philippines. Hong Kong. Boyd Studios.* "If this was somehow coordinated with Bobby Pearl, maybe it's him. You ever considered that"

"Or somebody who knows him," Woofter said. "Yes, we've thought of that."

"The world grows curiouser and curiouser," Hipp said. He wrote *Motive of a mad colonel.* He underlined *Supplier* and *Why?* Jake Hipp had gone through this drill almost every day, trying to make the links, but he still couldn't figure Bobby Pearl.

An hour later, Jake Hipp received an E-mail message from David Wong in Hong Kong; Wong sent the face photo of one of the cigar smokers, a dark-complexioned man with curly black hair who had been photographed entering the toilet at Most Hipp, plus a short note: *This customer on his way to take a piss at Most Hipp visited the Kowloon studio of Sing Sing Boyd's favorite special-effects artist James Chan twice within the last year. We don't know who he is or what he bought or ordered, if anything, but Chan is said to be one of the best in the business. Over the years, he's done a lot of contract work for Roger Korman's Hollywood cheapies. He's extremely skilled at silicon masks. For whatever it's worth . . .*

Hipp's stomach twisted with anxiety. He studied the doodles on his legal pad, then quickly checked his watch. He grabbed his phone and punched up the number of Most Hipp in Cebu. He was relieved when Gina answered.

"Hey, Jake! Where are you?"

"On my way to the Philippines as soon as I can get to the airport. I want you to go to that place we used to visit at Moalboal. Take Felix with you. Hire a cab. Change cabs once at Danao City, watching to make sure nobody is following you. Tell nobody, but nobody, that I called or where you are going. Just turn the place over to Bonny." Bonny, a gay man who was officially the manager of Most Hipp, worked the night shift and took over completely when Gina was out of town. Hipp said, "Tell Bonny to develop all the pictures that our camera is taking in the john. Tell him to switch to twelve-frame cartridges of film, so he can have them developed quicker."

"What?"

"This is extremely important. Please don't argue. Do it now. I'll call you when I get there." Hipp hung up and waited.

A minute later, the phone rang. He picked up the receiver. "Dammit, Gina. I said, 'Do it now.' Please do as I say."

"Does this have to do with Bobby Pearl?"

"Yes, it does. You know I wouldn't make a call like this unless it was something important. This is for your own good. I'll explain everything when I get there."

"For my own good. You mean for my own safety."

"Yes. I mean exactly that."

Gina laughed. "I love you, Jake."

"I love you too, which is why I want you to do what you're told. No more questions. Just do it."

"Okay, Jake. I'm on my way."

three

An electronic bell bonged softly and the seat-belt light began to blink on the plastic bulkhead above Jake Hipp. Hipp was resigned to the long, boring transpacific flight. He took a deep breath and buckled his seat belt. He had brought a book about the latest round of speculations on the nature of the universe—occasioned by a series of new photographs from the Hubble space telescope—plus the latest editions of *TIME, Newsweek,* and *U.S. News & World Report.* He had also brought along a portable chess set, although the prosperous-looking suit next to him didn't have the look of a chess player.

Hipp looked out at the tarmac of the Portland Airport as a pretty Asian flight attendant went through her safety spiel. It had begun to rain lightly. The flight attendant made him think of Gina. Gina loved him and cared about what happened to him. That was the bottom-line requirement of anything that could reasonably be called home. Gina was home. He was going home.

Hipp opened his *TIME* as the male flight attendant passed by, checking the laps of passengers. He knew he wasn't going to read, so he closed the magazine.

He thought about the nearly nightly appearance of the ghostly cocked hammer, and Lynn Vaughn reporting the numbers of dead.

The engines of the Boeing 747 began to whine.

Hipp had choked in Tangier, yet he knew that Bobby Pearl too had something to prove. Or thought he did. The question was, what?

The plane began to taxi slowly onto the runway.

He had his snake kit with him. Of all the weapons he

could use against Rattler Four, the snake kit—an inspired, if diabolical, Company invention—was clearly the most appropriate, and there would be not a little irony in using it on Bobby Pearl. The snake kit had been kept secret for better than two years, although everybody in Mongoose knew there would come a day when it would be leaked and civil libertarians would lobby furiously against its use. Why they would do this exactly, Hipp could not immediately fathom, but he knew they would, just as they had resisted the use of DNA to identify criminals. The snake kit, after all, was used to bring international terrorists to justice. It was as though in their heart of hearts, they felt that closing all avenues of escape, even for rampaging, homicidal maniacs, was bringing the world closer to the world George Orwell had prematurely predicted for 1984.

No, Hipp did understand the objection of civil libertarians. It was human nature to want to keep whatever little space remained in the world. Whatever freedom remained was precious. Nobody wanted to be closed in entirely, smothered by technological pens—never mind that psychopaths like Bobby Pearl thrived on what otherwise was liberating ambiguity.

The plane turned into position on the runway.

But for now at least, Hipp had a snake kit. This time, perhaps he would get an opportunity to use it. He couldn't imagine anybody objecting to its use on Bobby Pearl. This was one of those logical exceptions to the rule, like the spike order he had been given in Tangier.

The engines began to roar.

Louder.

Then louder.

Hipp felt himself pressed against the back of the seat, just as he had been emotionally pinned by his failure in Morocco. He was thus propelled forward for his rendezvous with Bobby Pearl.

The plane rose from the tarmac.

Hipp remembered Hemingway's definition of courage: **"Grace under fire."**

* * *

Carl Czez had flown from Manila to Cebu several times before, and in anticipation of the best view, had wangled a window on the left side of the cabin of the Philippine Airlines Boeing 727. He finished his copy of *The Philippine Daily Enquirer* and sat back, looking at patches of blue between the clouds below. Staring at the sea without seeing it, he thought back to his days as Cadet Carl Czez at The Citadel in Charleston, South Carolina. Pearl always thought of Carl Czez in the past tense and in the third person. Physically transformed, from the crowns on his teeth to his new nose and fingerprints, Czez was everything but literally dead.

The young Carl Czez had been required to read Edward Gibbon's epic *Rise and Fall of Roman Civilization.* He had read the entire twenty-eight volumes, a fascinating march through political, military, and cultural history that had required hours of reading in the library and his quarters, but his was no casual assignment by some out-of-control professor; there was a purpose behind it.

Cadet Czez had followed the growth of Rome from its founding, allegedly by Romulus in 753 B.C., through its heyday of triumph and power to the final tragic days. He had learned about the logistics of maintaining the remarkable legions, which had grown to nearly 350,000 legionnaires by the time of Augustus Caesar in 20 B.C., and the tactics of the successful Roman generals who had twice defeated the Carthaginians and conquered England. He read what happened when, in order to maintain the empire's remarkable growth, the emperors began turning the legions over to mercenaries and allowing foreigners to become Roman citizens. In the end, the emperors and the idle rich wallowed in gluttony and self-indulgence while the wretched poor became uncontrollable. And finally, in A.D. 476, after Rome had been captured and sacked by Visigoths and Vandal tribes, Romulus Augustulus was deposed as the last Roman emperor.

Czez's professor, citing the historian Oswald Spengler,

urged his students to consider the possibility that a similar cycle of growth and decay might be charted for all ancient civilizations, from the Egypt of the pharaohs to the fallen Mayans. To understand the cycle, he said, was mandatory for all officers in the legions of the current empire that dominated the world. It was their lifelong charge to defend and advance the interests of the United States.

Czez was jarred from his reverie by the realization that the plane was beginning its descent to the airport on Mactan Island. It was late afternoon and the sun was a dying ember to the west. Cebu was close enough to the equator that the sun rose and set plus or minus five minutes of six o'clock every morning and night. When the sun set, it was six o'clock, bet on it. Czez, looking out of his window, saw the orange-tinted sprawl of the city on the edge of the mountainous ridge that dominated the island of Cebu. He loathed Manila, which was to Cebu as New York was to Atlanta. The culture of metropolitan Manila was fast-paced and grasping; Cebu was laid-back and friendly.

As the plane descended, he saw the warehouses and office buildings of the international trade zone on Mactan Island by which Japanese, German, and American firms took advantage of smart, educated, but cheap Filipino labor. Czez had a difficult time placing a whole lot of faith in the macho Filipino pilot who had boarded the plane with a swagger and a jaunty tilt to his captain's cap, but he landed the 727 with hardly a bump.

A few minutes later, Czez stepped through the door into the familiar tropical heat, the first step of his rendezvous with Jake Hipp. He joined the departing passengers in a stroll across the tarmac to the terminal. He merged with the line to have his passport checked, and after a cursory examination of his baggage, he was waved through to join the usual lineup of jockeying cabbies—legal bandits in the Philippines, as they were in nearly all Third World countries. The Philippines, which had a barely functioning economy of its own, had, in addition to pineapples and sugarcane, two principal exports: educated, English-speaking labor whose foreign income was taxed by Manila, and beautiful daughters, loyal to their families, who sent money back home. Those who had become citizens abroad were called *balikbayans*.

In Cebu, the cabbies greeted each arriving white male with the expectation that he was a pen pal coming to visit a Filipina. These Americans, Australians, and Europeans, ordinarily newcomers to Third World travel, were used to paying real money for a taxi and so were prime targets for the big rip. Their pen pals had warned them to be careful, but they were idealistic and wanted to believe in the inherent goodness of Filipinos—that is, in the inherent goodness of their wives-to-be. In Czez's opinion, a belief in the inherent goodness of any culture was a virtue of fools. Individual humans were capable of being virtuous; to believe virtue applied in any aggregate was folly.

Carl Czez had been to Cebu several times before and so knew that a trip from the airport to the Ramada Hotel above Robinson's Department Store on Fuentes Circle was a 100-peso ride, 150 pesos tops—a four- to six-dollar ride. The Ramada was a three-block walk up Osmena Boulevard to Most Hipp, opposite Cebu Doctors Hospital.

After haggling for a ride, and yielding to a 150-peso tab, Czez slid into a dilapidated Toyota for the run from Mactan Island, through Mandaue City, to Talamban Street and uptown Cebu City. He had agreed to the 150 pesos because this was an air-conditioned cab, but it turned out that the air conditioner was broken. Never mind. Czez rode in his private world, remembering . . .

With Gibbon and Spengler on his mind, Lieutenant Czez, fresh from The Citadel, had helped with the withdrawal from Saigon in 1974. That stupid, unwinnable intervention in a civil war halfway around the planet had cost the lives of fifty thousand American soldiers and hundreds of thousands wounded and maimed, not to mention the beginning of The Great Debt, from which the country still suffered decades later.

As the years passed, Czez had looked upon his countrymen with increasing dismay. The spoiled boomers, the me-

me-me generation, had moved from pot and protest to the herpes and disco of their yuppie years, and then on into middle age, always demanding—and nearly always receiving, because of their cumulative buying power and influence of numbers at the polls.

Looking back, Czez understood clearly what had happened on the eve of his promotion to brigadier general. The self-indulgent Angie and George, caring only for the pleasures of the moment—forbidden romance, a quick fuck—had failed to grasp the elemental responsibilities of wives and friends. They were a microcosm, reflecting the deteriorating larger culture. The enraged Colonel Czez had been an agent of the inevitable. In fact, Angie and George had brought their fate on themselves; they deserved everything they got.

Czez had served the republic by devoting his life as a military officer. In his demonstration of the dangers of the new century, Bobby Pearl, the resurrected Czez, was no less devoted to his countrymen.

The last of the orange sun was setting to their left as the cab approached the bridge between Mactan Island and Mandaue City. The traffic suddenly slowed. As dusk settled in, it became clear that soon they would be unable to move. Czez had been in Bangkok before and so knew what traffic jams were really about. Besides, on the eve of his confrontation with Jake Hipp, he was in a contemplative frame of mind. What was a couple of hours' delay when he got to look forward to snuffing that mother's lights?

The President and his people were impotent before a phantom predator who operated from the sanctuary of cyberspace. If it hadn't been Bobby Pearl, operating out of duty and honor, the terrorist of the hour would be somebody else: a crazed Arab locked in the grip of *jihad,* an amateur hero like the OK bomber, a demented intellectual like the Unabomber.

To Czez, the question of his pedagogic mission was abundantly clear and instructive: how was his country to cope with easily obtainable g-agents and biologicals, combined with the growing, spookily uncontrollable cyberspace? A government official didn't know for sure whether an E-mail threat was a security check coming from the next office, a practical joke from a teenager in the suburbs, or the genuine article from a psychopath halfway around the planet. Add to that the wildfire of paranoia and bizarre tales that were spread in Internet chat rooms by the powerless, the isolated, the ignorant, and the gullible: mysterious black helicopters flying over Utah, the United Nations controlling secret bases in Kentucky, the navy accidentally downing commercial airliners.

What were the lives of a couple of thousand victims of Czez's measured terrorism if their demise taught the public the essential requirements of defending itself against the awful succession of terrorists that was sure to come?

Czez had had no trouble at all in hiring self-indulgent scumbags to act as his gophers. Dan Merrill and Slick Smith had no idea of who they were working for or where the money was coming from, and they obviously didn't care. Were they any different than narcissistic television journalists like Joaquin Hurtado, who casually reported whatever he wanted, whenever he wanted, without regard to anything except his own glory and bank account? In an odd way, Czez respected Merrill and Smith's unembarrassed greed. They were have-nots who wanted to have. One was a gambler, the other was a loud-talking alcoholic; they didn't try to dress their greed in the fanciful rhetoric of public service. Czez thought that they, like Angie and Hollins, lacked the basics of civilization: *purpose, discipline,* and *loyalty.*

Czez had considered the possibility that he had somehow become demented, but he knew that was wrong. He was no madman. Carl Czez had always been cool, clear, and rational.

In Tangier, Colonel Sayani had laid down a straightforward requirement that if Czez was to receive BCs, he would have to prove he could use them in a way that couldn't be traced. That hadn't been difficult. He'd simply used the Internet to hire and instruct surrogates to release mustard gas at the San Francisco Food Fair.

It was the second requirement, the purchase price, that had been tougher to meet. Sayani had said the supplier wasn't interested in money, so Czez would have to come up with something else. *Think of motive and proceed from there.*

Later, Czez had lain awake at night considering the permutations of desire. He remembered the words of the song by The Rolling Stones: "I can't get no satisfaction. No, no, no." Mick Jagger's lament was memorable because it was a universal complaint. Most people thought they could buy satisfaction, but that was an illusion or a delusion, Czez knew. The potential supplier of CBs was a head of state who was presumably sated with worldly goods. What on earth could possibly give him satisfaction? That was the question. A trinket or a bauble? A beautiful woman? Certainly none of those.

Czez had been stumped for months, until that sweltering day in Cebu City. He had been drinking San Miguel in Most Hipp with a loudmouthed drunk named Ralph Snow, watching student nurses *twitch, twitch, twitch* their splendid little butts down the street to Cebu Doctors Hospital, when he happened onto the answer without knowing it. The idea of swapping satisfaction for g-agents and biologicals did not become clear until his *My Side* interview on Negros the following week. Then it came in a flash. Bingo! Pow!

Czez was not surprised that his nemesis should later turn out to be Jake Hipp, the owner of Most Hipp. As Czez had learned from reading Gibbon at The Citadel, life turned on itself and looped back.

He was suddenly aware of the driver looking at him through the rearview mirror. The man was obviously amazed that his passenger was so calm in all the traffic.

"They're fixing the road on the other side of the bridge," he said. "Yesterday it took me over an hour to get across."

Czez, looking at the night lights of Mandaue City on the island of Cebu, said, "I've been in traffic before."

"I had German man as a passenger. He got hot and impatient and finally lost his temper. He began to shout, but what could I do? I couldn't go forward. I couldn't back up. I was trapped, just like now."

Czez smiled.

"Hard to be patient in traffic like this," the driver said. "He was anxious to meet his pen pal. You here to meet a pen pal?"

"A pen pal?" Czez laughed. "In a manner of speaking. But not a Filipina."

The driver looked surprised. "You don't like Filipinas?"

"I think Filipinas are wonderful," Czez said. He thought of Hipp's girlfriend, the proprietress of Most Hipp. Now there was a delightful little beauty.

"Are you an American?" the driver asked, still watching him in the rearview mirror.

Czez nodded.

The driver said, "I have a niece who is interested in meeting an American. She's tall, almost five-three. You interested?"

Czez laughed. "I believe I'll pass. I'm here on business. In and out."

The driver looked disappointed. "Too bad. You're missing a good bet." The traffic inched forward. He moved the Toyota ahead a few feet.

"Must be hard on clutches," Czez said. He swiped at the sweat on his forehead with the back of his hand. "Stop and go. Stop and go."

The driver grimaced. "Hard on patience. Terrible on clutches."

four

What with the highest murder rate in the world, the Republic of the Philippines was dangerous in the extreme. The Filipinos were so wretchedly poor they had the lowest daily intake of calories of any place in Asia. The cops were crooked. Corruption was rampant. Warlords with private armies ruled over sections of the provinces. The mountains were infested with Marxist rebels. Muslim rebels controlled large areas of Mindanao, just south of Cebu.

It seemed that all the things Jake Hipp wanted to buy, and which were casually found everywhere in the United States—dill pickles, say, good cheese, meat that had been properly hung—were not to be found in the Philippines except at an outrageous price. Cebu, just five degrees north of the equator and isolated from the rest of the world, was eternally hot except in April and May, when it got hotter still, then impossible. It was merely humid the year-round until July and August, when it was like walking through hot water. In addition, the air was filthy, the streets dirty, and in the rainy season, when the clouds opened up, the streets in downtown Cebu were turned into rivers. It was crowded; there was no open space anywhere. The traffic was impossible. It was noisy what with the rattle of motorcycle exhausts and the crowing of fighting chickens. Owing to corrupt officials running the power plants, the island was constantly plunged into darkness in what locals called "brownouts." On, off. On, off. On, off. Each surge of electricity took its toll on air conditioners, computers, and appliances. Cebuanos had never experienced the pleasure of constant electricity. For them, brownouts were a fact of life, to be endured.

All of that was true. But still, there was something about the Philippines in general, and Cebu in particular, that appealed to Hipp. Here was the raw stuff of life. Here, people struggled merely to survive, and to do that, they banded together into families and clans, where loyalty was everything. When you got to know them, Cebuanos could be sweet and generous in the extreme.

Compared to all this, life in the United States, which was clean and where department stores allowed the return of defective goods, was, well, sterile and boring. Every time Jake Hipp heard some alleged victim of this or that outrage boo-hooing on American television or complaining because a garment in Wal-Mart was sewn in Bangladesh, the Dominican Republic, or the Philippines, he wanted to puke.

Wearing his Third World traveler's uniform of sandals, walking shorts, short-sleeved shirt, multipocketed vest, and floppy cricket-player's hat to keep the sun off his face, Hipp did not go straight to Most Hipp after he arrived from the airport at one o'clock. He went to the house on Don Jose Avila Street that he had bought for Gina and stashed his bag. Then he took a leisurely hike down Osmena Boulevard, named for one of the Osmenas, a longtime family of power and influence in Cebu. He circled Fuentes Circle and went downstairs to the grocery store at Robinson's to see what fish they had for sale and for how much. He determined that they had fresh Lapu-Lapu, one of the most delicious fish in the world—and named for the man who had killed Francis Magellan—for the U.S. equivalent of a buck and a half a pound.

He finished the loop around Fuentes, going past Shakey's Pizza—where the pizzas were as good as they were in the United States—and started back up Osmena, in the direction of the provincial capital.

He took one quick detour down a side street to check out the fruit being peddled by sidewalk vendors. He bought some lanzones, a small yellow fruit about halfway in size between a marble and a Ping-Pong ball. The skin peeled off, revealing a succulent, translucent meat around the fruit's pit.

From the vendor camped out at the sidewalk entrance to Most Hipp, he bought a handful of national daily newspapers out of Manila—*The Globe, The Star,* and *The Enquirer.* Hipp loved Filipino journalism; here was a country where a nationalistic columnist could get away with calling Americans "assholes" and "dumb shits" in print, no problem. American editors, bowing to the wishes of Bible-thumping complainers, were so foolishly prudish that they took all the fizz out of the language; in Hipp's opinion, the vernacular was where the action was. On the box and over the Internet, boobs and buns hopped and bounced most joyfully along with language, opinion, and ideas. No damned wonder the circulations of the American newspapers kept plunging. It was as though honesty could be spoken, but not printed.

Lusting for a cold San Miguel, Hipp bounded upstairs and into the bar.

"Hey, it's Jake! The Hipp returneth!" exclaimed Bonny, who was wearing ball-busting tight jeans and his shirt unbuttoned to the middle of his chest.

"A cold one for Jake, coming up," said Gemid, a doe-eyed beauty who was a longtime waitress at Most Hipp.

Bonny asked, "Have you had lunch yet? Melissa, get Jake his usual."

Pretty Melissa, another longtime waitress, smiled broadly. "A bowl of chili coming up." She hurried for the kitchen to place the order.

Bonny arrived with a sweating bottle of San Miguel. "Gina took off, Jake. She didn't say where to. Said for me to take care of the place until you showed up." He paused, then said, "Is something going on that I don't know about?"

"Everything's cool, Bonny."

"Some juicy gossip, perhaps?"

"No gossip."

"You're no fun. We've added Australian sausages, did Gina tell you that? The Aussies love 'em. Say they taste just like home. Big, long ones. Mmmmmmm." He raised an eyebrow suggestively.

Hipp grinned. "So Gina tells me. Harold ever beat you at Scrabble?"

Bonny laughed. "He gave up after a hundred losses in a row, poor man." Harold, a regular at Most Hipp, was a professor of anthropology at the University of San Carlos. Although he sported a Ph.D. from the University of Pittsburgh, try as he might, the pompous Harold couldn't beat Bonny at Scrabble, and English was Bonny's second language. Actually, it was Bonny's fourth language. In addition to his native Visayan, he was fluent in Tagalog and Chinese, as it was spoken in Fukien Province.

It was at times like this, having fun with the effervescent Bonny, that Hipp never again wanted to take that long ride to Mactan to fly anywhere. This was where he wanted to be, not out somewhere chasing a snake like Bobby Pearl. He said, "You got a new roll of faces for me to look at, Bonny?"

"A new batch of twenty-four. Gina said I should have them developed for you and switch to twelve-shot film pack. I've got them in back. You want them now?"

"When my chili's ready. And keep the cold beer coming."

Bonny grinned. "You got it, Jake."

Most Hipp was on the second floor, and the bar itself was in the middle of the room so customers could sit at tables and look down on passersby on Osmena Boulevard. Hipp's formula for the bar was probably not fully understood by Gina or Bonny, but under their watchful eye, the place had prospered.

The walls of Most Hipp were covered with books. There were sections of mysteries and thrillers of one sort or another, plus westerns, novels of ideas, Penguin classics, and sections of history, geography, philosophy, government, and politics. There was a substantial section of books in German, and smaller collections in Dutch and Swedish.

The ceiling was festooned with a thicket of sports pennants that flapped lazily in the breeze created by the overhead fans. The pennants were international. They included the most famous Dutch and English football sides, plus the major sides in the German *Bundesliga*—Dortmund, Bayern Munich, and the rest—and Australian footie and cricket sides, from Adelaide and Goolagong to Cairns and Perth. Most of the professional American football, basketball, and baseball teams were there, as well as many college and university teams. Most Hipp's regulars knew that if they brought a pennant of their alma mater from home, Gina or Bonny would add it to the growing collection on the ceiling. Fans of Ajax and the Glasgow Celtics and the Vancouver Grizzlies had all added their teams to the ceiling, along with American college teams such as the Marshall University Thundering Herd and the Rice University Owls. Hipp had learned not to say that he "rooted" for the Oakland Athletics, say, in front of an Australian. To an Aussie, "to root" meant "to fuck."

Filipinos were rabid basketball fans, and playing half-court basketball with netless rims and thongs for shoes was a national pastime; they liked to associate themselves with winners; no self-respecting Filipino would wear anything other than a Chicago Bulls T-shirt. When Georgetown won the national championship, they wore Hoya T-shirts; when Duke won cup, they wore Blue Devil T-shirts. The Filipinos had their own professional league in Manila, the Philippine Basketball Association. The PBA teams were sponsored by companies, and Hipp thoroughly enjoyed their wonderful names, going so far as to add the San Miguel Beermen and the Pure Foods Tender Juicy Hot Dogs to his modest gallery of posters. Coming from a country whose teams called themselves Lions, Tigers, Cougars, and Panthers, Hipp thought it was a wonderful culture that could field a team of Tender Juicy Hot Dogs with an outsized wiener on the backs of their jerseys, looking like a giant phallus.

Hipp understood what expat and long-term travelers craved—in addition to sex. For the Germans, it was sausages and hot potato salad. The Americans wanted chili and generous hamburgers with big slices of onion. Aussies liked loud talk and getting tanked on cheap beer—skip the grub, Mate.

But all three cultures, plus the Canadians, Brits, Dutchmen, and Scandinavians, were isolated from home and so craved books and magazines; expats were explorers of sorts, and books explored the highways and byways of the imagination.

Gina Jumero's idea for competing with the established expat bars in Cebu was to provide sexy Filipina waitresses, good food, and loud music. An unbeatable combination, she thought. Hipp agreed on two out of three, but insisted on altering her formula. That Most Hipp would have sexy waitresses went without saying. And good food, yes, but more than that, authentic good food. For the Germans, for example, that meant mustard. For all Europeans and North Americans, that meant proper bread and salads. Proper bread meant whole-wheat bread, dark bread, and crusty loaves of French bread, not the ubiquitous loaves of white foam spiked with sugar so beloved by Filipinos. And salads? Filipinos were astonished that anybody would want to eat carabao food. For them, eating raw vegetables was like eating raw meat. They didn't eat salads themselves, unless it was a macaroni or potato salad, which they destroyed by dumping in copious quantities of sugar.

And no loud music, Hipp had added. While it was true that the Filipino love of romantic ballads was more acceptable than hard rock or rap, Hipp felt that one man's music was another man's noise. Quiet music maybe, on tape and controlled by the bar—some country-and-western, a little jazz, or classic Golden Oldies, depending on who was in the bar. But expats liked good talk most of all: of women, ideas, cultures, travels, and adventures. And watching the student nurses coming and going on the sidewalk below was great sport.

Gina had initially been bewildered by Hipp's plan to buy part of a transpacific shipping container and load it with paperbacks. Books? She and her friends were dubious, but Hipp had insisted, maintaining that he knew the desires of long-nose travelers. Authentic food. Salads. Very cold beer. Books.

As promised, Bonny delivered the twenty-four new photographs of cigar smokers along with Hipp's chili, which was piled high with chopped onions and grated cheddar cheese. As Hipp ate his chili, he began examining the photographs. The last picture was a stunner. He waved for Bonny. He did this with his fingers turned down, not up, which was offensive to a Filipino.

"Bonny, when did this man come in?" He showed him the picture of a blond man stepping through the door to the toilet.

Bonny pursed his lips. "Oh, that one. End of the roll. Last night. He didn't stay long. Had one beer and left." He glanced at the photograph. "Is this somebody we should know, Jake?"

"Last night. He was here last night? You're sure?"

Bonny made a face. He was the dependable one. Famous for it. "Of course I'm sure. Ask Gemid."

"Smoking a cigar, or you wouldn't have taken his picture. Has he been here before that you can remember?"

Bonny studied the picture. "He used to drop by once in a while, but I haven't seen him in months. One of those times, he brought us a pennant for the ceiling."

"The Citadel?"

"Yes, I think that was the place. It's up there in that mess somewhere." He looked up at the upside-down forest of pennants.

"That's okay, I believe. It'll have a bulldog on it," Hipp said. "Did he give you a name?"

Bonny shook his head. "First Gina takes off without so much as a how-do-you-do. Then you pop in wanting to see the pictures of the cigar smokers before you finish your bowl of chili. That's not like you, Jake." Bonny gave Hipp a look of admonition. He examined the picture with renewed interest. "This isn't Bobby Pearl, is it?"

"That's Colonel Carl Allen Czez, retired."

"Bobby Pearl?" Bonny said again. "I like that nice white skin. Mmmmm."

Hipp thought it was curious that Czez was wearing a

long-sleeved shirt. "Colonel Czez was in charge of a unit that traced hot money in the arms and NBC trades."

"What does NBC mean? Not National Broadcasting Corporation."

"Nuclear-biological-chemical." Hipp fished a photograph from the pocket of his vest. "You remember this individual?" He showed Bonny a swarthy-complexioned, curly haired man who had visited James Chan in Hong Kong.

Bonny said, "That's one of our cigar smokers. I sent you his picture."

"Correct."

Bonny studied the face. "Can't remember his name. Only came in a couple of times, and that's been some time ago. Who is he?"

Hipp, frowning, took a closer look. "Other than he has possibly been a customer of a special-effects artist for Sing Sing Boyd, it beats hell out of me, and that's a fact."

"Boyd Studios in Hong Kong?"

Hipp nodded.

"A customer? What did he buy?"

"Silicon masks, possibly. Hard to tell." Hipp showed Bonny a copy of the photograph of the Bang suspect taken by the CNN security cameras. "How about this guy? Has he ever been here? He's not a cigar smoker that I know of, but you might remember him."

Bonny grinned. "Oh, sure. Ralph. Hard to forget him. He used to be a regular here. Couldn't take his eyes off Gemid's butt. He loved his chili, just like you."

"Ralph who?"

"Ralph Snow. A big talker when he got drunk. Brag, brag, brag. Hasn't been by in months, though. Gemid's been wondering what happened to him." Bonny grinned. "She thought he was her ticket to the United States."

Hipp put his hands behind his head and stretched his arms. "I'm going to Gina's house to crash for a few hours. This is Saturday, isn't it? Tonight should be a big night here in Most Hipp, so I'll be back. If any one of these three men comes in while I'm out, I want you to save something with his fingerprints on it and put it in a paper bag for me."

"Ooooh. Like in the movies," Bonny said. "Done."

"It should be something dry—a spoon, a bowl, or an ashtray. Whatever. Glass is good, but not if it's wet."

five

Most Hipp was a favorite spot for a satisfying early morning meal after a horny tour of the girlie bars. There were ambitious young ladies of Cebu who, knowing this, trolled the establishment with stretch jeans. Veteran travelers knew that if a Filipina in a bar drank beer or smoked cigarettes, she was likely a prostitute; if she drank Coke and giggled, she was looking for a husband. At this hour of the night, the Filipinas in Most Hipp were drinking beer and smoking cigarettes.

When Jake Hipp stepped through the door at nearly one o'clock in the morning, Bonny grabbed him immediately, murmuring in his ear, "He's here, Jake. He's here."

Hipp's stomach leaped. "Colonel Czez?"

"Hong Kong man. I've got a soup bowl and a saucer for you. He handled them both."

"Good work. Thank you, Bonny."

"It's fun. Like being in the CIA."

Hipp spotted the dark-complexioned man watching MTV on the tube above the bar. MTV was a favorite of Bonny and Gemid and the other waitresses, not of their Australian, European, and North American customers, who ordinarily preferred CNN, Fox News, or The NET. Hipp found it mildly annoying that the box was tuned to MTV.

With Bonny at his side, he headed for the bar. As he drew close to Hong Kong man, he said, "I think I'll have some Wiener schnitzel tonight, Bonny. We've got somebody back in the kitchen, don't we?"

Bonny said, "Wiener schnitzel it is. With German potatoes." By this, he meant hot German potato salad. In Most Hipp, the German potato salad was made with Filipino bacon that was imitation American bacon—that is, with smoke flavor—and sugarcane vinegar rather than cider vinegar, and chopped purple onions rather than yellow onions, but no German traveler complained about the difference.

Hipp said, "Sounds good. Jon and Harold been in?"

"The droner and the Scrabble man." Bonny made a face of disgust. "Both came and went. The word is they turn into toads after six o'clock." Bonny grinned. "They'll see you tomorrow, they said."

Hipp always looked forward to bullshitting with longtime Cebu expats Droner Jon, who was obsessed by chess and military tactics, and the tall, potbellied Idaho Harold, but tonight he was glad he could choose his own company. "And a green salad," he said, heading for the bar. "And tell them to back off just a tad on the vinegar. The last time I was here, the dressing about curled my feet."

Behind him, Bonny made a face. "And a green salad. Yuch!"

Hipp took a seat near Hong Kong man, who was about fifty years old. He had light-brown eyes, good teeth, and an aquiline nose that was almost Charlton Heston.

Gemid, who was working the bar, quickly gave Hipp a cold beer. "Cigar, Jake?"

"Sure," Hipp said.

Gemid retrieved a box of Tony Valenzona cigars from behind the bar and opened it for Hipp. Hipp took one, eyeing Hong Kong. "Cigar?"

Hong Kong ran his fingers through his curly black hair. "Sure. I'll have a cigar."

Gemid handed him a cigar.

Hong Kong man studied the label on the cigar. "What is this? A Valenzona? A Filipino cigar? I didn't know they made cigars in the Philippines." He started to reach into his pocket, then stopped. "You have to cut the ends off these things, don't you?"

Hipp retrieved his nipper from his pocket. "Use this. Works like a tiny guillotine. You just nip the end off—like chopping off a head." He snipped the end from his cigar and handed the nipper to Hong Kong man.

Hong Kong grinned and used the guillotine to trim his own. "Say, that's pretty neat."

Hipp grabbed a package of Most Hipp matches and lit Hong Kong's cigar, studying his face as he did. Above them, on MTV, Michael Jackson, now reconciled with his sister Latoya, was singing a duet with her, "Restless Nights," from his new album, *Faces*. MTV was featuring all the videos on the album. As Michael and Latoya closed the song, it occurred to Hipp that if Michael's ambition was to be more beautiful than his sister, he had at last succeeded.

Hong Kong got his cigar going and puffed twice, savoring. "Sooie piggy. Mighty good smoke!" He made a circle with his mouth and sent a blue ring of smoke sailing. "Isn't this what you're supposed to do with cigar smoke? Gentlemen enjoying a good smoke and all that. Say, you must have some pull here. Bonny rushes over to take your order. Gemid has free cigars waiting for you."

Sooie piggy. Mighty good smoke! Hipp was momentarily startled. "My girlfriend and I own the place."

"Pretty Gina," Hong Kong said. "Where is she tonight?"

"Out of town," Hipp said.

Hong Kong glanced at Gemid. "She called you Jake. You're Jake Hipp."

"That's me."

"The famous Mongoose man."

Hipp smiled. "Infamous Mongoose man, the Charlie who couldn't pull the trigger on a cosmic motherfucker. Sweet fame. Follows me everywhere."

The Hong Kong man extended his hand. "I have to admit, I saw Joaquin Hurtado's interview with Bobby Pearl. I'm Bill Noble."

Hipp shook his hand. "Pleased to meet you, Bill." Was this man a friend of Bobby Pearl's? Was that the connection?

As if reading Hipp's mind, Noble said, "You people ever get a hint as to who Bobby Pearl is?"

Hipp nodded and took a puff on his cigar. "Sure, we got a line on him. We know who he is."

"Oh?" Noble waited. "And that would be?"

"A former military officer, it turns out. Almost made general."

"Army? Air Force? Marines?"

"Army." Hipp sent forth a circle of smoke. "A cigar smoker in addition to being a raging prick. I've been smoking cigars myself ever since I bumped into Pearl on the ferry between Algeciras and Tangier. He was smoking something big and black. Cuban or Central American. Honduras, but maybe Nicaraguan. Hard to tell."

"You think you're gonna get him?"

"Oh, hell yes, we'll get him," Hipp said. "His ass is grass, guaranteed." He thought for a moment, then pulled a photograph of Carl Czez out of his vest pocket. He showed it to Noble.

Noble studied it. "I've seen that guy in here before."

"He was in here last night, as a matter of fact."

Noble glanced up at the tube where Michael Jackson, in a skintight, metallic jumpsuit, danced down a rainy street in an apparent parody—or casual rip-off—of Gene Kelly in *Singing in the Rain:*

> *Faces, faces all the same*
> *Dancing, dancing*
> *Dancing, dancing in the rain.*

Noble, his eyes on Michael Jackson, said, "I was watching The NET down at Our Place. A man with your influence might be able to get Gemid to switch channels." Our Place, a downtown bar, was Most Hipp's competition.

Hipp waited for Gemid to finish taking an order from two Aussies who had arrived, their faces flushed from booze. They were hungry and wanted some of Most Hipp's good Australian sausages.

Noble said, "They're saying that Dani Bernardi's sister is taking over as permanent host of *My Side.*"

Hipp was stunned. He blinked. "She's what?"

Noble said, "Heard it on the BBC this morning. Frances Bernardi is her name. The producers are saying she showed up from Costa Rica or wherever she's been living and asked for an audition. They couldn't say no, what with her being Dani Bernardi's sister and all. Turns out she's a natural."

Hipp said, "Gemid, could you give us The NET, please?"

Noble went on: "They probably found it hard to turn her down after Bang killed Joaquin and her sister. Wonderful gambit, you have to give them that. Standing up for her fallen sister and all that. Heroic stuff."

Gemid punched up The NET, which was on the commercial break preceding *My Side*.

On the screen: the familiar *My Side* opener, a single figure sitting on a stool addressing the camera. Frances Bernardi, not surprisingly, turned out to be exactly like the photograph Jake had seen in Dani's office—a copper-skinned young woman who looked very much like her sister. She wore a low-cut dress showing a generous cleavage of light-brown breasts, and her nose was broader on the bridge than Dani's. She was blessed with Dani's rich, warm voice. She appeared sincere and courteous without being fawning. She had a way about her that commanded trust and respect. She looked straight at the camera.

Bernardi said, "Today I step into my sister Dani's shoes as she stood in for Joaquin Hurtado. We continue the march of truth with this special program so their deaths will not have been in vain. In view of our tragic losses, Elia Khardonne and The NET producers have given *My Side* free run to pursue the Bobby Pearl and Bang stories at will, without regard to time or day."

Hipp glanced at his watch. "It's ten o'clock in the morning on the West Coast and one in the afternoon, East Coast. This must be a helluva story."

Bernardi paused for a moment, looking resolved, then continued.

"As you likely know, *My Side* has often been criticized for its practice of inviting criminals to tell their stories in confidence. It's true we're willing to give them electronic masks and alter their voices if necessary. We'll also go anywhere and talk to anyone. Our critics tell us this is a reprehensible practice that glorifies megalomaniacs and criminals and that we are guilty of harboring felons and obstructing justice. If we know the whereabouts of a criminal, these critics argue, we should report this fact to the proper authorities. That's what they say. They're also fair-weather friends of the First Amendment. They believe in freedom of speech only when it suits them.

"We also encourage snitches and whistle-blowers to the point of paying for facts that would otherwise remain secret. Is this also reprehensible? Every once in a while we get a story that clearly justifies our kind of journalism. Today it is my sorrowful duty to begin my duties as host of *My Side* with a story of grave misconduct at the heart of American democracy. Callous as we have become to the arrogance and casual abuse of power in Washington, this surely is the worst of the worst—an American nightmare come to pass.

"I don't report this story lightly or without having considered fully the consequences. I'm a reporter, not a prosecutor. I seek only the truth. The issue of justice is for Congress and the courts. I report the facts in the name of Joaquin Hurtado, CNN's Roger Tarnauer and Belinda Lovewell, and of course my sister, Dani.

"The day after Joaquin Hurtado was murdered, the media were filled with speculation that the assassin was most likely a right-wing militiaman acting out of a misguided sense of patriotism. That Bang might be a renegade government agent was thought possible, but a suggestion of government conspiracy was beyond the pale—the fantasy of paranoids. The government, seemingly impotent to deal with Bobby Pearl, certainly had a motive. But whether Bang was a renegade or a militiaman, the will to ask pointed questions was blunted by Joaquin's death. Every journalist in the land had to ask himself or herself: *What if I'm next?* This is a fear well understood by anybody who has lived under murderous authoritarian regimes. From Argentina, Brazil, and Greece, through Zaire, the bloody list of murdered journalists in recent years runs the alphabet.

"Among many of the confidential sources Dani had

encouraged over the years was a woman in the Justice Department with a special loathing of greed and corruption. Dani, looking for anybody with a personal connection to higher levels of government, asked this woman for a list of all persons with access to FBI records of the E-mail codes and addresses used by professional criminals and mercenaries. Her source set to work. She provided Dani with a lengthy list of names, but none were suggestive of a conspiracy.

"Dani's source then turned her attention to persons outside the FBI headquarters, and immediately she happened onto a name that jumped right out at her: Tom Boso, brother of the President's chief-of-staff, Charlie Boso, had been hired as a White House data analyst shortly after the present administration took office and so had access to FBI computer banks. He had a virtual free run of computer data throughout the capital city."

Frances Bernardi fell silent, staring at her viewers straight-on. "At Dani's urging, her source hacked her way into Tom Boso's PC and entered a program to secretly record his communications over the Web. If Boso used his laptop to contact Bang in the future, *My Side* would have a record of it. He did and we do."

Bonny took a seat beside Hipp. "Your Wiener schnitzel is ready, Jake. You want to eat it here or at a table?"

Hipp said, "I'll eat it here, Bonny. I want to watch this show."

Frances Bernardi stared at her feet, clenching her jaw. She looked up again. "Dani's source did not check her tap on Boso's communications until the day after Dani was killed. She was stunned to find Tom Boso casually agreeing to pay a man named Ralph Snow a quarter of a million dollars to murder my sister. Fearing for her life, Dani's friend in the Justice Department remained silent. Her fear was understandable. Tom Boso was in daily contact with his brother in the White House."

Bernardi fought back the tears. "We now show you again the tapes that have quickly become familiar to all Americans: the man thought to be Bang as taped by security cameras at the entrance and exit of the CNN studios and above the desk of the Southern Comfort Hotel in Atlanta."

The Bang suspect was shown entering and departing the CNN studios and checking into the Southern Comfort. Then it was back to the distraught Frances Bernardi, whose eyes were still wet with tears. "And this is the same man in a videotape we bought from a law-enforcement official in Taipei who recognized the figure captured by the CNN and Southern Comfort security cameras. This man understood the commercial value of his tape and was determined to get the highest price possible. *My Side,* after examining it carefully to determine its authenticity, paid him one million dollars. It would have been a bargain at ten times the price."

On the monitor, the same middle-aged man could be seen walking down a cluttered Asian street, with Chinese language on the storefronts.

On the tube, Bernardi struggled to maintain her composure. "This is Ralph Snow walking down a Taipei street. Snow is a professional criminal who has for years been the Caucasian front man of a Chinese gang smuggling heroin and illegal immigrants into the United States. He communicated with the smugglers over the Internet, routinely changing his identity and E-mail addresses in order to stay ahead of government hackers; the FBI was thus able to contact him in cyberspace, but couldn't locate him physically.

"Only when it was announced that I was to take over from Dani did her fearful source speak up. The question I now put to you, the American people: are we to believe that Tom Boso hired Bang independently of the White House? That the Boso brothers would do this on their own, keeping the President ignorant? Where would a government employee come by a quarter of a million dollars? Break his piggy bank?"

Bernardi openly wept, both for her sister and for her country. It was the most dramatic moment on television in Jake Hipp's memory. He remembered watching the Green Bay Packers' Bart Starr follow Jerry Kramer's block into the end zone against the Dallas Cowboys in December 1967. He remembered Neil Armstrong stepping onto the surface of the moon in July 1969. Now this. The unmasking of a murderer in the White House.

Bernardi, fighting to regain her composure, said, "As I report the results of her investigation, my sister's source is in seclusion, supported by *My Side*. She will remain there until her safety is guaranteed."

Hipp was dumbfounded. Frances Bernardi had launched her new career with the biggest story since Bob Woodward and Carl Bernstein had led the media charge against Richard Nixon. But Nixon's transgressions were shoplifting compared to this. Dani had hated her sister, Frances. Now Frances Bernardi, using the results of her sister's covert inquiry, had unmasked a murderer in the White House—an American President with the imagination of a banana republic dictator. Irony, irony. Sweet irony ruled the world.

Hipp said, "Dani Bernardi must be twisting in her grave."

Noble looked surprised. "Why do you say that? I'd think she would be proud that her sister picked up where she left off."

Hipp, thinking of Michael and Latoya Jackson, said, "Frances Bernardi sure as hell looks like her sister, don't you think?"

Bill Noble furrowed his brow. "I don't know that I've ever seen her sister except for maybe a replay of the program that got her killed."

"Looks just like her," Hipp said. "Amazing resemblance. Darker complexion. Their maternal grandmother was an African-American."

Leaning to one side so Bonny could serve his Weiner schnitzel, Hipp looked thoughtful. Her rich, copper-colored skin reminded him of CNN's two famous Lynne/Lynns— Lynne Russel of the wonderful mouth, and the breathy-voiced Lynn Vaughn, who haunted his dreams night after night, reminding him of his failure at Tangier. "Her nose is different, too. A little broader. And she has bigger bazooms," he added.

Hipp studied Noble, wondering about the swarthy man.

Noble was a cigar smoker, which was why his picture was among those taken by Most Hipp's hidden camera, yet tonight he had pretended not to know that the end of a cigar had to be trimmed. Why was he trying to hide his knowledge of cigars?

David Wong's people had taken Noble's photograph when he was visiting the Hong Kong special-effects artist James Chan. What was his business with Chan?

Who the hell was Bill Noble?

six

Jake Hipp sat on the porcelain throne facing a wall of books while he talked to Joe Woofter on his cellular phone. Customers with full bladders would just have to go outside and pee on the side of a building like the Filipinos did. This was not a practice that Hipp recommended—there were walls in Cebu that were so foul you had to hold your breath when you walked past them—but right now he needed a little privacy. Most Hipp was his joint, and if he wanted to Bogart the john, it was his privilege.

Joe Woofter said, "I think I should start by telling you that one of our Charlies found a girlfriend of the prostitute in Amsterdam who was able to solve that part of the puzzle. Before she died, the prostitute told her girlfriend the probable reason for Pearl's fury. Turns out he barely got his gentleman in when it went limp. The girl used her womanly guilt to get it hard again, but the same thing happened. She was trying to get it up a third time when he went off his rocker and bragged that he was Bobby Pearl."

"After which, he started beating on her."

"Exactly."

"So that's his problem!" Hipp said. "He couldn't get it up for Greta, either."

"She should thank the gods he didn't give her the same treatment as the girl in Amsterdam."

"A close call on her part, but now we know his pathetic little secret. Things are beginning to come together, Joe."

Woofter said, "The President says that Frances Bernardi is lying through her teeth. He has agreed to a polygraph examination, which he's going to take within the hour at the White House."

"Fast acting."

"He knows he can't sit on an allegation like this. He's got to respond pronto. He can't just hole up on Pennsylvania Avenue and let his press secretary do the talking. He has to put this smoke out and put it out now, not later, or he'll have a political firestorm on his hands."

"God, let's hope he passes," Hipp said.

"You got that right."

Hipp said. "Could you get back to me immediately when you learn the results of the polygraph exam? I'm convinced that this Bang business dovetails with Carl Czez in some kind of way that's not immediately obvious."

"Sure, no problem. I'm too little potatoes to have scored an invite to the party, but the polygraph operator is a Company man and a friend of mine. By the way, one of the anthrax victims in Manhattan had a dried raccoon penis around his neck."

"The man from Charleston. He's hiring gophers."

"Looks that way. The guy with the coon's dick and his pal both died in fancy digs at the Waldorf-Astoria Hotel. We ran their prints and found they were ex-cons, Daniel Merrill and Thomas Smith, a.k.a. Elephant Dan and Slick."

"Plenty more shits where those came from."

"If you've got the bucks, and Czez can come up with whatever is necessary. We're talking a big, big sewer here, Jake."

Hipp glanced up as somebody rattled the locked door. "Listen, Joe, in a few minutes I'm going home to lift some fingerprints from an ashtray. I'll beam them to you with my laptop. I'll be wanting a check on them immediately, if not sooner. Can you get right on that when you get them?"

"Consider it done, Jake."

"Also, I want you to find a good dermatologist. I have a question to ask that might bear on all this. Roust one out of his or her office, or at home if that's what it takes."

"A dermatologist?" Woofter sounded puzzled. "I can do that. What's your question?"

"I'm interested in skin."

Woofter said, "Aren't we all, in one way or another?"

Hipp laughed. "A particular, specific interest, Joe. Light skin and dark skin."

All professional politicians knew better than to lie outright. The gotcha masters of the media went for an outright lie like sharks after blood. The trick always was to dodge the truth. In keeping with the dignity of the office, the extraordinary scene of the President of the United States undergoing a polygraph examination was not videotaped. The stated official reason for this decision was suspiciously similar to the gambit pioneered by Richard Nixon nearly thirty years earlier—that it would be undignified and harmful to the majesty of the office if the President of the United States should turn out to be a commonplace liar. The office of the presidency, not an individual president, was the issue. Let the curious gather around the tube to watch O.J.'s dodge if they wanted to. This was not spectacle; it was serious business that cut to the heart of democracy. Et cetera.

A second, perhaps less noble reason for the decision was that a videotape would erode the worth of the many nonfiction books that would later detail the scene. Nobody wanted that. Better to retain the profitable ambiguity.

To add to the credibility of his performance, not to mention the intimidating effect on the witnesses, the President chose his private office in the White House rather than the Executive Office Building. The office was lined with books, a testament to the President's education and sense of history. Here was an honorable and honest President, sincerely beloved by millions of the faithful, who would never believe he would lie about something so abjectly crass. Never mind what the polygraph said. Lie detectors weren't perfect, were they? A subject's state of mind would affect the results. Didn't everybody say that? The President might lie through his teeth in the Executive Office Building, but not in the White House. To do that would be to piss on the republic.

Merely being present would justify a handsome publisher's contract. Of course some contracts would be worth

more than others, that went without saying. Publishers
would spring for big bucks according to the author's power
and position, plus the quality of remembered details. Those
present would understandably attempt to observe and com-
mit to memory every conceivable detail, inflection of voice,
and nuance of emotion and meaning. This was rather like
prepping for an exam. After the session, the ghosts would be
standing by to test their memory.

It was inevitable, given the participants, the location, and
the stakes, that the scene—later told from multiple points of
view—was to have a *Rashomon*-like quality about it.

The largest publisher's contract almost certainly would go
to the polygraph operator, the tall, curly haired Leon Mandel, known from his childhood by the nickname of Dutch.
Dutch Mandel, it was said, was the best in the business.
After Aldrich Ames and Harold Nichols, the Company
decided that its counterintelligence section should get serious about internal security and so got the best-of-the-best to
check its officers and operatives. Nobody, but nobody, lied
to Dutch Mandel and got away with it. Since the analysis of
a subject's response was not an exact science, the polygraph
operator's interpretation of the telltale graphs was crucial.
Serious readers springing for a twenty-five-dollar hardcover
book would likely go straight to the polygraph operator,
screw the pols trying to dodge responsibility or score a fast
buck.

Just as Barry Scheck had become a celebrity DNA lawyer
following the trial of O. J. Simpson, Dutch Mandel was des-
tined to become a much-quoted and frequently interviewed
celebrity polygraph operator, and the payoff, come time to
sit back and enjoy retirement, would be significant. Mandel's efforts would be bought largely by the President's
detractors, and by those readers—a minority of the book-
buying public—who were interested solely in ascertaining
the truth.

The second-best contract, the profits from which would
likely be sucked up by legal fees, would no doubt be scored
by a spirited defense of the President, allegedly written by

his controversial wife, Anne, an activist First Lady much beloved by feminists. The First Lady's book would be panned by critics but snapped up by female soldiers of the gender wars, some of whom never read books, as a general in-your-face gesture to males.

The third-best score, owing to the passionate denial by people who had voted for the President, would likely go to his attorney, the wildly expensive celebrity lawyer Todd Singleton, who had once been a professor at Harvard Law School. In addition to his legal work, Singleton, a small, brown-eyed man once described in *The New York Times* as having "the demeanor of a hungry ferret," was famous for spouting controversial opinions and so was omnipresent on the tube. The people buying his book would be paying for confirmation of what they already believed—that the President, likely framed by conniving agents of the opposition party, was completely innocent.

Lesser, six-figure contracts would likely go to Sally Holtzbrinck, the tall, auburn-haired attorney general, who would write a lengthy legal analysis in order to dodge the central question: was the son of a bitch lying through his teeth, or was he telling the truth? The aging chief justice of the Supreme Court, John Brooks, would weigh in with a befuddled and confusing account, filled with irrelevant precedents and questionable conclusions. The House speaker, the Senate majority leader, and the House and Senate minority leaders, would get decent advances if they hired ghostwriters capable of producing a manuscript that would likely be well reviewed; otherwise, they would have to settle for more modest hits in magazines and fees for lecture-circuit discussions of the episode; those who later qualified for an autobiography could devote an entire chapter to rehashing the oft-told tale.

Singleton, determined to limit possible damage by any ambiguous or suggestive responses by the President, had talked Attorney General Holtzbrinck into limiting the inquiry to a single germane question: did or did not the President of the United States specifically order anybody to assassinate journalists? That was it. No more. Ms. Holtzbrinck, who looked forward to reappointment during the President's second term, relented in the interest of fairness and elementary justice.

Dutch Mandel chafed under Singleton's restriction, which, under the circumstances, he considered obscene. He was CIA, not Justice Department, and he did not want it said that he was supine in this situation. He was determined to ask whatever questions he thought ought to be asked. If the President's counsel or the attorney general objected, then up their hole with a telephone pole. Let the President's refusal to answer be recorded for the public to consider.

The witnesses gathered 'round, uneasily cracking wise as Mandel placed his machine on the President's polished cherrywood desk and wired the President so that his pulse, blood pressure, and sweating fingertips might be monitored. The President was flanked by the First Lady and his lawyer.

Mandel asked, "Are you comfortable, Mr. President?"

The President said, "Hardly comfortable, but I'm ready. Ask your questions."

"I'll ask you some questions to establish a baseline; then we'll get down to business. I want the truth to the first three questions, followed by lies for the next three. You understand?"

"Got it. Shoot."

"Do you wear boxers or jockeys, Mr. President?"

"Boxers," the President said.

The witnesses all laughed.

Mandel glanced at the attorney general and the First Lady. "I won't ask you on which side you hang."

Everybody laughed again.

"Do you eat whole-wheat or white?"

"Whole-wheat."

"What is your mother's name?"

"Grace."

"Would you like to see the House speaker reelected next November?"

"I hope he wins by a landslide," the President said, suppressing a grin.

The room erupted with laughter.

Mandel grinned. "That was a real whopper, Mr. President. Now, have you ever made a promise in a political speech that you knew was impossible to keep?"

"Never. Not once," the President said. Again, he looked amused. The President was nothing if not a charmer, which was essential for politicians who offered the voters an attractive image on the tube in lieu of sensible issues and policies.

Mandel grinned.

Singleton said, "Mr. Mandel, if you please."

Mandel said, "Sorry, Mr. President. Tell me, have you ever thought about peeing in a sink?"

The President grinned. "Of course not."

The spectators all laughed again.

Mandel glanced at the President's lawyer. "Good to relieve the tension."

Singleton said, "Please get on with it, Mr. Mandel. This is not a comedy club. We have serious business."

Mandel smiled. "Mr. President, have you and Charlie Boso ever considered the possibility of murdering journalists in a national emergency?"

Singleton held up his hand. "We have an understanding, Mr. Mandel."

Mandel looked annoyed. "An understanding. Right, right."

"The President declines to answer that question on the grounds that no president in recent memory hasn't felt a murderous urge with respect to journalists at one time or another. Read Jefferson's letters. Lincoln was enraged by the press of his day. How do you suppose Richard Nixon felt about Bob Woodward and Carl Bernstein? Do you suppose any president in American history could truthfully answer no to a question like that?"

Mandel ran his fingers through his curly hair. He regarded the President mildly. "At any time in the search for Bobby

Pearl, did you ever suggest to Charlie Boso that by murdering journalists, you might stop the reporting of leaks from the Justice Department?"

"Same objection," Singleton said. "We're dealing with a specific charge here, not the President's idle fantasies. Harboring a fantasy is not a crime. Acting on a fantasy is. Did the President or did he not order his chief-of-staff, Charlie Boso, to arrange the assassination of journalists? That's the only question at issue here. Did he or didn't he? Ask that question, and the President will be pleased to answer."

Mandel grimaced. "Mr. President, were you aware that Charlie Boso's brother, Tom Boso, had access to FBI data that included the E-mail addresses of known or suspected criminals or mercenaries?"

"Not specifically."

Singleton frowned.

"No?" Mandel asked.

"Well, I suppose I had some idea."

Singleton said, "Tom Boso is a data analyst for the White House. He presumably has access to FBI data. Be specific, Mr. Mandel. We're not interested in circumstance here. Did the President of the United States order journalists killed? You might try getting to the point. We have an agreement, remember." He looked at the attorney general.

Holtzbrinck said, "Mr. Mandel!"

Mandel looked sideways at Singleton. He did not admire lawyers in general, and the President's counsel was an obvious asshole. Mandel ran his fingertips down his jaw. "Okay, Mr. Singleton. Mr. President, did you ever ask—"

"Order," Singleton said. "Did the President 'order.' Not suggest or hint or anything like that. 'Order' is the operative word. Only 'order.'"

"Mr. President, did you ever order Charlie Boso to secure the help of his brother, Tom Boso, in hiring a potential assassin?"

Singleton interrupted quickly. "There might be legal reasons for hiring potential assassins. What if the CIA had been considering an action, however illegal, that involved murder and the President knew about it? The allegation is that the President ordered someone to murder Joaquin Hurtado, Dani Bernardi, William Tarnauer, and Belinda Lovewell. Be specific."

"Mr. President, did you ever instruct anyone to hire a killer to assassinate television journalists?"

"Not instruct. Order," Singleton said.

"Mr. President, did you ever order anyone to hire a killer to assassinate journalists?"

"No. Never. Absolutely not," the President said.

Mandel, studying the graph, glanced up at Holtzbrinck. The attorney general pursed her lips.

"Mr. President, did you ever suggest the murdering of journalists to Charlie Boso, with the request that you not be told about it if he followed through?"

The President licked his lips.

Singleton said quickly, "You're back in the territory of fantasy again. The President might well have had such a fantasy and mentioned it to Charlie Boso in a moment of stress. If Charlie Boso acted on a fantasy without the President's specific authorization, the President is not responsible or legally accountable. Did he or did he not order an assassination? That, I repeat, is the only relevant question here, and the President answered it. He said unequivocally no, he did not order anybody to kill journalists."

"Mr. President, how did you feel when Joaquin Hurtado was assassinated?"

Singleton's eyes widened. "The President's reaction is not at issue here. There is only one question to be answered. At the risk of sounding like a stuck record, I feel obliged to say again, did or did not the President order that journalists be murdered? The answer is no, negative, he did not."

The President held up his hand. "No problem. I'm glad to answer that question. I was horrified when I learned that somebody had shot Joaquin Hurtado. I was shocked to learn of Dani Bernardi's death. I was stunned when I found out what had happened to William Tarnauer and Belinda Lovewell."

Mandel, watching the graph, arched an eyebrow.

The President said quickly, "I was no admirer of Joaquin Hurtado, I admit. It's possible that I harbored some ambivalent feelings toward him. But I didn't order him killed. I was shocked at all four deaths. I knew Bill Tarnauer well. I considered him a friend. Ms. Lovewell was a beautiful and talented woman. Her loss was everybody's loss."

Mandel said, "You say you had ambivalent feelings toward Joaquin Hurtado. He reported administration secrets with an apparent disregard for any larger public interest. He was obviously thinking only of his Nielsens and personal glory. Considering all that, do you think he got what he deserved?"

Singleton glared at him.

"I'll withdraw the question," Mandel said quickly.

seven

It was a lonely walk home, but at 3:00 A.M., Jake Hipp was not alone. To his best knowledge, it was impossible to walk down a deserted street in any Filipino city, except perhaps at 4:00 A.M. on Christmas morning. At this hour, the humid tropical air was nearly balmy, and Hipp, who had not recovered from jet lag despite a nap, felt almost invigorated. He was running on nervous energy, he knew, and would sleep late from sheer emotional and physical exhaustion.

Carrying the paper bag with the print-laden saucer and soup bowl, he crossed Osmena Boulevard, thinking about all that had happened. He walked east, toward the provincial capital and the mountainous spine of the island. He felt that his failure to pull the trigger of a pistol had thrust him into a vortex of American history. The ultimate truth was simple enough, but almost impossible to accept: if Hipp had spiked Bobby Pearl as he had been ordered to do by Joe Woofter, none of the subsequent tragedies would have happened.

Had the President of the United States ordered the murder of journalists whom he felt were endangering the public interest? Jake Hipp sincerely hoped not. There had been some real White House numbskulls in recent history. One paranoid and insecure president, already all but assured of reelection, had ordered a break-in of the headquarters of the opposition party. Another chief executive, intent on buying reelection by massive television advertising, had solicited financial donations from Intelligence operatives of the Chinese communists—going so far as to invite them into the White House for coffee.

Hipp turned right on Don Jose Avila and two blocks later, arrived at the house he had bought for Gina Jumero, whom, he knew, he would one day marry. The house was surrounded by a wall made of cement blocks and topped by shards of broken Coke bottles. Hipp and Gina had planted their yard with tropical fruits: guavas; star fruits; papayas, and even a large mango tree that yielded the sweet little mangoes for which Cebu was famous. Hipp had had mangoes in many countries, but none, absolutely none, were as delicious as the variety grown on Cebu.

He stopped at the gate, which was made of a heavy iron grille, and unlocked the huge, Japanese-made padlock. He had no sooner stepped inside and relocked the padlock than he saw a glow on the front steps of the house. His mouth turned dry and his stomach raced.

He squatted in the shadows of the spreading mango tree and retrieved his .38 Smith & Wesson from one of the pockets of his vest. Was this it then: was this to be his confrontation with Bobby Pearl?

The ash on the steps glowed. A familiar voice said, "Jake? Is that you?"

Hipp grinned and put the pistol back in his pocket. He headed for the front door. "Felix! *Oy! Gino-o-ko!* I told Gina to stay in Moalboal." *Oy! Gino-o-ko!* was a familiar expression among Cebuanos, translating roughly as "Oh, God help me!" This was not to be confused with the Yiddish *Oy* as in *"Oy vey!"* The Philippines were a former Spanish possession, so Hipp assumed that the oft-used *Oy!* in Cebu was a corruption of the Spanish explective *Ay!*, as in *"Ay Dios!"*

"You know women," Felix said. "All she could do was worry, worry, worry. Finally, she couldn't take it any longer. Had to come back. I told her she should do what you said, but it didn't do any good."

As Hipp drew near, Felix's broad form and curly black hair became visible. In an effort to foil thieves, Hipp always spread out his money in the many pockets of his vest. Now he unsnapped the pocket where he had stashed an American fifty-dollar bill. He retrieved the bill and slipped it into the hand of his future brother-in-law. He said, "You stick with the job until I say otherwise, okay? Don't let her out of your sight. It's dangerous if you do. Got it?"

Felix squinted at the bill in the dim light. He looked pleased. "Got it. Done. Thank you."

Hipp left Felix on the porch and went inside and into the bedroom, where he saw Gina's slender form sit up in the bed. "Jake?"

"Me."

"I'm sorry, Jake."

Hipp sighed. He sat on the edge of the bed and put his arms around her. *"Gihigugma-koi-kau."*

"I love you, too. You know that."

"It was dangerous to come back. I told you to stay put."

"I'm sorry, Jake. I couldn't help it."

"So Felix said. Never mind, you're here now. I want you to call your brother Rudy tomorrow. I want Rudy to help Felix out. Tell them to hire some of your cousins. You can get Ben and Elvis, can't you? Until this business is settled, I want a relative on that doorstep, armed and alert, at all times."

"Is he here? Bobby Pearl."

"He's here," Hipp said. "We got his picture on the john camera last night." He stood at the barred window, looking out into the shadows of the yard.

"What are you going to do now?"

"I'm going to lift some fingerprints from a saucer and a soup bowl and zap them to Joe Woofter, then get quietly stoned and do some thinking. You been watching the news on the tube by any chance?"

"No, I haven't. What happened?"

"Where I grew up in Montana, the expression was, 'The shit hit the fan.' In this case, it's turds the size of watermelons." He exhaled. "Let me lift the prints and send them to Joe, and I'll be back to wait for his answer." Hipp grabbed his Charlie gear from the bureau drawer and went into the kitchen, where the light was good.

* * *

When Jake Hipp had finished lifting Bill Noble's fingerprints and sending them to Joe Woofter on the Web, he
returned to the bedroom and retrieved his bag of Filipino
bud from the corner of a bureau drawer. It wasn't green and
sticky and aromatic like the high-powered hydroponic weed
in the United States, but it got the job done. He loaded his
bong and lit a match. He took a hit of cannabis and sat squat-
legged on the bed beside the sleeping Gina—that is, Gina
who was pretending to be asleep—and smoked pot as he
waited for the call from Joe Woofter. The Company computers could run a fingerprint check in minutes.

Sooie piggy. Mighty good smoke.

Stoned, drifty, Hipp thought about all that had happened
and what he had learned in his long day:

Bobby Pearl, a.k.a. Carl Czez, had made an appearance in
Most Hipp the previous night. There was no denying the picture taken by the camera in the toilet.

The British Secret Service had photographed the swarthy-
complexioned Bill Noble visiting Sing Sing Boyd's special-
effects artist.

Ralph Snow was a former regular at Most Hipp. A big
talker when he got drunk, Bonny had said.

Frances Bernardi, up from Costa Rica to take over from
her fallen sister, had launched her new career as host of *My
Side* by accusing the President of the United States of murdering journalists.

The single connection or connections between or among
Pearl, Noble, and Snow was Most Hipp; each man, at one
time or another, had been a customer of Most Hipp. Of all of
Carl Jung's interesting speculations, the one Hipp found
most dubious was Jung's idea of synchronicity, an attempt to
explain the psychological origins of coincidence. Hipp
believed that there was only one kind of coincidence: a statistical anomaly devoid of logical links. Other so-called
coincidences were no such thing; somewhere beneath the
surface fact of happenstance, there lurked cause and effect.
Hipp believed that to be the case in the puzzle before him.

Bobby Pearl connections. He closed his eyes.

Carl Czez. Ralph Snow. Bill Noble.
Hong Kong. The Philippines. Most Hipp.
Moamar Qadhafi. Dani Bernardi. Frances Bernardi.

Three plus three plus three. Nine. Nine little Indians. Or was it two plus three plus two? Hipp opened his eyes and smiled. Seven, not nine. That was a possibility, depending. He was thinking about the web of cause and effect when the cellular phone rang on the nightstand beside the bed. He grabbed the phone.

"Jake? Joe here."

"What've you got, Joe?"

"The President passed the lie-detector test, sort of."

"Sort of?"

Woofter said, "He had Todd Singleton there to help him steer clear of any real danger. If you ask the President if he specifically ordered the murders, he passes the test. But Dutch Mandel says the President's secondary answers, combined with the answers of Charlie and Tom Boso, suggest that the situation is more complicated."

"Mandel is the polygraph operator?"

"Right."

"Charlie Boso is chief-of-staff. Tom does what, exactly?"

Woofter said, "He's a data analyst for the White House, with access to computer banks throughout the government. The President's designated nerd. Charlie Boso denied asking Tom to contact a professional killer on the Internet."

"Truth?"

"A lie," Mandel says. "Charlie also denied asking his brother to hire a professional killer to murder journalists. A generic question. Another lie."

"What about brother Tom?" Hipp asked.

"Tom Boso denied contacting Ralph Snow. A lie, Mandel says. He also denied asking Snow if he would be willing to murder journalists. A lie."

"Now we're getting to it."

"Dutch then asked Tom specifically if he had hired Snow to murder journalists. He said no. Mandel says he was telling the truth."

Hipp grimaced. "I don't understand. What do we conclude from all that?"

"We conclude that they're keeping tight sphincters at the White House. Charlie and Tom Boso no doubt did explore the possibility of murdering journalists, and probably at the suggestion of the President. Tom Boso likely contacted Snow as a possible hit man, but never went through with it. The President either discussed the idea with Charlie Boso and changed his mind or he suggested the notion with the request that it not be done with his knowledge. If that's the case, it wouldn't be a White House first. Nobody gets to be President who doesn't know how to avoid accountability."

Hipp said, "Hear no evil. See no evil. Speak no evil."

"The official dodge. We think so. Lyndon Johnson and Richard Nixon both probably harbored such murderous thoughts toward journalists at one time or another. I've even thought about it myself, to tell the truth. The President's reluctance to be asked whether or not he had harbored murderous feelings simultaneously made sense and finessed the polygraph examiner."

Hipp laughed. "If stupidity or bad taste were felonies, we'd have all journalists on death row."

"Joaquin Hurtado would at least have been doing hard time, that's a fact."

"Life without parole. How about the fingerprints?"

Woofter said, "No record of those prints anywhere that I can find. I checked the FBI. The Defense Department. The INS. Nothing."

"Nothing in the Defense Department?"

"Zero, I'm afraid."

Hipp thought about that for a moment. "Well, that may be no surprise, depending. I got a positive I.D. on another kind of fingerprint."

"Oh? And that would be?"

Hipp said, "The expression 'Sooie piggy. Mighty good smoke!' "

"Say again?" Woofter sounded puzzled.

"You always nag us to include the nonphysical fingerprints in our reports. Body language. Nervous tics. Emotional fingerprints. Tell me, Joe, how many people have you met lately who say, 'Sooie piggy. Mighty good smoke,' when they savor a stogie?"

"None. Not in a week or two at least," Woofter said.

"Been a while for me, too. Did you talk to a dermatologist?"

"Yes, I did. She says the answer to your question is yes. It turns out that folic acid is comprised of something called pteridine, plus para-aminobenzoic acid and L-glutamic acid. Pteridine is an enzyme that helps produce tyrosine, which is necessary for the production of melanin."

"Which makes skin dark."

"Correct. Africans have lots of melanin in their skin. Europeans don't. Also, para-aminobenzoic acid administered in large doses will darken your hair. But for the folic acid to produce tyrosine, it has to be stabilized and reduced to tetrahydrofolic acid. Ascorbic acid, vitamin C, will stabilize it. Vitamin B-twelve will reduce it to tetrahydrofolic acid."

"And the short of it in layman's language?"

"The short of it is that if you take a two-milligram tablet of folic acid twice a day, a five-hundred-milligram tablet of vitamin C twice a day, plus a hundred-milligram shot of vitamin B-twelve every two weeks, you can darken your skin and keep it that way. Dermatologists use this to help mask vitiligo, where patients have patches of skin without pigment. The patient will end up with a darker complexion, which is your question, right? You can give the process a boost by spending an hour in the sun or a tanning room each day."

"How long will it take?"

"She says quite rapidly, a couple of weeks maybe. But while you're waiting for the vitamins to have their effect, you can use cosmetics designed to cover up vitiligo. You want to tell me what you're thinking?"

"I . . . I'm not sure, Joe," Hipp said. "No, that's not correct. I'm thinking about motive and means and the technology of molting. The world gets curiouser and curiouser."

"You think he's there, Jake?"

Hipp sighed. "Very likely."

"Jesus, you and him again."

"I know. I know. I know. No time to send help, and if you did, he might recognize them and go to ground again. No telling what he learned when he was at NSA. For the moment, it's me he's after. I have to take him on."

"You have your snake kit?"

"Yes, I do, and this time it looks like I'll have a chance to use it."

"If you can, it's the safest way, Jake. Fuck that John Wayne boom-boom stuff. That's not you anyway."

Hipp smiled grimly. "Isn't that the truth?"

"You've got the kit. This is what it's designed for. Use it. Maximum lock. And put the son of a bitch on a short tether."

"If I have this business figured, you're right, it is made to order for the kit. Either way, tomorrow I should know."

"Good luck, Jake."

"Thanks, I'll need it." Hipp hung up, looking at the shadows in the yard. The shards of glass on top of the wall were silhouetted against the pale light. A gecko called *fuck-you, fuck-you!* A motorcycle without a muffler roared down Osmena Boulevard.

Gina, who had been listening to the conversation, slipped her arm around him. "What happens now?"

Hipp didn't answer. He packed the bowl of his bong with another pinch of cannabis. He struck a match and took a hit, holding it in his lungs. He exhaled. "I'm going to sleep in tomorrow morning. Tomorrow afternoon I'll buy a *lechon* and take it down to your folks, together with the bottles of Scotch I bought for your dad and brothers. I'll buy your dad a big chunk of *tanqueqe*. Cading'll make me some *kinilaw*, won't he?"

Kinilaw was a Filipino dish of raw Spanish mackerel, locally called *tanqueqe*, marinated in coconut milk, juice from *kalamansis*, a.k.a. *lemoncitos*, chunks of fresh ginger, chopped onions, hot peppers, and tomatoes. Hipp was not a great fan of *lechon*, which was suckling pig roasted over charcoal until the skin became a rich mahogany-brown. This crisp skin was much beloved by Filipinos, Gina included. In the United States, to say that a future father-in-law treated you like a son was usually pretense and affectation. Not so in the Philippines. Jake Hipp had already been taken into the family as Cading and Celing's long-nosed son.

Gina was pleased at Hipp's request. "Of course he'll make you some *kinilaw,* silly. What do you think? Clam soup too, if you want. And tomorrow night, what about tomorrow night?"

Hipp shrugged. "Maybe tomorrow night I'll finish the assignment Joe Woofter gave me to do in Seville."

eight

The gang at Most Hipp was gathered before the tube, where all channels were covering the aftermath of the allegation that the President of the United States, frustrated in his pursuit of Bobby Pearl, had hired a professional killer, Ralph Snow, to murder uncooperative television journalists. They watched a press conference wherein the President's lawyer, Todd Singleton, a master at delivering colorful sound bites, said the charges against the President were ridiculous; he had passed a lie-detector examination with flying colors. The President had not ordered anybody murdered, Singleton said. He was clearly innocent. This was a no-brainer lynch mob led by partisan pip-squeaks.

After Singleton's press conference, it was back to the rush of charge and countercharge. Some conniving skunk had leaked the fact that the President had refused to say if he had ever entertained the thought of murdering journalists. This was smoke of the most obvious sort, the President's eager critics charged, and the leaders of the opposition party, offended that the chief executive had declined to incriminate himself by answering all of Dutch Mandel's questions, were calling for him to resign.

To all of this, the beleaguered President issued a reply through his press secretary saying there was no crime in thinking untoward thoughts, which he hadn't done; only acting on them was a crime, which he hadn't done either. The polygraph examination confirmed that he hadn't acted on them. The press secretary said the President refused to answer questions about what he may or may not have been thinking, out of respect for his office. He didn't want to set a debilitating precedent for future presidents whereby opposition politicians would be demanding lie-detector tests as quickly as they now called for special counsels.

Fox News sponsored a session in which psychologists and historians solemnly discussed the wisdom of subjecting untoward presidential thoughts to a lie-detector test. One secret presidential thought that had backfired big time was Jimmy Carter's revelation, in a *Playboy* magazine interview, that he had "lusted in his heart" for women other than Rosalyn. In straightforward English, this meant that Georgia Jimmy got horny when he browsed through the skin pics in *Playboy.* Oh shock, shock! This had led to all manner of jokes about the presidential pee-pee being pulled in the White House john. The panel on presidential thoughts was split on the subject of presidential fantasies: half thought the President should have fessed up to having murderous thoughts about journalists; half thought he shouldn't have.

Hipp watched the unfolding hysteria with Bonny and the ruddy-faced Dieter Schultz, a German ship's captain from Hamburg; also with Mike Clarke, a mining engineer up from Sydney, and Paddy O'Ryan, a retired Irish building contractor, and the enigmatic Bill Noble. The San Miguel was cold, the Spanish peanuts were fresh and delicious, and the circus of American politics was never livelier and more fun to ridicule.

The speaker of the House, answering a question from a Fox News reporter, said, "The very fabric of the republic is at stake!"

O'Ryan made a snorting sound. "Fabric of the republic? What the hell does that mean? Is that fabric made of wool like the Aussies shear off of sheep, or is it something else? Nylon or polyester, perhaps."

"Spun bullshit," Clarke said quickly. "A new American technology. Cheaper than oil. More plentiful."

"They say we Americans recycle everything," Hipp added dryly. "Paper, bottles—"

O'Ryan burst out laughing. "By God, that's gotta be it. Recycled bullshit is the fabric of America, and here I thought it was only in Ireland."

Finding itself in a political firestorm, the administration was responding by spilling its guts on everything. There would be no more secrets in their pursuit of Pearl and Bang, none. Now on The NET, the director of the FBI was telling a reporter what the government knew about Ralph Snow, who had for years been serving as a Caucasian front man for a Chinese triad on Taipei.

Hipp had secured Bonny's help by prepping him in advance. He now gave Bonny his cue, a simple nod of the head.

Bonny said, "Ralph Snow used to be a regular here."

Clarke looked amazed. He tilted his head. "Bang hung out in Most Hipp? Are you sure?"

O'Ryan said, "Oh, hell yes. He consumed many a San Miguel right where you're sitting. No surprise that he was a crook. Big talker when he got tanked, though. Even I couldn't compete with him, and I was born in County Cork."

Bonny said, "Had his eye on you, didn't he, Gemid? It was well known that he was a butt man." Bonny raised an eyebrow.

Gemid blushed.

Bonny said, "He loved our pepper steak. We have nothing but class customers in this place, right, Jake?"

"Nothing but gentlemen and scholars," Hipp said. "And perhaps Bang."

Bill Noble said nothing. He clearly wasn't feeling well.

O'Ryan said, "Tell us, Jake. You're the house Mongoose man. What do you make of this?"

"*My Side* interviewed Bobby Pearl on Negros, one island over. Bang was a regular here. Makes a person think." He gave Bonny another cue.

Bonny said, "Bobby Pearl used to be a customer here, too. Isn't that right?"

Hipp said, "We think so. Like I said, nothing but gentlemen and scholars in Most Hipp. Anybody else, we give the boot." He said, "Tell me, Paddy, are you familiar with how Mongoose got its name?"

"You chase snakes."

"Right. Quicker than snakes we are."

Noble mopped some sweat from his forehead. "Except for Bobby Pearl."

Hipp said, "Except for Pearl. We call them snakes because snakes molt, but I suppose everybody knows that by now."

"They shed their skins," Bonny said.

Clarke said, "You must have a point to make with the business of molting. How does Bobby Pearl shed his skin? Have you Americans figured that out?"

"Good question," Hipp said. "Yes, we have. By plastic surgery and with silicon masks he had made by a special-effects artist in Hong Kong who does work for Sing Sing Boyd. He could be any one of us right here at the bar, as a matter of fact. We're all about the same age. Also, in the Old Testament, the snake is an incarnation of Satan. You feeling okay, Bill?"

Noble's hands began to tremble slightly.

Clarke said, "Lucifer slithering around Eden. Right? Some Eden this is, brownouts every half hour."

Carl Czez regarded Jake Hipp mildly. He hated the son of a bitch. Hipp thought he had it all figured. All his talk about snakes and molting. And here Czez was, Bobby Pearl, sitting right in front of Hipp. And Hipp had no idea. None. Blathering on to the stupid Australian and the Irishman. Talk, talk, talk. Hipp might have had the notion that he had used a plastic surgeon. New nose maybe. A new hairline. A different chin. All that. And he'd likely figured the masks. That wasn't hard. All anyone had to do was go to a movie to figure the masks. A good special-effects artist could make any kind of mask.

But had Hipp figured out that Czez had used the masks to transform himself into Ralph Snow? Czez didn't think so. It would be fun to go into the john and put on his Snow mask, then return and blow away the television set, but Czez wouldn't be doing that.

And Hipp hadn't figured the darkened skin, either. No

way. Czez could sit here as the dark-complexioned Bill Noble and drink all the San Miguel he wanted, and Hipp would be none the wiser.

Czez would never forget Hipp looking back at him in Seville, waving at him from the backseat. His sexual trouble might have started before Hipp, but Hipp had made the situation worse. Czez could have gone for Hipp's girlfriend straight off, but this was the way to savor triumph. Walk right into Most Hipp and sit at the bar and let the terrorist chaser talk on—blah, blah, blah.

Czez was a veteran traveler in the Third World, and he had learned, through hard experience, that someone coming from North America or Europe had to get used to a whole shitload of new bugs and bacteria. It was impossible to anticipate everything. There had come a time with nearly every trip when he had come down with a fever, or puked his guts out, or had got a good dose of the pineapple quick-steps. It was especially annoying, now that he was at last getting his chance to have a little fun with Hipp before he put his lights out, that he was coming down with some horseshit fever.

If Czez got too sick, he decided, he would just go back to his hotel and wait it out. Hipp wasn't going anywhere. When he got better, he'd come back to Most Hipp, where the stupid bastard would be waiting, holding court. A couple of days wouldn't make any difference.

Czez had to admit that it was sick sport listening to Hipp brag about how much he had figured out. If Hipp really had any brains, he'd shut the fuck up.

Jake Hipp retrieved a small black box from his pocket and put it on the bar. He opened the box, which contained six red capsules, three yellow capsules, and one green capsule. He handed Noble a red capsule. "Take this. You'll feel better, guaranteed."

Noble mopped more sweat from his forehead. "What?"

"Just do it."

Noble popped the capsule into his mouth and chased it down with beer.

Hipp, addressing Clarke as though nothing had happened, said, "Goethe called him Mephistopheles in his poem. You want to tell us about Dr. Faustus, Dieter?"

Dieter took a sip of San Miguel. "Dr. Faustus swapped his soul to the Devil."

Hipp said mildly, "I suppose we all make our private deals one way or another, don't we? Right, Bill?"

Noble smiled. "Well, yes, I guess we do."

"Feeling better?"

"Well, yes I am, as a matter of fact."

Hipp said, "I saw that woman up there last night, Frances Bernardi—Dr. Frances Bernardi—and I saw nothing but raw ambition. Her sister was murdered, so she pops up like a jack-in-the-box to take her place. We're supposed to believe she's all heroic, what with Bang still on the loose, but I wonder."

"Wonder what?" Noble asked. His good spirits had returned.

"Well, isn't it true that television celebrity journalists routinely swap their souls for fame? I'm not talking about the wannabe stars on the bottom. I mean those who have made it to the top."

Clarke looked disbelieving. "Their souls? You believe in souls? I wouldn't have thought that for some reason. I mean, what with you being an American and all." He grinned. He couldn't help himself.

"Of course he believes in souls," O'Ryan said. "Another beer, please, Gemid."

Hipp said, "I'm not talking about soul in the religious sense. I mean soul as an animating and vital principle in human beings. A matter of the cortex. We contemplate, so we have souls. We're amazing animals, that's a fact. Gemid, let's have cigars for everyone. On the house."

Gemid grabbed the box of Valenzonas as she served O'Ryan his beer. O'Ryan, Dieter, Clarke, and Noble all helped themselves. This was to be a speculative, philosophical conversation of the sort enjoyed by strangers isolated from their home culture. Expats ordinarily were of an adventurous, inquiring imagination or they would have stayed home, where life was known and predictable.

Except for Bill Noble, Hipp knew all of his companions from previous nights of drinking San Miguel in Most Hipp. Dieter was quiet, but capable of penetrating observations. Clarke was ordinarily barely able to suppress his animosity toward Americans, but in their presence, he contained his feelings admirably. Paddy O'Ryan, who had had stories of supervising construction projects in Miami, Nigeria, and Hong Kong, was a voluble lover of talk. O'Ryan was not above being a provocative gadfly if he thought he could keep the lively talk flowing.

Carl Czez was puzzled by Jake Hipp's blathering on about Frances Bernardi and Goethe's Dr. Faustus and the business of selling one's soul to the Devil. What the fuck was that all about? Hipp couldn't have figured the scam. Just couldn't . . . though it did look like Hipp, by whatever convoluted route, was thinking along the right lines. He was close perhaps, but as they say, no cigar.

Czez found the business of the cigars unnerving. Hipp appeared to be making much of Bobby Pearl's cigars. Maybe Hipp did have him figured, and he was fancying himself a regular Inspector Maigret, setting up a denouement in an expat bar.

Was that it? Was that what Hipp was doing? One thing was certain, his little red pill was quick-acting shit.

Jake Hipp gave O'Ryan his cigar trimmer. "Here, try this on the end. I grant you that I'm talking about an intangible quality, but we all know what soul means, don't we? Think about it. Responsibility and civility are soulful qualities. Concern for a greater good. When these television people are shallow and crass and get in the way of the government's hunt for Bobby Pearl, do they know it's wrong?"

"Wrong? Is it?" O'Ryan said.

"Sure it is."

O'Ryan lit up and took a puff. "What about your famous

First Amendment and the public's right to know and the rest of it? You're ready to blow that off?"

"By 'wrong,' I mean ethically, not legally, but they know they're cluttering the pursuit of justice, not aiding it. They're serving the public, they say. Everybody does it. Truth is the only line of defense against authoritarians. Secrecy is a scourge of democracy. Et cetera. If they ever displayed any common sense, we could accept their special pleading as more than a sack of shit. How about you, Mike, would you buy that?"

"For the sake of argument, sure," Clarke said.

Noble was again looking out of sorts.

Glancing at him, Hipp said, "Remember *The Dallas Morning News* breaking a story about the kid charged with the Oklahoma City bombing? One month before the trial, they saw fit to print a story, based on documents either stolen from Defense computers or leaked to them, that Timothy McVeigh had admitted the crime. He allegedly said he needed a 'body count' to prove his point, whatever that was. The newspaper defended itself by saying the story was in the 'compelling national interest.' The compelling national interest was in trying and convicting the little chickenshit, wasn't it? It was in nobody's interest to risk letting him walk because a fair trial was impossible."

"We'd have had them in the slammer Down Under," Clarke said.

"One case," O'Ryan said.

Noble swallowed. He was once again beginning to sweat.

Hipp said, "If you want, I could bore you with a list of examples that we could agree on. I'm not saying that if you sat down with any single editor, he or she wouldn't agree that there are occasions when the country would be better served if they sat on a story. It's just that no single editor or producer wants to be made a chump of, a Little Goody Two-shoes doing the right thing when everybody else is pursuing their self-interest."

Clarke shrugged.

Hipp said, "Joaquin Hurtado kissed Moamar Qadhafi's

ass for what must qualify for a Guinness record—a full two hours! Here we have an egomaniac who without a doubt sponsored the bastards who knocked Pan Am 103 out of the skies, and we know the Libyans are manufacturing g-agents and biologicals at Tarhunah."

"So the government thinks," O'Ryan said.

Noble's hands began to tremble again.

"Thinks? It *knows*," Hipp said. "I'm a Charlie, remember. We traced the mushrooms from a company in Italy. I've seen the satellite photos of Tarhunah. Hurtado preceded his visit to Libya with six weeks of nonstop promotions, then went along with the horseshit of letting Qadhafi pretend he's growing mushrooms there, solemnly telling his viewers they should make up their minds. Right! Now don't you think that's going a bit too far?"

"Only in America." Clarke waved for another beer. "Di! Di!"

Hipp said, "Take the case of Dani Bernardi. The Israelis would never try to frame Arabs for killing innocent Americans with mustard gas and sarin. Dani knew that was preposterous, didn't she? All Qadhafi wanted to do was suck up to the public. I ask you, truly, what kind of individual would suck up to a chickenshit like that? One with his soul intact?"

Noble, eyes wild, licked his lips.

O'Ryan said, "You sound like Bang, for Christ's sake."

"Or *her* soul in the case of Dani Bernardi. The Nielsen ratings for the Qadhafi special must have been out of sight, but would any soulful journalist sell out that cheaply?" He looked at Noble.

Noble looked positively stricken.

Hipp opened his black box and retrieved another red capsule, which he gave to Noble. "Take this."

Noble, eyeing the contents of the box, blinked.

"Don't argue. Just do it. The other one worked, didn't it? You'll feel better."

Noble took the capsule and quickly downed it.

The pill gave Carl Czez immediate relief. It seemed to him too damn easy that Hipp just happened to have a little red pill that instantly eased his symptoms. How had that happened?

After Tangier, Mongoose had to be suspicious about Moamar Qadhafi, but Czez suspected there was more to Hipp's enigmatic little discourse than that. Everybody knew that Dani Bernardi had been a crass opportunist who would suck Lucifer's asshole if it scored better Nielsens. That wasn't a state secret.

Czez eyed Hipp. Maybe Hipp was ahead of *him,* not the other way around, but Czez found that hard to believe. He had never met anybody who could outsmart him in the long run.

One thing Mr. Wise Guy had done that was flat-out dumb was to put all that sexual horseshit on the Internet. Czez might have let the Seville incident ride. But the Internet message was too much. That was going to cost Hipp dearly.

In the meantime, Czez was content to let Hipp talk. Better to listen to his little set piece and wait. In the end, Czez would win because he knew how to win. Czez felt that Mongoose should have its Charlies study the Japanese Code of Bushido. A samurai never embarrassed himself by letting his mouth flap. A winner let victory do the talking.

Jake Hipp said, "You know, the big question about Bobby Pearl is who the hell sold him the sarin and the anthrax? That's a pretty stiff risk for a horseshit raghead. What if Mongoose or the International Terrorist Watch found out? Selling g-agents and biologicals to a terrorist? The public would demand retaliation big time." Hipp rolled his eyes. "Shit, oh dear! Talk about spitting in a tiger's face. Do you think Moamar or Saddam would sell Bobby Pearl that crap just to make a fast buck?"

O'Ryan said, "Hard to believe."

Noble grinned broadly. He was feeling better. "Another beer, please, Gemid."

Hipp said, "Moamar and Saddam both have oil to sell, which is partly the reason they can get away with strutting around like fighting chickens. Poor countries have to go with the flow or starve. But if you define currency as anything you can use to purchase something, there are all kinds of currency—not just American greenbacks or the Eurodollar or whatever."

"I see what you mean," O'Ryan said. "I'll concede that."

"Celebrity is a form of currency for athletes and entertainers. For politicians, that currency is public approval. 'Positives,' in the pollster's lingo. Politicians covet positives because they're essential to maintaining power. A president with sixty-percent positives is on top of the world. If those numbers turn into negatives, he can't do anything." He glanced at Clarke. "Tell me, Mike, have you ever heard the expression 'land poor'?"

Clarke squinted one eye.

"I grew up in Montana," Hipp said. "Montanans say a man is 'land poor' if he has a lot of land but no money for a tractor or seed or anything else that it takes to grow a crop. He's invested everything in land."

"Our entire country is land poor," Clarke said. "Good for 'roos jumping about, but not much else."

Hipp said, "Moamar Qadhafi is a president, but he doesn't have any power, because people won't do business with him. He's title poor. He might swap sarin straight-up for a prime-time, two-hour special, mightn't he? Juice those positives. Get that power back, so he could swagger around on the world stage."

O'Ryan laughed. "How on earth would Bobby Pearl deliver a prime-time special to Moamar Qadhafi?"

Hipp pursed his lips. "By fast-talking the producer of *My Side* into giving Qadhafi a two-hour, ass-kissing, prime-time special."

O'Ryan said, "Why on earth would Dani Bernardi give Moamar Qadhafi a two-hour, ass-kissing special?

"For the same currency that Pearl used to buy the sarin and anthrax."

O'Ryan cocked his head, looking puzzled. "Say again."

"Ms. Bernardi coveted Joaquin Hurtado's spot as host of *My Side*. Fame, she wanted. Celebrity. And she got it, didn't she? Complete with a once-in-a-hundred-years story, or close to it. Unmasking the President of the United States as a murderer of journalists. Hard to top that."

Noble took a puff on his cigar. "Her sister, Frances, got the fame and celebrity. Dani Bernardi is dead."

Hipp laughed. "Is she? You believe that? Bobby Pearl almost pulled it off. He understands the human animal. If you accept the nature of the beast, the motive is easy enough to figure."

"And you think you've found him, do you?"

"Oh, hell yes. I *know* I've found him. He's a snake, remember. He molts. He has a new exterior, but he's still the same on the inside, poor fucked-up son of a bitch."

Noble's face tightened almost imperceptibly. "Fucked-up?"

Hipp looked at O'Ryan and Clarke. "We know that Bobby Pearl gets his gun up and ready to go. Cocked, in a manner of speaking. But he can't pull the trigger. He gets it in and it wilts. He chokes. Chokes! Impotent is the word."

Noble clenched his jaw. He was looking out of sorts again. He took a deep breath and rested his forehead in the palm of his hand.

Hipp said, "And the pathetic scumbag had the nerve to call me a choke artist on *My Side,* with the whole world watching. 'All you have to do is point the damn thing and pull the trigger. Ha, ha, ha?' Isn't that something? The pot calling the kettle black. One of us can't fire his piece, and the other can't get his gun off. The old yin and yang."

Beneath his calm, bemused exterior, Carl Czez was enraged, exploding. Fucked-up! Impotent! Pathetic scumbag! Hipp *was* talking to him. Ridiculing him. Laughing at him in front of these assholes. Czez had to concede that Hipp had the story figured, or most of it. But did he understand all of it? Czez didn't think so.

Czez knew how to play a dangerous game. His molting, as Mongoose called it, was total. As far as anybody at the bar knew, including Hipp, Carl Czez was the dark-complexioned Bill Noble. Czez regarded himself as a warrior. He understood the value of discipline. He would keep his composure and show no emotion whatsoever. He would remain silent in face of the worst provocation. Let Hipp talk. Let him prove his case. Let him say anything he wanted. The more insults Hipp offered, the harder it would be on his girlfriend, then on him.

Jake Hipp took a hit of San Miguel. "Be fun to sit down at a bar like this and tell the cocksucker you knew he couldn't maintain a hard-on. Grind it in big time. He'd have to suck it up if he wanted to maintain his cover. He's a careful kind of guy. He'd just sit there with his guts grinding, getting more and more pissed. Knowing I was doing it deliberately wouldn't help matters. But you know, after what he did to me, I wouldn't give a flying fuck how he felt. A challenge is a challenge. I'm up for the competition." Hipp blew a circle of blue smoke. "Feeling crappy again, Bill?"

"What's wrong with me?" Noble asked.

"Here." Hipp retrieved another red capsule and gave it to him.

Noble snatched the capsule from Hipp's hand and studied it for a moment before taking it. He looked annoyed. "What the hell are these things?"

"Tethers," Hipp said. "I'm hungry. What do you say, will you join me for a hamburger and a bowl of chili?"

"Tethers?" Noble looked puzzled. "I'm feeling better now. A hamburger and a bowl of chili? Sure, I can go for that."

nine

Jake Hipp and Bill Noble settled in at a table overlooking Osmena Boulevard, which was packed with cabs and jeepneys—the latter being colorful homemade vehicles into which were packed from eighteen to twenty passengers. After Bonny had taken their order for chili and hamburgers and given them new bottles of San Miguel, Hipp regarded his companion thoughtfully and sucked in air between his teeth.

"Another smoke?" Hipp offered Noble a Tony Valenzona. Noble said, "Why not?"

Hipp retrieved his nipper and snipped the end of his cigar. He gave the nipper to Noble. "I knew you'd show, and I was right. Here you are, all pumped with testosterone. Ready to rumble."

"Me? Pumped with what?" Noble trimmed his own stogie. "I'm game. What on earth are you talking about?"

Hipp said, "It's the never-ending tournament. I inadvertently learned something about you that embarrassed you. You dissed me. I returned tit for tat. You felt compelled to settle the score. You felt your manhood was at stake. I understand that." Hipp lit up. "The logic isn't complicated. I've spent most of my life studying animal behavior. I understand the nature of testosterone. And here you are, predictably, ready to have it out."

Noble laughed. "I don't know what you're talking about."

"Yes you do. We're like a couple of bull walruses on the beach or buck mule deer having it out in a meadow. Which one of us is the winner and which is the loser? Not one damned whit of difference between us and walruses in that respect."

Noble looked amused.

"If it weren't for your genes, you'd have kept killing people and let me go my way. But you couldn't do that, especially after the E-mail message I advertised on *My Side*."

Noble took a puff on his cigar. "You want to tell me who you think I am?"

"You're Carl Czez, also known as Bobby Pearl, chicken-shit terrorist."

"Bobby Pearl?" Noble grinned. "How in hell did you come up with an idea like that?"

"In the end, it was the skin that did it."

"The skin?" Noble was beginning to sweat.

Hipp took a puff on his Valenzona. "Bobby Pearl had fair skin when I saw him in Tangier." He spread some photographs of Carl Czez on the table. "The kind of skin that sunburns easily. See there?"

Noble picked up a photograph. "This is Bobby Pearl?"

"Carl Czez was formerly a bird colonel in charge of an NSA unit that used computers to trace arms money. I bet he had to stay out of those ultraviolet rays in the summertime."

"How does his skin come into it?"

"Dani Bernardi had skin like that. Very white. I know. I saw her in the altogether. She was too busy to spend time in a tanning salon or on the beach. No tan whatsoever. When Frances Bernardi gave her big scoop last night, she looked just like Dani, only she had darker skin and a broader nose. A plastic surgeon could change her nose in a few minutes. But it was the skin that got me thinking. Light skin. Dark skin."

Hipp fell momentarily silent. He took a contemplative puff on his cigar. "When people talk about cosmetic surgery, they ordinarily mean face lifts—new noses and that kind of thing. When they think of skin, they mean tightening it or removing blemishes. I didn't think about color until last night when I was watching Michael Jackson's video on MTV. Way back, Michael wanted to look white, so he got his skin lightened. I remembered a novel from years ago, *Black Like Me*, in which a man had his skin turned dark so he could experience life like an African-American. Could that really be done, I wondered. I checked, and the answer is yes. No problem. He wouldn't look like Sidney Poitier, but dark enough."

"Oh? How is that?" Noble mopped his brow.

"By pumping melanin. As you know, it's not esoteric," Hipp said. "You knock back a tablet each of folic acid and vitamin C twice a day and give yourself a shot of vitamin B-twelve every other week, and there you have it. You were fair-complexioned when I saw you on the ferry and at William Burroughs. But you darkened your skin and got yourself a new nose and jawline, plus a change of teeth and fresh fingerprints. You're not packing Czez's fingerprints. I had them checked."

Noble sat up straight and smiled.

"You probably went to Dr. Wu Feng, a plastic surgeon in Hong Kong. I don't know for a fact that Wu was the surgeon, but I do know that you visited a Hong Kong special-effects artist named James Chan at least twice in the last year."

Noble cocked his head, looking puzzled.

"The British have been watching Chan for years," Hipp said.

"Ahhhh. I see." Noble looked at his hand, which was beginning to tremble again.

Hipp said, "Once you admit cosmetic surgery and silicon masks to the Bobby Pearl puzzle, logical possibilities pop up like mushrooms. For example, look at this picture of Czez that was taken here last night." Hipp picked up the photo and handed it to Noble.

Noble looked puzzled. "Who the hell is this guy?"

"Carl Czez. You, wearing a silicon mask of your face *before* you had plastic surgery. You can become the old Carl Czez whenever you want. Clever as hell, I'll give you that."

Noble burst out laughing.

"Of course that wouldn't last forever—Czez would begin to age, just like the rest of us. But it was a neat trick for a while. Dani Bernardi pumped melanin so she could look like her sister, Frances. It was a Faustian bargain she made with you, just like I said at the bar."

"You deduced all that from folic acid, vitamin C, and vitamin B-twelve?"

"Most of it," Hipp said. "But there's also something about your voice and manner that's familiar. When somebody scares the piss out of you, like you nearly did to me on the ferry between Algeciras and Tangier, you never forget what he sounds like."

Noble considered that. "You want to tell me the full story as you think you've got it figured?" He was beginning to sweat harder. He bit his lower lip.

Hipp fished his black box out. This time he handed Noble a yellow capsule.

Noble hesitated.

Quickly, Hipp said, "The yellow works as well as the red, only it lasts longer."

Noble turned it in his hand before chucking it into his mouth. "You want to tell me what's with these capsules? You know what's wrong with me?"

"I've got a good idea."

"Something going around?"

Hipp shook his head and continued. "You tried to buy chemicals and biologicals from Moamar Qadhafi, but he said no, so you hired two ex-cons to deliver mustard gas. Mustard is low-tech, and you're a no risk kind of guy. They could easily have made it themselves. Then you went to Asia to get your face changed. That's when you bumped into Ralph Snow here in Most Hipp, bragging about how someone was interested in knocking off television journalists, and he had deduced that it was someone in the White House. How am I doing?"

"Interesting story."

"Since you were going to get a new face anyway, you agreed to a *My Side* interview here in the Philippines. That's where you got your inspiration. You told the ambitious producer of *My Side* that the great Libyan narcissist could almost certainly be talked into swapping BCs for a flashy television special. If Dani Bernardi scored your BCs, you'd put her in Joaquin's on-camera slot as Frances Bernardi and launch her new career by pinning the President for murder."

"Not me. Czez maybe."

"Which you did as Bang, using silicon masks!"

Noble took a puff on his cigar.

"Such a deal. Moamar Qadhafi starts turning the tide of public opinion in his favor. You get your BCs. Dani Bernardi gets her dream job."

"But supposing Carl Czez did that? Why? He's gotta have a motive. You have that figured, too?"

"There are two kinds of motive. Up here." Hipp pointed to his temple. "And down here." He tapped his crotch. "The up here reason"—he tapped his temple again—"was the official justification. The Unabomber thought he was pissed off by technology; the truth is that he was a filthy hermit, a social misfit. The kid who blew up the Federal Building in Oklahoma City thought he was defending the people's liberties against an arrogant government. The truth is that he was a misguided twerp, a failed Special Forces wannabe with no future and an exaggerated sense of self-importance. You took it upon yourself to give the rest of us a lesson in tactics and technology that we were ignoring, dangerously in your opinion."

" 'Dangerously' hardly covers the territory. Terrorists are operating from the cover of cyberspace."

"Hand-carrying chemicals and biologicals—poor man's nukes," Hipp said. "I get the point, but that's the bogus motive you used so you could live with yourself. The 'purpose, discipline, loyalty' horseshit. The real motive is down here." He tapped his crotch again. "Manhood. A limp dick. Proving yourself."

Noble's face froze.

"You get it in and it wilts. Not good."

Noble said nothing.

"The best guess is that it's related to your having murdered your wife and George Hollins."

"Say again."

"You were cuckolded. Hard to take, I'll give you that."

Noble studied Hipp. "Somebody made you a cuckold, have they?"

"Guilt probably took your cock down," Hipp said. "Both of us have a genetic compulsion to demonstrate prowess. What you've really been doing with this Bobby Pearl horse-shit is showing us all what a big, hairy-chested man you are. You might have a soft dick, but you're a world-famous hard man. Sick shit, but a form of prowess nevertheless."

Noble took a swig of beer. "You want to tell me about those capsules of yours?"

Hipp smiled. "Getting a little suspicious?"

Bonny arrived with a tray loaded with their food and more San Miguel.

Jake Hipp loaded his hamburger with ketchup, thumping the bottom of the bottle with the heel of his hand. He removed the top of the bun, looking pleased. "See those onions? That's the way a hamburger ought to be. Lots of onions. These little purple numbers are good too, you have to admit. By the way, why don't we drop the Bill Noble crap? Carl Czez, you're Bobby Pearl."

Pearl confirmed his identity by not denying it. He sampled his chili.

"You like that chili?" Hipp asked.

Pearl nodded yes. "You were going to tell me about the capsules and whatever's ailing me."

Hipp looked down on the street, then returned his attention to Pearl. "You've got good reason to wonder about the capsules. They're all about tactics and technology."

Pearl waited.

Hipp took a bite of hamburger. Munching placidly, he said, "From the day of its inception, Mongoose anticipated the time when a solo Charlie in the field might have to bring in a snake by himself—a dangerous business, especially across international borders. Say, from here in the Philippines. A tough assignment."

"I'll give you that," Pearl said.

Hipp chewed contentedly, then swallowed, washing the hamburger down with San Miguel. "Ideally, the cooperation of the snake had to be assured, and there should be no physical indication to guards or customs agents that a prisoner was being transported. No visible chains or handcuffs or anything like that. So the Company came up with a snake kit, my little black box. The capsules are chemical tethers."

"Chemical tethers?"

"Helluva lot better than leather or metal." Looking mildly disappointed that his hamburger was gone, Hipp turned his attention to his chili, digging in with gusto. "I had Bonny slip a pill into one of your bottles of San Miguel. That's the part of the kit we call the 'lock,' which comes in a tasteless, odorless liquid, or pills that dissolve almost immediately. Once your system is locked, you can't go far without a 'tether,' an antidote that delays the effect of the drug. A physical tether—a rope or a chain, say—is measured in length. A chemical tether is measured in time. With a knock-out lock, you pass out if you don't renew your tether. With a killer lock, you have a massive heart attack and die."

"What?"

"The tethers in a snake kit are color-coded to signify different lengths. You ever hear the rhyme used to teach kids the meaning of traffic lights? 'Green means go. Yellow means slow. Red means stop, stop, stop.' A green tether is good for about twenty-four hours. A yellow is good for roughly an hour. A red is worth fifteen minutes, give or take five minutes. The exact length depends on your body weight. When the tether draws short, you start sweating and feeling jittery, like you're speeded up."

Pearl blinked.

Hipp, eating chili, said, "I gave you three reds at the bar. Now you're on a yellow. I wanted to give you an idea of what the action is all about. Incidentally, it's impossible for me to remove the lock permanently. A Mongoose doctor can do that back in the United States, but by then, you'll be behind bars." Hipp looked pleased. "Take off on me, pal, and you croak. Slick shit, huh?"

Pearl looked disbelieving. "You're telling me that after the last 'tether,' as you call it, I've got an hour to live?"

Hipp finished his chili. "Unless I'm a sport and give you another capsule, correct. When a Charlie is sent after a terrorist, he is issued a kit, snake, one each. You know the lingo. Each kit contains one green, three yellows, and six reds."

"Just one kit?"

"One is all it takes. We've got one green, two yellows, and three reds. That's about twenty-six hours and forty-five minutes, give or take ten minutes or so, to get this settled." Hipp paused, watching Pearl's reaction. "You don't like it?" He slumped his shoulders in disappointment. "What with you being such a high-tech fan of BCs and all, I thought you'd be pleased."

Hipp stared at the empty chili bowl and slapped his stomach with satisfaction. "Man, that was good stuff. Authentic Tex-Mex with a Filipino touch. The trick is to make your own seasoning, generous with the cayenne and lots of cumin. The plum tomatoes they grow here in the Philippines are just perfect. Also, this isn't beef, it's carabao. More flavorful. Goat's good too, but it's a tad expensive. If the cook doesn't make the chili right, I have Bonny give her hell. Don't want to be losing customers to Our Place."

Pearl glared at him. "You want to tell me who in hell dreamed up this bullshit 'snake kit,' as you call it?"

"An acquaintance of mine in T-Cell who was tired of dealing with assholes like you. The kit's not entirely esoteric if you think about it; all it does is replace handcuffs and shackles. I've been dreaming of this moment for some months now, I have to admit. Pretty sweet for me."

Pearl shifted in his chair.

Hipp held up a finger. "Ah-ah. Don't get violent on me. Remember, you have to keep me alive. This is bad, bad shit, guaranteed." Hipp looked concerned. "You're beginning to look a little pale around the gills. The way I feel about you, I'd just as soon drift on out of here and let you croak, but Mongoose wants to know for certain how you got the sarin, so we can be assured that another asshole doesn't repeat this same crap. Not good to send you under until we get that cleared up."

"Good thinking."

"To find out for certain if we've got this thing completely contained, I just might have to shove a cattle prod up your asshole or wire your balls with an alternating current. Better to do it on some isolated place in the Philippines than back in the United States, where it'd eventually get leaked. There's an island just south of Cebu called Siquijor that the Filipinos believe is haunted. They'll just think the screaming was done by ghosts."

Watching Hipp, Pearl momentarily rested his fingers on his chin. "You don't have the stomach for it."

"On a guy who ambushed innocent people with mustard gas and sarin? I'll do what I have to do."

"You're basing all this on circumstance."

"Tangier was a different place and another time. 'Sooie piggy. Mighty good smoke!' Remember that?" Hipp watched Pearl's eyes. "Sure you do. Your pet phrase." He took a swig of San Miguel.

Hipp said, "Fun to regard the lock as the hammer of a cocked pistol. You get to think about it as you watch it coming at you, just like we're all supposed to think about those lethal pearls of yours tumbling from the corner of the screen. Each passing minute is like subtracting years from your life." Hipp looked wistful. "You know, I've been watching a damn hammer fall every night for months—heading straight for my eyes. The hammer that didn't drop on you. Then there's the image of Lynn Vaughn giving a body count on CNN. In fact, that was my body count. I had my chance to stop you." He shook his head at the memory. "Awful nightmares."

Pearl stared down at the traffic on Osmena Boulevard.

Hipp looked solicitous. "Say, your chili and hamburger are cold! You didn't eat a bite. You must be getting hungry. Nothing to say? No? You fuck over me, Bub, I fuck back. Cubed. No Marquess of Queensberry here. It's Charlie Darwin all the way."

Pearl turned in his chair. "Tell me, Jake, how many people are you willing to sacrifice to bring me down? Ten thousand? Twenty thousand? How many?"

"I can't imagine I'll have to sacrifice anybody."

"No? I tell you what, let's the two of us make a deal. You release my tether and pop my lock. I'll let a whole shitload of people live to see another day. Then we can both go our way like a couple of gentlemen. What do you say?"

ten

Jake Hipp had not believed for a second that Bobby Pearl, a cornered snake, would placidly bow to the choice of committing suicide or going off to Langley with his tail tucked between his legs. Pearl was both determined and smart. What the hell was he up to now? Hipp sat for a moment thinking, aware that the former army officer was watching him attentively, assessing his reaction.

A tether for a tether?

Pop the lock?

Finally, Hipp said, "Okay, tell me what you've got."

Pearl said, "You figured it. I did use gophers in San Francisco, Charleston, and New York, but I burned them and got myself some new suckers. Easy score on the Internet. Since I didn't know for certain how much you'd figured out, I ordered an insurance hit before coming here tonight. I'm the only one who knows how to call it off."

Hipp felt a rush of anxiety in his stomach. "What?"

"Tabun this time. Bad, bad shit. The Red Sox are playing the White Sox in Fenway tomorrow afternoon; the Orioles are playing the Blue Jays in Camden Yards, and the Marlins are home against the Colorado Rockies. There are other possible release points—wherever people are gathered in numbers. There are tanks used to hold gas to put the fizz in soft drinks, tanks to fill balloons with helium. Also, tabun can be stored and released from custom-built containers made out of plastic. The short of it is that unless I call them off, my gophers will eliminate a stadium full of sports fans. Strike all fucking three."

Hipp blinked.

"What are you going to do, shut down Boston, Baltimore,

and Miami? If you try, I'll simply have my gophers deliver the goods somewhere else, at a soccer game, say. Easy enough to do. D. C. United is playing the Metro Stars in Washington. There'll be a crowd there. If you take me out, you take out a stadium full of sports fans. There are other possibilities. Anyplace where people are gathered in numbers." Pearl looked amused. "But maybe you want to tell everybody on the East Coast to stay home tomorrow afternoon because your horseshit government can't stop me. Easy enough for me to let the media know what happened."

Hipp ground his teeth. He didn't think it was possible for one human being to hate another as much as he hated Bobby Pearl at that second.

"You thought you had me beat, didn't you? Sitting there crowing." Pearl looked scornful.

On the tube behind them, CNN was vigorously promoting a Larry King interview of the new hero of the hour, Frances Bernardi. Never mind that Ms. Bernardi was from the NET, CNN's competitor; the people in the Atlanta-based network were furious at the deaths of Tarnauer and Lovewell. CNN wanted Bang's hide. If ever there was a time for the media to put their competitive differences aside for the greater good, this was it; in the pursuit of Bang, The NET and CNN were as one. If Frances Bernardi was helping bring the murderous President to justice, CNN would gladly spread the word.

Frances was wasting no time in following in her sister's steps; she had already scheduled an interview of Saddam Hussein, one of the Arab leaders suspected of supplying chemical- and biological-warfare agents to the terrorist Bobby Pearl.

Hipp, listening to the promo, suddenly brightened. Maybe there was a way out after all.

Pearl checked his watch. "It's now one A.M. here in the Philippines; that's one P.M. on the East Coast. Those ball games all have a three-o'clock start, give or take a half hour. I want a twenty-four-hour capsule now. That'll give you plenty of time to fly a doctor here. I'll arrange the time and place for him to pop my lock. When he's finished, I'll be on my way. This is the way gentlemen do business. Like scholars."

Hipp took the snake kit from his pocket. He opened it and retrieved the green capsule, which he gave to Pearl.

Pearl took the capsule and downed it quickly, chasing it with a gulp of San Miguel. "You gotta remember, Jake, the game ain't over until one of us fucks the pretty girl."

Jake Hipp's stomach twisted while he waited for Joe Woofter's response to the bad news. The phone was silent for so long that he wondered if Woofter was still on the other end.

Finally, his voice filled with disgust and dismay, Woofter said, "Jesus Christ Almighty! What does it take? Just what the hell does it take with this guy?"

Hipp said, "He never quits. But we don't waste our tether, Joe. We've got twenty-four hours. We put them to good use."

"Meanwhile, I put a lock doctor on the plane for Cebu?"

"I suppose we don't have any choice. I see by the tube that Larry King is going to have Frances Bernardi as his guest tonight. King is an okay kind of guy, isn't he? An amiable, responsible sort. Certainly not the kind of guy to blow us off in a national emergency."

"Go ahead. Tell me what's on your mind, Jake."

"The business of Frances Bernardi scheduling Saddam Hussein as her guest got me thinking . . ."

"About what?"

"About deals and Arabs. It's now one o'clock your time. That gives us eight hours. King can beam a guest in from Cebu, can't he? CNN has a correspondent based in Manila, Caridad Sanchez. That's an hour away by Philippine Airlines. Plenty of time for Ms. Sanchez to fly down with a cameraman."

"A guest? Who?"

"Me. I want you to get on the phone to Atlanta pronto. I've got a modest proposal for Larry King, and a chore for your fingerprint people, but they'll have to move quickly."

"A proposal for Larry King." Woofter sighed audibly. "Okay, let's hear it."

Hipp said, "Don't be so down. We're not out of this one yet. Bobby Pearl thinks he's found a way to break his tether. If we're lucky, there just might be a way to shuck ours."

eleven

Most Hipp had become a breakfast favorite of politicians in the provincial capital at Cebu, ordinarily opening at eight o'clock, but on this Saturday morning, Bonny opened the doors at seven to prepare for the visit of Caridad Sanchez and her CNN crew. Sanchez, a small Filipina with a professional television voice, her cameraman Winston Monzon, a slender, mustached Filipino, and two sound-and-transmission technicians arrived at 7:30 A.M. Gina was late, but Hipp knew she'd show soon. She wouldn't want to miss the fun.

The solicitous Bonny, a charming host, treated them all to a splendid breakfast of brewed coffee, omelets, and Australian sausages while they waited for *The Larry King Show* to begin. Instant coffee was the usual in the Philippines, and rich, flavorful, brewed coffee was a treat.

The show opened with the ordinarily placid King looking more serious than customary. Like all journalists, King was sore as hell over what had happened to William Tarnauer and Belinda Lovewell, both of whom had been his friends. The television icon was wearing his favorite red suspenders over a blue-striped white shirt. Opposite him, Dr. Frances Bernardi wore a simple black dress in keeping with the solemnity of her job of running the murderous Bang to ground—that is to say, the murderous liar who was President of the United States.

Bernardi obviously possessed those oft-repeated qualities of concentration and perseverance that virtually all biographers said were necessary for success. To be thus interviewed by the reigning international master of talk-show hosts was to officially become a world-class heroine and celebrity journalist. As the newly designated people's champion, Bernardi was above such bothersome concepts as irony and hypocrisy.

King opened with a series of questions intended to guide his viewers through Frances Bernardi's amazing allegations of the previous night. One at a time, he covered the major figures and what they did: the confidential *My Side* informant in the Justice Department; Charlie Boso, the President's chief-of-staff; Charlie's brother Tom, the White House data analyst; Ralph Snow, mercenary Asian hand; Tom's hiring of Snow to murder Dani Bernardi. This was the murderous trail of deceit and treachery that led straight to the White House, and almost certainly to the President, never mind his evasive denials.

King repeated the conclusions of his earlier guests, the CIA polygraph examiner, Dutch Mandel, and the President's lawyer, Todd Singleton. Singleton had maintained that the President had clearly passed the test and was innocent. Mandel had disagreed, saying the President and his lawyer had so framed the allowable questions as to leave the President with an out.

Here King put the bottom-line question to his viewers: had the President suggested that an assassin be hired to murder journalists, but without his specific knowledge? The practice of hear no evil, speak no evil, therefore do no evil— called "plausible deniability"—was commonplace among politicians and Intelligence officials.

Bernardi listened gravely to King's suggestive summary. In keeping with the requisite image of sacrifice, duty, and high calling, she dutifully followed the script of pretense, suppressing her joy in favor of sorrow over the damage done to the republic. Woe, woe, woe was she, poor humble journalist, being forced to destroy the President. She loved her country and hated doing this. Loathed it.

Loathed it? Hipp thought of the Filipino admiration of Whitney Houston and the lyrics of Houston's famous song, "One Moment in Time." This truly was Bernardi's one memorable moment in time. Here was a woman who would prove the validity of John Milton's lovely conceit that truth, when pitted against falsehood, would always prevail. She personally would see to it; she was confident, determined to follow the facts of this high tragedy to their inevitable conclusion. Unstated in her dramatic charade was the assertion that an occasional knockdown like this justified the general shedding of all taste and ethics.

As he watched the program, Hipp began to worry about Gina. Why was she late? He was aware of Ms. Sanchez watching him, wondering what his role was in all this that she should arrange to beam him live from Cebu. Ordinarily she dealt with CNN's international news desk, not with Larry King. The people at CNN, following Joe Woofter's request, had told her nothing.

Winston Monzon got his camera set up, focusing it at the window table where Hipp would sit. The two technicians set the lighting and sound and put the transmission gear into place.

With fifteen minutes remaining in King's scheduled program, and Gina still unaccounted for, Hipp took his place. Sanchez fitted him with a tiny ear receiver so he could hear King and his guest in Atlanta. She then stepped in back of the camera, where Bonny and Most Hipp's waitresses and cook stood in a semicircle to watch their employer on camera.

After a commercial break, King returned, and Hipp could hear him clearly in his ear receiver. Hipp took a deep breath to help himself relax.

"And now, joining us from the island of Cebu in the Philippines, we have Jake Hipp, a Mongoose Charlie pursuing the terrorist Bobby Pearl. Mr. Hipp, a sociobiologist and one-time college professor, was formerly in T-Cell, the Mongoose research wing and think tank. Can you hear us, Mr. Hipp?"

Hipp, addressing the red light in front of him, saw himself appear in the tube above the bar. "Yes, I can, Larry. I can see you also, and dapper you are in your red suspenders."

"I understand you have a couple of questions of Ms. Bernardi."

"Why, yes, I do. I was wondering, Ms. Bernardi, if you

remembered to remove that little scar from your tailbone? In the shape of a fishhook, it is. You told me your sister pushed you over on the beach and you landed on a broken Pepsi bottle. Remember that?"

Bernardi's eyes went wide.

"In the last few hours, Mongoose matched your fingerprints with those of your sister Dani. Plenty of Dani's fingerprints are still around. You want to tell Larry's viewers what we found?"

King raised an eyebrow. "Frances?"

Bernardi blinked, her face an uncomprehending mask.

"Dani," Hipp said. "She's Dani Bernardi, Larry, not Frances. Frances is dead, along with Ralph Snow, Nadia Heimbigner, William Tarnauer, and Belinda Lovewell—all murdered by the same man, Ms. Bernardi's accomplice, Bobby Pearl."

King looked amazed. "Ms. Bernardi?"

Dani Bernardi looked stricken.

"Been loading up on those vitamins, have you, Dani? Folic acid, vitamin C, and vitamin B-twelve. Put that natural melanin to work, eh? Pumping vitamins is how she faked the color of her sister's skin, Larry. Easy enough to do. That plus the broader nose and bigger boobs she got from Dr. Wu Feng in Hong Kong. One week, Dani. The next week, *voilá*, Frances! Fun flashing all that cleavage, is it, Dani? All the men eyeing your chest out of the corners of their eyes. By the way, those wonderful numbers are called Wu Boobs in Hong Kong. They're quite fashionable among the actresses in Sing Sing Boyd's movies."

Behind the camera, the grinning Bonny raised his fist in triumph.

The way Hipp saw it, Dani Bernardi had made a deal with Mephistopheles. She had bargained with Muslim fanatics to deliver poison and disease to the serpent; in return, the snake had given her sweet triumph.

Jake Hipp said, "Finally, Larry, I would like Dani Bernardi to tell us now whether or not Saddam Hussein delivered the tabun to Bobby Pearl before his fancy *My Side* special, or does he want payment up front just like Moamar Qadhafi did? The quid before the quo. It's essential that we know this in order to prevent more tragedy."

King said, "Ms. Bernardi?"

While he waited for her answer, Hipp's stomach fluttered. Where was Gina?

twelve

Carl Czez took a sip of Chivas Regal and considered Gina Jumero, lying on the bed with her wrists tied to the headboard. She was wearing a form-fitting knit dress, a sexy little witch. Czez would have liked to fuck the bejesus out of her, but he could not risk that. If she was a shouldn't, he'd have to kill her, and he couldn't do that just yet. For the moment, he had to keep her alive. If he wasted her prematurely, he risked his own neck.

The announcer said that Larry King's guest was to be the new *My Side* hostess, Frances Bernardi, who would talk about the White House conspiracy to murder journalists, after which she would take calls.

On the bed, Gina kept wiggling. Frances Bernardi and White House conspiracies meant little to her. Only when King said he would have another guest, a terrorist chaser live from the island of Cebu in the Philippines, did she stop squirming. She glanced at Czez.

Czez frowned. "The clever stud."

"Jake?" she asked.

"Did he mention anything about Larry King to you?"

She shook her head.

Czez looked out of the window at the city of Cebu, spread below them. The Plaza Hotel, located on top of a hill, was a refuge for wealthy tourists—mostly, Japanese men—who wanted to play golf and screw Filipinas without having to deal with local people.

Gina said, "What's it all about, do you think?"

Czez raised an eyebrow. "Me, most likely." He took another sip of Scotch. "Motherfucker never gives up. I'll give him that."

Gina said, "He'll never quit."

Czez pursed his lips. "For you, he will, little Gina. He's in love with you. For that reason, I've got him right here." He grabbed his crotch by way of demonstration. "Gonna make him squeal like a piggie-wig. Wee, wee, wee!"

"I wouldn't be so confident if I were you," Gina said mildly. "He's changed."

"Oh?"

"He's different now."

"Different from when?"

"From what happened at Tangier. From the humiliation. From losing his job."

Czez grinned. "It was good for him in the long run. Taught him the meaning of discipline and duty. He should have pulled the trigger. It was his job. Mongoose was right to fire him."

"He's a good person."

"He's an idiot. You should have seen him eyeing me over that pistol. The hammer was cocked. He was a coward. No other word for it. No balls."

Czez reached over and ran the palm of his right hand across Gina's chest. He smiled as she flinched. "You've got a nice little pair of tits, you know that? Jake have fun with these, does he?"

Gina twisted, trying to escape his hand.

"When this is over, I think I'll fuck you blind." When his personal struggle with Jake Hipp was over, Gina would be a should. No doubt about that. He said, "Are you sure he didn't say anything about Larry King?"

Gina shook her head. "I told you no."

The program started. They watched in silence as Larry King and Frances Bernardi discussed the awful case of the President ordering journalists assassinated.

Then King abruptly switched to Jake Hipp in Cebu, and Hipp, without ado, unmasked Frances Bernardi. She was not Frances at all. She was Dani Bernardi, Cosmic Bitch of the Western World.

Czez looked grim as King asked her the fateful question

near the end of the program: had Saddam Hussein paid for his television special in advance, or was his payment yet to be made in chemical- or biological-warfare agents?

Czez, scowling, picked up the remote and punched off the set. He took a sip of Scotch and sat, looking down on the city.

On the bed, Gina said, "He figured you out, didn't he?"

"He's a smart son of a bitch, I'll give him that. But he loses."

"Oh?"

"He figured that I can't release tabun on the stadiums because few Arabs would trust a Westerner to deliver on his end of the bargain—certainly not Saddam Hussein. Jake has his mind chock-full of Charles Darwin, stupid asshole. But that's not really what it comes down to in the end, is it? Love and hate. I've got you. That's what matters. To him, that's more important than a stadium full of baseball fans that he's never met. He loves you."

"And hates you."

Czez laughed. "What's the phone number at Most Hipp?"

"There's a telephone directory in the end table."

"You'll get yours, stubborn little bitch." Czez looked up the number. He punched up the hotel operator and gave her the number. He waited, then said, "I'd like to speak to Jake Hipp, please. Tell him it's Colonel Czez."

thirteen

Jake Hipp was ripped by anguish. How in hell had this happened? He had left Gina in the care of her brother Felix and his *barkada*. She was safe with them, he had thought. They were inside a walled compound. Now Gina was in the hands of Bobby Pearl.

Gina. Bobby Pearl had Gina.

Hipp, accompanied by Bonny and his boyfriend, the son of a wealthy Chinese-Filipino businessman, hurried down the stairs from Most Hipp and headed up Osmena Boulevard for Don Jose Avila Street. When he got to the heavy iron gate in front of Gina's house, he could see activity in the yard. He was mildly surprised that Felix, a stocky, short Filipino with curly black hair—alive and apparently unharmed—met him at the gate and popped the heavy brass lock.

"What happened?"

Felix stared at his feet. "Gina wanted to buy some stuff at Rustan's, so she took off with Donde. After they had been gone an hour and a half, we got worried and called you."

Hipp's body slumped. "Didn't you try to stop her?"

"Of course we tried to stop her, but she wouldn't listen. Out and back. A quick trip. 'What can go wrong?' she said."

"Jesus!"

"She's a woman," Felix said.

"When you're dealing with Bobby Pearl, what can go wrong will. I thought she understood that."

"What do we do now?" Felix asked.

Hipp thought for a moment. "All is not lost. We stay cool. He figures that Gina is his ticket out of here, so he won't do anything to her yet. How many of you are there?"

Felix said, "Eight, including Rudy and me. Henry, Ben, Elvis, and their *barkada*." A *barkada* was a friend in the singular or a close circle of friends. A *barkada* was second to family in a Filipino's hierarchy of loyalties. In the case of Henry, Ben, and Elvis—cousins of Felix and Rudy—Hipp knew that this was likely a tough crew indeed.

Hipp said, "His tether is running short, so he'll have to make his move soon. I'll do the talking. I want everybody to stay well back. I say again: I don't want anybody to get hurt. When it's all over and we have Gina back, we send out for three or four *lechons*, plus all the San Miguel we can drink."

"All this is our fault. We shouldn't have let her go." Felix was disconsolate.

"She's a good woman, but there are times when she can be stubborn as hell. We both know that."

"But we will get her back, won't we?"

"We'll get her back," Hipp said.

Bobby Pearl called fifteen minutes later. "I'll make you a simple deal, Hipp. I'll give you Gina safe and unharmed; you give me the rest of your primary snake kit plus your backup."

"I don't have a backup," Hipp said.

Pearl groaned. "Come on now. I was a career military officer, remember. All tactical systems have a built-in redundancy in case something goes wrong. I say again, I want the remainder of the primary kit plus the backup."

"Shit," Hipp muttered.

"Has the lock doctor arrived?"

"He's on Cebu. You can arrange a rendezvous by calling the American consul."

Pearl said, "Write the name of the lock doctor and the consul's number on a piece of paper and tuck it inside the back-up kit. By my calculations, the combined tethers in both kits will give me roughly thirty hours to arrange a meeting with the lock doctor and free myself of this shit."

"Give me Gina and I'll give you the tethers. No problem."

"You'll get Gina when the doctor pops the lock, not

before. Those are my terms. If you don't want me to get nasty to your lady friend, you'll do what I say."

"Where's Donde?"

"Pushing up sugarcane. He was an idiot. Do we have a deal?"

Hipp sighed. "We have a deal."

"If I see any of your people on the street, your girlfriend is dead. If they're there, I'll spot them. You know I'm good."

"I made a deal. I'll stick with it," Hipp said. "How do you want to proceed?"

"For one thing, I want this connection kept open so we can talk."

Hipp hesitated, then said, "Done."

Felix was disbelieving. "Are you just going to do what he says?"

Hipp held his finger to his mouth for Felix to be quiet.

Pearl said, "Put the kits on the sidewalk. When I'm satisfied it's safe, Gina will pick them up. I'll be back here in the shadows with a piece. If I detect any motion or suspect that anything has gone wrong, I'll drop her with a round to the back of the head. Do you understand?"

"I get the picture."

"Begin."

"I'll have to go inside to get the kits."

"Do it now."

Hipp trotted inside Gina's house and retrieved a Most Hipp business card from his wallet. He jotted the lock doctor's name and the consul's number on the back of the card and tucked it into a snake kit. He returned quickly to the gate. He reached around and pitched the two snake kits onto the pavement.

Pearl said, "Hipp?"

"I'm here," Hipp said.

"Remember, I've got your lady in my sights."

"Hard to forget that."

"You'll get yours later."

"We'll see," Hipp said.

Gina appeared on the far side of the street and walked

across. She stooped and picked up the kits. As she did, she whispered, "He shot Donde in the back of his head. He'll kill me after he gets his way."

"That won't happen," Hipp whispered, "I love you."

"I love you, Jake."

As Gina turned to go back, Pearl said, "The problem with you is that you think too much, Jake, and you're not half as smart as you think you are. Look who gets to fuck the pretty girl."

Jake Hipp watched Gina disappear into the darkness to join Bobby Pearl.

Jake Hipp slumped onto the ground and leaned against the courtyard wall. His mouth was dry. His stomach fluttered. He felt like vomiting. He glanced at his watch again.

Felix glared at him. "Is that all you're going to do, sit there?"

"It's all I can do. A long wait though, I have to admit."

"What are you talking about?"

"He'll be back," Hipp said.

"He will?"

"Any second now. He'll be in a sour mood, guaranteed."

From the darkness across the street, Pearl yelled, "Hipp!"

Hipp grinned at Felix. "See. What did I tell you?"

Hipp rose and looked through the bars of the gate. Pearl stood in the middle of the street, using Gina as a shield.

Pearl looked shaken. "What's wrong with me?"

"You take the greenie in the back-up kit?"

Pearl nodded.

"A back-up kit has a yellow dot on the bottom. You want to check the underside of your backup?"

Pearl glanced down.

Hipp said, "What do you see?"

"Red dot." Pearl's voice was trembling.

"That's the kit we pack for smart guys like you who think they're going to run off with the tethers and get their lock popped. We call it 'Cobra Six,' meaning it'll put you six feet under. All the pills in a Cobra Six are poison. Why else do you think I'd be dumb enough to explain the system to you? I do have a white pill in my pocket that might interest you—given the circumstances and your symptoms."

"Give it to me."

"First let Gina go."

Pearl gave her a push.

Gina sprinted through the gate to safety.

Pearl dropped to his knees, his face wet with sweat. He had a silenced automatic pistol in his hands, but his life was on the line and he knew it. "I want that pill."

"Get rid of the piece."

Pearl flung the pistol to one side, where it clattered to rest on the pavement. "A deal's a deal," he said.

Hipp stepped through the gate and squatted in front of the distraught Pearl. "You remember our encounter on the ferry from Algeciras to Tangier? The Brit was telling me about the fourteen sieges of Gibraltar, and you interrupted with your neat little knife, claiming that the Spanish and French were idiots to have stubbornly stuck with the same old dated tactics. Simple enough to slip ashore in the dark of night and slit a few throats. Use a little stealth, you said. Guile. I figured I'd take you at your word."

"I gave you your girlfriend back. I kept my end of the bargain."

"Sure you did. Right about now, your heart ought to be doing a regular rumba. Thump, thump, thump. Got a splitting headache, too. Am I right?"

"Just give me the goddam pill."

"If you really had any class, you'd confirm what I've already figured out. Then I'll help you out. You got the balls for that?"

Pearl clenched his jaw. "Yes, yes, I did it. I knew Moamar Qadhafi would swap his mother's eyes for a *My Side* special. Dani Bernardi pretended to be shocked at first. Murder her sister? But when I sweetened the deal by offering her the President, she hesitated. I knew I had her. She was a whore. They all are. I hired gophers on the Internet. Easy to do. Now gimme the goddam pill."

"That. Oh, sure." Hipp reached into his trousers and retrieved a small bottle. He spilled several white pills into the palm of Bobby Pearl's outstretched hand. "Here you are. Don't let anybody tell you Jake Hipp is not a sport."

Pearl quickly popped the pills into his mouth and swallowed. "What are these? They taste like aspirin."

"They are aspirin," Hipp said. "Some people take Advil or Aleve or Tylenol when they get a headache, but I've always stuck with plain old aspirin. A genuine wonder drug. A natural anti-inflammatory. It coats those blood platelets so your blood won't clot as easily. Can't be beat."

"Aspirin?" Pearl looked disbelieving. He opened his mouth to say something more, but all he could manage was an *aaaaaarrrrrkkkk* sound.

"You want Tylenol?" Hipp turned and called into the house. "Gina, hon, do we have some Tylenol? Extra strength."

Bobby Pearl, staring up at Hipp, clutched his chest with both hands. "Youuuuuummmmmottttthhhherrrrrrrrrrffffff."

Hipp said, "See there? No problem pulling the trigger any more. The good guy gets the girl this time around."

Pearl tumbled onto the sidewalk. His eyes were open. He did not blink.

Hipp look at Felix and shrugged.

"What do we do now?" Felix asked.

"Why, we drag this corpse inside and start the party, in memory of Donde and in celebration for Gina and me."

Hipp noticed something in Pearl's trouser pocket. He wondered if it might not be Bobby Pearl's spring-loaded knife. He checked it out. It was. He retrieved the knife and flipped it in his hand; this knife, which had once been used to tickle Hipp's carotid artery, would be his souvenir. He found two Cuban cigars in Pearl's shirt pocket. He took those, too.

Jake Hipp didn't especially go for loud music, but when in the Philippines, well, hey! There were times when the best thing to do was to loosen up a little. Besides, the Filipinos

were given to romantic ballads, and while Barry Manilow's
syrupy crooning got on Hipp's nerves, he liked Karen Carpenter's good rich voice. He liked Whitney Houston, too.

Bonny and Gina took over the details of the party, dispatching Felix and Rudy and their cousins and *barkadas* for
two *lechons* and several cases of San Miguel.

Hipp said, "Mongoose is springing, so don't be cheap,
Bonny. Go for it."

Bonny raised an eyebrow. "Pricey imported cheese?"

"Sure. Fritos, Corn Curls, and potato chips. Stuffed green
olives."

Bonny grinned. He was good at managing things and
loved parties. "Okay, everybody, listen up. Here's what I
want."

Leaving Bonny inside to take care of the party, Jake went
outside with a Tanduay rum spiked with a squeeze of
lemoncito and enjoyed one of Bobby Pearl's cigars. In a few
minutes he would call Joe Woofter and tell him what had
happened. The American consul would wake someone up to
come fetch the corpse, which would have to be examined on
the off chance it contained some telltale detail that Carl Czez
had overlooked in his reincarnation as Bobby Pearl. There
would certainly be no fishhook scar, but perhaps something
else.

Jake Hipp felt that Czez, however demented, had had a
legitimate point to make about purpose, discipline, and loyalty, except that with him, it was only an excuse to murder
and murder and murder.

The more high-blown and grand the rhetoric, the greater
the delusion. Hipp thought of two lines from a poem by
Percy Bysshe Shelley:

> *My name is Ozymandias, king of kings.*
> *Look on my works, ye Mighty, and despair!*

After Jake Hipp called Woofter, he would have to call Jerry
Czez and tell him what had happened to his older brother.
He wondered if Bonny and his boyfriend, gay men routinely

ridiculed and scorned by insecure straights, might not be fortunate, in an odd way, to be spared the kind of frustration suffered by Carl Czez. But he knew that they too had their private torments. In the end, nobody, straight or gay, was spared the grip of demanding genes.

Hipp listened to Gina and the celebrants inside laughing and partying out. Bonny had sent word out, and the waitresses and cooks from Most Hipp began arriving, along with more of Gina and Bonny's friends, and friends of Felix and Rudy. As news spread that the owners of Most Hipp were springing for a party big time, the gathering of celebrants would get larger and larger. Filipinos made first-rate beer, rum, and cigars, and they knew how to sing and dance and tease and tell jokes and laugh. They were the entertainers of Asia; their talents were found everywhere. As the promotions for Philippine Air Lines said, this was Asia with a smile. Good for the Filipinos. There was a lot to be said for enjoying the present.

Jake Hipp's Cebu Libre was finished, and so too was his guilt about his failure at Tangier. He stood to go inside with the others. He knew that Bonny had made the *kinilaw* just right—giving it an extra spike of hot pepper and ginger. Everybody knew that if Donde could have a say, he would want the party to go on, as life went on. If ever an occasion called for pigging out, this was it, but rum was not good for washing down properly spiced *kinilaw*. That called for San Miguel, and lots of it. In the morning, Jake Hipp would curl up with Gina Jumero to sleep off the inevitable hangover.